Kuno Meyer

**Aislinge Meic Conglinne**

The vision of MacConglinne - a Middle-Irish wonder tale

Kuno Meyer

**Aislinge Meic Conglinne**
*The vision of MacConglinne - a Middle-Irish wonder tale*

ISBN/EAN: 9783337088620

Printed in Europe, USA, Canada, Australia, Japan

Cover: Foto ©Andreas Hilbeck / pixelio.de

More available books at **www.hansebooks.com**

# AISLINGE MEIC CONGLINNE

---

## THE VISION OF MacCONGLINNE

### A MIDDLE-IRISH WONDER TALE

EDITED

*WITH A TRANSLATION (BASED ON W. M. HENNESSY'S),*
*NOTES, AND A GLOSSARY*

BY

## KUNO MEYER

WITH AN INTRODUCTION BY

## WILHELM WOLLNER

LONDON

DAVID NUTT, 270-271, STRAND

---

1892

TO

# WHITLEY STOKES.

# CONTENTS.

# PREFACE.

THE famous Irish tale known as "The Vision of Mac-Conglinne" is now for the first time printed in the different versions which have come down to us. The longer of these versions, to which, on account of its literary merits, I have assigned the chief place, is taken from the huge vellum codex known as the *Leabhar Breac*, or *Speckled Book*, now preserved in the Royal Irish Academy, Dublin, by which it was published in fac-simile in 1876. This MS. was compiled from various sources in the fourteenth century. It is noteworthy that, with the exception of the Vision and a version of the mediæval legend of Alexander, the contents of this MS. are almost wholly ecclesiastical and religious.

The second shorter version, printed *infra*, pp. 114-129, and translated on pp. 148-155, is taken from a paper MS. of the end of the sixteenth century, preserved in the library of Trinity College, Dublin, where it is classed H. 3. 18 (pp. 732-742).

In printing the text, I have added a punctuation of my own. I have separated words according to the method followed by Windisch and Stokes. I have extended contractions, using italics in all cases where there could be the smallest doubt as to the correctness of such extensions. Long vowels are marked by an accent wherever this is the case in the MS., and by a horizontal line in cases where the scribe has omitted

to put the accent. Obvious corrections are received
into the text, but the reading of the MS. will then be
found at the foot of the pages, where I have also put
some few conjectural emendations. After the text was
in print, I had an opportunity of comparing the fac-
simile of *Leabhar Breac* with the original. The results
of this comparison will be found in the Corrigenda.

As regards the translation, my first intention was
simply to republish the late W. M. Hennessy's spirited
rendering of the *Leabhar Breac* version in *Fraser's Maga-
zine* of September 1873. However, on carefully comparing it with the original, I soon became convinced
that this was not feasible. Mistakes, inaccuracies, and
omissions were too frequent. I should have had to alter
and to add so much that the character of Hennessy's
work would have been completely changed. Nor did
I feel that Hennessy had been happy in his style.
Like many of his countrymen, he seems to have been
over-fond of Romance words, and to have preferred
these where the simpler Saxon equivalents were at
least as effective. For these reasons I decided to make
a translation of my own, basing it on Hennessy's, and
adopting his rendering wherever it seemed accurate and
forcible. I thought it right, however, in the notes to
indicate where my rendering differs most from his, as
also to give a list of the more serious mistakes into which
he has fallen. I hope no one will think that this was
done in a fault-finding spirit. I honour the memory of
W. M. Hennessy as one of the few native scholars who
did not shut their eyes to the progress of Celtic research
on the Continent, and as one who was generous enough
to place his intimate knowledge of his mother-tongue
at the disposal of any student wise enough to consult

him. It is always instructive to see how and where a man of Hennessy's learning went astray. One of the snares into which he often fell was his habit of reading older Irish with modern pronunciation, as I have repeatedly heard him do: a source of error, against which native students cannot too carefully guard themselves.

In the Glossary I have collected all words not found in Windisch's *Wörterbuch*, as well as some the form or meaning of which he has left doubtful. Although many riddles offered by the text remain unsolved, I hope my work will be of some use to the Irish lexicographer, whose advent we are still expecting.

"The Vision of MacConglinne" will prove a mine where the folk-lorist as well as the student of mediæval institutions may find much precious material. It is rich in allusions to customs and modes of thought, many of which I at least was unable to illustrate or explain· But wherever I was able to throw light on these, either from Irish or general literature, I have done so in the notes.

As to the place of the Vision in Irish and general mediæval literature, its source and origin, and its author, I do not feel myself entitled to speak. Division of labour is as yet unknown in Irish studies, and the editor of an Irish text, besides adding a translation and a glossary, without which his work would only serve the very small number of Irish students, is also expected to say something on such points. But this implies a knowledge of the most varied branches of mediæval learning and literature, a knowledge which I do not possess. Under these circumstances, I rejoice that my friend, Professor Wilhelm Wollner, of Leipsic University, has consented to contribute an Introduction treating the problems indicated above.

There remains only one question on which the reader may desire me to say something, the question as to the probable age of the Vision. In the absence of any published investigations into the characteristics of the Irish language at different periods, I cannot speak with certainty. But from a comparison of the language of the *Leabhar Breac* text with that of a fair number of dateable historical poems in the *Book of Leinster* and other early MSS., I have come to the conclusion that the original from which this copy is descended must have been composed about the end of the twelfth century. That the tale itself, in some form or other, is older, is proved by the second version, which, though much more modern in its language, represents, as Prof. Wollner will show, an older form of the tale.

I may add that an incident in the story itself seems to confirm the date of the *Leabhar Breac* version. The ironical conscientiousness, with which MacConglinne offers the monks of Cork tithes on his bit of bread and bacon (p. 22), seems to me to derive its point from the novelty of the introduction of tithes into Ireland, and from the strictness with which they were then first exacted. Though mentioned earlier, tithes were not generally paid in Ireland till the second half of the twelfth century, and then not without much opposition. At the synod of Kells, in 1152, Cardinal Paparo, the Pope's legate, ordained that tithes should be paid. On this, Lanigan, in his *Ecclesiastical History of Ireland*, iv, p. 146, remarks : "On this point he was very badly obeyed ; for it is certain that tithes were, if at all, very little exacted in Ireland until after the establishment

of the English power." In 1172, at a synod held at
Cashel, it was again ordered that tithes should be paid
to the churches out of every kind of property. See
Lanigan, *ib.*, p. 205.

In conclusion, I wish to thank the several friends
who have encouraged me by their interest, and aided
me in various ways by advice and help. Dr. Whitley
Stokes has throughout assisted me with most useful
criticism and many valuable suggestions, more especially
in the Glossary. My kind friends and colleagues, Pro-
fessors J. M. Mackay and W. A. Raleigh, have ever
been ready to help me in my endeavours to make the
translation as faithful and idiomatic as the great difference between the two languages will allow. To the
Rev. Professor E. O'Growney, Maynooth, I am indebted
for many a fruitful suggestion drawn from his scholarly
knowledge of the modern language. Lastly, Mr. Alfred
Nutt has, by his generous offer of bearing the risk of
publication, as well as by the liberality which he has
shown in the worthy equipment of the book, added
another to the many claims which he has on the grati-
tude of Celtic scholars.

Kuno Meyer.

*University College, Liverpool.*

# INTRODUCTION.

In the following investigation into the nature, origin, and authorship of the curious Irish mediæval tale called The Vision of MacConglinne, we have first to consider the mutual relations of the two versions which have come down to us. I hope to show that the shorter of the two, that contained in the MS. H. 3. 18 (H.), the later in point of date as far as MS. tradition is concerned, represents an older and purer stage of the story, though one far removed from the original form, and that the longer version, that of *Leabhar Breac* (B.), which supplies the staple of the present volume, is the extravagantly embroidered production of a minstrel genius who had a special grudge against the Church. An analysis of the various portions of our tale shows that the origin of this luxuriant growth of fanciful imaginings must be sought for in a group of popular tales, allied to those found among other pastoral peoples, concerning a wonderful land of abundance, and not in such mediæval lore as the *fabliaus de Coquaigne*, or the *Bataille de Karesme et de Charnage*. Finally, the central conception of the story, that of possession by a devouring demon of voracity, is shown to be a favourite one on Irish soil, and to have retained its vitality among the people to the present day.

## I.—The Two Versions.

In the two versions of the tale known as The Vision of
MacConglinne[1] we can more or less clearly distinguish
two elements differing in treatment—a poetical one, the
Vision itself, and an historical one, comprising MacConglinne's quarrel with the monks of Cork, the revealing
to him of the vision by means of which he cures King
Cathal, and his reward for the cure. The treatment of
the Vision is equally confused in both versions, and is
interlarded with various obscure allusions, whilst the
historical part contains much that clearly points to a
common original source, the very wording of which can
in some cases be established. On the other hand, dis-
crepancies are found which lead to the conclusion that
different versions of this original must have existed, and
that B. and H. each go back to one or more of these
versions, though not to the same, a relation which may
be expressed graphically thus :

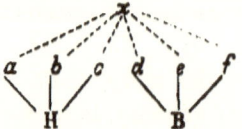

Lastly, much is found in B. of which we can say with
certainty that it belongs to that version only.

The author of H. is a sober and modest man. He is
a mere copyist, who adds nothing of his own, keeping
strictly to tradition. His object is the faithful rendering

---

[1] It is noteworthy that the title, "The Vision of MacConglinne", occurs only in *Leabhar Brear* (B.), whilst *II.* 3. 18 (H.)
is without any heading, and concludes : " Thus was Cathal
cured from his craving, and MacConglinne honoured."

of the story as it has been handed down. His narrative is simple, terse, logical. Rarely does he make a small mistake.

The author of B., on the other hand, is a man of poetical ambition. He has imagination and humour, and does not scruple to show them. He puts himself freely into his work. His defects are neglect of logical consistency and a want of restraint. He spends loving skill in devising variations of an existing motive rather than in inventing new situations. Detail is his delight. Absorbed in the pleasure of adorning and illustrating the matter in hand, he generally forgets what went before and what is to follow. Thus it happens that he often contradicts himself, that he repeats himself, that he piles up effects. He will describe something with the nicest precision, exhaust himself in minute details, and a few lines further on a new idea crops up at complete variance with all that he has just said.[1]

The narrative in B. is therefore neither accurate nor faithful; and if we want to know how the original version may have run, we must turn to H., where, in many cases, we actually find it, as a few examples will show.

The verses—

    " My lad,
    Why should we not have a duel in quatrains?
    A quatrain compose thou on the bread,
    I will make one on the condiment,"

are, on p. 14, addressed by MacConglinne to the servant

---

[1] As a typical instance of his manner, I may mention his description of the woman on p. 96, where he sets down thirty-five details as against five in H. (p. 153). On p. 98, 3 and 5, all this is forgotten.

of the monastery. This is senseless. He surely cannot expect a response from the lay-brother. But they would be in their place if addressed to a companion in misery who could take his share in the satire. Now this is the case in H. (p. 148), where MacConglinne in the church at Kells obtains food by a poetical duel with his attendant, the Scabbed Youth. This quatrain in B. is thus a trace in that version of how MacConglinne and his companion obtained food by a satirical contest.

In a further quatrain (p. 16), MacConglinne speaks of the "oaten ration of Cork", although he has been offered nothing but a cup of the church whey-water (p. 14, 1). Again, on p. 18, 25, in answer to Mac-Conglinne's complaint of having been left without food, the Abbot says : "Thou hadst not gone without food, even though thou hadst only got a little crumb, or a drink of whey-water in the church." Observe : Mac-Conglinne is offered whey-water, his satire is directed against an oaten ration, and here he is told, "You cannot speak of having been left starving, even if you had obtained nothing but whey-water"; but this is exactly what he did get. It is beyond doubt that the ration offered to MacConglinne in the original of B. was oats. A combination of the two quatrains and the mention of whey-water by the Abbot lead to the supposition that we have here another trace of the episode mentioned above.

On p. 24, the words "now take me to the Lee", and again, "he was taken with all his bonds and guards towards the Lee", stand in no connection whatever with the preceding narrative. MacConglinne had asked (p. 22) as a boon to be allowed to eat the portion of food he had in his satchel. This was granted, and, according to an Irish custom, pledges were given for the fulfilment of the request, as is the case everywhere where the narrator inserts a "boon", which he does often. He then eats, and the pledges are redeemed. But, without further intimation, he is taken to the Lee. For what object? To be once more soused and drenched? The drinking-scene with the brooch follows, MacC. abuses the monks, and tells them that he will not move, "for I have pledges in my hands" (p. 26). The monks, in their perplexity, treat with him, that he may restore the pledges to the guarantors.

Meanwhile it grows late, the monks themselves ask for delay of the execution. But first MacC. fetches his "passion-tree". It is evident that this form of the episode is not original, and merely furnishes a desired opportunity of inserting a tirade against tithes, abuse of the monks, and a parody on the passion of Christ.

The clumsiness of this whole episode of the tithes is shown by MacC.'s address to the people (p. 22). He wants to make out that no one stands in greater need of the tithes than he. He has eaten and drunk nothing since his arrival in Cork. Why then did he not touch his provisions? The reason cannot be found in B. Here, again, H. has the true original version. The festival of St. Barre and Nessan is being celebrated in Cork, and the men of Munster go to Cork to fast, as a preparation for the festival. B. says no word of this, but it does mention "bacon with a streak across its middle" (p. 8, 23), which, being no food for fasting, had to remain untouched. MacC. goes on to say that on the day before he had travelled farther than any of his audience—probably originally an allusion to the people

*b*

who had come to Cork for the festival. "I had eaten nothing on the road." Why not?

In H., MacC., after he had spent the night in the abbot's bed, where St. Mura appears and relates the vision to him, is brought in the morning before Cathal and the nobles of Munster, who, we must assume, were in Cork for the festival. He asks to be allowed to drink, and to draw the water himself. He then drinks with the brooch, receives respite till the next day, the story thus developing naturally and logically, whereas the author of B. sacrifices everything to the drastic description of MacC.'s bad treatment by the monks.

After he has been soused in the Lee, beaten, stripped naked, and locked up, judged unjustly on the next day, he is compelled to cut and fetch his own "passion-tree", and then, tied naked to a pillar-stone, left to suffer hunger and cold (p. 30). True, this latter circumstance contradicts MacC.'s own statement in the Vision (p. 70, 7), that he passed the night in a beautiful canopied bed; but then the Vision is a long way off yet. The author kills two birds with one stone: he rouses pity for the miserable plight of his hero, and, in making an angel reveal the Vision, the truth of his narrative is borne out by the "Angel's Ridge", near Cork. To the local name we doubtless owe the introduction of the angel, who has supplanted in B. the patron saint of H.

The vision "revealed by the angel" is put into rhyme by MacC., and his authorship is thus established.

In H., St. Mura of Fahan comes to the assistance of his countryman. He sings a song to him, by which to cure Cathal and thus save his own life. In B. the angel says no word of the salutary power of his story; yet MacC. turns it into verse, "which would serve to relate what had been manifested to him". To whom is he going to relate it?

It is now necessary for B. to bring Cathal and MacC. together. This is again unskilfully managed. The abbot has had a dream revealing to him that Cathal would be cured by the Vision. The simplest thing would surely have been that when MacC., without any apparent motive, unless to show off, asks the boon of reciting his poem, the abbot should remember his dream. But no! he refuses to listen to the Vision. MacC. has to press it on him; and then only, reminded of his dream, does he command MacC. to go to Cathal.

The bargain about MacC.'s reward, which now follows, is quite out of place, as MacC., who has tried everything to prolong his life, would, one would fancy, be content with getting off on any terms. However, he demands the abbot's cloak, and, in spite of the latter's remonstrance, this has to be deposited with the bishop.

Here MacC.'s quarrel with the monks ends. He binds himself, in return for his spared life and for the cloak, to cure Cathal.

One would think his having come to cure Cathal would be the best introduction to Pichan. But that would be too simple for our author, so MacC. must dress himself up and begin, quite unexpectedly, a juggling performance of the lowest kind (the disapproval of which is evidently pretended), in order to attract attention (p. 42). Having succeeded, he makes a special bargain with Pichan, though he has already had his reward for curing Cathal. He engages to restrain Cathal from eating for twenty-four hours. Cathal comes, and begins to eat. MacC. enters upon his bargain by preventing him from eating all the apples. Cathal falls into a rage, and here the anecdote of the scholar of Emly Ivar is introduced not unskilfully.

MacConglinne now says he is going away; but first he craves a boon, and is, as usual, very particular about pledges. Why he should demand, and Cathal grant, a boon, the fanciful author alone knows. Cathal soon has occasion to repent of his readiness when he hears that he is to fast. The preliminary cure now begins, a fast of thirty-six hours. "What is the good of all this, son of learning?" the tormented king cries out, and we cannot but echo the cry. The good is that the author gets an opportunity of making MacC. preach a sermon which draws three showers of tears from his audience (p. 58). Then he dresses as cook, has Cathal bound fast, and tantalises the demon in him by passing food before Cathal's mouth, after which he wishes Cathal to expound the Vision which he is going to tell. Meanwhile, three days have passed since the Vision; yet MacC. begins (p. 66, 12):

"A vision I beheld *last night*";

and again (p. 70, 7): "As I lay *last night* in my beautiful canopied bed." The pillar-stone, as we saw before, has entirely escaped his memory.

In H. the opening is quite logical, as MacC. saw the Vision in the preceding night, which he spent in the abbot's bed.

After the demon has been expelled through the Vision, MacC., according to B., receives rich reward, among other things, the abbot's cloak. A jester's family then appears on the scene, and makes a satire on the abbot, beginning (p. 108):

"Manchin went (a brilliant feat!)
To *plead* against MacConglinne."

The preceding narrative is here contradicted in three points : (1) Nothing has been heard previously of Manchin's pleading; (2) Manchin has deposited the cloak, much against his will ; (3) Manchin has remained in Cork, and has not met Cathal at all. The song is, therefore, unintelligible as it stands. It is again in H. that we find the solution. Here Manchin is present at the cure, he and his monks having accompanied the king to Pichan, in order to crucify MacC. on the next day. MacC. is granted his life by Cathal, whereupon the abbot protests against the slanderer of the Church getting off scot-free. MacC. then proposes to call to-gether the brehons, and let them decide whether or no he has slandered the Church. He deposits a sum ; so does Manchin. The brehons decide that the remark on the oaten ration was no slander. MacC. is thus awarded Manchin's deposit, and asks for the cloak. "Thou shalt have it, with my blessing."

Manchin's presence did not suit the author of B., who had made MacC. go to Cathal alone. But, as he did not want to lose the effect of the satirical poem at the end, he simply cut out the episode of Manchin's pleading ; but he did not cut out enough. On p. 104, while the demon sits on the roof, MacC. says quite unexpectedly :

"Well now, ye men of Munster, yonder is your friend."

If we here alter "Munster" into "Cork", we have a natural taunt addressed by MacC. to his enemies, the monks, whom he further annoys by calling the demon "an unworshipful monk".

So far concerning what I have called the historical part. I have, I trust, made it clear that H. represents in the main a more original version, which however, amplified and mixed up partly with the author's own fancies, partly with popular traditions, can also be recognised in B.

## II.—THE VISION.

Our investigation so far shows that, of the two versions which have come down to us, H. approaches the original nearer than does B., which must be regarded as an amplified and frequently corrupted form of that original. This result, however, applies only to the narrative which precedes and follows the Vision, not to the Vision itself. Several details in the latter do indeed show a like relation of B. to H.; yet, on the whole, the account of MacConglinne's journey to the Wizard Doctor, of what he saw on this journey and at the Hermitage, is equally confused and full of unintelligible matter in both versions.

It might be assumed that this is owing to corrupt tradition, but the same obscure passages occur in both versions, and must have formed part of the versions from which B. and H. sprang; these we have seen reason to consider as different forms of one common original, which must thus itself have contained these obscurities. Technically speaking, the tradition is good rather than bad.

The reason must be sought elsewhere. The Vision consists of poetry and prose. It is introduced by two poems connected by the words "and he said further" (pp. 66, 68). That they are actually two poems is shown by the different metres. Then follows a new section called "the Fable", in prose, without any connection with the preceding poems, and with a new and separate beginning. We are told, briefly in H., with great detail in B., how MacConglinne is met by a Phantom, who, on his complaining of great hunger, directs him to the Wizard Doctor.

The description of MacConglinne's journey follows. He sails across New-Milk Lake. Here H. interrupts the prose by a poem. The land and residence of the Wizard Doctor (Chief Cleric in H.) are described. Mac-Conglinne appears before him. Here H. again inserts a poem. The Doctor asks after his complaints, and prescribes a cure. B. then adds : " Thus far the Vision, etc." (*ocus araile*). H. relates how the Chief Cleric gives his blessing to MacConglinne, who sets out for the Tribes of Food. Then follow the names of these Tribes, which are no names at all, and finally : " Those are the chiefs of the Tribes of Food."

The narrative then returns to Cathal, whose cure is described.

B., it will be seen, includes the narrative of Mac-Conglinne's journey in the Vision, while H. does not so include it.

Before we proceed, some remarks on the relation between H. and B. are necessary. The reader is at once struck by the different use made of two poems, the first of which, that inserted in the Vision in H., describes the voyage across New-Milk Lake. B. does not include it in the Vision or Fable related to Cathal at all, but, on p. 34, makes MacConglinne recite it to Manchin as the vision revealed by the angel. The second poem, beginning " Wheatlet, son of Milklet", contains in H. the answer to MacConglinne's question respecting the name of the Chief Cleric. It is quite out of place, as MacConglinne has just addressed to the Cleric the same elaborate pedigree which in B. he addresses to Manchin before relating the Vision to him (see pp. 22 and 151).

B. makes use of the poem "Wheatlet" as an answer to MacConglinne's question respecting the name of the Phantom. But here, again, it is out of place, as the Phantom has just given his name (Buarannach, etc., p. 74, 9). ·

Thus, in "Wheatlet, son of Milklet", we have a poem which neither in H. nor in B. stands in its proper place.

The poem on p. 34 (B.) is used in H. in a still more curious manner. It contains, to a large extent, the same things as the prose in which it is inserted, and it is evident, from a comparison of the two, that the prose must be regarded as a paraphrase of the poem. That this poem originally belonged to a tale dealing with Cathal is probable, from the mention of Cathal in the last stanza.

The following points are to be considered :

(1) The poem is found in both versions, and therefore existed in the versions from which B. and H. sprang.

(2) It is quite out of place in H., and must therefore have had a different function in the original version.

(3) The poem seems to show by its close that it originally belonged to some narrative about Cathal.

(4) In B. the poem is recited to Manchin as the vision revealed by the angel.

I conclude as follows :

It is no mere arbitrary whim of the author of B. to call this poem "The Vision". For once in a way, B. is right. In an earlier version this poem actually was the Vision, and, as I think, the whole of the Vision. It was only later that, in place of this poem, those additions were introduced which in B. and H. represent the

Vision, viz., the poems on pp. 56 and 68, and the prose
of "The Fable".

The original signification of the poem on p. 34 is
almost wholly obliterated in the present form of the
work. The poem has been superfluously inserted in H.,
whilst in B. it is wholly left out where the Vision is
dealt with (p. 66). The replacing of the Vision proper
(the poem on p. 34) by what now stands in its stead
must have taken place in the version underlying B. and
H., as both these agree in their treatment of the Vision.

The pedigree of the two versions which I sketched on
p. x can be thus carried back a step further. I assume
an oldest version, in which the Vision was the poem on
p. 34, and I call it the Source (S.):

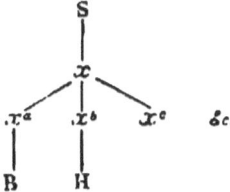

We must imagine S. as a shorter narrative of Cathal's
cure by a recitation of the Vision. Whether S. was wholly
in verse or prose I leave undecided. The cure was
effected by the scholar MacConglinne. S. further contained something about a mantle as the subject of a
quarrel between MacConglinne and the abbot Manchin,
and which the former obtained. What kind of episode
this was we cannot judge from H. and B. Of one
thing we can be sure, namely, that this episode of the
mantle stood in connection with the cure of Cathal, as
is proved by the jester's song on p. 108. In this the
name of MacConglinne is handed down. This song

already existed in S., and was mechanically taken over by the author of X.[1]

The shorter narrative S. was then remodelled by a later hand into a longer work, X. The existing motives were utilised and given a new turn. The figure of MacConglinne stepped into the foreground and became the centre of interest, whereas in S. Cathal had been the chief person. Cathal and his cure now served merely as a foil to MacConglinne.

The quarrel about the mantle developed into a conflict between MacConglinne and the monks of Cork. The author thus obtained an opportunity for invectives against the clergy generally, and he could endow his hero with new and interesting features. By this expansion of the figure of MacConglinne the narrative part of the work assumed larger dimensions. In comparison with the rest, the Vision, which consisted of about sixty lines, may have appeared too scant to the redactor. At any rate, he set about expanding the Vision as well. For this purpose he found material ready to his hands in a folk-tale cycle of which I shall treat more in detail later on. I will here only remark that he seems mainly to have drawn on a tale the figures of which are partly found in the poem "Wheatlet, son of Milklet." It treated of a wonderful people living in a land of abundance. All that the redactor had to do was to combine this material with the story of Cathal's cure, and embody it in the Vision. This problem he solved, or at any rate tried to solve, at the

---

[1] In H. as well as in B. the episode of the mantle plays quite a secondary part. Even H. is content with a mere allusion to a jester's family, who recite the poem, without giving us any information about these people, who lost all significance as soon as the episode in which they played a part ceased to be of interest.

same time providing his favourite hero with a further adventure. Wheatlet was changed into a *fáthliaig*, *i.e.*, a Seer-Leech or Wizard Doctor, a kind of medicine-man combining the gift of prophecy with medical skill,[1] a figure well known from other Irish tales.

That he makes a pagan *fáthliaig* appear amid the Christian surroundings of a Hermitage, or himself play the part of a Cleric, might seem strange in any other redactor but ours, who, as we have repeatedly seen, is by no means consistent.

That the Wizard Doctor has taken the place of Wheatlet I conclude from the following circumstances.

In H. the Wizard Doctor, answering MacConglinne's question concerning his name, says, " Not hard to tell .... Wheatlet, son of Milklet," etc. As I have shown above, both answer and poem are out of place here. Now, this interpolation can best be explained by the author's wish to establish the identity of the Wizard Doctor and Wheatlet. The simplest means to effect this was to make the Wizard Doctor himself say that he is Wheatlet. This is no doubt a clumsy proceeding, but it is not the only one in the prose. The son of the Wizard Doctor is called Ugadart in H. In the household of Wheatlet the bridle-boy of Wheatlet is called Ugadarc. I shall endeavour to show presently that this figure Ugadart-Ugadarc belonged to the legend used by the author. But in our narrative it is episodic,

---

[1] One of the things a *fáthliaig* was evidently expected to do was to be able to tell, from the aspect of a wound, what sort of person had inflicted it. See the story of Fintan mac Cethirn and the *fáthliaig* Fingin, who was leech of the Ulster King Conchobar (*Book of Leinster*, p. 89*b*). The pupils of another *fáthliaig*, on approaching the house in which a wounded man lay, and hearing his cries, were able to tell from them what instrument had inflicted the wound (*ibid.*, p. 329*a*).

and has no significance whatever. Hence I conclude
that it was mechanically taken over from the original
source. And I further conclude, from the parallelism
Ugadart-Wizard Doctor and Ugadarc-Wheatlet that the
prose is derived from a legend of Wheatlet, and that
just as Ugadart = Ugadarc, so the Wizard Doctor =
Wheatlet.

I assume, then, that the author of X. changed Wheatlet into a *fúthliaig*, to whom MacConglinne travels to
find a cure. A cure from what? As he is travelling
into a land of plenty, it was natural to make him suffer
from hunger.

In carrying out this idea the author took little trouble.
The original Vision, changed into prose, supplied him
with a description of the journey. But the Vision
being thus used up, the difficulty arose that MacConglinne's adventures had still to be related in the form of
a vision.

The redactor had another happy thought. To form
an introduction, MacConglinne has a vision of the Phantom, who comes from the land of plenty, and directs
him to the Wizard Doctor.

In B. the Phantom says that he comes from the
Fairy-knoll of Eating. One would imagine that the
Wizard Doctor dwelt there too. But no. The Fairy-
knoll of Eating is not mentioned again, and the Hermitage of the Wizard Doctor, according to the description
on p. 84, lies at the mouth of the pass to the country
of O'Early-eating, that is, at the entrance of this
country, and not in it. If this country of O'Early-
eating is an Irish land of Cockayne, this would be interesting.

H. has a similar allusion. The Church lies in the
pass of Meat-juice, in the land of O'Early-eating.

But the author was either unable or too careless to carry out his plan of treating the prose as a vision.

He begins quite logically : " As I lay last night in my beautiful canopied bed, I heard a voice, but I answered not. Whereupon it said again." Then H. goes on : " When the voice had spoken to me again, I arose. Then I saw a phantom approaching me," and then the narrative proceeds. MacConglinne is no longer dreaming ; he relates his actual experiences.

In B. this is still more striking. MacConglinne does not stir when he hears the voice, but sleeps calmly on. " At early morn on the morrow I arose, and went to the well to wash my hands, when I saw a mighty phantom approaching me" (p. 70). Here, again, we have not a vision, but experience.

And yet I am almost inclined to believe that the author's original intention was to parody in his vision the celebrated visions of Irish saints. I see indications of such an intention in the voice[1] which MacConglinne hears in his sleep, in the " dark, lardy mist,[2] that arose around us so that we could see neither heaven nor earth"; in the church[3] of the Wizard Doctor—motives which occur in several visions ; lastly, in the Phantom,

[1] Compare *e.g.* the vision of the monk of Evesham in Matthew of Paris (*sub anno* 1196), ed. Luard, ii, 427). Thurchill's vision, Matth. Par., ii, 497.

[2] "Nigra erat terra, et regio tenebrosa" (*Patrick's Purgatory* Matth. Par., ii, 195), "venerunt ad vallem valde terribilem ac tenebrosam et mortis caligine coopertam" (*Visio Tnugdali*, ed. Wagner, p. 12).

[3] Thurchill is led by Julianus hospitator, who appears to him, to a *basilica mirae structurae* (Matth. Par., ii, 498). In the *Purgat. Patr.* the knight Owen comes to an *aula . . . . . parietes non habebat, sed columnis erat per gyrum subnixa, ut claustrum solet monachorum* (*ib.*, ii, 194).

who has taken the place of the guardian angel who receives the soul on leaving the body.[1] However, if a parody was intended, it has not been carried out. The parody on the greeting of welcome (p. 150), that of the benediction (p. 82, p. 154), "In the name of Cheese," are simply such parodies of sacred things as occur throughout the narrative.

Thus the prose narrative was not cast into vision form. The poem of p. 34 was used up, and therefore not at the author's disposal. Yet the story demanded a vision.

The redactor took things easily. He inserted before the prose narrative two popular poems, which, like that on p. 34, treated of eatables, and which profess explicitly to be dreams. These are the poems on pp. 66 and 68.

He also kept the poem on p. 34, in order to use it at a fitting opportunity. It was handed down with the rest; and thus we find it in B. recited to Manchin as the Vision; its curious position in H. may be set down to the helplessness of the author, who could find no better place for it. The poem "Wheatlet" supplies, as we have seen, a like instance of helplessness.

The assumption that the author of X. and his successors held in reserve such unemployed materials as the poem of p. 34 and "Wheatlet" may seem strange. Let me therefore anticipate what I shall endeavour to demonstrate in the following chapter, namely, that the Vision of MacConglinne is the work of a gleeman. If I succeed in this demonstration, the above assumption follows naturally from the known character of such works.

---

[1] Cf. the address of the guardian angel in Tnugdal's Vision! "*Ave, Tnugdale, quid agis?*" with that of the Phantom.

It has been assumed that native legends were used for the amplification of the Vision. I cannot claim to have recovered the several materials in whole or in part. The indications in the "Fable" are not sufficient for that. But it is possible to argue from them the general character of the legendary cycle and of its heroes.

MacConglinne stands in marked contrast to the other persons of the fable. One and all treat him contemptuously as an inferior being. So does the Phantom, so does Ugadart (in H.), the doorkeeper (in B.), and so, finally, does the Wizard Doctor himself.

What is the significance of this? Says Ugadart to MacConglinne: "You are the first face that appears in this isle to which you have come," that is to say, "You are a specimen of a race different from us."

The apparition is called "a mighty phantom" (*scál mór*) in B. It tells MacConglinne, when he longs to go to the land of plenty, that if he wants to get on well there, he must have a very broad, four-edged belly, five hands in diameter, etc., *i.e.*, a belly such as people there have. He is directed to Becenat, the daughter of the son of Baetan, the monstrous eater (*brasslongthech*). He comes to an enormous fort. The crown of the doorkeeper (the Chief Cleric in H.) consists of seven times the produce of seven ridges of leek. The cords of his whip consist of twenty-nine puddings; every drop that fell to the ground from the end of these would be enough for a priest (p. 88); every drop trickling down from his stick would contain the full of seven vats. The angling-rod of the Wizard Doctor's son is thirty hands long.

It is indifferent how much of this description was contributed by the redactor. We at any rate see his endeavour to produce the impression of something colossal. This intention is manifest in both versions, *e.g.*, in

II., in the contemptuous remark of the Wizard Doctor :
"That meal (*i.e.*, the meal you call great feeding) is not
greater than what a child of one month would eat in
this island."

In short, MacConglinne has here to do with giants
who despise him, the puny imp.  That is why he seeks
courage in a draught from the well of tremanta, "that
my heart may not fail me on the road".

The residence of the Wizard Doctor lies between
Butter-mount, Milk-lake, and Curd-point ; and Butter-
mount, Milk-lake, and Curd-point are about the limits
of the gastronomic imagination of the prose.  The range
of this rustic *gourmandise* includes no more than, firstly,
white-meats (*bánbiad*), then milk, and its endless prepara-
tions—buttermilk, butter, various kinds of cheese, curds,
custard ; further, fat, suet, lard, tallow, bacon, flitches
of boar, tripes, sausage, corned beef, pot-meat, hung
meat.  Of vegetables we have onions, leek, carrots.
Then soups, meat-juice, broth, pottage, porridge, gruel.
Of baked food, bread, cakes, wheaten cakes.  Hardly
any game ; the boar and deer are mentioned once or
twice.  The only condiments quoted are honey and salt.

It is noteworthy how little stress the Vision lays
upon intoxicating drinks.  Mead and bragget are mentioned incidentally, but one has the impression that this
is done for completeness' sake.  Compare, on the other
hand, the recipe for MacConglinne's "little drop" (p.
100).  With what gusto is not the favourite drink of
the people between Butter-mount and Milk-lake described !

A hasty comparison of the descriptions of the Irish
story with those of the Land of Cockayne, the Pays de
Coquaigne, the German Schlaraffenland, etc., shows at

once an essential difference between the two. In these latter we have the ideal picture of a life of lazy enjoyment, extravagant as the fancy of the people and of the poet could make it. This lazy life stands in direct contrast to that of the ordinary workaday world. On the one hand, scanty dress, toil, lack of money; on the other, undiluted idleness, all the dainties of the world, flying into the very mouth of the recipient—whose laziness will not even allow him to stretch out his hand for them—dresses of the most precious materials, gold, silver, and jewels strewn in the streets; in fine, miserable reality here, there the most wonderful of dreamlands.

This Utopian trait is wholly wanting in the Irish "Fable". True, plenty reigns in the land of the Wizard Doctor, nor is aught talked of but eating; but this plenty is of a most primitive kind—abundance of the simplest materials. Of precious things—gold, silver, and the like—not a word; nor do the inhabitants lead a lazy life.

It is, then, a vain endeavour to seek points of contact between our "Fable" and those French and English poems with which, at first blush, it would seem to be connected. At most one might be inclined to see, in the description of the doorkeeper and his horse, an analogy with the accoutrement of Charnage or Karesme.[1] But the similarity consists merely in this, that the dress is made of various kinds of food. The point of the French poem—the fight between Lenten foods and meat foods—is wholly foreign to the Irish work. For the same reason, it would not be permissible to seek, in the war between the Tribes of Butter-pat and Cheese (p. 86, 20) and the Wizard Doctor, an analogy with the battle between Karesme and Charnage. Whence this

---

[1] *Bataille de Karesme et de Charnage*, Méon, iv.

c

essential difference between the Irish narrative and the non-Irish mediæval descriptions of Cockayne? The subject did not demand it; a picture of Cockayne would have answered the redactor's purpose as well as that he has given.

The explanation is simple. The redactor mechanically followed his original, the contents of which were no version of the Cockayne story, but a legend of a vanished golden age, a tale told by shepherds or peasants of the days of their forefathers.

Only among a cattle-breeding population of a primitive stage of culture could a legend arise, the epical apparatus of which is so entirely taken from peasant life as is the case in our tale. What do we find in the " Fable" save the products of agriculture and farming, of the dairy and beehive? Wheat, oats, barley are the only cereals, leek, onions, carrots the vegetables, the apple- and nut-tree the only fruit-trees.

The primitive character of this cycle of legends has been preserved with distinctness, though the single legends are no longer to be clearly recognised.

It is well known that similar legends of a golden age exist among other peoples. I may instance the description of the *aurea aetas* in Ovid (*Metam.*, i, 89), in Hesiod ("Εργα καὶ ἡμέραι, 109), and the old Norse legend of King Fróði's rule.[1]

The following piece of Swiss folk-lore has a special interest in this connection. It is orally current in the Kanderthal, in the Berner Oberland:

[1] See Uhland, *Schriften zur Geschichte der deutschen Dichtung und Sage*, iii, 237. Compare also, on this as well as on the descriptions of Cockayne, Fr. Joh. Poeschel, *Das Märchen vom Schlaraffenlande*, Halle, 1878; and Menzel, *Odin*, Stuttgart, 1855, p. 196 : **Vom Wunschland.**

"There lived formerly a tall race of people in the Simmenthal. They had cattle which were too big for stables, and were therefore always kept in the open air. Every cow yielded daily three vats of milk, for which reason they were milked into a lake instead of into a pail. The staircase that led down to this lake was made of cheeses. The butter was stored in hollow oak-trunks. The walls of the houses and the barn-doors were polished with butter, and floors and dishes were washed with milk. The people sailed on the lake in an oak-trunk to skim the cream, which was cast on the bank with shovels. Once a violent gale blew, the milk-lake flooded the land, and drowned the tall people."

A variant from the Berner Oberland and the Frei-burger Ormund says: "Every evening the cowherd (*Sennbub*) sailed in a boat on the milk-lake and skimmed the cream. Once he struck against a rock, consisting of a large lump of butter, and was drowned. How-ever, when all the milk had been churned into butter, they found his body, which was buried in a cave of wax made by bees, every comb of which was bigger than the town-gate at Brugg or Freiburg."[1]

Uhland[2] quotes the following variant as a shepherd's tale among the Romance population in the Ormont Alps. "One day, when a beautiful shepherd went on the lake to skim the cream, the boat was capsized by a vehement gust of wind, and the poor youth was drowned. Lads and lasses put on mourning and searched for the body, which was at last discovered in a gigantic butter-keg in the midst of the foaming waves of cream.

[1] See E. L. Rochholz, " *Gold, Milch und Blut*," *Germania*, vii, p. 400.

[2] In his *Abhandlung über das Volkslied*, Schriften iii, p. 238.

They carried it into a spacious cave, the walls of which were wainscoted with honeycombs as big as the former city-gates of Lausanne."[1]

Uhland compares this Swiss legend with the Norse tale of King Fróði of Denmark and King Fiölnir of Sweden. Both were kings of the golden age; both lived in superfluity. Fróði once treated Fiölnir to a drinking-banquet on a mead-vat, which was many ells high and made of rafters. The mead was drawn through a hole between the top-rafters; but, in the night, Fiölnir, overcome with sleep and drink, fell in, and, as a skald sings, "the windless sea (*vágur vindlaus*) drowned him."[2]

There can be no doubt that Ugadart's death in the lake of lard, as told in our "fable" (p. 90), belongs to the same group of legendary lore. The *tertium comparationis*, the drowning in plenty, is found. But a mere indication of the legend is all that remains. In H. (p. 151), Ugadart fishes in a lake of new milk, but no mention is made of his drowning. B. has substituted a lake of lard (*loch usca*). It seems certain to me that the lake was originally of milk, and I think it highly probable that the Irish legend, of which a remnant has been preserved in this episode of Ugadart, was one very like the Swiss.

Ugadart angles in a lake of milk, or catches flitches of bacon and salt-beef in a lake of lard. This is obviously wrong. It is possible that Ugadart, or whatever else

---

[1] Uhland quotes as source Fr. Kuenlin, *Die Schweiz und ihre Ritterburgen*, i, 113. Cp. *Deutsche Sagen*, p. 150. W. Menzel, *Odin*, quotes *Mémoires de l'Acad. Celtique*, v, 202; Wyss, *Reise ins Berner Oberland*, 416; and Schwab, *Ritterburgen der Schweiz*, i, 113.

[2] Uhland, *l. c.* Cp. the quotations on p. 338, *Anmerkung*, 269.

he was called, originally played the same part in the
Irish tale as the cowherd in the Swiss one. Neither in
H. nor in B. is anything said about Ugadart's attitude,
nor how he came to be drowned. The reader pre-
supposes that he was sitting on the bank angling; but
this may have been different in the original, where,
perhaps, he sailed about on the lake skimming the
cream. This trait may not have suited the redactor,
who made him angle.

In the variant quoted by Uhland, lads and lasses go
out dressed in mourning to search for the body. It is
buried in a specially-prepared cave. In our tale it is
said that a celebrated elegy was made on Ugadart's
death. In both cases the death of the young hero is
an event of importance for his people.

The setting of both legends is similar. The scene of
both is among a giant race, in both the milk-lake plays
a part, and dairy-products are similarly used in both.[1]

I have tried to show that the heroes of the Irish
legend underlying the prose narrative are giants. It is
true, we find no trace of gigantic cattle; but, if I am
right in my equation of Ugadart with the cowherd,
Ugadart's employment as skimmer of the milk-lake
would presuppose these.

Finally, Wheatlet, whom the poem makes the master
of Ugadart, while in the prose the Wizard Doctor is
called his father, is to be regarded as the patriarchal
ruler of this Irish shepherd-people.

What Beccnat (lit. "The Little Woman"), the Tribes
of Food, and the Children of Early-Eating are to signify

---

[1] Would it be too daring to see a trace of the original story
in the servants of the Wizard Doctor, with their shovels of dry
bread (p. 90, 11)?

—whether they belong to the same legend or are remains of other legends—I do not venture to say.

The prose narrative is called "the fable". The Irish _fúball_ is also said to mean "a lie". One might suppose that our "fable" is a kind of _Lügenmärchen_. These stories, which are to be found in most popular literatures, are mixtures of impossibilities, contradictions, and absurdities. Several details in our "fable" are of this nature, _e.g._, "I struck with my back against a tombstone of curds. It almost shattered the bones of my skull to pieces" (p. 150) ; or, again, many details in the description of the door-keeper.

But these absurdities are restricted to the description in which food is exclusively employed. The narrative itself is lacking in the essential of the _Lügenmärchen,_ the intentional and wild improbability of the story, as an example of which may be quoted the well-known English nursery-rhyme :

> "Hey diddle diddle,
> The cat and the fiddle,
> The cow jumped over the moon ;
> The little dog laughed
> To see the sport,
> While the dish ran after the spoon."

Some of the mediæval and modern _Lügenmärchen_ also employ descriptions of Cockayne ; but in these Cockayne rather has the significance of an inverted world, and the whole is conscious nonsense.

The prose narrative does not, then, seem to me to have the character of a _Lügenmärchen ;_ so it is likely that the expression _fúball_ does not mean "lie", but simply "narrative". Perhaps the Irish gleeman rendered by it the expression *fable*, by which his French colleagues denoted their smaller stories.[1]

---

### III.—THE AUTHOR.

B., after having in the Introduction (p. 2) mentioned MacConglinne himself as the author, repeatedly quotes the *Books of Cork* as one of the sources from which the story is drawn, as well as the oral tradition of "elders and shanachies", *i.e.*, professional story-tellers. H. says nothing either about author or source.

MacConglinne's authorship is of course a pious fancy of the redactor of B.; but it is worth close examination. H. calls him a splendid "scholar". MacConglinne himself tells the phantom that he is a poor "scholar". Cathal speaks of him as a "bard", and, as such, refuses to crucify him. This is all consistent : at the suggestion of the Scabbed Youth, MacConglinne had given himself out to be an ollave. B. has much to say about the personality of our hero. He is a famous scholar, with abundance of knowledge, a dreaded satirist, to whom no one dare refuse anything (p. 8). Cathal calls him "student" or "son of learning". On p. 30 he is spoken of as a "sage", and regarded as an instrument of divine power. On p. 12 it is considered extraordinary that no one came to visit him or do reverence to him. He preaches with great success (p. 58). The devil himself says that he possesses the grace of God, abundance of wisdom, acuteness of intellect, etc. (p. 104). According to MacConglinne's own words (p. 40),

---

[1] See Gaston Paris, *La Littérature Française au Moyen Age*, p. 111.

Heaven is open for him, and the heavenly hosts im
patiently await his soul; and on p. 56 he says
himself that his treasure is only in Heaven, or in the
wisdom and poetry of earth.

From all this, then, it would seem that he was
a learned, wise, pious, and generally-esteemed man; at
the same time, a poet and satirist, whom the people
respected.   But the description which the Wizard Doctor
gives of him to his people contradicts this (p. 86).   He,
too, attributes several good qualities to him, but calls
him also "a troublesome party, fierce, furious, impatient, voracious, ungenerous, greedy—a man who
must be fed well or he will abuse his host".[1]

Again, he is not received in Cork as an honoured
guest; on the contrary, he is most ignominiously treated.

He himself behaves in an extraordinary fashion for
a grave and respected scholar (p. 42).   He puts on
a peculiar "short" dress, and begins to juggle before
Pichan and his guests, like a buffoon of the lowest
degree, *obscenis partibus corporis*, like those, *qui crebro
sonitu aerem foedant, et turpiter inclusum turpius pro-
dunt*, of whom John of Salisbury marvels that they are
not turned out of the house (*Polycrat.*, i, chapter viii,
quoted by Warton (ed. Hazlitt), iii, p. 162, note 3).

How are we to understand this?   Simply, I think,
by assuming that in MacConglinne we have one of those

---

[1] It is important to note that this description by the Wizard
Doctor is only found in B.   It is, again, one of those passages
ntroduced with a view to the audience, but quite inconsistent
with the context.   Even the Wizard Doctor himself seems
afraid of MacConglinne's satire, and gives orders to have him
well served.   Immediately after the author forgets his part,
and, in spite of this admonition, MacConglinne is by no means
honourably received, but slips with difficulty into the house.

vagrants (*vagantes*) which were at the same time the
plague and the delight of mediæval Europe.

The one other place in Irish literature in which
MacConglinne's name occurs is a poem in the notes on
the *Calendar of Saints*, ascribed to Oengus, a poem
much like the one in our tale on p. 6. Here he is
mentioned, together with some of his fellow-students at
Armagh :

> " Critan was MacRustaing's name,
> Garbdaire was MacSamain's name,
> Aindiairr was MacConglinne's—
> Many lays he made."[1]

The popular conception of MacConglinne thus seems
to have been that of a clerical student, who was also
a poet. As we have seen, our tale represents him as
a jongleur or jester. An expression which occurs twice
in our tale seems to corroborate this latter view. On
p. 12, while MacConglinne is left starving in the guest-
house at Cork, it is said : " This came of original sin,
and of MacConglinne's hereditary sin, and his own bad
luck." A similar expression occurs on p. 18. I take
this to mean that, beyond the general consequences of
the fall of man and the blows of fortune, MacConglinne
suffered from the discredit attaching to his hereditary
profession as a gleeman or jongleur, a profession that
was always regarded by the Church as one of the most
sinful. Gleemen were not admitted to communion,
and were only allowed exceptionally to partake of the
sacraments, under condition of abstaining from their
trade two weeks before and after. Hugo a Sancto Victore
doubts whether jongleurs should be admitted to mon-
astic life : *joculatores ante conversionem leves, cum ad*

[1] See Stokes' edition, p. cxlv.

*conversionem veniunt, saepius usi levitate, leviter recedunt.*
They have no hope of salvation.[1]  The secular law was
no less severe on them: the *Sachsenspiegel* declares
gleemen to be outlaws; they forfeit their right of inheritance, unless the father has also been a gleeman
who has sold his honour.

The costume which MacC. assumes as he approaches
Pichan's house is none other than the professional garb
of the minstrel or jester.  A *short* cloak and *short*
garments.  Strutt (*The Sports and Pastimes of the
People of England*, p. 189) relates the following anecdote from the time of Edward III.  A young nobleman appears at a festival in a dress called coatbardy,
cut short in the German fashion.  This causes great
stir, and an old knight, well known to him, asks:
"Where, my friend, is your fiddle, your ribible, or such-
like instrument?"  The young nobleman replying that
he could play none of these, "Then," returned the
knight, "you are much to blame, for if you choose to
debase yourself and your family by appearing in the
garb of a minstrel, it is fitting you should be able to
perform his duty."[2]  Strutt further instances a pillar in
St. Mary's Church, Beverley, Yorkshire, bearing the
inscription: "This pillar made the mynstrells."  The
capital of this pillar is adorned with the figures of five
men in short coats, one of whom holds an instrument
like a lute.[3]

[1] *Habent spem ioculatores?  Nullam; totâ namque intentione
sunt ministri Satanae.* (Honor. August., quoted by Scherer,
*Deutsche Dichtung im* 11 *und* 12 *Jahrhundert*, p. 19.)

[2] Strutt quotes as his authority Harl. MS. 1764.

[3] In older Russian literature the short-skirted garment (*kroto-
polie*) of the minstrels is likewise mentioned.  These minstrels
came to the S.E. Slavonic countries from Germany and the

It is true that the two passages from B. referred to above proceed from the last redactor, and did not exist in the versions on which B. and H. are based ; but the fact that B. added them shows, I think, that they were regarded as being in harmony with the character of the hero.

MacConglinne, then, is a vagrant scholar, or one of those vagrant clerics called *lotrici* (*loterphafen* in the German of the Middle Ages) or *goliardi*,[1] who were the rivals of gleemen and jugglers, and who allowed their hair to grow, in direct opposition to the clerical order (*loterphafen mit dem langen hâre*—*lotrici et vagi scolares cum longâ comâ*).

The intention of presenting the condition of the vagrant scholar as advantageously as possible, and of abusing the hated clergy, the hereditary enemy of gleemen, as much as possible, is specially clear in B. We have seen above how MacConglinne is extolled. The

West generally. They even kept their German name (*šp̌ilman*). See Alex. Wesselofsky's excellent paper on mediæval minstrels and jugglers in his *Roumanian, Slavonic, and Greek Christmas Carols* (*Researches in Russian Spiritual Popular Poetry*, vii, ii, p. 128-222, St. Petersburg, 1883, written in Russian), from which the above remarks are mostly taken.

[1] "At the end of the twelfth and during the thirteenth century we meet with frequent mention of a class of persons distinguished by the jocular name of goliards. In Latin they were termed *goliardi* and *goliardenses;* their profession was termed *goliardia;* the verb *goliardizare* was used to signify *goliardorum more agere* .... The *goliardi*, in the original sense of the word, appear to have been in the clerical order somewhat the same class as the jongleurs and minstrels among the laity, riotous and unthrifty scholars who attended on the tables of the richer ecclesiastics, and gained their living and clothing by practising the profession of buffoons and jesters." (Thomas Wright, *The Latin Poems of Walter Mapes*, p. x.)

spite against the clergy vents itself repeatedly. In B. the quarrel with the monks is protracted for the sole reason that the author may have an opportunity for invectives against the monks : "Ye curs and robbers and dung-hounds, ye monks of Cork !" (p. 22, 30). "Your own treachery has come about you, ye curs and robbers, ye monks of Cork !" (p. 24, 26). "It is a sentence of curs" (p. 26, 21). "Ye curs and ye robbers and dung-hounds and unlettered brutes, ye shifting, blundering, hang-head monks of Cork !" (p. 28, 21). When the demon has been expelled, MacConglinne says : "Well, now, ye men of Munster" (instead of "ye monks of Cork"), "yonder is your friend" (the devil). "Shut your mouths, that I may speak with that unworshipful monk" (p. 104, 8). Where anything good is said of the monks, there is a special reason for it. Two passages occur to me ; on p. 20, when MacConglinne is being judged, it is said : "Though a deal of wisdom and knowledge and learning had they, lawfully he was not convicted on a point of speech for which he could be crucified." Here the mention of their wisdom merely serves to set off MacConglinne's innocence. Another laudatory passage, on p. 104, is clearly meant ironically, being put in the mouth of the devil.

At the conclusion of the tale, MacConglinne is greatly honoured by the king, at whose right hand he is to sit, and whose food he is to carve. The abbot, on the other hand, is disgraced, and is left to the mockery of the jesters.

Such a glorification of the vagrant state can only be conceived of as penned in the interest of gleemen or vagrant scholars, and as originating in their circle.

We have seen that in B. the original form of the

tale is much disguised by additions of various kinds;
but these very additions are of great importance in
determining the question of authorship.

The parading of the *soi-disant Books of Cork*, the
acquaintance with other versions of story-tellers, the
statement about the heavenly origin of the Vision—all
this is quite in the gleeman style. He insists upon the
high value of his tale : it was revealed to MacConglinne
by an angel of the Lord ; its truth is undoubted ; it
has been transmitted from of old by elders and historians ; it is written in the annals of Cork ; the scene of
the revelation, the Angel's Ridge, is still to be seen at
Cork ; proverbial sayings have their origin from inci-
dents of the tale (p. 62, p. 64). The narrator is
thoroughly well informed ; he knows the history of how
Cathal became possessed ; he inserts an anecdote of
the scholar of Emly-Ivar, to explain Cathal's favourite
oath ; in short, he seeks to make the impression of a
earned and credible man.

A further characteristic of the gleeman's workman-
ship is his anxiety for reward. Though he does not
interrupt his narrative at some point of thrilling interest
by the remark that he will not continue, or that he will
kill off his hero, unless he is given something to drink,
as is the case in German productions of the kind, yet
the Irish " reader" takes his opportunity to remind his
hearers of the reward to be given him. Shortly before
the end, he says : " Cathal left his grace and blessing
on every one who would read and preserve it" (p. 108).
To "read" here means, of course, not to read by oneself, but to read aloud to others—to recite. The " pre-
server" is the reciter.

The hearers are promised that nothing sorrowful shall

be heard by them ; that it will be a year's protection to them. To hear the tale recited will be of special benefit to them in thirty cases, four of which are specified (p. 112).

Lest there should be any mistake, the reciter himself says what his dues are. A cow, or a shirt, or a woollen cloak with a brooch, from a king and queen, and from married couples; and then follows an enumeration, from which the reciter probably selected what was suited to the present circumstances, and omitted the rest.

In the same way, the hero of the tale demands a boon wherever he can. He makes both the abbot and Pichan reward him for curing Cathal, quite apart from what he gets from the king himself. Nor does the author fail to detail these rewards minutely.

The characteristic description which the Wizard Doctor gives of MacConglinne is directed at the same time *ad auditores.* Not only MacConglinne, but the gleeman, is "fond of eating, voracious, greedy, charming, if he will, but provided he is well served. He is a man great at thanksgivings and upbraidings ; and no wonder, for he has wit both to censure and to praise the hearth of a well-appointed, gentle, rich, merry, mead-circulating house. 'Let me have my proper food and drink,' is his cry, ' or woe to you ; I shall abuse you.'"

The form of the narrative also points to a gleeman. Consider the frequent display of learning in matters religious and ecclesiastical (p. 12, 9 ; 18, 27 ; 40, 10 ; 50, etc.) ; the constant repetitions, the Vision repeated no less than three times, according to the indications of the author, and actually related twice ; the return of runs and typical passages ; the amplifications ; the satirical treatment of Church-matters, and the parody of sacred things ; and compare with all these features what F. Vogt, in his Introduction to *Salman und Morolf*, p. cxviii, says of the manner of composition of gleemen, and it will be allowed that, *ceteris paribus*, the treatment described is that of B.

To sum up, I am convinced that we have here to do with the work of a gleeman. H. is a shorter version, in which much is only indicated. B. is the copy of a detailed gleeman's book, which served for recitation.

If this supposition is correct, the loose patching together of the various sections becomes explicable. In a book intended for private reading, such rude patchwork would not be permissible ; but in a libretto used for recitation, the extent of which might vary, and which might often be interrupted, the patchwork arrange·ment is highly useful, if merely as allowing for pauses, which the reciter makes when collecting money or comforting himself by a drink ; or facilitating the selection made by the reciter according to the character of the public actually before him.

---

## IV.—PARALLELS.

In conclusion, a few analogues to the story of Cathal's cure require notice. Only remote parallels are afforded by Greek legend, as in the case of Erysichthon plagued by Demeter with a demon of voracity for having done violence to a sacred tree.[1] In Ovid's description the culprit is embraced by Fames :

> " altoque sopore solutum
> (noctis enim tempus) geminis amplectitur ulnis,

---

[1] Callimachus, Hymn. 6.

seque viro inspirat, faucesque et pectus et ora
afflat, et in vacuis spargit ieiunia venis."[1]

Fames then returns to his solitary haunt, while Eri-
sichthon, tormented by hunger, consumes all he has and
is beggared. Ovid finally makes him sell his daughter,
and when he has spent the purchase-money :

"ipse suos artus lacero divellere morsu
cœpit, et infelix minuendo corpus alebat."[2]

In mediæval literature, the following story, told by
William of Malmesbury (ii, p. 164), may serve as an
example of other similar ones: "Ruricola quidam in
viciniâ Melduni, notus monachis et urbi, pessimo afflatus
demone torquebatur, cibos nec humanos nec coctione
conditos voragini ventris immergens." He was cured
by St. Aldhelm, who had him placed before the altar.

These three analogues, to which others might no doubt
be added, have nothing else in common with the case of
Cathal but the personification of an unnatural craving
for food in the shape of a demon. The superstition
that such craving originates from a devil having taken
up his abode in the body of the patient is found in
modern times as well.[3] Thus, before a Court of Inquisi-
tion in the last century, a young girl stated that an old
woman had given her a piece of bread smeared with old
fat. When she had eaten it, her bowels began to creak
like a cart, whence she concluded that she had a devil

---

[1] *Metam.* viii, 817-20.                    [2] *Ib.* 877.

[3] There may possibly be a realistic basis for the conception in
the existence of persons with a diseased craving for food. See
the very repulsive cases cited by Tardieu. The "great eater" is
a constant figure of the folk-tale, and appears in Wales as early
as the twelfth century (Kulhwch), and in Iceland in the thirteenth century (Snorri's Edda). Herakles, under one of his
aspects, probably goes back to an early Greek "great eater".

in her body. When he wanted to eat, he made himself
small, crept up into her mouth, and pinched her till she
was forced to eat something, when he was appeased.
If he wished to eat "Eierback" or "Stuten", he would
call to her out of her body, "Stuten!" "Eierback!"
and when he was satisfied he said "Stop!" after which
she was unable to eat anything more.[1]

In a dissertation for the degree of doctor at Witten-
berg, written in 1757, the candidate treats the case of
a celebrated eater of the time, whom the people considered possessed. The Senate of the University had
instituted an inquiry into this case, and placed the
minutes at the disposal of the author.[2]

According to an English superstition, it is the presence
of a wolf in the stomach that produces an unnatural
craving for food. Thus, in *The Dialect of Craven in the
West Riding of York* (2nd ed., London, 1888), vol. ii,
p. 8, the word "wolf" is explained—"an enormous
unnatural appetite, vulgarly supposed to be a wolf in
the stomach."[3] Or take this passage from the *Vocabu-
lary of East Anglia*, by Robert Forby, London, 1830 :
"Wolf, (1) a preternatural or excessive craving for

[1] Ernst Gottfried Kurella, der Arzneygelahrtheit Doktors,
*Gedanken von Besessenen und Bezauberten*, Halle, 1749. On
p. 12 the author quotes the proceedings of the Court of In-
quisition from a disputation by Prof. Detharding of Rostock,
*Von Besessenen und von besessen-Gehaltenen.*

[2] Christ. Godofred. Frenzelius, *De polyphago et allotriophago
Wittenbergensi*, p. 4 : "Putabant vero plurimi illum miraculosâ
et præternaturali ratione ea peragere, ideoque suspectum et a
diabolo forte obsessum esse communiter dicebant." In chapter
ii the author, with much learning, gives "alia phagonum ex-
empla".

[3] Cf. the slang use of " to wolf" = to eat gluttonously.

*d*

food—'Surely he must have a wolf in his stomach'; (2) a gnawing internal pain proceeding from cancer or other ulcer, which, as a ravenous beast, preys upon the intestines." The author tells that a poor woman, whose husband had been dissected, informed him that the doctors had found the wolf and carried it away. He adds these remarks: "Had she supposed it to be a morbid part of the body, she would certainly not have allowed this; but she believed *bonâ fide* that it was a voracious animal, which had somehow found its way in, and had been detected and turned out too late."[1]

In his paper *Deutscher Aberglaube*,[2] Liebrecht quotes from the *Myreur des Histors, Chronique de Jean des Preis dit Doutremeuse*, the story of Eraclius, Bishop of Liéges, who in a dream was cured by St. Martin of an ulcer on his leg. The chronicler says that the Bishop had "une plaie qui mangoit cascon jour dois gros porcheais, si la nommons le louve".

Finally, I would quote a modern Greek incantation, in which the stomach-ache (γαστήρ) is personified[3]: Γαστήρ, γαστέρα τρομερέ, τρομερέ καὶ φοβερέ! κάτω 'ς τὸ γιαλό, κάτω 'ς τὸ περιγιάλι εἶνε τρία σκουτελάκια, τ' ἕνα μέλι, τ' ἄλλο γάλα, τ' ἄλλο τ' ἄντερα τ' ἀνθρώπου. Φάε μέλι, φάε γάλα, κι' ἄφες τ' ἄντερα τ' ἀνθρώπου. "Stomach-ache, terrible stomach-ache, terrible and horrible! Below on the shore, on the beach are three dishes, one with honey, another with milk, another with human entrails. Eat honey, eat milk, and leave the human entrails."

All these legends are various forms of the belief, prevalent at all times and with all peoples, that certain

[1] Quoted by Felix Liebrecht, *Otia Imperialia*, p. 171.
[2] *Zur Volkskunde*, p. 348.
[3] See Liebrecht, *l. c.*

diseases are evil beings, which can only be expelled through witchcraft and incantation.

But these parallels are insufficient to explain the definite form which this idea has assumed in Irish legend, and of which we have an early example in the specific Irish form of Herod's punishment preserved in the *Leabhar Breac* (p. 143*a*), according to which he was possessed by a demon of voracity called a *lon cráis*, as in the Vision of MacConglinne.

The following curious tale of the Irish saint Fursa, from the notes on the *Calendar of Oengus*, may also be quoted[1] :

Now Fursa chanced to visit Maignenn of Kilmainham. They make their union, and exchange their tribulations in token of their union, viz., head-ache or piles[2] (?) that was on Fursa to be on Maignenn, and a beast that was in Maignenn to go into Fursa, so that it was his custom every morning for ever to eat three bits of bacon, so that he might suppress the beast's violence. Fursa happened to go over sea, and came to a certain great city, where he observes his usual practice, and he is brought to the Bishop of the city to be censured. "Not good devotion is thy life," quoth the Bishop. "Thou art permitted, O cleric," quoth Fursa, "to try that which inflicts this on me." Forthwith then leaps the beast into the Bishop's throat. Now, when every one knew that, Fursa calls the beast back to him again.

The way in which the demon is enticed out of Cathal's throat by food being shown to it reminds one of numerous stories of snakes that have been swallowed and are

---

[1] *Félire Oengusso*, ed. Stokes, p. xxxv.
[2] Lit. red-disease.

made to come forth by milk being placed for them. I might quote many versions, but believe the thing itself to be too well known.

All the analogues hitherto mentioned stand, however, only in a more or less remote relation to the story of Cathal. Indeed, a wholly analogous legend is not known to me. The form that comes nearest to it is found on Gaelic ground.

Campbell of Islay, in his *Popular Tales of the West Highlands*, ii, p. 366, has the following story of an Islay doctor (*ollamh Ileach*) :

He was called to see a young lady, daughter of Mackay of Kilmahumaig, near Crinan. When approaching the house, attended by a servant, the latter remarked a sweet female voice which he heard singing a song :

"''S binn an guth cinn sin,' ars 'n gilleadh.
''S binn,' ars ant Ollamh, 'air uachdar losguin.'"

"'Sweet is that head's voice,' said the lad.
'Sweet,' said the Doctor, 'above a toad.'"

The poor young woman had an enormous appetite, which could not be satisfied, but she was reduced to a skeleton. The doctor, on hearing her voice, knew what her disease was, and ordered a sheep to be killed and roasted. The lady was prevented from getting any food, from which she was in great agony.

She was made to sit by the sheep while it was being roasted, and the flavour of the meat tempted the toad she had swallowed to come up her throat and out of her mouth, when she was completely cured. The reptile she had swallowed was called the *lon craois*.

A similar story is found in Douglas Hyde's collection

of Irish tales called *Beside the Fire*,[1] p. 47. According
to a note on p. 183, traces of this story are found
throughout Ireland.

I believe, then, that the story of Cathal's cure is of
Irish local origin; for, whether the cause of the unnatural appetite is a *lon cráis* or demon, as in the case
of Cathal, of Herod, and the lady of Islay, or a newt
(*alp líachra, lissotriton punctatus*), as in Hyde's version,
in each case the essential element of the story is the
bringing out of the monster by exciting his appetite,
either through hunger or thirst.

[1] *Beside the Fire*: A Collection of Irish Gaelic Folk-Stories.
Edited, translated, and annotated by Douglas Hyde. With
Additional Notes by Alfred Nutt. London: David Nutt. 1890.

W. WOLLNER.

# THE VISION

OF

# MacCONGLINNE.

# VISION OF MacCONGLINNE BEGINS.

THE four things to be asked of every composition must be asked of this composition, viz., place, and person, and time, and cause of invention.

The place of this composition is great Cork of 5 Munster, and its author is Aniér MacConglinne of the Onaght Glenowra. In the time of Cathal MacFinguine, son of Cúcengairm, or son of Cúcenmáthir, it was made. The cause of its invention was to banish the demon of gluttony that was in 10 the throat of Cathal MacFinguine.

Cathal MacFinguine was a good king, who governed Munster ; a great warrior prince was he. A warrior of this sort : with the edge of a hound, he ate like a horse. Satan, viz. a demon of gluttony that was in 15 his throat, used to devour his rations with him. A pig and a cow and a bull-calf of three hands, with three score cakes of pure wheat, and a vat of new ale, and thirty heathpoults' eggs, that was his first dole, besides his other snack, until his great feast 20 was ready for him. As regards the great feast, that passes account or reckoning.

The reason of the demon of gluttony being in the throat of Cathal MacFinguine was, because he had, though he had never seen her, a first love for Lígach, 25 daughter of Mældúin, king of Ailech; and she sister to Fergal, son of Mældúin, also king of Ailech, who

# AISLINGE MEIC CONGLINNE.

CETHARDAI as cuintesta da cach elathain, issed as
cuintesta don eladain se .i. locc [ocus persu] ocus
aimser ocus fáth airicc.

Locc don eladain se Corcach Mōr Muman, ocus
persu dī Anér mac Conglinde di Eoganacht 5
Glennabrach. I n-aimsir Cathail meic Fhinguine
meic Concengairm nū meic Concenmūthair dorónad.
Is hē didíu fáth airicc a dēnma .i. do díchor in luin
crūeis bói i m-brāgait Cathail meic Fhinguine.

Cathal mac Finguine, rí maith rogab Mumai : araile 10
lǣch māl mór ēsside. Amlaid bōi in lǣch sin: co
n-gēri chon, co longad chapaill. Sattan (.i. lon crūis
bōi ina brāgait) nomeled a chuit laiss. Mucc ocus
mart ocus ag trora ferglacc, la trī fichte bairgen do
fhírcruithnecht, ocus dabach do nūa chorma ocus 15
tricha og rerchirce, ba hí insin a prīmairigid,[1] cen-
motha a [fh]rithairigid,[1] co m-ba herlam a mōrfheiss
dó. Dāig in mōrfheiss, nī thalla rím nū āirem
furri-sene.

Is hē tra fáth airicc in luin crūis i m-brāgait Cathail 20
meic Fhinghuine: daig bōi cētshercus ēcmaise dó fria
Lígaig ingin Mōile Dúin rīg Oilig, ocus derbshiur side
do Fhergal mac Mōile Dúin, rí Oilig beos, ocus ba

airaigid

· was then contending for the kingship of Ireland
against Cathal MacFinguine, as is plain from the
quarrel of the two hags, when they had a duel in
quatrains at Freshford :

5      "He comes from the North, comes from the North,
       The son of Mældúin, over the rocks,
       Over Barrow's brink, over Barrow's brink,
       Till kine he take he will not stay."

       " He shall stay, shall stay," said the Southern hag ;
10     " He will be thankful if he escapes.
       By my father's hand, by my father's hand,
       If Cathal meets him, he'll take no kine."

Then kernels and apples and many sweets used
to be brought from Lígach, Mældúin's daughter, to
15 Cathal MacFinguine, for his love and affection.
Fergal, son of Mældúin, heard this, and his sister was
called unto him.   And he gave her a blessing if she
should tell him truth, and a curse if she should deny
him it.   The sister told him ; for great as was her
20 love and affection for Cathal MacFinguine, she
feared her brother's curse reaching her.   Then she
told the true story.

The brother told her to send the apples to himself.
And a scholar was summoned unto him, and he
25 promised great rewards to the scholar for putting
charms in those numerous sweets, to the destruction
of Cathal MacFinguine. And the scholar put charms
and heathen spells in those numerous sweets, and
they were delivered to Fergal, who despatched
30 messengers to convey them to Cathal. And they
entreated him by each of the seven universal things,
sun and moon, dew and sea, heaven and earth, day
[and night . . . . that he would eat] those apples,

cosnamaid[1] Érenn ēsside an inbaid sin i n-agaid
Cathail meic Fhinguine, am*al* is follus a himarbáig
in dā chaillech dīa n-de*rn*sat in dí chammrand i
n-Achad Ūr saindrud :

> "Dosfil atūaid, dosfil atūaid  5
> mac Mōile Dúin dar ailechu,
> dar Berba brú, dar Berba brú,
> co ruca bú nī aineba."

> " Anfaid, anfaid,"—ar in chaillech aness—
> " bid buide lais dīa n-ērnaba.  10
> Dar laím m'athar, [dar lāim m'athar,]
> dīanustáir Cathal, nīsbēra bā."

Dobertīs īarum ettne ocus úbla ocus ilblassa ō
Lígaig ingin Mōli Dúin do Cathal mac Finguine for
a sheirc ocus inmaine. Atcūala Fergal mac Mōile Dúin  15
inní sin, ocus dogarad a shiúr a dóchumm. Ocus
dombert bennachtain dī for fír d' indissi dó, ocus
mallacht dīa sénad fair. Ro-indis in shiur dó ; ar cīa
bói dīa sheircc ocus grād Cath*ail* m*ei*c Fhinguine
aicce, rop ōmun lee mallacht a brāthar dīa rochtain.  20
Ro-indis īar sin in scél fíre.

Atbert in brāthair fria na húbla do tachor chuice.
Ocus rogairmed scolaige ina dóchumm, ocus doruachell
lógu mōra don scolaigi ar thūathi do chur isna
hilblassaib út do admilliud Cathail meic Fhinguine.  25
Ocus rolā in scolaigi tūathi ocus gen*tl*echt isna
hilblassaib sin, ocus rothidnacit chuca ina hilblassa,
ocus cartaid timthirid dīa tidn*a*cul do C[h]athal.
Ocus rogāidetar for nach sech*t*a coitcend .i. grian
ocus ésca, drúcht ocus muir, nem ocu*s* tal*am*, lā . . .[2]  30

---

[1] cosnamaig     [2] Space left vacant for about ten letters.

since it was out of love and affection for him they
were brought from Lígach, daughter of Mældúin.

Cathal thereupon ate the apples, and little
creatures through the poison spells were formed
5 of them in his inside. And those little creatures
gathered in the womb of one—in that animal, so
that there was formed the demon of gluttony.
And this is the cause why the demon of gluttony
abode in the throat of Cathal MacFinguine, to the
10 ruin of the men of Munster during three half-years;
and it is likely he would have ruined Ireland during
another half-year.

There were eight persons in Armagh at that time
of whom these lays were sung :

15    I heard of eight to-night
In Armagh after midnight ;
I proclaim them with hosts of deeds,
Their names are no sweet symphonies.

   Comgán was the name of the Two Smiths' son.
20    Famous was he after the hunt.
Critán was Rustang's noble son,
It was a full fitting name.

   The Two Tribes' Dark One, a shining cry,
That was the name of Stelene's son,
25    Dun Raven, a white nun, of Beare,
Rough Derry was the name of Samán's son.

   Never-Refused was MacConglinne's name,
From the brink of the sweet-crested Bann.
Wee Man, Wee Wife, bag of carnage,
30    Were Dead Man's sire and dam.

   My king, king of high heaven,
That givest hosts victory over death,
Great son of Mary,—Thine the way—
A confluence of cries I heard.

na n-uball út, ūair is ar a grūd ocus inmaine tuccad
ō Lígaig ingin Móli Dúin.
Doromel Cathal na húbla īarum, ocus dorigne míla
eptha dib ina medōn. Ocus timoirsit na míla eptha
sin i m-broind ōen . . . . . .¹ isin anmunna sin, co 5
n-derna lon craís de. Conid hē sin *fāth* o[i]ricc in
luin chráis do attreib i m-brágait Cathail meic
Fhinguine do aidmilliud fer Muman co cend *teora*
lethbl*iadan* ; ocus is dōig nomille[d] Ēirinn co cend
lethbl*iadna* ele. 10

Bōi *ochtar* i n-Ard Macha an inboid sin. ocus is
dōib-side rocanait in lūid se :

Atcnala *ochtar* anocht
i n-Ard Macha īar midnocht :
fortgillim co m-búidnib band, 15
nīdat cuibde a comanmand.

Comgán ar mac Dā Cherda,
ba herdraic i n-dīaid shelga,
Critān for mac Rustaing rán,
ba hainm comadais comlán. 20

Dub Dā Thūath, ba togairm n-glō,
ba hē ainm meic Stelene :
Don[n]fliach² caillech Berre bán, ʌ[i]
Garbdaire for mac Samán. ʌ[i]

Aniér for mac Conglinde 25
do brú Banda barrbinde,
Becān, Becnait, bolg donī ār,
athair sceō māthair Marbán.

Mo ríg-se, ri nime nāir,³
dobeir for buidne būad nāis, 30
*mac* mūad Muire, mod notba,
comur n-gāire rochūala. Atcūala ochtar.

¹ Space left vacant for about sixteen letters.
² There seems to be *punctum delens* under *th*. ³ nais

One of these eight, then, was Aniér MacConglinne, a famous scholar he, with abundance of knowledge. The reason why he was called Aniér was because he would satirise and praise all.  No wonder, indeed ;
5 for there had not come before him, and came not after him, one whose satire or praise was harder to bear, wherefore he was called Anéra [*i.e.* Non-refusal], for that there was no refusing him.

A great longing seized the mind of the scholar, to
10 follow poetry, and to abandon his reading.   For wretched to him was his life in the shade of his studies.   And he searched in his mind whither he would make his first poetical journey.   The result of his search was, to go to Cathal MacFinguine,
15 who was then on a royal progress in Iveagh of Munster.   The scholar had heard that he would get plenty and enough of all kinds of whitemeats ; for greedy and hungry for whitemeats was the scholar.

This came into the mind of the scholar on a
20 Saturday eve exactly, at Roscommon ; for there he was pursuing his reading.   Then he sold the little stock he possessed for two wheaten cakes and a slice of old bacon with a streak across its middle.   These he put in his book-satchel.   And on that night two
25 pointed shoes of hide, of seven-folded dun leather, he shaped for himself.

He arose early on the morrow, and tucked up his shirt over the rounds of his fork, and wrapped him in the folds of his white cloak, in the front
30 of which was an iron brooch.   He lifted his book-satchel on to the arched slope of his back.   In his right hand he grasped his even-poised knotty staff,

Ba hǣn tra don ochtar sin .i. Aniēr mac Conglinne,
scolaigi amru ēsside co n-immad eōlais. Is aire
atbertha Aniér friss .i. no-ǣrad ocus nomolad cāch.
Deithbir ón, ūair nī thānic remi ocus ní ticc dīa
ēissi bu duilge ǣr nō molad, conid aire atbertha 5
Anūra friss, iarsinnī ní fētta éra fair.


Tānic móit mōr for menmain don scolaigi .i. dol
ra filidecht ocus a lēgend do [fh]ācbāil. Ar ba
doinmech dó a betha for scáth a fhogluma. Ocus
roscrūtust*air* ina menmain cīa leth nob*e*rad a 10
chétchūai*r*t fhilidechta. Issed tra tucc dīa scrūt*ain*, a
dula co Cathal mac Finguine bói for cūairt rīg i
n-Ūib Ech*ach* Muman. Atchūala in scolaige immad
ocus oirer cacha bánbíd do fhāgbāil dó; ūair ba
sánntach soaccobrach mbánbíd in scolaige. 15


Is and tānic inní sin im-menmain in scolaigi
aidche Sath*air*n saindrud ic Russ Commán; or is
ann bói oc dēnmus[1] a légind. Iarsin recaid in
m-bec sprédi bōi acca .i. for dā bairgin do
chruithnecht ocus for thócht sensaille co sīthfi[2] dar a 20
lār. Dosrat sin ina théig lib*air*. Ocus c*u*mmais dī
chūarán corra coidlide[3] do dondleth*ar* sechtfhillte
dó in adaig[4] sin.


Atraacht moch īarnabárach ocus gabaid a lēnid
i n-ardgabāil ōs mell*ach* a lāruc, ocus gab*aid* 25
a lummain find fortōcbalta i forcip*ul* imme.
Mílec[h] īarnaide[5] ūasu ina brutt. Tūarcaib
a théig lib*air* for stūagleirg a dromma. Rotgab

---

[1] den*m*uu*s*   [2] tithfi   [3] coidlige   [4] agaid   [5] iarnaige

in which were five hands from one end to the other.
Then, going right-hand-wise round the cemetery, he
bade farewell to his tutor, who put gospels around
him.

5   He set out on his way and journey, across the
lands of Connaught into Aughty, to Limerick, to
Carnarry, to Barna-trí-Carbad, into Slieve-Keen,
into the country of the Fir-Féni, which is this day
called Fermoy, across Moinmore, until he rested a
10 short time before vespers in the guest-house of
Cork.   On that Saturday he had gone from Roscommon to Cork.

This was the way in which he found the guest-
house on his arrival, it was open.   That was one of
15 the days of the three things, viz., wind and snow
and rain about the door ; so that the wind left not
a wisp of thatch, nor a speck of ashes that it did
not sweep with it through the other door, under the
beds and couches and screens of the princely house.
20  The blanket of the guest-house was rolled,
bundled, in the bed, and was full of lice and fleas.
No wonder, truly, for it never got its sunning by
day, nor its lifting at night ; for it was not wont to
be empty at its lifting.   The bath-tub of the guest-
25 house, with the water of the night before in it, with
its stones, was by the side of the door-post.

The scholar found no one who would wash his
feet.   So he himself took off his shoes and washed
his feet in that bath-tub, in which he afterwards
30 dipped his shoes.   He hung his book-satchel on the
peg in the wall, took up his shoes, and gathered his
hands into the blanket, which he tucked about his
legs.   But, truly, as numerous as the sand of the sea,

a t[h]rostán comthromm cōicduirn (.i. ón beind
co a chēli) cutruma fo*r*bolcsén ina desláim. Dolluid
desel relci. Bendachais dīa fithir (.i. aite). Atnagar
sosc*ē*la imme.

Docummlai i cend shētta ocus imdechta dar crīch   5
Connacht i n-Echtgi, do Luimnech, do Charnd
Feradaig, do Berna Trī Carpat, i Sléib Cāin, i tīr Fer
Fhéni, frisi rūite*r* Fir Muige indíu, dar Mónaid Móir,
co n-dessid sel becc rīa n-espartain i taig áiged
Chorcaige. Ō Ross Comān co Corccaig dia Sathai*r*n  10
saindrud.

Is am*laid* dorala in tech āiged, oslaicthe for a
chind. Hil-lathi na teorai in lá sin .i. gāth ocus
snechta ocus fleoch*ud* ina dorus, conā fārcaib in
gāth sifi*nd* tuga nō minde lúatha cen scūabad lee  15
dar in dorus aile fo cholbaib ocus fo immdadaib
ocus fo clīathaib in rīgthige.

Sētigi in tige āiged ocus sē timmthasta timmairethi
ina lebaid, ocus ba mīlach dergnatach ēside. Deithbir
ón, ar nísfūgbad[1] a grīanad il-lō nō a thōcbáil i  20
n-aidche, ar nī ba gnāth dó beith folam fria thōcbāil.
Lothomur in taige āiged co n-us*ci* na haidche remi
ind, cona clochaib hi tāib na hursand.

Niconfūair in scolaige āen dogneth a fhósaic. Benais
fén īarum a chūarānu de, ocus iudlais asin aithindlat 25
út. Mescais a chūarānu and iarum. Tócbais a thēig
liba*ir* for a luirg isin fraigid, ocus tecbaid a chūarānu,
ocus teclumaid[2] a lāmu laiss isin sētigi, ocus
inmaiscis imma chossa. Acht cena ba liridir fri

---

[1] fadbad
[2] Sign of aspiration added over t in paler ink.

or sparks of fire, or dew on a May morning, or the
stars of heaven, were the lice and fleas nibbling his
legs, so that weariness seized him.   And no one
came to visit him or do reverence to him.

5    He took down his book-satchel, and brought out
his psalter, and began singing his psalms.  What
the learned and the books of Cork relate is, that the
sound of the scholar's voice was heard a thousand
paces beyond the city, as he sang his psalms, through
10 spiritual  mysteries,  in  lands,  and  stories,  and
various kinds, in dia-psalms and syn-psalms and
sets of ten, with paters and canticles and hymns at
the conclusion of each fifty.   Now, it seemed to
every man in Cork that the sound of the voice was
15 in the house next himself.  This came of original
sin, and MacConglinne's hereditary sin and his
own  plain-working  bad  luck ;  so  that  he  was
detained  without  drink,  without  food,  without
washing, until every man in Cork had gone to his
20 bed.
      Then it was that Manchin, abbot of Cork, said,
after having gone to his bed : " Lad," he said, " are
there guests with us to-night ? "
      " There are not," said the attendant.
25    However, the other attendant said : " I saw one
going hastily, impatiently across the green a short
time before vespers, a while ago."
      " You had better visit him," said Manchin, " and
take him his ration.  For he has been too lazy to
30 come back for his allowance, and moreover the
night was very bad."
      His allowance was brought out, and these were

gainem mara nō fri drithrenna tened nō fri drúcht
im-matain cétamain nō fri renna nime míla ocus
dergnatta ic guilbniugud a choss, condagaib emeltius.
Ocus nīstānic nech dia fhiss nō dia umalōit ina
dochum.                                                    5
    Tucc fadessin a théig lib*air* chuca, ocus benais a
shaltair essi, ocus forbairt cantain a shalm.  Is*sed*
atfīadat eōlaig ocus libair Chorccaige, co closs míle
cūmend sechtair cath*raig* immach son a gotha in
scolaigi oc cētul a shalm tria rúnib spīr*t*alta, for aillib 10
ocus annālaib ocus ernaḻib, for diapsalmaib ocus
sinsalmaib ocus decáidib, co paitrib ocus cantaccib
ocus immnaib hi forba cacha *coc*ait.  Ba dóig
im*moro* fria cach fer i Corccaig, bá isin tig ba nessa
dō nobith son in foguir.  Issed ró-imfulaing, in 15
comra*r*gu bunatta ocus a p[h]eccad búnadgendi ocus
a mīrath follusgnéthech fodēin, corerfhuirged cen dig
cen bīad cen indlat, co n-dech*aid* cach duine i
Corccaig ina immdaid.


    Con[id] ann asbert Manchīn abb Corccaige iar 20
n-dul dó ina lepaid : "A scolócc," ol sē, "in filet
áigid occaind innocht?"
    " Nī filet," ol in timthirid.
    Ar sē in timthirid aile : " Itconnarc-sa ēn co díscir
denmnetach dar fiarut na faigthi gar becc rīa 25
n-espartain ō chīanaib."
    " Is ferr a fhiss," ol Manchín, " ocus a chutig do
br*eith* dó.  Or bōi dia lesca les-side tidecht 'na
[fh]rithing aridisi for cend a chota, ocus bōi tra d'
olcc na haidche."                                          30
    Berar a chuitig-sium amach, ocus is ī proind ruccad

X comrorcu, cuar

the rations that were taken to him : a small cup of
the church whey-water, and two sparks of fire in the
middle of a wisp of oaten straw, and two sods of fresh
peat.

5    The servant came to the door of the guest-house,
and fear and terror seized him at the gaping open
pitch-dark house.   He knew not whether anybody
was within, or not; whereupon one of the two asked,
in putting his foot across the threshold :

10    " Is there any one here ? " says he.

" There is some one," answered MacConglinne.

" It is a breaking of the spells that are on this
house to put it in order for one man."

" If ever the spells on it were broken," said
15 MacConglinne, " they were to-night ; for their
breaking was fated, and it is I who break them."

" Rise," said the attendant, " and eat thy meal."

" I pledge my God's doom," said he, " that since I
have been kept waiting till now, until I know what
20 you have there, I shall not rise."

The gillie put the two sparks of fire that were
in the middle of the wisp of oaten straw, on the
hearth, and pulled another wisp from the bed.
He arranged the two sods of fresh peat round the
25 wisps, blew the spark, lighted the wisp, and showed
him his repast ; whereupon MacConglinne said :

"My lad," said MacConglinne,
" Why should not we have a duel in quatrains ?
A quatrain compose on the bread,
30    I will make one on the relish.

Cork, wherein are sweet bells,
Sour is its sand,

ann : cūachān (.i. corcca) do médgusci na heclaise, ocus dā óibell tened im-medón suipp silcātha corcca, ocus dā fhót do úrmónaid.

Ticc in timt[h]irid co dorus in taigi óiged, ocus rosgab gráin ocus ecla frisin tech n-óbéla n-oslacthi 5 n-imdorcha. Niconfetar in rabi ēn and, fó nū rabi. Conid ann atbert indalanāi oc tabairt a choisse dar in tairsech :
    " In fil nech sund ? " ol sē.
    " Fil ēn," ar Mac Conglinde.              10
    " Is cóll gessi don tig sea a thachur for ēnfer."

    " Mārocollit rīam a gessi," ar Mac Conglinne, "rocollit innocht, .i. bōi a n-dán a coll, ocus is mē choilles."
    " Erg," ol in timthirid,[1] " ocus tomil do próind ! " 15
    " Atbiur mo dēbroth," ol sē, " ōramfuirged cusin trāth sa, nocofesser cid fil and, noco n-ērus."

Atnaig in gilla in dī ōibill a medōn int shuip shílcātha corcca isin tellach, ocus ticc sopp asin lepa chuca, cōirgis in dí fōt úrmónad imna suppu, sétis 20 ind óibill, lassais in sopp, ocus follsigis dō a proind. Ut dixit Mac Conglinne :

        " A scoló[i]c," ar Mac Conglinne,
        " cid nā dénum dá chammrand ?
        Déna-su rand ar arán,                          25
        co n-dēn-sa rand ar annland.

        Corcach i fil cluca binde,
        goirt a gainem,

                    [1] timthirig

Its soil is sand,
Food there is none in it.

Unto Doom I would not eat,
Unless famine befel them,
5       The oaten ration of Cork,
Cork's oaten ration.

Along with thee carry the bread,
For which thou'st made thy orison ;
Woe worth him who eats this ration,
10      That is my say, my lad."

The attendant remembered the quatrains, for his understanding was sharp.

They take the food back to the place where Manchín was, and declared the quatrains to the
15 abbot.

"Well," said Manchín, "the ill word will tell you the boy. Little boys will sing those verses,, unless the words are avenged on him who made them."

20 "What do you mean to do, then ?" said the gillie.

"This," said Manchín ; "to go to the person who made them, to strip him of all his clothes, to lay scourges and horsewhips on him, until his flesh and
25 skin break and sever from his bones (only let his bones not be broken): to put him in the Lee and give him his fill of the muddy water of the Lee. Then let him be put into the guest-house, without a stitch of clothing." (And there was no clothing in
30 that house but the blanket, in which lice and fleas were as plentiful as May dew.) "There let him sleep that night, in the most wretched and darkest plight he ever was in.  Let the house be closed on

gainem a grīan,
noconfil bīad inde.¹

Co brāth noco n-ísaind-sea,
acht minustecma gorta,
cūachān corca Corccaige,      5
cúachān Corccaige corca.

Geb-si chucat in n-arān
ima n-dernai[s]-siu t' oróit.
In chuit si is mairg dosméla :
is īat mo scéla, a scoló[i]c." A scoló[i]c.     10

Mébraigis in scolōc² na runda, ūair bā háith á
inntlecht.

Atnagut leō in m-bīad co hairm a m-bōi Mainchín,
ocus taisselb*ait* na runna don abbaid.

"Maith," ol Mauchín, "atmait meicc mífhoccuil. ¹⁵
.Gébdait mecc beca na runda sin, minā dīgailt*ir*
forsintí dorigne."

"Cid fil lat-su desin ?" or in gilla.

"Fil liumm," or Mánchín, "dul cusintí dorigne,
ocus ulidétaid a ētaig do bein de, slipre ocus 20
echlusca do gabáil dō, coromuide ocus coroet*ar*scara
a fheōil ocus a chraiccend ō chnámu, acht nammū nā
robrist*er* a chnámu ; a chor isin Sábraind, ocus a
bodarshāith d' usc*i* na Sábrainde dó. A chor isin tech
n-ōiged īarum cen meth*er* n-étaig do lōcud leis 25
inund." (Ocus nī bōi tall d' étach acht in sétige,
ocus ba lilithir drucht cētemain a mīla-side ocus a
dergnuta.) "Fessid ind in aidche sin feib as doccra
ocus as dorcha bōi rīam remi. Forīatar in tech fair

¹ si*n*de           ² scolaigi

C

him from outside until morning, in order that he
may not escape, until my counsel together with the
counsel of the monks of Cork shall be held on
him to-morrow, even in the presence of the Creator
5 and of St. Barre, whose servant I am.   Our counsel
shall be no other than his crucifixion to-morrow, for
the honour of me and of St. Barre, and of the Church."

So it was done.   And then it was that his
hereditary transgression and his own plain-working
10 sin rose against MacConglinne.   The whole of his
clothing was stripped off him, and scourges and
horsewhips were laid on him.   He was put into
the Lee, and had his fill of its dead water.   After
which he lay in the guest-house until morning.

15   Early at morn Manchin arose on the morrow ; and
the monks of Cork were gathered by him, until
they were in one place, at the guest-house.   It
was opened before them, and they sat down on
the bed-rails and couches of the house.

20   "Well, you wretch," said Manchin, "you did not
do right in reviling the Church last night."

"The church-folk did no better," said MacConglinne, "to leave me without food, though I was
only a party of one."

25   "Thou hadst not gone without food, even though
thou hadst only got a little crumb, or a drink of
whey-water in the church.   There are three things,
about which there should be no grumbling in the
Church ; viz. new fruit, and new ale, and Sunday
30 eve's portion.   For however little is obtained on
Sunday eve, what is nearest on the morrow is psalm-
singing, then bell-ringing, Mass, with preaching

co matain dianechtair, ardāig nū roélád, coraib mo
chomairle-si fair le comarli muntiri Corccāige im-
mbūrach i fiadnaise in dúilemun cena ocus Barre
'gátó-sa.  Nī ba comairle aile acht a c[h]rochad imbūrach imm enech-sa ocus enech Barra ocus ina  5
heclaisi."

Dorigned am*ail* sin.  Ocus is ann sin tānic a chom-
rarcu bunata ocus a p[h]eccad follusgnēthech féu
fri[s]-sium.  Robenad ulidétaid a étaig de, ocus
rogabad slipre ocus echlusca dó.  Rofuirmed hē isin  10
Sábraind co tartad nī fair,[1] a sháith do bodarusci na
Sabrainde dō.  Fessid īar sin isin tig óiged co
matain.

Atracht Manchīn matain moch īarnabūrach, ocus
rotinōlit muinnter Chorccaige ō Manchīn, co m-bātar  15
i n-ǣnbaile .i. isin tech n-óiged.  Auroslaicther
rempu, ocus fessait for colbadaib ocus immdadu in
tigi.

" Maith, a t[h]róig," ol Manchín, "ní dernais cóir
in eclais do écnach aréir."                                20

" Nīrbo fherr do lucht na heclaisi," ar Mac
Conglinde, " mo beth-si cen bīad occu, ocus rob
ūathad mo dám."

" Nīrbeith cen bīad deitt, cein co fāgtha acht
ablaind m-bic nō dig do medgusci isind eclais.  Fil  25
tréda darnā dlegar oirbire ind-eclais .i. nūathorud
ocus nūa cornma ocus cuit aidche Dómnaig.  Ar
cid bec isna haidchib Domnaig, issed is nessam ara-
būrach : sailm do ghabāil, cloc íar sin, celebrad la
precept ocus oiffrend, sāsad bocht.  Esbuid na haidche  30

[1] *fora*

and the Sacrament, and feeding the poor. What
was a wanting on the eve of Sunday will be got on
Sunday or on the eve of Monday. You began
grumbling early."

5      "And I profess," said MacConglinne, "that we
acted in humility, and there was more than enough
in requital."

"But I vow before the Creator and St. Barre,"
said Manchín, "thou shalt not revile again. Take
10 him away with you, that he may be crucified on the
green, for the honour of St. Barre and of the
Church, and for my own honour."

"O cleric," said MacConglinne, "let me not be
crucified, but let a righteous, just judgment be
15 given on me, which is better than to crucify
me."

Then they proceeded to give judgment on Mac-
Conglinne. Manchín began to plead against him,
and every man of the monks of Cork proceeded,
20 according to rank, against MacConglinne. But,
though a deal of wisdom and knowledge and learning had they, lawfully he was not convicted on a
point of speech for which he could be crucified.

25      Then was he taken without law to Ráthín Mac n-
Aeda, a green in the southern quarter of Cork. He
said :

"A boon for me, O Manchín, and ye monks of
Cork !"

30      "Is it to spare thee?" asked Manchín.

"That is not what I ask," said MacConglinne,
"though I should be glad if that would come of it."

"Speak," said Manchín.

Domnaig is dia Domnaig nō aidche Lūain fogabar.
Ocus moch dorindis oirb*ir*e."

"Fuisidim-si tra," ar Mac Conglinne, "co n-d*er*n-
samm i n-umalōit, ocus fuilled ro-imarcraid ind-
aithi."                                                           5
"Acht gillim fīad n-duilemain ocus Barri," ol
Manchín, "nī ba hāir bess duit. Tucc*ar* lib siut co
croch*ar* i n-enech Barri ocus na heclaisi ocus im'
enech-sa forsin fhaithche."[1]

"A c[h]lērig," ar Mac Conglinne, "nīdamcrochtar, 10
acht berar br*eth* fírian indraicc form is ferr oltū mo[2]
chrochad."

Atnagar ann sin hi cend br*eith*i do br*eith* for Mac
Conglinne. Atnaig Manchīn oc taccra friss. Atnagar
cach fer īar n-urd do muintir Chorcc[aig]e co Mac 15
Conglinne. Cīa bói d' immbud ēcnai ocus eōlais
ocus aircetail leō, nī [fh]rith loc laburtha i n-dligud
dō trīasa crochthá.

Berair īar sin cen dlig*ed* co Ráthín Mac n-Aeda
i n-descertleth Cho[r]ccaige (.i. fai[th]chi). Co 20
n-epert budessin :
"Asccaid dam, a Manchín ocus a muinter Chorccaige !"
"Ōt anocul sin ? " ol Manchín.
"Nī head condaigimm," ar Mac Conglinne ; "fó 25
liumm cé notísad de."
"Apair," ol Manchīn.

---

[1] faichthe        [2] mo mo

" I will not speak," said MacConglinne, " until I
have pledges for it."

Pledges and bonds stout and strong were im-
posed on the monks of Cork for its fulfilment, and
5 he bound them upon his pledges.

" Say what it is you want," said Manchín.

" I will," said Aniér : " to eat the viaticum that is in
my book-satchel before going to death, for it is not
right to go on a journey without being shriven.
10 Let my satchel be given to me."

His satchel was brought to him, and he opened it,
and took out of it the two wheaten cakes and the
slice of old bacon.   And he took the tenth part of
each of the cakes, and cut off the tenth of the
15 bacon, decently and justly.

" Here are tithes, ye monks of Cork," said Mac-
Conglinne.   " If we knew the man who has better
right, or who is poorer than another, to him would
we give our tithes."

20 All the paupers that were there rose up on seeing
the tithes, and reached out their hands.   And he
began looking at them, and said :

" Verily before God," said he, " it can never be
known if any one of you stands in greater need of
25 these tithes than I myself.   The journey of none of
you was greater yesterday than mine—from Roscommon to Cork.   Not a morsel or drop tasted I after
coming.   I had eaten nothing on the road, I did not
find a guest's welcome on my arrival, but I received
30 [insult], ye curs and robbers and dung-hounds, ye
monks of Cork !   The whole of my clothing was
stripped off me, scourges and horsewhips were
laid on me, I was plunged into the Lee, and

" Ni epér," ar Mac Conglinne, "co m-bet cuir dam
fria."

Atnagar rátha ocus nadmand tenna ocus *trebaire*
for muintir Chorccaige fria comall, ocus naidmis for
a churu.                                                          5

"Apair," ol Manchīn, "cid condige."

"Atbēr," ar Aniér ; ".i. pars fil am' théig lib*air* do
chaithem ré n-dul for cel ; ar nī dlegar escómlad cen
dol do láim. Tucthar mo thīag lib*air* dam !"

Doberar a théig dó, ocus oslaicis hí, co m-ben dī 10
bairgin (.i. cruith*nechtu*) essi la tócht senshaille.
Ocus gab*ais* dechmaid cechtarnūi ocus b*en*ais dechmaid in tóchta co himargide ocus co hindraicc.

"Fil dechmaid sund, a muinter Chorccaige," ar
Mac Conglinne. " Dīa fhesmais intí bud chóru nō 15
is bochta a céli, dó dob*ē*rmais ar n-dechmaid."

An rob*ō*i ann do bochtaib atrachtatar s*ūas* ic
décsi na dechmaide, ocus sínid a lámu ūadib. Ocus
gab*ais* sill*ed* forru iarum ocus atbert :

"Fīa[d] Dīa ūm," ol s*ē*, "nī festa cid mó nórís*sed* 20
*ō*n ūaib a less in dech*mad* si oldá-su fessin. Nī bā
mó uide neich ūaib indé oldá m' uidi-sea .i. ō Rus
Chommán co Corccaig. Nīrthóimless mír nō banna
iar tidecht, nī rochaithes for s*ēt*, nī fūarus fīad
fhīróiged iar tidecht, acht fūarus [      ], a matadu 25
ocus a latrannu ocus a c[h]onu cacca .i. a muinter
C[h]orccaige ! Robenad ulidēta[i]d m' étaig[1] dimm,
rogabad slipre ocus echlusca dam, domratad isin

[1] *in ētaid*

clean injustice was practised upon me. Fair play was not given me. In the presence of the Maker," said MacConglinne, "it shall not be the first thing the fiend shall lay to my charge after going yonder, 5 that I gave to you these tithes, for ye deserve them not."

So the first morsel that he ate was his tithes, and after that he ate his meal—his two cakes, with his slice of old bacon. Then, lifting up 10 his hands, and giving thanks to his Maker, he said :

" Now take me to the Lee!"

On that he was taken, bonds and guards and all, towards the Lee.

15   When he reached the well, the name of which is " Ever-full", he doffed his white cloak, and laid it out to be under his side, his book-satchel under the slope of his back. He let himself down upon his cloak, supine, put his finger through the loop of 20 his brooch, and dipped the point of the pin over his back in the well. And while the drop of water trickled down from the end of the brooch, the brooch was over his breath.

The men that guarded him and held him in bonds 25 grew tired.

" Your own treachery has come about you, ye curs and robbers, ye monks of Cork ! When I was in my cell, what I used to do was to hoard what bits might reach me during five or six days, 30 and then eat them in one night, drinking my fill of water afterwards. This would sustain me to the end of three days and three nights without anything

Sábraind, rohimred fír n-indlig*id* form, ni rodamad
fír dlig*id* dam. I fhīadnaise in dūileman," ar Mac
Conglinne, "nī ba hū cētní aicūras demun form-sa
īar n-dul anúnd, in dech*maid* sa do thabairt dūib-si,
ar nīsdligthi."                                                    5

Conid é cētmír adūaid indsin, a dech*mad*; ocus
caithis a próind īarum .i. a dí bairgin cona thócht
senshaille. Tócbaid a lámu ocus atlaigis buide dia
dúilem*ain.*

"Mo br*eith* inn-dóchum na Sábrainne festa!" ar 10
Mac Conglinne.
Īar sin berair hū lín a chuimrig ocus a chométaid[1]
a dóchum na Sabrainne.
In tan rosīacht in tiprait dīanad ainm Bithlán,
romben a lumain fhind de, ocus dosrat foa thōeb, 15
ocus a théig lib*air* fo leirg a droma. Roslēic fūn
for a lummain, atnaig a mér trīa drol a delci, ocus
tummais rind in delgai dar a ais isin tiprait. In
céin nobíd banna oc snige a cind in delca sís, nobid
in delc ūas a anáil.                                               20


Rostorsig in lucht coimēta ocus c*u*mrig.


"Tānic in brēc *for* timchell, a matuda ocus a
latranda, a muinter Chorccaige! Inbuid robá-sa
'cóm boith, issed dognínd: inamtoirched co cend
cūic trāth nō sé do blogaib, a taiscid co caithind i 25
n-ōen-adaig,[2] mo sháith do us*ci* ina n-dīaid sin,

---

[1] chométaig
[2] adaid

else, and it would not harm me. I shall be three
days and nights subsisting on what I ate just now,
three days and nights more doing penance, and
another three days and nights drinking water,
5 for I have pledges in my hands. I vow to God
and St. Barre, whose I am here," said MacConglinne, "though neither high nor low of the
monks of Cork should leave the place where
they are, but should all go to death in one night,
10 and Manchín before all or after all, to death and
hell,—since I am sure of heaven, and shall be in the
Presence, to which there is neither end nor decay."

This story was told to the monks of Cork, who
quickly held a meeting, and the upshot of the meet-
15 ing was that MacConglinne should have a blessing on
his going in humility to be crucified, or else that
nine persons should surround him to guard him
until he died where he was, that he might be crucified afterwards.

20      That message was delivered to MacConglinne.

" It is a sentence of curs," said he. " Neverthe-
less, whatever may come of it, we will go in
humility, as our Master, Jesus Christ, went to His
Passion."

25      Thereupon he rose, and went to the place where
were the monks of Cork. And by this time the
close of vespers had come.

" A boon for us, O Manchín!" said the monks of
Cork themselves.

30      " O my God, what boon ?" cried Manchín.

" Respite for that poor devil until morning. We
have not tolled bells, neither have we celebrated

no[m]be*r*ed co cend nómaide ce*n* ní īar sin, ocus
ní lāud fo*r*m. Bĕt nómaide for ar'chaithius ō
chīanaib ; bĕt nómaide aile oc athrige, ocus nómaide
aile ic ól us*ci*, or atāut cuir frim' lāmaib. Fortgel-
laimm Dīa ocus Barre 'catú," ar Mac Conglinne,  5
"cen co tig ūasal nō ísel do muintir C[h]orccaige
asin baile itāt, co n-digset écc uli i n-ǣnaidchi,
ocus Manchīn rīa cách ocus īar cách, do bás ocus
dochumm n-iff*ir*n ;—or am derb-sa do nim, ocus
bīat i frecnarcus forsnā fil crích nō erchra."        10


Rohindissed do muintir Chorccaige in sc*ŭ*l sin,
ocus dorigset lūathchomarc, ocus issed tuccad asin
chom*ar*c : bendacht do Mac Conglinne for a dul fé*n*
ar umalōit dia chroch*ad*, nō nónbur timchill*ed* dia
chom*ēt*, co n-dig[s]ed éc áitt a m-bōi, ocus co ro- 15
croch*ad* īar tain.

Rorāided fri Mac Conglinne inní sin. Asbert
Mac Conglinne :
"Is matroga," (.i. is ro*g*a mataid, nō is mat*ad* intí
hō tuccad in roga.) "Acht ōenní chena, cid ed bess 20
de, ré*g*mait fri hum*al*óit feib rochōid ar mágist*ir*
Īsu Crist fria c[h]ésad."
Atraig co háit i m-bātar muinter Chorccaige.
Ocus tāncatar crícha espartan ann sin.


"Ascaid dún, a Manchīn!" ol muinter C[h]orccaige 25
fodēin.
"A mo Dé, cissi ascaid ?" ol Manchīn.
"Dál co matain[1] cen croch*ad* don tróg út. Nī
                          [1] commatain

Mass, nor preached, nor made the Offering. The poor have not been satisfied by us with food against the Sunday, nor have we refreshed ourselves. Grant us a respite for him till morning."

5    "I pledge my word," said Manchín, "that respite shall not be given, but the day of his transgression shall be the day of his punishment."

Ochone ! in that hour MacConglinne was taken to the Foxes' Wood, and an axe was put in his hand,
10    his guard being about him.    He himself cut his passion-tree, and bore it on his back to the green of Cork.    He himself fixed the tree.    And the time had outrun the close of vespers, and the one resolve they had was to crucify him there and then.

15    "A boon for me, O Manchín, and ye monks of Cork!" said MacConglinne.

"I pledge my word," said Manchín, "that no boon shall come from us."

"It is not to spare me I ask you, for, though it
20    were asked, it would not be granted to me of your free will, ye curs and ye robbers and dung-hounds and unlettered brutes, ye shifting, blundering, hang-head monks of Cork !    But I want my fill of generous juicy food, and of tasty intoxicating
25    sweet ale, and a fine light suit of thin dry clothing to cover me, that neither cold nor heat may strike me ; a gorging feast of a fortnight for me before going to the meeting with death."

"I vow to thee," said Manchín, "thou shalt not get
30    that.    But it is now the close of the day ; it is Sunday.    The convent, moreover, are entreating a respite for thee.    But thy scanty clothing shall be stripped off thee, and thou shalt be tied to yonder

rosbensom clucu, nō nī dernsamm celebrad nō
precept nō oiffrend. Nī rosásta boicht lind 'na
caithium co cend in Domnaig, cen sāssad dún
fessin. Cairde dún co matin dō !"
"Atbiúr brēthir," ol Manchīn, "nā rega in dál 5
sin, acht lathi a imorbois bid hō lū a phennati."

Monūar ! Isin ūair sin berair Mac Conglinne fo
Chaill na Sindach, ocus doberair bīail 'na láim, ocus
lucht coimēta immaille friss. Benais fén a chōsad-
c[h]rand, ocus nosimarchuir fri ais co faithc[h]i 10
Chorccaige. Sáidis fén in crand. Ocus lingis ind
amser dar crīch n-espartan, ocus nī bōi comairle aile
leō, acht a chrochad in tan sin.
"Ascaid dam, a Manchīn ocus a muinter Chorccaige !" ar Mac Conglinne. 15
"Atberim mo brēthir tra," ol Manchīn, " conā tāt
ascaid ūaind."
" Nī maithem n-anocuil connaigimm foraib ; or
cīa chuinger, nīstá dam dia bar n-deoin, a matuda
ocus a latranda ocus a chonu cacca ocus a brúti 20
nemliterdhai .i. a muinter chorrach cómraircnech
cendisel Corccaige ! Acht mo sháith do biud olardai
inmárdai ocus do lind shoōil shomesc shomilis ; ocus
clith n-ūlaind n-étrom do étach thana thīrmaide
torum, nā romforrgi fūacht nō tess, corup lōnfheiss 25
cūict[h]igis dam rīa n-dul i n-dáil báis."

"Fortgillim," ol Manchīn, "nī fhúigbel-siu inní
sin. Acht is derind lái, is Dómnach and. Fil didu
in popul oc irguide dála duit. Acht benfaider dít

---

[1] fhúidbo

pillar-stone, for a fore-torture before the great torture to-morrow."

So it was done. His scanty clothing was stripped off him, and ropes and cords were tied across him 5 to the pillar-stone.

They turned away home, Manchín going to the abbot's house, that the poor and guests might be fed by them. They also ate something themselves. But they left that sage to fast, who came, having 10 been sent by God and the Lord for the salvation of Cathal MacFinguine and the men of Munster, and the whole Southern Half to boot. The justice of law was not granted him.

He remained there until midnight. Then an 15 angel of God came to him on the pillar-stone, and began to manifest the vision unto him. As long as the angel was on the pillar-stone it was too hot for MacConglinne, but when he moved on a ridge away from him, it was comfortable. (Hence the "Angel's 20 Ridge" in the green of Cork, which was never a morning without dew.) At the end of the night the angel departed from him.

Thereupon he shaped a little rhyme of his own, which would serve to relate what had been mani-25 fested to him, and there he remained until morning with the poetical account of his vision ready.

Early at morn the chapter-bell was tolled on the morrow by the monks of Cork, and all came to the pillar-stone.

30    " Well, you miserable wretch," said Manchín, "how is it with you to-day?"

" It is well," said he, " if I am allowed to make known to thee a few short words that I have,

do bec n-étaig, ocus cengelt*ir* don chorthi út, corob¹
frithpīan fogab*ar* rēsin mōrphéin imbūrach."
 Dorónad fon sam*ail* sin. Bent*air* de a bec n-
ētaig, ocus rocengl*ad* téta ocus refeda taris don
chorthi.                                                       5
 Tīagat ūad dia tig. Luid Manchīn don tig abbad,
corosásta boicht ocus óigid leō. Rothomailset fén
ní. Rolécsit troscud in ecnadu út tānic īarna fóided
do Dīa ocus don Choimdid do thesarcain Cathail
meic Fhinguine ocus fer Muman ocus Lethi Moga 10
Nūadat olchena. Noch*a* damad fír n-dligid dó. *Nocho n-damad*

 Fessid co medōn óidche ann. Īarsin ticc aingel
Dé chuci for in corthi, ocus fororbairt in aislingthi do
foillsiugud dó. Cēin bói int aingel forsin cloich, ba
rothē dó. Intan téged for imaire ūad, bā sofhulaing 15
dó. (Conid de sin fil Imaire in Aingil hi fhaichthi
Chorccaige ; nī bōi-sium matain cen drúcht.)
Doll*uid* ūad int aingel deōd n-aidche.

 Cumaid-sium īarum cennpurt m-bec ūad fodén
bīd imchub*aid* re aisnē*is* amail rofhaillsiged dó ; 20
ocus ataig annsin co matain co cendport a aislingt[h]i
do léri lais.
 Bent*air* cloc tinōil oc muintir Corccaige matan
moch īarnabūrach. Tecat uli cusin corthi.

 "Maith, a t[h]róig," ol Manchīn, "cindus filt*er* lat 25
indíu ?"
 "Is maith," or sē, "dīa lécther dam in cumair

¹ coro*m*

for a vision appeared to me last night," said Mac-
Conglinne, "and, if a respite is given me, I will
relate the vision."

"By my word, I say," quoth Manchin, "if the race
5 of Adam were of my thinking they would not give
thee respite even for a day or a night. As for
myself, I will not give it."

"We pledge our word," said the monks, "though
it be disagreeable to you, he shall have a respite,
10 that he may relate his vision. Inflict on him
afterwards whatever you wish."

Then it was that he traced Manchin up to Adam.
according to the pedigree of food, saying :

"Bless us, O cleric, famous pillar of learning,
15 Son of honey-bag, son of juice, son of lard,
   Son of stirabout, son of pottage, son of fair speckled fruit-
       clusters,
   Son of smooth clustering cream, son of buttermilk, son of
       curds,
20   Son of beer (glory of liquors!), son of pleasant bragget,
   Son of twisted leek, son of bacon, son of butter,
   Son of full-fat sausage, son of pure new milk,
   Son of nut-fruit, son of tree-fruit, son of gravy, son of
       dripping,
25   Son of fat, son of kidney, son of rib, son of shoulder,
   Son of well-filled gullet, son of leg, son of loin,
   Son of hip, son of flitch, son of striped breastbone,
   Son of bit, son of sup, son of back, son of paunch,
   Son of slender tripe, son of cheese without decrease,
30 Son of fish of Inver Indsén, son of sweet whey, son of
       biestings,
   Son of mead, son of wine, son of flesh, son of ale,
   Son of hard wheat, son of tripe, son of  .  .  .
   Son of fair white porridge, made of pure sheep's milk,

m-brīathar fil occum do rélad duit-siu .i. aislingt[h]i
domarfaid arér," ar Mac Conglinne, " ocus dia léctber
dál dam, indisfet in aislingthi."
"Atbiur dom' brē*th*ir," ol Manchīn, "dīa m-betís
sīl n-Adaim dom' rēir, conū tibratís dál lái nū aidche    5
duit.  Mē fēn nīcontibér."

"Atberam ar m-brē*th*ir," ol in popul, " cid lonn
lat-su, léchthír dál dó, coro-indise a aislinge.  A
n-us tol lat-su īarum, tab*air* fair."

Conid indsin ruc-som Manchīn iar n-genel*ach* bíd  10
co hAdam :

" Bennach dūn, a c[h]lérig,  a c[h]lī cloth co cómgne,[1]
Mac midbuilce mela,   meic bela, meic bloince,
   Meic buaidrén, meic brothchāin,   meic borrthoraid brec-
      bāin,                                                          15
Meic borrchrothi blāthi,  meic blāithche, meic brechtāin,
   Meic beōiri būaid mbainde,  meic brócoti binde,
   Meic cainninde caimme,  meic shaille, meic imme,
   Meic indrechtāin lānméith,  meic lemnachtai immglain,
Meic messai, meic thoraid,  meic holair, meic inmair,      20
   Meic hítha, meic ārand,  meic clethi, meic gūaland,
Meic lonloingen láinte,  meic láirce, meic lūabann,
   Meic lessi, meic lethind,  meic loinge brond ballai,     ᴧ[*ch*]
Meic míre, me[i]c lommai,  meic drommai, meic tharrai,
   Meic thremantai thanai,  meic thainghe cen trāethad,     25
Meic ēisc Inbeir Indsēn,  meic millsēn,[2] meic mōethal,    ᴧ[*i*]
   Meic meda, meic fhína,  meic cárna, meic cornu,
Meic cruithnechta rigne,  meic inbe, meic onba,
   Meic fhindlitten gile  d' ass chōerach co n-glaine,

---

[1] leg. comge        [2] me*ic* míllsén me*ic* millsén

Son of soft rich pottage, with its curls of steam,
　Son of rough curds, son of fair oatmeal gruel,
Son of sprouty meat-soup, with its purple berries,
　Son of the top of effeminate kale, son of soft white
5 　　midriff,
Son of bone-nourishing nut-fruit, son of Abel, son of Adam.
　Fine is thy kindred of choice food, to the tongue it is
　　sweet,
　O thou of staid and steady step,—with the help of pointed
10 　　staff."

"That hurts me not, MacConglinne," said Manchin. "Little didst thou care about slandering me
and the Church when thou didst compose a food-
pedigree to commemorate me, such as has not been
15 invented for any man before me, and will not be
invented till Doom."

"It is no slander at all, O cleric," said MacConglinne, " but a vision that was manifested to me last
night. That is its prelude. The vision is not out
20 of place, and, if respite or leave be granted me, I
will relate it."

And Manchin said, as before, that he would give
no respite. But MacConglinne began to recount his
vision, and it is said that from here onward is what
25 the angel manifested to him, as he said :

　A vision that appeared to me,
　An apparition wonderful
　　I tell to all :
　A lardy coracle all of lard
30 　Within a port of New-milk Loch,
　　Up on the World's smooth sea.

　We went into the man-of-war,
　'Twas warrior-like to take the road

Meic scaiblín buic bládmáir cona gáblaib gaile,
  Meic gruthraige gairge, meic garbáin cháin chorcca,
Meic cráibechán cráebaig cona chöeraib corccra,
  Meic bairr braisce bíthe, meic bolgáin buic bánghlain,
Meic cnómessa cnáimfhéil, meic Ábéil, meic Ádaim.
  Maith do dú[th]chus dégbíd, is milis re tengaid,
A chéim fosad fostán al-los trostán bennaig.' Ben. b. d.   ‸[ċ]

" Nocon-olc dam-sa ón, a Mic Conglinne," ol Manchin. " Bec lat-su áil form-sa ocus forsind eclais co
n-dernais genelach bíd i cúmni dam nā dernad do 10
duine romum is nā dignestar co brunni brātha."[1]

" Nī háil etir sin, a c[h]lérig," ar Mac Conglinne,
" acht aislingt[h]i domarfás aréir. Is ed siut a
cennport. N'imcubaid[2] in aisslingthe, ocus dia
tucthar dál nō cairde dam, innisfet in aislingt[h]i 15
īarsin."
  Ocus atbert Manchín in cétnai, nā tibred dál.
Téit-sium īarsin hi cend a aislingt[h]i, ocus atberut
is ōthá sin sís rofhaillsig int aingel dó, ut dixit :

  Aislingi domarfas-[s]a,                            20
  taidbsi ingnad indisimm
    i fhīadnaise cháich :
  curchán gered gerthige
  i purt locha lémnachta
    ōs lind betha[3] bláith.                          25

  Lódmar isin lóechlestar,
  láechda in chongaib chonaire

---

[1] „cobratha„ cobrunni   [2] leg. Is imchubaid ?   [3] bethad

O'er ocean's heaving waves.
Our oar-strokes then we pulled
Across the level sea,
Throwing the sea's harvest up,
5    Like honey, the sea-soil.

The fort we reached was beautiful,
With works of custards thick,
Beyond the loch.
New butter was the bridge in front,
10   The rubble dyke was wheaten white,
Bacon the palisade.

Stately, pleasantly it sat,
A compact house and strong.
Then I went in :
15   The door of it was dry meat,
The threshold was bare bread,
Cheese-curds the sides.

Smooth pillars of old cheese,
And sappy bacon props
20   Alternate ranged ;
Fine beams of mellow cream,
White rafters—real curds,
Kept up the house.

Behind was a wine well,
25   Beer and bragget in streams,
Each full pool to the taste.
Malt in smooth wavy sea,
Over a lard-spring's brink
Flowed through the floor.

30   A loch of pottage fat
Under a cream of oozy lard
Lay 'tween it and the sea.
Hedges of butter fenced it round,
Under a blossom of white-mantling lard,
35   Around the wall outside.

dar bolclenna lir ;
[corbensom] na sesbēmend
dar muncind in murtráchta,
co tochrad a murthorud
   murgrīan amal mil.     5

Cöem in dúnad rāncamár,
cona rāthaib robrechtán,
  resin loch anall :
bā himm úr a erdrochat,
a chaisel bā gelchruithnecht,     10
  a shondach bā sáll.

Bā suairc segda[1] a shuidiugud
in tige trēoin trebarda,
  i n-dechad īartain :
a chomla do thīrmcharnu,     15
a thairsech do thurarán,
  do mæthluib a[2] fraig.

Ūaitne slemnaɪ sencháise,
sailghe saille súgmaire
  serndais imasech ;     20
scssa sena[3] senchrothi,
fairre finda fírgrotha
  foloingtís in tech.

Tipra d' fhín 'na fhírīarthar,
áibne beóri is brocóti,     25
  blasta cech lind lán ;
lear do braichlis blāithlendai
ōs brú thopair thremantai
  dorói dar a lár.

Loch do braisig belaiche     30
fó barr úscai olordai
  eturru ocus muir ;
erbi imme oc imaire
fo chír blonci bratgile
  imon múr amuig.     35

---

[1] sin         [2] do         [3] segda H. 3. 18.

A row of fragrant apple-trees,
An orchard in its pink-tipped bloom,
  Between it and the hill.
A forest tall of real leeks,
Of onions and of carrots, stood
  Behind the house.

Within, a household generous,
A welcome of red, firm-fed men,
  Around the fire.
Seven bead-strings, and necklets seven,
Of cheeses and of bits of tripe,
  Hung from each neck.

The Chief in mantle of beefy fat
Beside his noble wife and fair
  I then beheld.
Below the lofty cauldron's spit
Then the Dispenser I beheld,
  His fleshfork on his back.

The good Cathal MacFinguine,
He is a good man to enjoy
  Tales tall and fine.
That is a business for an hour,
And full of delight 'tis to tell
The rowing of the man-of-war
  O'er Loch Milk's sea.

He then narrated his entire vision in the presence
of the monks of Cork until he reached its close (but
this is not its close), and the virtues of the vision
were manifested unto Manchín.

 "Excellent, thou wretch," said Manchín, "go
straight to Cathal MacFinguine, and relate the vision
to him; for it was revealed to me last night that this
evil which afflicts Cathal would be cured through
that vision."

Ecor d' áblaib fírchumra,
fid cona bláth barrchorcra
  etuira ocus slīab ;
daire forard fírlossa,
do chainnind, do cherrbaccán.       5
  for cúl tigo tīar.

Muinnter cnig inichin
d' ócaib dercaib tennsadchib
  im thenid astig :
socht n-allsmaind, socht n-opislo      10
do cháisib, do chōelánaib,
  fo brágait cech fhir.

Atconnarc nī, in airchindech
cona brot[h]raig bóshaille
  'má mnái mīadaig maiss ;      15
atconnarc in luchtaire
fó inbiur in ardchori,
  'sa cehel ria ais.  A.

Cathal maith mac Finguine,
fó fer dīanad oirfited      20
  airscéla bind braiss ;
maith in menar ōenūaire,
is áibind ria indisi,
immram luipe lœchlostair
  dar ler locha ais.[1]  A. d. a.    25

Ro indis-[s]ium a aisl*ing*i uli annsin i fīadnaiso muintire Corccaige, coroacht a deriud (cencop ē so a deriud), ocus rofallsiged do Manchīn rath in aisl*ing*i.

"Maith, a t[h]róig," ol Manchīn, "ǥirg do s[h]aigid Cathail meic Fhinguine, ocus indis dó 30 in aisl*ing*i ; ūair rofallsiged dam-sa arēir int olc su fil i Cathal do híc trīasin aisl*ing*i sin."

      [1] lais

"What reward shall I have for that ?" asked MacConglinne.

"Is not the reward great," said Manchín, "to let thee have thy body and soul ?"

5 "I care not for that, though it should be done. The windows of Heaven are open to receive me, and all the faithful from Adam and Abel, his son, even to the faithful one who went to Heaven in this very moment, are all chanting in expectation of my soul,

10 that I may enter Heaven. The nine orders of Heaven, with Cherubim and Seraphim, are awaiting my soul. I care not, though Cathal MacFinguine and the men of Munster, along with all the southern Half, and the people of Cork, and Manchín first or last,

15 should go to death and hell in one night ; while I myself shall be in the unity of the Father, and the Son, and the Holy Ghost."

"What reward dost thou require ?" asked the monks of Cork.

20 "Not great indeed is what I ask," said Mac-Conglinne, "merely the little cloak, which he re-fused to the clergy of the Southern Half, and for which they fasted on the same night, viz., Manchín's cloak ! "

25 "Little is that thing in thy sight, but great in mine," said Manchín.

"Verily," he added, "I declare, in the presence of God and of St. Barre, that if the whole country be-tween Cork and its boundary were mine, I would

30 sooner resign it all than the cloak alone."

"Woe to him that gives not the cloak," cried all present, "for the salvation of Cathal and Mog's Half is better than the cloak."

"Cia lóg dobērad dam-sa aire?" ar Mac Conglinne.

"Nach mōr in lōg," ol Manchín, "do chorp ocus t 'anim do lēcud duit?"

"Cumma lem inní sin, cia dognether. Senistre 5 nime at urslacthi frim, ocus in uile fíreon atō Ādam ocus Ābēl a mac ocus cosin fírian frecnairc dolluid docúmm ríchid isin punc amsire hitāmm, atāt uli oc clascetul for cind m' anma *cot*ías in-nem. Atāt nōi n-grāid nime im Hirophín ocus Sarophín i frestul 10 m' anma. Is cumma leam cia dig Cathal mac Finguine ocus fir Muman co Leth Mog Nūadat ocus muinter C[h]orccaige ocus Manchīn ría cách ocus īar cách ind-éc ocus ind-illirn a n-ænoidche ; ūair bēt fessin i n-æntaid in Athar ocus in Meic ocus in 15 Spir*ta* N*æm*."

"Cia lóg condigi?" ar muinter C[h]orccaige.

"Nīt mór ēm a n-condigim," ol Mac Conglinne, " .i. in cochall bec ima ro-éraid clērig Lethi Moga, ocus 'bár-troiscset i n-ænaidchi .i. cochall Manchīn." 20

"Bec fīad-su inní sin ocus mōr fíadum-sa," ol Manchīn.

"Acht ænnī," ol Manchīn, "dobiur-sa br*eth*ir i fíadnaise Dé ocus Barri, damad lemm-sa a fíl eter Corccaig ocus a te*r*mu*n*d, robad usa a sechna uli 25 oltās in cochall a ænar."

"Mairg nach tibre" ol cách, "in cochall ; ol is ferr in Cathal ocus Leth Moga do tesarcain oldās in cochall."

" I will give it then," said Manchín, " but I never
gave, nor shall I give, a boon more disagreeable to
me ; that is to say, I will give it into the hands of
the bishop of Cork, to be delivered to the scholar if
5 he helps Cathal MacFinguine."

It was then given into the hands of the bishop of
Cork, and the monks of Cork were to deliver the
cloak with him ; but in the hands of the bishop it
was left.

10    " Now go at once to Cathal ! "

" Where is Cathal ? " asked MacConglinne.

" Not hard to tell," answered Manchín.   " In the
house of Pichán, son of Maelfind, King of Iveagh, at
Dún Coba, on the borders of Iveagh and Corcalee,
15 and thou must journey thither this night."

MacConglinne thereupon went hastily, eagerly,
impatiently ; and he lifted his five-folded well-
strapped cloak on to the slope of his two shoulders,
and tied his shirt over the rounds of his fork, and
20 strode thus across the green to the house of Pichán,
son of Maelfind, to Dún Coba, on the confines of
Iveagh and Corcalee.   And at this pace he went
quickly to the dún.   And as he came to the very
meeting house where the hosts were gathering, he
25 put on a short cloak and short garments: each upper
garment being shorter with him, and each lower one
being longer.   In this wise he began juggling for
the host from the floor of the royal house, (a thing
not fit for an ecclesiastic) and practising satire and
30 buffoonery and singing songs ; and it has been said
that there came not before his time, nor since, one
more renowned in the arts of satire.

When he was engaged in his feats in the house of

"Dob*er*-sa amail seo," ol Manchīn, "ocus nī tardus
ocus nī thibar ascaid is andsa lemm .i. dobūr hū.i
n-ērlaim esp*uic* C[h]orccaige fria aisec don scolaige,
dīa cobra Cathal mac Finguine."

Rohaithned iarsin i n-ērlaim esp*uic* C[h]orccaige, 5
ocus m*uinter* C[h]orccaige dia hidnocul leis in
cochaill ; acht is al-lūim in esp*uic* rofācbad.

"Imthig fodechtsa do saigid Cathail ! "
"Cia hairmm i fil Cathal ? " ar Mac Conglinne.
"Nī *hansa*," ol Manchīn. "I taig Pichāin meic 10
Mōile Finde rīg hūa n-Echach ic Dún Choba i
cocrīch hūa n-Echach ocus Corco Lāigde; ocus soch-
si innocht conuice indsin."

Luid Mac Conglinne iarum co daidbir[1] díscir deinmnetach ; ocus tōcbais a lummain cōicdiabulta cen- 15
galta i fán a dá gūaland, ocus cenglaid a lēnid ōs
mellach a lūrac, ocus cingis dar fiarlāit na faithchi[2]
fon samail sin co tech Pichā[i]n meic Mōilfinde co
Dún Coba i cocrīch hūa n-Echach ocus Corcu Lāigde.
Ocus cingis co dīan a dóchumn: in dúnaid fon tǫchim 20
sin. Ocus feib rosīacht in slūagtech saindrud i m-
bádus oc tinōl na slóg, gab*ais* gerrchochall ocus
gerrétach imme : girru cach n-ūachtarach lais, ocus
libru cach n-īchtarach. Fororbairt fuirseōracht fon
samail sin dont shlōg do lár in rīgthige (.i. ní nārba 25
comadais dia p[h]ersaind) [ocus] cáintecht ocus
bragitōracht ocus dūana la filidecht do gabūil, coro-
hasblad[3] hē nā tānic rīam nō iarum bīd errdarcu
i cerdu cáintechta.

Intan bōi forna splegaib[4] i tig Pichāin meic Mōil-

---

[1] leg. dethbir ?    [2] faichthi    [3] leg. hasbrad ?    [4] spledaib    30

Pichán, son of Maelfind, then it was that Pichán
said aside : " Though great thy mirth, son of learning, it does not make me glad."

" What makes him sad ? " asked MacConglinne.

5 " Knowest thou not, O scholar," said Pichán, " that
Cathal MacFinguine with the nobles of Munster is
coming to-night ; and though troublesome to me is
the great host of Munster, more troublesome is
Cathal alone ; and though troublesome is he in his
10 first meal, more troublesome is he in his prime
feast; but most troublesome of all is his feast again.
For at this feast three things are wanted, viz., a
bushel of oats, and a bushel of wild apples, and a
bushel of flour-cakes."

15 " What reward would be given me," said MacConglinne, " if I shield thee against him from this hour
to the same hour to-morrow, and that he would not
avenge it on thy people or on thyself? "

" I would give thee a golden ring and a Welsh
20 steed," said Pichán.

" By my oath, thou wilt add unto it when
accepted," said MacConglinne.

" I will give thee besides," said Pichán, " a white
sheep for every house and for every fold, from Carn
25 to Cork."

" I will take that," said MacConglinne, " provided
that kings and lords of land, poets and satirists are
pledged to me for the delivery of my dues and for
their fulfilment, so that they shall reach me in full,
30 viz., kings to enforce the dues, lords of land to keep
spending on the collectors while they are levying
my dues, food and drink and necessaries ; poets
to scathe and revile, if I am cheated of my dues ;

finde, conid ann asbert Pichān secha: "Cid mōr do
muirn-si, a mic lēgind, nīmdēnann-sa subach di."

"Cid dosgní mifech?" or Mac Conglinne.
"Nū fet*ara*-su, a scolaige," ol Pichān, ".i. Cathal
mac Finguine co maithib Muman do thidecht 5
innocht; ocus cid doilig lemm mōrshlúag Muman, is
annsa Cathal a ēnur ; ocus cid doilig ēssium ina
p[h]rímchutig, is doilge ina p[h]rímairigid, ocus is
doilgíde a fhrithairigid[1] doridisi. Fil trēdi condagur
icon [fh]rithairigid sin .i. mīach cūachūn ocus 10
míach fīaduball ocus míach mináráin."


"Cia lóg dobē*r*tha dam-sa," ar Mac Conglinne,
"dīa n-dīngbaind ditt hē ōn trāth sa cusin trāth
arabárach, ocus nū dīgnesta a aithe for do[2] thūaith
nū fort fén." 15
"Dosbē*r*aind fal*aig* n-oír ocus ech Bretnach duit,"
ol Pichān.
"Dom' débroth! fullfi friss," ar Mac Conglinne,
"intan gébth*ar*."
"Dobē*r*-sa beos" ol Pichān, "cēra find cacha tige 20
ocus cacha trillsi o Charnd co Corccaig."


"Gébut-sa sin," ar Mac Conglinne, "acht corab rīg
ocus brug*aid*, filid ocus cáinte dam fri taisec fhīach
ocus da comall*ad* conomtorsit immlán .i. rīg do
aithne na fhīach, briug*aid* do imfhulang do chaithem 25
bíd ocus lenda ocus lessaigthi leō cóin bēd ic tobach
m' fhīach. Dīa fhéllt*air* form' fiach*aib*, filid dia n-
āir ocus glūim n-dícind, cáinte dia sílad ocus dia n-

[1] rithairige       [2] da

and satirists to scatter the satires, and sing them against
thee and thy children and thy race, unless my dues
reach me." And he bound him then on his pledges.

Cathal MacFinguine came with the companies and
5 hosts of horse of the Munstermen; and they sat themselves down on bed-rails and couches and beds.
Gentle maidens began to serve and attend to the
hosts and to the multitudes. But Cathal MacFinguine did not let the thong of his shoe be half-
10 loosed, before he began supplying his mouth from
both hands with the apples that were on the hides
round about him. MacConglinne was there, and
began smacking his lips at the other side of the
house, but Cathal did not notice it. MacConglinne
15 rose and went hastily, impatiently, like the fiend, in
his furious rush and warlike bold pace across the
royal house. And there was a huge block and
warriors' stone of strength on which spears and
rivets were wont to be fastened, and against which
20 points and edges were wont to be ground ; and a
warrior's pillar-stone was that flag. And he lifted
it on his back and bore it to the place where he had
been before on the bed-rail, thrust the upper end of
it in his mouth, rested the other end of it on his
25 knee, and began grinding his teeth against the stone.

What the learned, and the elders, and the books of
Cork relate is, that there was no one in the neigh-
bourhood of the dún inside or outside, that did not
hear the noise of his teeth against the stone, though
30 it was of the smoothest.

Thereat Cathal raised his head.

"What makes thee mad, son of learning ?" asked
Cathal.

gab*ail* duit-siu ocus dot' chloind ocus dot' c[h]en*ēl*,
m̄inamtísat mo fhéich." Ocus nádmis īarum for a
chura.

Tūnic Cathal mac Finguine co m-búidnib ocus
marcshlōg fer Muman, co n-dessitar for colbadu ocus 5
imscinge ocus imdadu. Gabsat ingenai mínc mac-
dachta fósaic ocus frithail*em* dona slōgaib ocus dona
sochaidib. Nīcon-dam Cathal mac Finguine fria
lethéill a bróci do bein de, intan bói oc tidnocul a
beōil ō chechtar a dí lám dona hublaib bátar forsna 10
sechedaib imme sechnón. Is andsin bói Mac Conglinne. Atnaig oc blassachtaig isin leth aile don
tig, ocus níc*on*ráthaig Cathal sin. Ērgis Mac Conglinne co díscir deinmnetach dīabulda ina rúath*ur*
bodbda ocus ina chēim curata dar fiarlūit in rīgthige. 15
Ocus buí rell dermáir ocus nertlia míled forsa n-
indsmatís slega ocus semmunna ocus fria meltís
renda ocus fæbra; ocus bā corthi curad in lecc sin.
Ocus tócbais fria ais co háit a m-bói remi for in
colba, ocus indsmais in cend n-ūachtarach ina beōlu 20
di, ocus araile for a glún, ocus forobairt ic tomailt a
[dé]t frisin cloich.

Is ed adfīadut eōlaig ocus senōire ocus libuir
Corccaige, nātbōi i fhoccus in dúnaid ar medōn
nō dīanechtair nā cūala fūaim a dét frisin cloich bōi 25
ina beōlu, cia bōi dia slémnu.

Tócbais Cathal a chend ársin.
" Cid dotgní mer, a mic légind ? " or Cathal.

" Two things," said MacConglinne ; " viz., Cathal,
the right-beautiful son of Finguine, the high-king of
the great Southern Half, the chief defender of
Ireland against the children of Conn of the hundred
5 battles, a man ordained of God and the elements,
the noble well-born hero of pleasant Onaght of
Glennowra, according to the kindred of his
paternity,—I grieve to see him eating anything
alone ; and if men from distant countries were
10 within, soliciting request or gift, they will scoff if
my beard wags not in mutual movement with
thine."

" True," said Cathal, giving him an apple, and
jamming two or three into his own mouth. (During
15 the space of three half-years that the fiend abode in
the throat of Cathal MacFinguine, he had not performed such an act of humanity as the giving of
that one wild apple to MacConglinne after it had
been earnestly asked.)

20      " Better two things than one in learning," said
MacConglinne.

He flung him another.

" The number of the Trinity ! "

He gives him one.

25      " The four books of the Gospel, according to the
Testament of Christ ! "

He threw him one.

" The five books of Moses, according to the Ten
Commandments of the Law."

30      He flung him one.

"The first numeral article which consists of its
own parts and divisions, viz., the number six;

" Fil dā ní," ar Mac Conglinne, ". i . Cathal mac
fīrālaind Finguine, ardrīg mōrlethi Moga Nūadat,
ardc[h]osnamaid¹ Ērenn fria clanna Cuinn Chētcha-
thaig, fer rohoirdned ó Dīa ocus ó dūilib, lǣch sǣr
sochenūlach d' Eoganacht gribda Glendabrach īar  5
cenēl a atharda, sǣth lem-sa a acsin a ǣnur ic tomaīlt
neich ; ocus dīa m-beth dóine a crīchaib cīana istaig
ic cuinchid ail nō aisc, dogénut ēcnach cen m'
ulchain-se² ic comscísachtaig friat' ulchain-sea."


" Is fír," for Cathal oc tabairt ōenuba[i]ll dó,  10
ocus ro-esairg a dó nō a trí ina beōlu fén.  Fri ré na
trī lethbl*iadan* bōi in demun i m-brāgait Cathail
meic Fhinguine, nī derna dōen*nacht acht* int ǣnuball
fiadain út do Mac Conglinne īarna athcuinch*id* co
trén.  15

"Ferr déda hō óin ind-ēcna," ar Mac Conglinne.

Snedis aroli dó.
"Umir na Trīnōti !" or Mac Conglinne.
Cuiris ōen dó.
"Ceth*ir* leba[i]r int soscēla īar timna Crīst !"  20

Tidnais óen dō.
" Cōic lebair Mysi īar *n-deich* timnai rechta !"

Cuiris ōen dó.
" Cētna airtecul ármide do-airis ō rainde ocus ō

¹ co*s*namaig         ² mulchai*n*fe

E

for its half is three, its third is two, [and its sixth
is one]—give me the sixth ! "

He cast him one apple.

" The seven things which were prophesied of thy
5 God on earth, viz., His Conception, His Birth, His
Baptism," etc.

He gave him one.

" The eight Beatitudes of the Gospel, O Prince
of kingly judgments ! "

10    He threw him one.

" The nine orders of the kingdom of Heaven, O
royal champion of the world ! "

He gave him one.

" The tenth is the order of Mankind, O defender
15 of the province ! "

He cast him an apple.

" The imperfect number of the apostles after sin."

He flung him one.

" The perfect number of the apostles after sin,
20 even though they had committed transgression."

He threw him one.

" The triumph beyond triumphs and the perfect
number, Christ with his apostles."

" Verily, by St. Barre !" said Cathal, " thou'lt
25 devour me, if thou pursue me any further."

Cathal flung him hide, apples and all, so that there
was neither corner, nor nook, nor floor, nor bed, that
the apples did not reach.   They were not nearer to
MacConglinne than to all else ; but they were the
30 farther from Cathal.

Fury seizes Cathal.   One of his eyes jumped so far
back into his head that a pet crane could not have
picked it out. The other eye started out until it was as

chotib fadén . i. in umir séda ; acht is a trī al-leth,
is a dō a trīan.    Tabair dam in sessad!"
Snidis urch*or* d' ōenuball dó.
" In *sechte* dorarngired dot' Dīa i tal*main* . i. a
chompert, a gein, a bathis," *ocus araile.*                    5

Tic ōen dó.
" Ocht m-biati int soscēla, a ruri rīgbre*th*aig !"

Beris ōen dó.
" Nói n-grāid nime, a mic, a rīgnīa in betha !"

Tidnacis ōen dó.                                              10
" Dechmad    grād    tal*man*,    a    chosnamaid[1]    in
chōicid !"
Tic uball dó.
" Āirem anfhurmithi na n-apstal[2] īar n-imorbus !"
Gnidis ōen dó.                                               15
" Numir forpthi na n-apstal[2] īar n-imorbus, cia
dorigset tairmthecht."
Ferais ōen fair.
" Bū hī in būaid ós būadu ocus in umir forpthi,
Crīst for a apstalu."[3]                                     20
" Indeo," or Cathal, " dar Barre, nom-ísa, dīa
nomlena ní as[4] mó."
_ Snédis Cathal in sechid cona húblaib dō, conā bōi
cúil nō frith(   ) nō lár nō lepaid nā ristís na hublai ;
conār nessa do Mac Conglinne inūs do cách, ocus bū 25
faide ō Chathal īat.

Gabaid feirg Cathal.    Lingid indala súil d*ó* ina
chend, conā tibred petta cuirre ass.    Gaba*id* in súil
<hr>
[1] chosnamaig       [2] asp-       [3] as-pn       [4] as is

large in his head as a heath-poult's egg. And he
pressed his back against the side of the palace, so
that he left neither rafter, nor pole, nor wattle, nor
wisp of thatch, nor post, that was not displaced.
5 And he sat down in his seat.

"Thy foot and thy cheek under thee, O King !"
said MacConglinne. " Curse me not, and cut me not
off from Heaven!"

"What has caused thee to act so, son of learn-
10 ing ?" said Cathal.

"Good reason have I," said MacConglinne. " I
had a quarrel last night with the monks of Cork,
and they gave me their malediction. This is the
cause of my behaving thus towards thee."

15 "Go to, MacConglinne," said Cathal. " By Emly-
Ivar, if it were my custom to kill students, either
thou wouldst not have come, or thou shouldst not
depart."

(Now, the reason why Emly-Ivar was an oath with
20 him was, because it was there he used to get his fill
of small bread ; and he used to be there, dressed in a
dun-coloured soft cloak, his hard straight-bladed
sword in his left hand, eating broken meats from one
cell to another.

25 One day he went into the cell of a certain student,
and got his fill of broken meats. He examined
the bits. The student examined the page that lay
before him ; and when he had finished studying the
page, he thrust out his tongue to turn over the
30 leaf.

' What has caused thee to do that, O student ?"
asked Cathal.

"Great cause have I," said he. " I have been

n-aile immach, co m-bā métithir ocus óg rérchirce
hī ina chind. Ocus bertais a druimm fria sliss in
rīgt[h]ige, conā fārcaib clūith nō slait nō scolb nō
dlai nō ūatni nā dicsed asa inad ; ocus saidis 'na
shuide.[1]                                                              5
" Do chos ocus do grūad fōt, a rī ! " ar Mac Con-
glinne. " Nā tuc mallachtain dam, ocus nā gat nem
form ! "
" Cid dotrigne, a mic légind ? " ol Cathal.

" Sodethbir dam," ar Mac Conglinne. " Dorala 10
dam arāir fri muintir Corccaige, ocus cotardsat a
n-osnaid dam. Issed fotruair dam aní sin frit-siu."

" Luid dó, a Mic Conglinne ! " ol Cathal. " Dar
Imbliuch n-Ibair, dīamad bés dam mac lēgind do
marbad, sech nī rista, nī tísta."                                      15

(Aire tra bá luige dó-sam Imbliuch n-Ibair ; ar is
innte fogebed a shūith minarūin ; ocus nobíd ocus
bratt bóinni odarda imme, ocus a c[h]loidem crūaid
coilcdīrech ina chlélāim ic tomeilt blog ó cech boith
i n-aroli.                                                             20

Atnaig and lā n-óen i m-boith aroli meic lēgind,
ocus tic lán dó do blogaib. Figlis na blogu. Figlis
in mac légind in lethenach bōi ara bēlaib. Feib
rosīacht in lethenach do fhigled, sínis a thengaid d'
impód na duille.                                                      25

" Cid dotrigne, a mic légind ? " ol Cathal.

" Dethbir mōr accum," or sē. " In slūaiged co

[1] suuide

pressed to go soldiering with a host in arms to the
world's borders, so that there is nothing that touches
ashes and fire, that has not been dried up by smoke
and wind during my absence, until there is neither
5 sap nor strength in it, not so much as a biscuit-rim.
I have not a morsel of bacon, nor of butter, nor of
meat, no drink of any sort, except the dead water of
the pool ; so that I have been bereft of my strength
and vigour.   But first and last—the hosting !"
10    " Verily!" said the son of Finguine, said Cathal.
" By St. Barre, henceforth whilst I live, no cleric
shall go a-soldiering with me."   And up to that time
the clerics of Ireland were wont to go a-soldiering with
the King of Ireland ; and he was therefore the first
15 that ever exempted clerics from going a-soldiering.

He left his grace and blessings, moreover, to the
pilgrims of Emly, and a profusion of small bread in
Emly.   And this is greatest in the south-western part
20 of it ; for there he used to get his fill.

(But this is a digression.)

" By thy kingship, by thy sovereignty, by the
service to which thou art entitled, grant me a little
boon before I go," said MacConglinne.

25    Pichán was summoned into the house.

" Yon student," said Cathal, " is asking a boon
from me."

" Grant it," said Pichán.

" It shall be granted," said Cathal.   " Tell me what
30 it is thou desirest."

" I will not, until pledges are given for its fulfilment."

" They shall be given," said Cathal.

marbad immel int shægail do thachur il-leth frim
.i. errandus do chimais na bairgine do neoch techtas
lūaith ocus tene īarna súgud do dethaig ocus do
gáith, conā bí súg nō seag innte; cen mír salle nō
imme nō feōla, cen dig nach ceneōīl, acht deoch do   5
bódarusci na cuirre, coramdīgaib fom' nert ocus fom'
tracht, ocus in slōgad rē cách ocus īar cách."


"Indeo," ar Mac Finguine .i. ar Cathal, "dar
Barre! céin bam beō-sa, nīconregu clērech i slōgad
lem-sa ó sund immach." Ocus tēgdis clērig Ērenn 10
slōgud cosin fri rīg n-Ērenn; conid ēssium benais
in slōgad do clērchib i tós rīam.


Fācbaid tra rath ocus bendachtn for deoradu Im-
blechu, ocus ana mhinaráin i n-Imblig. Ocus is mōu
isin leth īarthardescertaig[1]; ar is ann dolínta hē 15
beos.

(Etaraissnēis didu sin remaind.)

"Ar do ríge, ar do [fh]laith, ar th'innram, tabair
ascaid m-bicc dam," ar Mac Conglinne, "rūsiú
imthiger."                                              20

Dogarar dó Pichán isin tech.

"Atā in mac lōgind út" or Cathal "ic cuinchid
ascada form."

"A tabairt," ol Pichān.

"Dobērthar," or Cathal. "Abair frim," ol Cathal, 25
"cid condigi."

"Nīcon-epér, corabat curu fria comall."


"Dobērthar," ol Cathal.

[1] dercertaig

"Thy princely word therein?" said MacConglinne.

"By my word," said he, "thou shalt have them, and now name the request."

"This is it," said MacConglinne. "I had a quarrel
5 with the monks of Cork last night, when they all gave me their curse, and ~~it was owing to thee that~~ ~~that trouble was brought on me.~~ And do thou fast with me to-night on God, since thou art an original brother, to save me from the malediction of the monks
10 of Cork; that is what I ask."

"Say not that, son of learning," said Cathal. "Thou shalt have a cow out of every garth in Munster, and an ounce from every house-owner, together with a cloak from every church, to be levied by a steward,
15 and thou thyself shalt feast in my company as long as he is engaged in levying the dues. And by my God's doom," said Cathal, "I had rather thou shouldst have all there is from the west to the east, and from the south to the north of Munster, than
20 that I should be one night without food."

"By my God's doom," said MacConglinne, "since thy princely troth has passed in this, and since it is not lawful for a King of Cashel to transgress it, if all that there is in the Southern Half were given me,
25 I would not accept it. Good reason have I, thou arch-warrior and king-hero of Europe, why I should not accept conditions from thee; for my own treasure is only in Heaven, or on earth, in wisdom, or in poetry. And not alone that—for the last thing
30 is always the heaviest—but I shall go to endless, limitless perdition, unless thou save me from the malediction of the monks of Cork."

"That shall be granted to thee," said Cathal, "and

"Do bríathar flatha ind?" ar Mac Conglinne.
"Dom' bréthir," ol sē, "dogēba, ocus slúind in
aiscid."
"Is ed inso," ar Mac Conglinne. "Tochar dorala
dam arūir fri múnntir Corccaige, *c*otardsat a mallacht 5
uli dam, ocus iss ed fodera in comrorcu sin dam il-
leth frit-sa. Ocus troscud cid duit-siu lém fri Dia
innocht, ár isat brāthair bunaid, dom' s[h]ǣrad for
mallachtain muintire Corccaige, iss ed condaigim."

"Nā hapair, a mic lēgind," ol Cathal. "Bó cach 10
liss i Mumain, ocus uinge cach comaithig, la bratt
cacha cille, ocus mǣr dia tobach, ocus tū fodén im'
f[h]ail-sea ic praindiud oiret bé ic tabach fhīach.
Ocus dom' débroth," or Cathal, "is ferr lemm ina
fil ō īarthar co hoirther ocus ō descert co tuaiscert 15
Muman duit, oltás beth adaig[1] cen bīad."

"Bam' débroth," or Mac Conglinne, "ō rosīacht do
f[h]ír flatha fris, ocus nā dlig rí Caissil tidecht taris,
dīa tarta dam-sa ina fil il-Leth [Moga] Nūadat nícon-
gēbthar. Fil tra, a ardgaiscedaig ocus a rígfhénnid 20
Eorpa, a adbar accum, cén cogabar cóma ūait; ar
ní fhil mo máin fén acht a nim nó i talm*ai*n nō[2]
i n-ēcna nō i n-aircetal. Ocus ní namá,—ar is
trumma cach n-dēdinach—regut a n-iffirn cen crīch,
cen forcend, minām-sǣra for mallachtain muintire 25
Corccaige."

"Dobērthar duit-siu sin," ol Cathal, "ocus ní
[1] agaid         [2] an leg. .i.?

there has not been given before, nor shall there be
given hereafter to the brink of Doom, a thing more
grievous to us than that."

Cathal fasted with him that night, and all that
5 were there fasted also. And the student lay down on
a couch by the side of a door-post, and closed the
house.

As he lay there at the end of the night, up rose
Pichán, the son of Mael-Finde.

10 " Why does Pichán rise at this hour ? " said Mac-
Conglinne.

" To prepare food for these hosts," answered
Pichán, " and 'twere better for us had it been ready
since yesterday."

15 " Not so, indeed," said MacConglinne. " We
fasted last night. The first thing we shall have to-
morrow is preaching." And they waited until
morning. Few or many as they were, not one of
them went out thence until the time of rising on the
20 morrow, when MacConglinne himself got up and
opened the house. He washed his hands, took up
his book-satchel, brought out his psalter, and began
preaching to the hosts. And historians, and elders,
and the books of Cork declare, that there was
25 neither high nor low that did not shed three
showers of tears while listening to the scholar's
preaching.

When the sermon was ended, prayers were
offered for the King, that he might have length of
30 life, and that there might be prosperity in Munster
during his reign. Prayers were also offered up for
the lands, and for the tribes, and for the province as
well, as is usual after a sermon.

tuccad rempi nā ina dīaid[1] co bruinde brātha ní as
lesciu lind oltás sin."

Troscis Cathal in oidche sin leis, ocus troscit a m-
bōi and uli olchena.   Ocus sāmaigis in mac légind i
túlg i tæb n-ursainde, ocus īadais in tech.                           5

Intan bōi and i n-déod aidche, ūrgis sūas Pichān
mac Mōle Finne.
" Crēt ūrgius Pichān an inbuid se ?" or Mac Conglinne.
" Do dénam bíd dona slōgaib se," ol Pichān ; " ocus  10
ba ferr dún comad erlum óné."

" Nithō ám sin," or Mac Conglinne. " Rot[h]rosc-
sium arūir.   *Precept* bus lind īarum imbārach i tos-
saig." Ocus ansit co matain.  Ūathad sochaide a m-bá-
tar, nī dechaid nech dīb anúnd nō amach co trāth érgi  15
īarnabārach.   Atracht Mac Conglinne fessin annside
ocus ro-oslaic in tech.   Ro-indail a lūmu, ocus tuc a
théig libair chucca, ocus bertais a s[h]altair essi, ocus
fororbart *precept* dona slógu.   Is ed atfīadut senCH-
aide ecus senóri ocus libair Corccaige, ūatbōi do  20
ūasal nō d' ísel nūrosteilg trī frassa dér ic éstecht fri
*procept* in scolaige.

Intan tarnic in *procept*, dognít*her* airnaigthi frisin
rīg, conambed fotsægail dó, ocus conambeth maithius
Muman fria remes. Dognīther ernaigthi frisna crīch*a*  25
ocus frisna cenēl*a* ocus frisin cóiced árchena, amal is
gnāth d' aithle *precept*ai.

                    [1] diaig

"Well," asked MacConglinne, "how are things over there to-day ?"

"By my God's doom," answered Cathal, "it never was worse before, and never shall be until Doom."

5  "Very natural it is that thou shouldst be in evil case," said MacConglinne, "with a demon destroying and ravaging thee now during the space of three half-years; and thou didst not fast a day or night on thy own account, though thou didst so for the sake of a

10 wretched, impetuous, insignificant person like me."

"What is the good of all this, son of learning ?" asked Cathal MacFinguine.

"This," said MacConglinne. "Since thou alone didst fast with me last night, let us all fast this night,

15 as many of us as there are; and do thou also fast, that thou mayest obtain some succour from God."

"Say not that, son of learning," said Cathal. "For though the first trial was hard, seven times harder is the last."

20  "Do thou not say that," said MacConglinne, "but act bravely in this."

Then Cathal fasted that night together with his host even until the end of the night.

Then MacConglinne arose.

25  "Is Pichán asleep ?" he said.

"I will tell truth," answered Pichán. "If Cathal were to remain as he is to the brink of Doom, I shall not sleep, I shall not eat, nor smile, nor laugh."

30  "Get up," said MacConglinne. And he called for juicy old bacon, and tender corned-beef, and full-fleshed wether, and honey in the comb, and English salt on a beautiful polished dish of white silver, along

" Maith," ar Mac Conglinne, " cindus atáthar annsin indiú ?"

" Darom' débroth," ol Cathal, " nī bás remi rīam ní is messu, ocus nī bether co bráth."

" Cubaid ém" or Mac Conglinne, " do beth cu holc 5 .i. demun 'cot áidmilliud ocus 'cot indrud fri ré trī lethbl*iadan* indorsa ; ocus nī rot[h]roscis lā nō aidche lat fén, ocus troscis fri persaind tróig n-discir n-deróil mo shámla-su."

"Cid is maith desside, a mic légind?" ol Cathal mac 10 Finguine.

" Nī *ansa*. Ō ratroscis-[s]iu t' ænur lium-sa aráir, troiscem-ni uli lín atāum innocht ; ocus troisc-siu fessin, co fhágba cobair écin ó Dīa."

" Nā ráid ind sin, a mic légind," ol Cathal. 15 " Cérba tróm in tóisech, i[s] sechttruma in déd- enach."

" Nā ráid-siu ind sin," or Mac Conglinne, " acht calma do dénam and."

Troscis tra Cathal in aidche sin cona shlóg ósin co 20 dēod n-áidche.

Érgis Mac Conglinne tra.

" In cotlad do Pichān ?" or Mac Conglinne.

"Atbēr fír," ol Pichān. " Darab Cathal co bruinde m-brátha amal atā, ní choitél, nī thoimél, ní dingēn 25 gen nō gáire."

" Érig," or Mac Conglinne ; ocus iarrais olar sen- shaille ocus mæth bōshaille, ocus lán charna muilt, ocus mil 'na crīathraib, ocus salann Saxanach for teisc fírálaind fhetta findairgit, la cethri bera 30

with four perfectly straight white hazel spits to support the joints. The viands which he enumerated
were procured for him, and he fixed unspeakable, huge
pieces on the spits. Then putting a linen apron
5 about him below, and placing a flat linen cap on
the crown of his head, he lighted a fair four-
ridged, four-apertured, four-cleft fire of ash-wood,
without smoke, without fume, without sparks. He
stuck a spit into each of the portions, and as quick
10 was he about the spits and fire as a hind about her
first fawn, or as a roe, or a swallow, or a bare spring
wind in the flank of March. He rubbed the honey
and the salt into one piece after another. And big as
the pieces were that were before the fire, there dropped
15 not to the ground out of these four pieces as much
as would quench a spark of a candle; but what there
was of relish in them went into their very centre.

It had been explained to Pichán that the reason
why the scholar had come was to save Cathal. Now,
20 when the pieces were ready, MacConglinne cried
out, " Ropes and cords here !"

" What is wanted with them ?" asked Pichán.
Now, that was a " question beyond discretion" for
him, since it had been explained to him before ; and
25 hence is the old saying, " a question beyond discretion."

Ropes and cords were given to MacConglinne,
and to those that were strongest of the warriors.
They laid hands upon Cathal, who was tied in
30 this manner to the side of the palace. Then Mac-
Conglinne came, and was a long time securing
the ropes with hooks and staples. And when this
was ended, he came into the house, with his

fírdīrge findchuill fóthib. Fogabur dō na bīada
rothurim, ocus sāmaigis stacci dī[fh]reccra dermáru[1]
forsna beraib. Ocus gab*ais* īarum línfhūathróicc
tīs ime, ocus a att leccda línaide ba clethi a chend-
mull*aig*, ocus atáid tenid cūin cethirdrumnig cethir-    5
dórsig cethirscoltigde úindsin, cen diaid, cen chiaig,
cen crithir. Sáidis bir cacha hordan dīb, ocus bā
lūathithir fria mai*ng* bá cūtlæg hé, nō fri heirb nō
fannaill nō fri gáith n-imluim n-errch*ai*de im bolg-
s[h]liss Márta hé 'mana beraib ocus 'mána ténntib.   10
Comlis in mil ocus in salann in cach staic īar n-urd.
Cīa robā do mét na staci bōi frisin tenid, nīcontanic
asna cethri[2] stacib sís co lár ní nosbáided crithir
chonnli ; acht a m-bōi d' inmar intib, ina medón fén
dochóid.                                              15


Rofaillsiged do Pichān conid dó tānic in scolaige
do thesarcain Cathail. Ocus intan tarnacar na staci
sin, is ann atbert Mac Conglinne : "Téta ocus réfeda
dam !"

"Cid is áil díb-side ?" ol Pichān. Ocus rop īar-   20
faige[3] dar cubais dō-sum sin, ūair rofaillsiged dó
remi ; conid [d]esin atū in senbrī*athar* .i. fiarfaige
dar cubus.


Atagur téta ocus reféda dó ocus do neoch ba calma
don lǣchraid. Furmit a láma tar Cathal, ocus rocen-  25
glad fōn samail sin hē do shliss in rígthige. Tic
Mac Conglinne īarum, ocus indlis baic ocus corrānu
ead imchīan forsna tétaib sin. Ocus feib tarnic sin,
tic-sium istech, ocus a cethri bera fria ais i n-ardgab-

¹ degmáru      ² cet*ra*      ³ iarfaide

four spits raised high on his back, and his white wide-spread cloak hanging behind, its two peaks round his neck, to the place where Cathal was. And he stuck the spits into the bed before Cathal's
5 eyes, and sat himself down in his seat, with his two legs crossed. Then taking his knife out of his girdle, he cut a bit off the piece that was nearest to him, and dipped it in the honey that was on the aforesaid dish of white silver.
10 "Here's the first for a male beast," said Mac-Conglinne, putting the bit into his own mouth. (And from that day to this the old saying has remained.) He cut a morsel from the next piece, and dipping it in the honey, put it past Cathal's mouth
15 into his own.

"Carve the food for us, son of learning!" exclaimed Cathal.

"I will do so," answered MacConglinne; and cutting another bit of the nearest piece, and dipping it as
20 before, he put it past Cathal's mouth into his own.

"How long wilt thou carry this on, student?" said Cathal.

"No more henceforth," answered MacConglinne, "for, indeed, thou hast hitherto consumed such a
25 quantity and variety of agreeable morsels, that I shall eat the little that there is here myself, and this will be 'food from mouth' for thee." (And that has been a proverb since.)

Then Cathal roared and bellowed, and commanded
30 the killing of the scholar. But that was not done for him.

"Well, Cathal," said MacConglinne, "a vision has

āil, ocus a lumman find fírscailti ina dīaid, ocus a
dá beind imo brágait, co hairmm a m-bōi Cathal.
Ocus sáidis na bera isin leba ina f[h]īadnaise, ocus
saidis fodén ina shuide, ocus a dí choiss imasech.
Ber̃dais a scín dia chris, ocus benais mír don staic   5
ba nessa dó. Tummais isin mil bói forsin teisc find-
argait út.

"A thosach ar míl firend so," ar Mac Conglinne, ic
tabairt in míre ina beōl fodén.   (Is ósin ille lentar
in senbrī*athar*.)   Benais mír don staic n-aile, ocus  10
tummais isin mil, ocus ataig tar beōlu Cathail ina
beōl fódén.

"Tinme dún in m-bīad, a mic légind !" ol Cathal.

"Dogén," or Mac Conglinne.   Benais mír don
staic ba nessa dó, ocus tumais fōnn samail cūtna  15
sech bél Cathail ina beōlu fodén.
"Cīa fot lenfa desin, a mic lēgind ?" ol Cathal.

"Nad lenab ō shunn ; acht ǣnní chena rothómlis-
[s]iu immad na m-blog n-imarcide n-écsamail cusin
trát[h]-sa ; in m-bec fil súnd, is mise dosméla, ocus  20
bid bīad ō beōlu duit-siu seo."   (Ocus senbrī*athar*
sin ille.)

Búraid ocus béccid Cathal īarsin, ocus fócrais a
marbad in scolaigi.  Ní dernad tra fair-siun innī
sin.                                                      25
"Maith, a Cath*ail*," ar Mac Conglinne ; "aislinge

F

appeared to me, and I have heard that thou art good
at interpreting a dream."

"By my God's Doom!" exclaimed Cathal, "though
I should interpret the dreams of the men of the
5 world, I would not interpret thine."

"I vow," said MacConglinne, "even though thou
dost not interpret it, it shall be related in thy
presence."

He then began his vision, and the way he related
10 it was, whilst putting two morsels or three at a
time past Cathal's mouth into his own.

"A vision I beheld last night:
I sallied forth with two or three,
When I saw a fair and well-filled house,
15      In which there was great store of food.

A lake of new milk I beheld
In the midst of a fair plain.
I saw a well-appointed house
Thatched with butter.

20      As I went all around it
To view its arrangement:
Puddings fresh-boiled,
They were its thatch-rods.

Its two soft door-posts of custard,
25      Its dais of curds and butter,
Beds of glorious lard,
Many shields of thin pressed cheese.

Under the straps of those shields
Were men of soft sweet smooth cheese,
30      Men who knew not to wound a Gael,
Spears of old butter had each of them.

domarfás, ocus itcūala it mait[h]-siu oc brei*th* for
aislingi."

" Dom' débroth !" ol Cathal, "dia m-bēraind for
aislingi fer talman, ní bēraind for th' aislingi-se."

" Fortgillim," or Mac Conglinne, "cén co ruca-su,    5
indisfith*ir* hī it' fīadnaise."

Fōbrais tra a aislingi.    Is amlaid did*u* ro indis,
ocus dū mír nō a trī sech bēl Cathail ina beōlu
fodén.

    " Aislinge itchonnarc arāir :                  10
    mo dul for fecht dís nō triūr,
    co n-acca in tech[1] find forlán,
    i rabā a lommnān do biūd.

    Co n-acca in loch lémnachta
        for lār muige find,                        15
    co n-acca in tech lērgníma
        īarna thugaid d' imm.

    Tan tānuc 'na mōrthimchell
        do fégad a uird,
    marōca [ī]arna cūtberbad,                       20
        ba hīat sin a scuilb.

    A dí ersaind bocai brechtáin,
    a leibend do gruth is d' imm,
    imdadai do blonaig bladaig,
    scūith iumdai do thanaig thimm.                 25

    Fir fo scīathraigib na scīath siu
    do mōethail buic mellaig mín,
    fir cen tuicse gona Gōedil,
    góei gruitne cech ōenfhir díb.

                    [1] findtech

A huge caldron full of .  .
(Methought I'd try to tackle it)
Boiled, leafy kale, browny-white,
A brimming vessel full of milk.

5      A bacon house of two-score ribs,
A wattling of tripe—support of clans—
Of every food pleasant to man,
Meseemed the whole was gathered there."

### And he said further :

10      " A vision I beheld last night,
'Twas a fair spell,
'Twas a power of strength when to me appeared
The kingship of Erin.

I saw a court-yard topped with trees,
15          A bacon palisade,
A bristling rubble dyke of stone
Of pregnant cheeses.

Of chitterlings of pigs were made
Its beautiful rafters,
20      Splendid the beams and the pillars,
Of marvellous . . .

Marvellous the vision that appeared to me
By my fireside :
A butter draught-board with its men,
25          Smooth, speckled, peaked.

God bless the words I utter,
A feast without fatigue !
When I got to Butter-mount,
A gillie would take off my shoes !"

30    Here now begins the fable.

Coire ramór lán do luabin,
darliumm rolámus riss gleŏ,
braisech bruithe duillech dóndbán,
lestar lommnán lán do cheŏ.

Tech saille dá fichet tŏebán,                                     5
cŏelach cŏelán comge[1] clann,
dá cech biŭd bud maith la duine,
darlium bātar uile and."
                    Aislinge itchonnarc.

Ocus dixit beos :                                                10

" Aislingthe itchondarc arāir,
    bā cáin gēbend,
bā balcc bríge co tarfás dam
    rīge n·Ērcnn

Co n-accaı in liss m-bilech m-barrach,[2]                        15
    bā sáill sondach,
caisel carrach[3] do miuscellcib
    tanach torrach.

Cádlai[4] mucc, is dc dorŏnta
    a cholbai cadlai,                                            20
suaire in sonba ocus ŭaitne
    ongha[5] amra.

Amra in fhís tarfás dam
    hi cind mo thellaig :
fidchell imme cona foirind                                       25
    blāith bricc bendaig.

Bendachad Dīa mo labra,
    líth cen tassa,
īar[6] techt dam hi Slīab n-Imme
    rolaad[7] gille fomm assai."  Aislingthe.               30

Incipit do fhábull[8] sísana budesta.

---

[1] coimgne  [2] mbairrach  [3] imme *add.*  [4] carna H. 3, 18.
[5] onba H. 3, 18.  [6] ria H. 3, 18.  [7] rolaitea  [8] leg. fhábaill

Though grievous to Cathal was the pain of being two days and a night without food, much greater was the agony of (listening to) the enumeration before him of the many various pleasant viands, and
5 none of them for him !

After this, MacConglinne began the fable.

"As I lay last night in my beautiful canopied bed, with its gilded posts, with its bronze rails, I heard something, viz., a voice coming towards me ;
10 but I answered it not. That was natural; such was the comfort of my bed, the ease of my body, and the soundness of my slumber. Whereupon it said again: ' Beware, beware, MacConglinne, lest the gravy drown thee ! '

15 "At early morn on the morrow I arose, and went to the well to wash my hands, when I saw a mighty phantom approaching me. 'Well, there,' said he to me. ' Well, indeed,' said I to him. ' Well, now, wretch,' said the phantom, ' it was I that gave thee
20 warning last night, lest the gravy should drown thee. But, verily, 'twas

> Warning to one fey,
> Mocking a beggar,
> Dropping a stone on a tree,
25 > Whispering to the deaf,
> A legacy to a glum man,
> Putting a charm in a hurdle,
> A withe about sand or gravel,
> Striking an oak with fists,
30 > Sucking honey from roots of yew,
> Looking for butter in a dog's kennel,
> Dining on ~~the husks~~/of pepper,
> Seeking wool on a goat,
> An arrow at a pillar,

*grains/*

Cūrba tromm in phīan les-sium beth dí laa co n-
áidche cen bīad, bū romó leis do phéin tuirem na
m-bīad n-imda n-imorcide n-ūcsamail ina fhīadnaise,
ocus cen ní dib dó.

Īarsin dó i cend na fáible. 5

" Intan tra rombū ann arūir im' lepaid cháin chumdachta cona hūatnib forūrda, cona colbaib créduma,
co cūala ní .i. in guth frim; ocus ní rof[h]recrus-[s]a
inní sin.  Deithbir dam ; robói do clithmaire mo
lepthai ocus do shádaile mo chuirp ocus do thressi 10
mo chodultai.  Co n-ebert aridisi : ' Fomna, fomna,
a Mic Conglinne, beochail nūrotbáda' (.i. faitches
lat nūrotbáde beoil).

"Atomraracht matain moch arnabárach don tiprait do indmad mo lám, co n-acca ní : in scál mór 15
am' dóchumm.  'Maith insin,' ol sū frim.  'Maith
ūm,' ol smū friss.  'Maith tra, a t[h]róig,' ol in
scál.  'Messi tidnus robud duit aráir, nūrotbáde
beochail.  Acht ūnní cenai,

|  |  |
|---|---|
| bū robad do throich, | 20 |
| bū hirchuitbed fri foigdech, | |
| bū tusliud clochi fria crand, | |
| bū sanais fri bodar, | |
| bū dībad for dubach, | |
| bid cor eptha i cléith, | 25 |
| bū gat im gainem nū im gñal,[1] | |
| bū esorcu darach do dhornaib, | |
| bū deol mela a mecna[ib] ibair, | |
| bū cuinchid imme il-lige chon, | |
| bū longad i scellaib scibair, | 30 |
| bū iarraid olla for gabur, | |
| bū saiget i corthi, | |

[1] leg. grían

*noped /*

Keeping a mare from breaking wind,
Keeping a loose woman from lust,
Water on the bottom of a sieve,
Trusting a <u>mad</u> (?) bitch,
5    Salt on rushes,
A settlement after marriage,
A secret to a silly woman,
(Looking for) sense in an oaf,
Exalting slaves,
10    Ale to infants,
Competing (?) with a king.
A body without a head,
A head without a body,
A nun as bell-ringer,
15    A veteran in a bishop's chair,
A people without a king,
Rowing a boat without a rudder,
Corn in a basket full of holes,
Milk on a hide,
20    Housekeeping without a woman,
Berries on a hide,
Warning visions to sinners,
Reproof to the face,
Restoration without restitution,
25    Putting seed in bad land,
Property to a bad woman,
Serving a bad lord,
An unequal contract,
Uneven measure,
30    Going against a verdict,
To outrage the gospel,
Instructing Antichrist,

to instruct thee, MacConglinne, regarding thy appetite.'

bā cosc lára do broimnig,

Ms boithe

bā cosc mnā bóithe do drúis,

bā usce for tóin créthir,

bā tǣb fri coin fholmnig,

bā salond for lūach*air*, 5

bā tinnsccra ı̄ar n-ındsma,

bā rún fri mnāi m-báith,

bā cīall i n-óinmit,

bā mórad mogad,

bā lind do bǣthaib, 10

bā himmthūs fria rīg,

bā coland cen chend,

bā cend cen chol*aind*,

bā caillech fri clog,

bā hathlǣch i cathair n-esp*uic*,[1] 15

bā tūath cen rīg,

Ms. lái.

bā himram luinge cen lai,

bā harbor i clīab tóll,

bā hass for sechid,

bā tigadus cen mhnāi, 20

bā cǣra for gaimen,

bā taidbsi (.i. messa) do p[h]ecdachu,

bā hathis i n-inchuib,

bā haisec cen taisec,

bā cur síl i n-drochith*lainn*, 25

bā tarcud do dhrochmnāi,

bā fognam do dhroch[fh]laith,

bā lethard cundartha,

bā tomus lettromm,

bā tidecht tar fuigell, 30

bā sārugud soscēla,

bā forcetul Ancrist,

t' f[h]orcetul-sa im do longad, a Mic Conglinne !'

"'I declare by my God's Doom,' said I, 'the reproof is hard and severe.'

"'How is that?' asked the phantom.

"'Not hard to say,' I answered. 'I know not
5 whence thou comest, nor whither thou goest, nor
whence thou art thyself, to question thee, or tell
thee again.'

"'That is easily known,' said the phantom. 'I
am Fluxy son of Elcab the Fearless, from the Fairy-
10 knoll of Eating.'

"'If thou art he,' I said, 'I fancy thou hast
great news, and tidings of food and eating. Hast
any?'

"'I have indeed,' said the phantom; 'but though
15 I have, 'twould be no luck for a friend who had no
power of eating to come up with it.'

"'How is that?' I asked.

"'Indeed, it is not hard to tell,' said the phantom.
'Even so: unless he had a very broad four-edged
20 belly, five hands in diameter, in which could be
fitted thrice nine eatings, and seven drinkings (with
the drink of nine in each of them), and of seven
chewings, and nine digestions—a dinner of a
hundred being in each of those eatings, drinkings,
25 swallowings, and digestions respectively.'

"'Since I have not that belly,' answered I,
'give me thy counsel, for thou hast made me
greedy.'

"'I will indeed give thee counsel,' said the
30 phantom. 'Go,' said he, 'to the hermitage from
which I have come, even to the hermitage of the
Wizard Doctor, where thy appetite for all kinds of

"'Atbiur mo dēbroth,' or Mac Conglinne, 'is crūaid codut in cosc.'

"'Ced sin ?' ol in scál.

"'Nī *ansa*,' or Mac Conglinne, 'nī fhet*ar* can tice, nō cīa thégi, nō can deitt fén friat' imchomarc 5 nō frit' aisnēs doridise.'

"'Nī *ansa* ēm,' ol in scál, '.i. Buarannach mac Elcaib Essamain a Síth Longthe domānaic-sea.'

"'Domúnim,' or Mac Conglinne, 'masathú, fileat scēla mōra lat, ocus di*du* fiss-scél ō bīud ocus ō 10 longad. In fil lat?'

"'Fil tra,' ol in scál, 'ocus matū, nirb' [sh]ursan do charait beth a n-díchumci longthi fri comrīachtain friss.'

"'Ced ōn ?' or Mac Conglinne. 15

"'Nī *ansa* ém,' ol in scál, '.i. cen broind cóicduirn comlethain ∧cethirochair acca, i tanfatís[1] na tr∤ nói n-ithe ocus na secht n-óla imm ól nónbuir cacha díb-side, ocus na secht tomaltais, ocus na nói n-díthata, ocus praind cē*it* cacha hithe ocus cacha 20 hōla ocus cach longthi ocus cacha díthata díb-side foleith.'

"'Or nā fil lem-sa in m-broind sin,' or Mac Conglinne, 'tidnaic[2] comarli dam, ar is acobrach[3] dam fritt.' 25

"'Dobēr-sa ón comairle duit,' ol in scál. 'Éirg,' ol sē, 'doc[h]umm in díserta ō túdchad-sa, .i. dísert ind Fháthlegai, ocus fogēba ann hícc do mīan do cach

---

[1] an leg. tallfatís?    [2] tidnais    [3] acomrach

food, which thy gullet and thy heart can desire, will
find a cure ; where thy teeth will be polished by
the many wonderful manifold viands of which we
have spoken; where thy melancholy will be attacked;
5 where thy senses will be startled ; where thy lips
will be gratified with choice drink and choice
morsels, with eating and putting away every sort
of soft, savoury, tender-sweet food acceptable to
thy body, and not injurious to thy soul,—if only
10 thou gettest to the Wizard Doctor, and to sharp-
lipped Becnat, daughter of Baetan the monstrous
Eater, the wife of the Wizard Doctor.

"'The day thou wilt arrive at the fort will be the
day on which his pavilion of fat will be raised about
15 him, on its fair round wheat plains, with the two
Loins, the Gullet, and the worthy Son of Fat-kettle,
with their mantles of . . ..: . about them.  It will
be a happy day for thee when thou shalt come unto
the fort, O MacConglinne,' said the phantom ;
20 'the more so as that will be the day, on which the
chieftains of the Tribe of Food will be summoned
to the fort.'

"'And what are their names ?' asked MacConglinne.

25    "'Not hard to tell,' said the phantom ; 'they are
Little Sloey, son of Smooth-juicy-bacon ; Cakey, son
of Hung Beef ; and Hollow-sides, son of Gullet, and
Milkikin, son of Lactulus, and Wristy-hand, son of
Leather-head, and young Mul-Lard, son of Flitch
30 of Old-Bacon.'

"'And what is thy own name, if we may ask ?'
"'Not hard to tell,' said the phantom.

bíud at accobor do crūes ocus do chride ; airm i n-
airlímthar do déta ōna bīadu immda inganta ilerda
itchōtamar; i n-indraithfither do dulas ; il-lūife do
chéill bidgu ; inbat budig do bēoil do shainól ocus
do shainait, do longad ocus do brondad cacha bíd 5
buic blásta blūthmilis bus tol dot' chorp ocus nū ba
tocrád dot' anmain, acht corís a dochumm ind
Fháthlega, ocus Becnat Būlathi ingen Meic Bǣtáin
Brasslongthig a ben ind Fháthlega.

" ' In laa ricfa-su dochum in dúnaid, is ū in lá sin 10
tóicūbthar a pupall hítha immpe for a crúndmuigib
córaib cruithnechta; in dū Loan, in Lonloingen[1] ocus
in dagmacu Lónchorūn cona cochull[2] do íthascaig
impu. Bid maith duit-siu in laa ricfa doc[h]úmm
in dúnaid sin, a Mic Conglinne,' ol sū in scál, ' ocus 15
didu conid hē sin laá gairfither tōisig Tūathi in Bíd
dochumm in dúine.'

" ' Ocus cīa a n-anmanna sin ?' or Mac Conglinne.

" ' Nī *ansa*,' ol in scál, '.i. Airnechūn mac Saille
Slemni Súgmaire, ocus Bairgenach mac Toraid 20
Tīrmcharnna, ocus Fastáib mac Lonlongen, ocus
Lachtmarān mac Blichtucán, ocus Lámdóitech mac
Lethirchind, ocus Ōcmǣl-Blongi mac Slessa Sen-
shaille.'

" ' Ocus cīa h' ainm-siu fodén fri īarfaige dīn ?' 25
" ' Nī *ansa*,' ol in scál.

_____
[1] lotloingen          [2] choll

 ' Wheatlet, son of Milklet,
 Son of juicy Bacon,
  Is mine own name.
 Honeyed Butter-roll
5 Is the man's name
  That bears my bag.

 Haunch of Mutton
 Is my dog's name,
  Of lovely leaps.
10 Lard, my wife,
 Sweetly smiles
  Across the kale-top.

 Cheese-curds, my daughter,
 Goes round the spit,
15  Fair is her fame.
 Corned Beef, my son,
 Whose mantle shines
  Over a big tail.

 Savour of Savours
20 Is the name of my wife's maid :
 Morning-early
 Across New-milk Lake she went.

 Beef-lard, my steed,
 An excellent stallion,
25  That increases studs ;
 A guard against toil
 Is the saddle of cheese
  On his back.

 When a cheese-steed is sent after him
30  Rapid his course,
 Fat . . . . is on his ribs,
 Exceeding all shapes.

'Cruithnechtán mac Lémnachtān
mac Saille Súgmaire
m' ainm-si fodén.
Brechtān fo Mil
comainm in f[h]ir                                5
bís fom' théig.

Hïar[sh]liss Cærech
comainm mo chon
cádla bánd.
Blonag mo ben                                    10
tibid a gen
tar braisce barr.

Millsén m' ingen
imthét n-inber,
gile a glond.                                    15
Böshall mo mac,
taitnid a brat
tar ethri n-oll.

Olor n-Olar
comainm inalta mo mná:                           20
mátan moch
tar Loch Lémnachta roslā.

Böger m' airech,
sall boc[c] braivech
brogas scuir :                                   25
din sæthra,
sadall mæthla
for a muin.

Intan locar ina dïaid oirech mæthla.
lūath a ruth,                                    30
híth ar all aig bid ar asnaib
sech cach cruth.   Cruth.

A large necklace of delicious cheese-curds
Around his back,
His halter and his traces all
Of fresh butter.

5 His bridle with its reins of fat
In every place.
The horsecloth of tripe with its . . . ,
Tripes are his hoofs.

Egg-horn is my bridle-boy
10 .        .        .        .

Before going to a meeting with death
.        .        .        .

My pottage tunic around myself
Everywhere,
15 *well boiled* . . . of tripe with its . *quantum*
Of uncooked food.

" ' Off with thee now to those delicious pro-
digious viands, O MacConglinne,' said the phantom,

' many wonderful provisions,
20 pieces of every palatable food,
brown red-yellow dishes,
full without fault,
perpetual joints of corned beef,
smooth savoury lard,
25 and heavy flitches of boar.

" ' Off with thee now to the suets and cheeses ! '
said the phantom.

" ' I will certainly go,' said MacConglinne, ' and
do thou put a gospel around me.'

30 " ' It shall be given,' said the phantom, ' even a
gospel of four-cornered even dry cheese, and I will
put my own paternoster around thee, and neither
greed nor hunger can visit him around whom it is
put.' And he said :

Mōrmuince do mulchán mellach
    ima chúl,
[a] adastar ocus a ellach
    d' imim úr.

A srīan cona aradnu hítha          5
    in cach dú,
inbert inbe cona tibrecht
    d' inbib crú.

Ugadarc mo gilla glomar,
    níta tuir,                10
rē n-dul i n-dáil báis dáig nibras
    dontī dotcuir.  C.

M' inar crúibechán imum-sa féin
    in cach dú,
imbert inbe cona tibrecht       15
    din bīd crú.  C.

" 'Cosna bīadaib oirerda[ib] ingantaib út duit festa,
a Mic Conglinne !' ol in scál,

    ' .i. bīada ile inganta,
    staci cach bíd belaide,      20
    mlissa donna dergbuide,
    lomnāna cen locht,
    aisle būana bōshaille,
    blongi bláthi belaide,[1]
    tarthrann troma torcc.      25

" ' Cusna blongib duit festa ocus cusna mǣthlaib !'
ol in scál.

" ' Regut ēm,' or Mac Conglinne, 'ocus tabar soscēla immum.'

" ' Dobērthar,' ol in scál, ' .i. soscēla do thirm-  30
chaisi cetharochair cutrumma, ocus gēbthar mo
pater-sa fodén imut, ocus nīstadaill athgēri nō oc-
curas intí ima n-gabar hī.'  Ut dixit:

          [1] belaige           G

" 'May smooth juicy bacon protect thee, O Mac-
Conglinne !' said the phantom.

" 'May hard yellow-skinned cream protect thee,
O MacConglinne !

5    " 'May the caldron full of pottage protect thee,
O MacConglinne !

" 'May the pan full of pottage protect thee, O
MacConglinne !'

" 'By my God's doom, in the presence of the
10 Creator,' said MacConglinne, 'I wish I could get to
that fortress, that I might consume my fill of those
old strained delicious liquors, and of those wonderful enormous viands.'

" 'If thou really so wishest,' said the phantom,
15 'thou shalt have them. Go as I tell thee ; but
only, if thou goest, do not go astray.'

" 'How is that ?' said MacConglinne.

" 'Not hard to tell,' said the phantom. 'Thou
must place thyself under the protection and safe-
20 guard of the mighty peerless warriors, the chiefs
of the Tribes of Food, lest the gravy destroy
thee.'

" 'How, then,' said MacConglinne, 'which of the
chiefs of the Tribes of Food are the most puissant
25 safeguards against the heavy waves of gravy?'

" 'Not hard to tell,' said the phantom. 'The
Suets and the Cheeses.'

"Thereupon then I advanced," said MacConglinne, "erect, with exultant head, with stout steps.
30 The wind that comes across that country—it is
not by me I wish it to go, but into my mouth.
And no wonder ; so heavy was the disease, so scant
the cure, so great the longing for the remedy. 1

" 'For foesam duit na saille slemni sūgmaire, a
Mic Conglinne ! ' ol in scál.

" 'For foesam duit na crothi crūadi cūlbudi, a
Mic Conglinne ! ' ol in scál.

" 'For foesam duit in chori lán do crūibechān, a   5
Mic Conglinne ! ' ol in scál.

" 'For foesam duit in[d] aigin lán do crūibecbān, a
Mic Conglinne ! ' ol in scál.

" 'Dar mo dēbroth i fīadnaise in dūileman,' ar
Mac Conglinne,.' ba maith lium co rísaind a dochum  10
in dúnaid sin, dūig cotormolaind mo lōr dona
lendaib senaib sīthaltai somillsi ocus dona bīadaib
inganta aidble út.'

" 'Mad maith lat-sa ém,' ol in scūl, 'fogēba sin.
Ocus ēirg amail asberim-si frit, acht namā dīa téis,  15
nīstéig a merachad.'

" 'Cid sin ? ' ol Mac Conglinne.

" 'Nī *ansa* ēm,' ol in scál. 'Acht focerd for
fæsom ocus comarci na n-óc n-antem n-anamail .i.
tōsig Thūath Bíd, nāratródbá beochoil.'   20


" 'Ced ón ? ' ol Mac Conglinne, 'cīa do tósechaib
Tūath Bíd is gératu comarci ar tromthondaib
beochla ? '

" 'Nī *ansa* ém,' ol in scūl, '.i. cusna Blongib ocus
cusna Mūthlaib.'   25

" Atomregar dō īarsin," or Mac Conglinne, " co
herard cendfhælid cuslūthmar. In gōeth nostic
darsin tīr sin, dūthracur conūb seocham notēissed,
acht co m-[b]ad a m-beōlu. Bā dethbir ōn, bōi do
thrumma in galair ocus do therci in legis, do  30
accobar na n-aicidi.[1] Atomraracht co dīan díscir

---

[1] leg. na hícce or na n-íccide. Cf. p. 93, 22.

advanced vehemently, furiously, impatiently, eagerly, greedily, softly, gliding, like a young fox
approaching a shepherd, or as a clown to violate a
queen, or a royston-crow to carrion, or a deer to
5 the cropping of a field of winter-rye in the month
of June.  However, I lifted my shirt above my
buttocks, and I thought that neither fly, nor gad-
fly, nor gnat could stick to my hinder part, in its
speed and agility, as I went through plains and
10 woods and wastes towards that lake and fort.

  "Then in the harbour of the lake before me I
saw a juicy little coracle of beef-fat, with its coating
of tallow, with its thwarts of curds, with its prow of
lard, with its stern of butter, with its thole-pins
15 of marrow, with its oars of flitches of old boar
in it.

  "Indeed, she was a sound craft in which we em-
barked.  Then we rowed across the wide expanse of
New-Milk Lake, through seas of broth, past river-
20 mouths of mead, over swelling boisterous waves of
butter-milk, by perpetual pools of gravy, past woods
dewy with meat-juice, past springs of savoury lard,
by islands of cheeses, by hard rocks of rich tallow, by
headlands of old curds, along strands of dry cheese:
25 until we reached the firm, level beach between
Butter-mount and Milk-Lake and Curd-point at the
mouth of the pass to the country of O'Early-eating,
in front of the hermitage of the Wizard Doctor.
Every oar we plied in New-milk Lake would send
30 its sea-sand of cheese curds to the surface."

  It was then MacConglinne said, at the top of
his voice : "Ha, ha, ha ! these are not the seas that
I would not take!"

denmnetach, co mianach michuirdech, co slemda
slithemda, amail sinchūn do leith[1] ægaire, nō aithech
do sleith banrigna, nō fendóc dochúm gairr, nō
ag n-allaid do gebbad guirt gemshecoil a mís Míthe-
main. Forcena tócba[i]m-sa mo lēnid ōs mell*ach*  5
mo lūrac, ocus midithir[2] lem nū tairissed cuil nō
crebar nō corrmíl form' íarcómla for a déni ocus
athluime, co rūnuc maige ocus feda ocus fúsaige
dochumm in lacha ocus in dúnaid sin.

"Conn-acca nī i purt in lacha for mo chind, .i.
ethar bec beochlaide bōshaille cona immchassal  10
gered, cona shessaib grotha, cona braine blongi,
cona erus imme, cona sculmarib smera, cona rūmaib
slessai sentuirc fair.

"Bā soccair tra in lestar i n-dechumar. Iarsin  15
tra imrāsium dar lethanmhag Lacha Lemnachta,
dar trethna tremunta, tar inberaib meda, tar
bolgonfad buptáid blāithche, tar baitsechaib būana
belaide, sech caille druchtbela, tar tibrén úscai
olorda, a n-indsib mōethal, tar crūadchaircib gered  20
gerthige, tar srónaib sengrothai, tar trachta
tana[ch] tīrmaide, corogaibsium calath comnart
cutruma eter Slīab n-Imme ocus Loch n-Aiss ocus
Bend Grotha ar bēlu belaig crīche hūa Mochlongthi
for dorus dīserta ind Fháthlega. Cach ráma do-  25
bermís il-Loch Lémnachta cotochrad a murgrīan
millsēn for ūachtar."

Conid ann atbert Mac Conglinne in guth a
n-ūachtar a chind : "Abb, abb, abb ! nīmtát muir
nādgaibend."  30

_____
[1] dosleith          [2] médith*ir*

"Then the Wizard Doctor spoke to his people : 'A troublesome party approaches you to-night, my friends,' said the Wizard Doctor, 'viz., Aniér Mac-Conglinne of the men of Munster, a youngster of
5 deep lore, entertaining and delightful. And he must be well served; for he is melancholy, passionate, impetuous, violent, and impatient ; and he is eager, fond of eating early ; and he is voracious, ~~niggardly~~, greedy; and yet he is mild and gentle, . . . easily
10 moved to laughter. And he is a man great in thanks-givings and in upbraidings. And no wonder ; for he has wit both to censure and to praise the hearth of a well-appointed, gentle, fine, mirthful house with a mead-hall.' "

*shameless*/

15 "Marvellous, indeed, was the hermitage in which I then found myself. Around it were seven score hundred smooth stakes of old bacon, and instead of the thorns above the top of every long stake was fried juicy lard of choice well-fed boar,
20 in expectation of a battle against the tribes of Butter-pat and Cheese that were on Newmilk Lake, warring against the Wizard Doctor.

"There was a gate of tallow to it, whereon was a bolt of sausage.

25 "I raised myself up then out of my boat," said MacConglinne, "and betook myself to the outer door of the entrance porch of the fortress, and seizing a branchy cudgel that lay directly on my right hand outside the porch of the fortress, I dealt
30 a blow with it at the tallow door, on which was the sausage lock, and drove it before me along the outer porch of the fortress, until I reached the splendid inner chief residence of the enormous

" Conid annsin atbert in Fáthliaig fria muintir :
' Fail dáim n-annsa in bar n-dochum anocht, a
muinter,' ol in Fáthliaig, '.i. Aniér Mac Conglinne
do Muimnechaib, glūim gilla ūasail oirchetail oirfitig
aín.   Dáig rocaiter a deg[fh]rithailem, or is dūb-    5
lathi díscir dīan dremun denmnetach ; ocus sū
mīanach mochloingt[h]ech, ocus sū ithamail anfhīal
occurach, ocus sū sām[fh]ind sobucc sotorchutbide.
Ocus is fer bret[h]i budi ocus oirbiri.   Dethbir ón,
dūig rofhétand āir ocus molad for tellach taige  10
trebargloin mín maisig medraig midchūartai[g].' "


" Ba hamra tra in dīsiurt i m-badus ann .i. *secht*
*fichit cēt* sónn sleman senshaille imme ; ocus bū hē
casdraigen bōi ūas clethi cendmull*aig* cacha suind
sīrfhota, .i. blonoc brothrach belathi tuirc trebair  15
taiscelta fria fómtin imbualta[1] fri Tūath*a* Mescān
ocus Mǣthal bátar for Loch Lemnachta i cocad frisin
Fáthliaig.

" Cómla gered friss, ocus gerrcend maróci furri.

" Atomcnireth*ar* sūas dó as mo ethar," or Mac  20
Conglinne, " co dorus érdaim imdorais in dúnaid
dianechtair, ocus gebim bulbi*n*g brusgarbán bói
for mo lūim dírig deiss fri himdorus in dúnaid
anechtair, ocus ticimm bulli de frissin cómla*id* n-
geriud bói co n-glass maróice furri, ocus foscer-  25
dimm sechum for fut immdorais imechtraig in
dúnaid, co ruachtus in prīmcathraig mōrglain
medōnaig in dúnaid dímóir.   Ocus indsmaimm mo

---

[1] im imbualta

fort. And I fixed my ten pointed purple-bright
nails in its smooth old-bacon door, which had a
lock of cheese, flung it behind me, and passed
through.

5   "Then I saw the doorkeeper. Fair was the shape
of that man ; and his name was Bacon-lad, son of
Butter-lad, son of Lard ; with his smooth sandals
of old bacon on his soles, and leggings of potmeat
encircling his shins, with his tunic of corned beef,
10 and his girdle of salmon skin around him, with
his hood of flummery about him, with a seven-
filleted crown of butter on his head (in each
fillet of which was the produce of seven ridges of
pure leeks) ; with his seven badges of tripe about
15 his neck, and seven bosses of boiled lard on the
point of every badge of them ; his steed of bacon
under him, with its four legs of custard, with
its four hoofs of coarse oaten bread under it, with
its ears of curds, with its two eyes of honey in
20 its head, with its streams of old cream in its two
nostrils, and a flux of bragget streaming down behind, with its tail of dulse, from which seven hand-
fuls were pulled every ordinary day; with its smooth
saddle of glorious choice lard upon it, with its face-
25 band of the side of a heifer around its head, with
its neck-band of old-wether spleen around its neck,
with its little bell of cheese suspended from the
neck-band, with its tongue of thick compact metal
hanging down from the bell ; and a whip in that
30 rider's hand, the cords whereof were twenty-nine
fair puddings of white-fat cows, and the substance
of every juicy drop that fell to the ground from the
end of each of these puddings would, with half a

deich n-ingne corra corcarglana isin cóml*aid*
slemain senshaille cona gl*ass* mǣthla furri, ocus
foscerdimm sec[h]umm ocus *con*ludimm sec[h]a.

"Co n-acca tra in doirrseōir.   Bā cáin delb in
óclaig sin, ocus bū hē a chomainm .i. Mǣlsaille mac 5
Máilimme meic Blongi ; cona assaib slemna sen-
[sh]aille ima[1] bunnu, cona ochraib do biud scaiblíne
ima lurg[n]ib, cona hinar bōshaille imme, cona
c[h]riss do leth*ar* fírésc taris, cona chochall di
thascaid imme, cona secht cornib imme ina chind; 10
ocus bátar secht n-immaire do f[h]írchainnind in
cach coraind díb-side fóleth ; cona secht n-epislib
do chǣlānu inbi[2] fo brágait, cona secht m-bille do
blonaig bruithi for cind cacha hepis*le* díb-side, cona
chapall saille foe, cona *cethri* cossa brechtūin, cona 15
cethri crú do garbarán chorca fou, cona chlūassaib
grotha, cona dá shūil mela ina chind, cona srothaib
senchrothi[3] i cechtar a dí sr*ón*, cona buindib brócoti
asa īarcómlaid sīar sec[h]tair, cona scóib dhulisc      *adv*
fair, dīa m-bendais secht n-glacca cach lathi aic*en*ta, 20
cona sadull blongi (nō bōs[h]ailli) būadaige fair,
cona drecho*n*gdás tóib samaisce fria cend, cona munci
do dressán senmuilt ba brūgait, cona c[h]luchín do     *Ms. bá brágait*
mǣthail asin munci, cona thengaid do métail tiag[4]
timmthasta asin clucín sís, cona s[h]rogill ina láim 25   *adv.*
in marcaig sin, bátir īalla būtar inde[5] .i. nōi n-in-
drechtāna finda fichet do indrechtānu bó bán-méthi,
ocus nobíd sáith sacairt fria lethbairgin in cach
bainde beochlaide nothuited a cind cach indrechtāin díb-side fria lár ; cona bachaill buic bruthi 30

----

[1] *ina*          [2] *inbíd*          [3] *crochi*
   [4] *leg. tiug*          [5] *inide*

cake, be a surfeit for a priest; with his slender
boiled stick of *bundrish* in his hand, and every
juicy drop that trickled from the end of it, when
he turned it downwards, would contain the full of
5 seven vats."

"'Open the hermitage to us,' said MacConglinne.

"'Come in, wretch!' answered the doorkeeper.

"On going in, then," said MacConglinne, "I saw
on my left hand the servants of the Wizard Doctor
10 with their hairy cloaks of . . . . . with their hairy
rags of soft custard, with their shovels of dry bread
in their hands, carrying the tallowy offal that was
on the lake-bridge of custard, from the porch of
the great house to the outer porch of the fortress.

*stone -*

15 "On my right hand I then beheld the Wizard
Doctor, with his two gloves of full-fat rump-steak
on his hands, setting in order the house, which was
hung all round with tripe from roof to floor.

"Then I went into the kitchen, and there I saw
20 the Wizard Doctor's son, with his fishing-hook
of lard in his hand, with its line made of fine

*shanks/*

brawn of a deer, viz., the marrow of its leg,
with its thirty-hand rod of tripe attached to
the line below, and he angling in a lake of lard.
25 Now he would bring a flitch of old bacon, and now
a weasand of corned beef from the lake of lard mixed
with honey, on to a bank of curds that was near him
in the kitchen. And in that lake it is that the Wizard
Doctor's son was drowned, for whom the celebrated
30 elegy was made :

'The son of Eoghan of lasting fame,' etc.

"Afterwards I went into the great house.  As I

bùndraisse ina lǎim, co m-bǐd lǎn secht n-dabach
cacha bainde beochlaide nosc͞c͞ed tar a cuirr, intan
nosfuirmed fri lǎr."

ᴬ ˢ "'Oslaicth*er* dùn in dísert!' ol Mac Conglinne.
"'Ā thrōig ém,' or in dǒirrseōir, 'tair amuig!'     5
"Co n-acca tra īar n-dul anúnd," ol Mac Con-
glinne, "for mo lǎim clíi .i. mogaid in[d] Fhǎthlega     *clíi ꝭs.*
cona m-broth*ar*lúmnib brothracháin, cona m-bro-
th*ar*certib boc-brechtāin, cona slūastib turarāin ina
lǎmu ic fochartad in ottraig ingerta bōi forsin loch-   10  *c[l]och-*
drochat brechtāin ōtha immdorus in tige mōir co         *drochat.*
himdorus in dúine inechtair.

"Co n-acca tra dom' lǎim deiss .i. in Fǎthliaig
cona dí lǎmaind do loncharna lǎn-mhc͞ith bǎ lǎmaib
ic lc͞rgním in taige lānimmerta do chǎ͞lánu inbe¹ ō  15
mull*uch* co talm*ain*.

"Atnaigim isin cuchtair, co n-acca tra .i. mac ind
Fhǎthlega cona dubǎn blongi ina lǎim, cona rūaimnig
do minscomartaig oige all*aid* ass, .i. smir a lurgḟn,   *a/*
cona slait co *tri*ch*a*t ferlǎm do chǎ͞lānu inbe asin  20
rūaimnig sin sís oc dubǎnacht for loch n-úsca.
Cumma nobered tinne senshaille ocus lonlongén
bōs[h]aille ar loch úsca cummascaig[th]e mela for
tír n-grotha bōi 'ma farrad isin cuchtair. Ocus isin     *ina/*
loch sin robǎided mac ind Fhǎthlega, dīa n-dernad in  25
marbnaid erdraicc, .i.

'Mac Eogain clù marind,' *ocus araile*.

"Ataigimm isin tech mōr īarum. Amail tucus
                    ¹ imbe

set my foot across the threshold into the house, I saw
something, viz., a pure white bed-tick of butter, on
which I sat ; but I sank in it to the tips of my two
ears.    The eight strongest men that were in the
5 king's house had hard work to pull me out by the
top of the crown of my head.

"Then I was taken to the place where the Wizard
Doctor himself was.

"'Pray for me!' said I to him.

10    "'In the name of cheese!' said he to me.   'Evil
is the limp look of thy face,' said the Wizard Doctor.
'Alas! it is the look of disease.   Thy hands are
yellow, thy lips are spotted, thine eyes are grey.
Thy sinews have relaxed, they have risen over thy
15 ~~brow~~/and over thy flesh, and over thy joints and
nails.   The three hags have attacked thee, even
scarcity and death and famine, with ~~sharp~~ beaks of
hunger.   An eye that sains not has regarded thee.
A plague of heavy disease has visited thee.   No
20 wonder, truly ; for thine is not the look of a full-
suckled milk-fed calf, tended by the hands of a good
cook.   Thou hast not the corslet look of well-
nourished blood, but that of a youth badly reared
under the vapours of bad feeding.'

25    "'Very natural that,' said MacConglinne.  'Such
is the heaviness of my ailment, the scarcity of cure,
the longing for the remedy.'

"'Tell me thy disease, my man,' said the Wizard
Doctor.

30    "'I will tell thee,' said MacConglinne, 'what it is
that shrivels me up and what makes me low-spirited,
inactive, even love of good cheer, hatred of bad
cheer, desire of eating early, the gnawing of my many
fancies, the gnawing of flesh, the consumption of

mo choiss darsin tairrsech istech, co n-acca ní .i. in
colcaid[1] n-éngil n-imme, *co* sess*ar* furri, conamtarrusar
innte co barr mo dī chlūas. In ochtar is calma bōi
isin rīgthig, a n-opar 'com tharraing esti for clethib
cendmull*aig*.                                                    5

" Nomcurth*er* īarsin áitt a m-bói in Fáthliaig
fodessin.

" ' Oráit, orāit !' ol mé friss.

" ' I n-anmam mǣthla !' or sē frim. ' Is olc in
féthán féths[h]nais fil for h'agaid,' or in Fáthliaig.   10
' Uchán ! is féth gal*air*. At buide do láma, at brecca
do beōil, at līatha do shúile. Rof[h]ánnaigsetar th'
féthi, atrachtatar ōs tuil ocus ōs t' feōil ocus ōs    *t'[sh]ūil/*
t' altaib ocus ōs t' ingnib. Ro[t]tairb*ir*setar t*eora*
mná : ūatha ocus ōca ocus gorta, .i. do gobaib   15
gorta galbigi. Ro[t]tāraill súil nát-athbendach,       *✗*
ro[t]táraill tám trómgal*air*. Sodethbir tra, ni féth
láig lilicca lachtmair lessaigthi latt fo lámu d*i*gchoca.   *a/*
Ni féth luric[2] fola lessaigthi latt, acht is féth mcic
mīaltromma fo múich milessaigt[h]i.'                    20

" ' Sodethbir ón,' ol Mac Conglinne, 'atā do thruime
mo gal*air*, do therci in legis, do accobar na hícce.'

" ' Asnéid dam do gal*ar*, a lāich,' or in Fūthliaig.

" ' Asnēdfit ēm,' ol Mac Conglinne, ' indrud mo
credba ocus a n-domgní miſſrech mígnīmach, .i.   25
carthain cǣmna, miscais míchūmna, mīan mochlongthi, minchirrad m' ilblass, cnám cárna, bronnud

_____

¹ colcaig            ² an leg. lúirig ?

white-meats, greed and hunger. The thirst and voracity which I feel in consuming my food, so that what I eat gives neither satiety nor substance; inhospitality and niggardliness, refusal and unchari-
5 tableness regarding what is my own, so that I am a burden to myself, and dear to none. Hunger, with its four-and-twenty subdivisions in addition thereto, sadness, niggardliness, anxiety to be welcomed before everybody to all kinds of food, and
10 the injurious effect to me of every food.

"'My wish would be, that the various numerous wonderful viands of the world were before my gorge, that I might gratify my desires, and satisfy my greed. But alas! great is the misfortune to
15 one like me, who cannot obtain any of these.'

"'On my word,' said the Great Doctor, 'the disease is grievous. Woe to him on whom it has fallen, and not long will it be endured. But as thou hast come to me to my hermitage and to my
20 fort at this time, thou shalt take home with thee a medicine to cure thy disease, and shalt be for ever healed therefrom.'

"'What is that?' asked MacConglinne.

"'Not hard to tell,' answered the Great Doctor.
25 'If thou goest home to-night, go to the well to wash thy hands, rub thy teeth with thy fists, and comb every straight rib of thy hair in order. Warm thyself afterwards before a glowing red fire of straight red oak, or of octagonal ash that grows near
30 a hill-side where little sparrows leave their droppings; on a dry hearth, very high, very low, that its embers may warm thee, that its blaze may not burn thee, that its smoke may not touch thee. Let

bánbíd, géri ocus gorti, ítmaire ocus ithemraige lemm
mo chuit fodéin, conū gaib g*r*eim nō gabūil ina
tómlim ; doichell ocus dochta, díultad ocus díchon-
nercli immonní is leamm fodén, conad am lista
liumm fodén ocus na*ch* am inmain frisnach ūn.  5
Gorta cona *cethri fichet fodlaib* airsin anūas .i.
dogaillsi, díbe, dál fria hēssamna lem rū cách i cénd
cach bíd, inriud cach bíd frim.

" ' Ba hed mo mían, bīada ilarda immda inganta in
betha i comair mo c[h]ráis, do dénam mo tholi, do  10
línad mo shánti.  Uch tra, is mōr in sæth sin do
neoch nūdosfāgaib uli.'

" ' Atbíur mo br*ēth*ir,' or in Fáthliaig, ' is olc ind
accidit.  Is margócán dīanostarla, ocus nī ba fota
foelustar.  Ar is co tuide[c]ht duit dom' dísiurt-sa  15
ocus dom' dúnad don chur sa, bēra midchuine
latt do tig d' ícc do gal*air*, ocus bid slán cáidche de.'

" ' Cade side ?' ol Mac Conglinne.
" ' Nī *annsa* ēm,' or in Fáthliaig.  ' Dīa téis do
tig innocht, ēirg don tiprait d' innmad do lám, co-  20
melfi dorni fri détu, ocus doch*b*sail each finda fíar
foltnide[1] īarna chōir dot' fhult.  Iarsin notgor fri
tenid trichemrūaid do daroich d*eir*g dírig nō do
ochts[h]lisnig úindsend fhásus i fhail airshlēbi
dú i caccut mingelbuind, hi tellach thīrmaide  25
irard airísel, coratgori a grīss, nūrotlosci a lassar,
nūrotbe*n*a a dé.  Scarth*ar* gemen findach fírgámna

---

[1] foltnige

a hairy calf-skin be placed under thee to the
north-east before the fire, thy side resting exactly
against a rail of alder. And let an active,
white-handed, sensible, joyous woman wait upon
5 thee, who must be of good repute, of good dis-
course, red-lipped, womanly, eloquent, of a good
kin, wearing a necklace, and a cloak, and a
brooch, with a black edge between the two peaks of
her cloak, that sorrow may not come upon her;
10 with the three nurses of her dignity upon her, with
three dimples of love and delight in her counten-
ance, without an expression of harshness in her
forehead, who shall have a joyous, comely appear-
ance, a purple five-folded cloak about her, a red-
15 gold brooch in her cloak, a fair broad face, a good
blue eye in her head, two blue-black brows of the
colour of the black chafer over those eyes, ruddy
even cheeks, red thin lips, white clear teeth in
her head as though they were pearls, soft tender
20 white fore-arms, two smooth snowy sides, beau-
teous shapely thighs, straight well-proportioned
calves, thin white-skinned feet, long ~~slender~~ fingers,
long pale-red nails. So that the gait and move-
ments of the maiden may be graceful and quick,
25 so that her gentle talk and address may be melo-
dious as strings, soft and sweet; so that, from her
crown to her sole, there may be neither fault, nor
stain, nor blemish, on which a sharp watchful
observer may hit.

30 "'Let this maiden give thee thy thrice nine
morsels, O MacConglinne, each morsel of which
shall be as big as a heath-fowl's egg. These morsels
thou must put in thy mouth with a swinging jerk,

fót fria tenid anairtūaid,[1] ocus do s[h]liss fri colba
findgel ferna saindrud. Ocus toirbered ben dīan
dóitgel imchīalla fhorbáilid, 'sí sochla sōacéallma,[2]
'sī bēlchorccra banamail, 'sī sobéōil sochenēlach, 'sī
muncach bratach brétrrusach,⁁ co m-brūach n-dub  5
eter dā ló a bruit, nāroshera brón fuirri. Teora muime
a hórdan fuirri. Teora hūible sercci ocus ana for a
hínchaib, cen fír doichle ina hétan. Ēcosc sūairc
sochóir lee, bratt corccra cóicdīabail impe, eō órderg
ina brut, agaid chāin forlethan lé, rōsc glass cáiu  10
ina cind, dā brā dóile dūbgorma ōsna rosca sin,
grūade corccra comarda lé, beōil deirg tanaide, dēta
gela glanide ina cind amail betís nemaind, rigthi boca
bláthgela, dí thǣb shlémna shnechtaide, slīasta sǣgda
sébcaide, colptha córa cutruma, traigthe tana tóungela,  15
méra sēta síthalta, ingne áidble iuchanta. Corab
álaind ocus corab gasta a focheím ocus a foimmthecht
na hinghene sin ; corab tétbind téthmilis a mínchom-
rad ocus a mīnacallam ; conāroib locht nō on nō anim
rism-benfa nach aicsed féig furachair ōthā a hind coa  20
bond.

" 'Tabrad in ingen sin duit do trī nói mírend, a
Mic Conglinne, corab médithir fri hog rerchírci
cach mír. Fodosceirdi for lūasc lūamnig it' beōlu

[1] uaig   [2] soacmallma

H

and thine eyes must whirl about in thy skull whilst
thou art eating them.'

  "'The eight kinds of grain thou must not spare, O
MacConglinne, wheresoever they are offered thee,
5 viz., rye, wild-oats, beare, buck-wheat, wheat, barley,
*fidbach*, oats. Take eight cakes of each ~~fair~~ grain
of these, and eight condiments with every cake,
and eight sauces with each condiment ; and let each
morsel thou puttest in thy mouth be as big as a heron's
10 egg. Away now to the smooth panikins of cheese-
curds, O MacConglinne,

    to fresh pigs,
    to loins of fat,
    to boiled mutton,
15   to the choice easily-discussed thing for which
the hosts contend—the gullet of salted beef ;
    to the dainty of the nobles, to mead ;
    to the cure of chest-disease—old bacon ;
    to the appetite of pottage—stale curds ;
20   to the fancy of an unmarried woman—new milk ;
    to a queen's mash—carrots ;
    to the danger awaiting a guest—ale ;
    to the sustenance of Lent—the cock of a hen ;
    to a broken head—butter-roll ;
25   to hand-upon-all—dry bread ;
    to the pregnant thing of a hearth—cheese ;
    to the bubble-burster—new ale ;
    to the priests' fancy—juicy kale ;
    to the treasure that is smoothest and sweetest of
30 all food—white porridge ;
    to the anchor . . . .—broth ;
    to the double-looped twins—sheep's tripe ;
    to the dues of a wall—sides (of bacon);

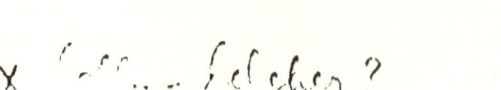

na mírenda, corusimpōat do shúile it' chloiceand
ocá n-ithe.'

"'Na hocht n-orbaind nídoscoicéla, a Mic Conglinne, cia bali adochrat duit: secul, seruān, mælān,
rūadān, cruithnec[h]t, eōrna, fidbach, corca. Ocht
m-bairgena cacha [fh]indorba dīb-side, ocus ocht
n-ándlaind cacha bargine, ocus [ocht] torsnu fria cach
n-andland, ocus mēdithir fri hog curri cach mír
foscerdi it' beōlu díb. Cosna corénaib míne millsén
duit festa, a Mic Conglinne,

*Right margin notes:*
nídoscoicéla *ōs.*
5
orbaind
10

co mucca úra,
co luna hítha,
co lunu messi (.i. muilt bruithi),
cosin tuicsenach soacallmach cosnáit na slōig .i.
cosin lónlongin bōshaille,
cosin sercoll sochenēlach, co mid,
co leiges in chlīabgalair .i. sean senshaille,
co tothlugud m-brothc[h]āin .i. sengroith,
co mīan ban ǣntuma .i. lemnacht,
co briscén m-banrīgna[1] .i. cerrbacan,
co héill fir cēlide .i. cuirm,
co cunnid corgais .i. coilech circe,
co hétan briste .i. brechtān,
co lám ar cách .i. turarán,
co torrach tellaig .i. tanach,
cosin m-brúchtaig m-bolgaig .i. nūa corma,
co mīan na sacart .i. braisech belaide,
cosin māin is mīne ocus is millse da cach bíud
.i. findlitte,
co hingur cingir cicharan .i. cráibechūn,
cosna lūbdiabulta émnaigib .i. cǣlūnu cǣrech,
co fīachu fraiged .i. cliathūnu,

*Right margin notes:*
15
sengruth *ōs.*
20
25
30

¹ bandrigna

K 2

to the bird of a cross—salt ;
to the entry of a gathering—sweet apples ;
to the pearls of a household—hens' eggs ;
to the glance of nakedness—kernels.'

5    " When he had reckoned me up those many
viands, he ordered me my drop of drink.  'A tiny
little measure for thee, MacConglinne, not too large,
only as much as twenty men will drink, on the top of
those viands : of very thick milk, of milk not too
10 thick, of milk of long thickness, of milk of medium
thickness, of yellow bubbling milk, the swallowing
of which needs chewing, of the milk that makes
the snoring bleat of a ram as it rushes down the
gorge, so that the first draught says to the last
15 draught :  " I vow, thou mangy cur, before the
Creator, if thou comest down, I'll go up, for there
is no room for the doghood of the pair of us in
this treasure-house."

    " 'Whatever disease may seize thee from it, Mac-
20 Conglinne, 'tis I that will cure thee, excepting one
disease, I mean the disease of sages and of gentle-
men, the best of all diseases, the disease that is
worth perpetual health—loose bowels.' "

    Thus far the vision, etc.

25    At the pleasure of the recital and the recounting
of those many various pleasant viands in the king's
presence, the lawless beast that abode in the inner
bowels of Cathal MacFinguine came forth, until
it was licking its lips outside his head.   The
30 scholar had a large fire beside him in the house.
Each of the pieces was put in order to the fire, and
then one after the other to the lips of the king.

    One time when one of the pieces was put to the

co hén crossi .i. saland,
co himdorus ænaig .i. úbla cumra,
co némannu tigi teglaig .i. uga cercc,
co brafud nochta .i. etneda.'
"Feib nosturim dam na hilbīadu īarsin, ordaigis 5
dam mo deog m-bolgaim. 'Metríne bec bec, nát
romór, cethri fichit ferbolcumm deit, a Mic Conglinne, for na bīadaib sin anūas : d'ass rothécht,
d'ass nāt rothecht, d'ass lebarthēcht, d'ass eter dū
thecht, d'ass buide bolcach, foloing in slucud 10
chocnum, don lomum daní in slaimegil rethid[1] oc
dul darsin m-brágait sís, co n-aprai in bolcum
tūisech frisin m-bolcum n-dédenach : "Fortgillim,
a charrmatraid, i fīadnaise in dúilemun, cia tís
anūas, regut-sa sūas ; ar ní thalla ar mataidecht ar 15
n-dís isin istadluc sa."

*this ðs.*

"'In galar notgébad desin, a Mic Conglinne,
cenmothā ænghalar, is misse not-ícfa .i. galar sruthi
ocus dágdāine, in galar is ferr cach n-galar .i. in
galar is fíu slánti suthain, .i. in búar fodessin.'" 20

Ind aislingthi indsin anūas, *ocus araile.*
Fri hairerdacht na hindlisen ocus fri tuirem na
m-bīad n-imda n-écsamail n-oirerda i fīadnaise in
rīg, int anmunna indligthech roaittrebastar a n-indib
inmedōnachaib Cathail meic Fhinguine tānic co 25
m-bói oc imnlīge a bél a bél fria chend anechtair.
Is amlaid bói in mac légind, co tenid móir occa
istaig. Doberthi cach staic īar n-urd dona stacib
frisin tenid ocus dosbertís īar n-urd co beōlu in ríg.
Tan ann tuccad staic dīb co beōlu in ríg, ocus lingis 30

---

[1] leg. sraindmegil rethi

king's mouth, the son of malediction darted forth,
fixed his two claws in the piece that was in the
student's hand, and taking it with him across the
hearth to the other side, bore it below the caldron
5 that was on the other side of the fire. And the
caldron was overturned upon him. (And hence
is said *lonchoire*, viz., from the demon—*lon*—of
gluttony that was in Cathal's throat being under
the caldron.)

10    This is not what (some) story-tellers relate, who
say that it was down the throat of the priest's
gillie he went, and that the gillie was drowned in
the millpond of Dún-Cáin opposite the fortress of
Pichán, son of Mael Finde, in the land of the men
15 of Féne. But it is not so in the books of Cork,
which state that he was put into the caldron, and
was burned under it.

"To God and Brigit we give thanks," said Mac-
Conglinne, clapping his right palm over his own
20 mouth, and his left palm over the mouth of Cathal.
And linen sheets were put round Cathal's head and
he was carried out.

"What is most necessary for us to do now?" asked
Pichán.

25    "The easiest thing in the world," said MacConglinne. "Let the hosts and multitudes, the kings
and queens and people, the herds, flocks and cattle,
and the entire gold and silver treasure of the fortress
be taken out beyond the fortress."

30    And the learned say, that the price of a chafer's leg
of any kind of property was not left in the large
central royal pavilion of the fort, except the caldron
that was about the demon's head.

in mac mallachtain corsháid a dí chrob isin staic bōi
il-láim in mec légind, ocus beris leis dar tellach
anúnd, ocus atnaig fón coire bói fri tenid anall.
Ocus impāither in coire fair.   (Conid de asberair
lonchoire .i. don crāes-lon bói i m-brága Cathail  5
meic Fhinguine do beith fói.)

Noco n-ead atfīadut scélaige, acht is a m-brāgaiᵣ
gilla int shacairt dochóid, corobáidead in gilla il-linᵈl
mulind Dúine Cáin for bélu puirt Pichāin meic
Mōile-Finde hi Feraib Fēni.  Noco n-ed sinfil il-  10
lebrᴘib Corccaige, acht conid isin coire tucad, ocus
conid fóe rolosced.

"Fri Dīa ocus fri Brigit berma a at[h]lugud," ol
MacConglinne ic tabairt a bossi deis[e] fria gin fodén,
ocus a chléboss fria gin Cathail.  Ocus atnagur lín-  15
scóti bá chend Cathail, ocus berair hē immach.

"Cid is nesem dún," or Pichān, "ifesta?"

"Iss asu chách lind," ol Mac Conglinne.  "Berair
na slōig ocus na sochaide, rīg ocus rīgna ocus muin-
tera, éte ocus alma ocus indile ocus a uli indmassa  20
óir ocus argait in dúnaid dar dún immach."

Ocus atberait eōlaig conārfārcbad lūag cossi cenbair do nach innmas i rīgimscing mōir medōnaig
in dūnaid, acht in cori bói imm chend in luin.

And the house was then shut on him from the outside, and four huge fires were kindled here and there in the house. When the house was a tower of red flame and a huge blaze, the demon sprang to
5 the rooftree of the palace above, and the fire was powerless to do anything to him, and he sat on the house that was next to it.

"Well, now, ye men of Munster," said Mac-Conglinne, "yonder is your friend. Shut your
10 mouths that I may speak with that . . . . . unwor-shipful monk."

"Now, wretch," said MacConglinne, "do obeisance unto us."

"And indeed I will," said the devil, "since I
15 can help it. For thou art a man with the grace of God, with abundance of wisdom, with acute-ness of intellect, with intentive humility, with the desire of every goodness, with the grace of the seven-fold Spirit. I am a demon by nature, of in-
20 frangible substance, and I shall tell thee my story. I have been three half-years in Cathal's mouth, to the ruin of Munster and the Southern Half besides, and if I were to continue three half-years more, I should ruin all Ireland. Were it not for the noble-
25 ness of the monks of great Cork of Munster, and for their wisdom, for their purity and for their honesty, and for the multitude of their bishops and their confessors, from whom thou hast come against me ; and were it not for the worth of the voice
30 and the word, honour and soul of the noble venerable king, whom thou hast come to save; and again, were it not for thy own nobility and worth, and purity and wisdom, and abundance

Ocus iatar in tech fair indechtair, ocus adaither
cethri tendti dermára sainchan isin tech. Intan bói
in tech ina thuir trichemrūaid ocus ina briaid adbul-
mōir, lingis in demun i féic in rīgthige sūas, ocus
nirchōem in tene ní dó, ocus saidis forsin taig bū 5
nessa dó.

"Maith tra, a fhiru Muman," ol Mac Conglinne,
"fil sund út bar cara. Ocus iadaid bar m-beōla,
corusacailler-sa in manach n-oibell n-dermitnech
út." 10
"Maith, a thróig," ol Mac Conglinne, "déna um-
alóit dún."
"Dogēn-sa ōn," or diabul, "or ní chumga[i]m cen
a dénam. Ūair at fer co rath Dé, co n-imma[d]
ĕcnai, co n-gĕri inntlechta, coll-léri umalóti, co 15
mīan cach maithusa, co rath in.Spīrta sechtaig. Am
demon-sa aicenta co n-ádbur nembrisc, ocus indisfet mo thindram det-siu. Atám teora lethbliadna
hi n-gin Cathail oc ádmilliud Muman ocus Lethe
Moga Nūadat olchena, ocus dīa m-beind teora leth- 20
bliadna ele, nomillfind Érinn uli. Minā beth dia
n-ūaisle ocus dia n-ĕcnaidecht, dia n-ógi ocus dia
n-indracus ocus d' immad a n-espoc ocus á n-an[m]-
charut muintire Corccaige móire Muman ō túdchad-
su dom' shaigid-sea, ocus do indracus a gotha ocus a 25
brēthri ocus enig ocus anmma in rīg ūasail oirmitnig
dīa tánac tesarcain ; ocus didu, minā beth dot' ūaisle-
siu ocus t' indracus ocus t' ógi ocus t' ĕcnaide, d'
immbud t' fhessa ocus t' airchetail, is it' brágait fén

of knowledge and lore—it is into thine own
throat I would go, so that they would lash thee
with dog-straps and scourges and horsewhips
through all Ireland, and the disease that would
5 kill thee, would be hunger."

"The sign of the Lord's cross between me and
thee," said MacConglinne, thrice threatening him
with the Gospels.

And the demon said : "Were it not for the little
10 fair woman from the Curragh, by my God's doom
before God, O Cathal MacFinguine, I would bear
thy body into the earth and thy soul into hell before
long to-night." After that he flew into the air
among the people of hell.

15 "What is to be done now, O MacConglinne ?"
asked Pichán.

"Not hard to tell," answered MacConglinne.
"Let new milk and fresh butter be boiled along
with honey, and drunk for a new drink by the
20 King."

That was done. A caldron of a hundred measures
of fully-boiled milk was given as a special drink to
the King. It was the last great bellyful that Cathal
took because of the demon.

25 A bed was afterwards prepared for the King on a
downy quilt, and musicians and players entertained
him from noon until twilight. The King lay in his
slumbering rest of sleep. The chieftains lay around
Pichán in as pleasant and honourable a manner as
30 ever before.

Great respect and honour had they that night for
the scholar.

The learned (viz. the story-tellers) say that the

noragaind, co n-gabdáis cointéill ocus slipre ocus
echlusca duit sechnón Érenn, ocus co m-[b]ad hé
galar notb*en*ad, gorta."


"Airde na crochi coimdetta ūam-sa it' agaid !" ol
Mac Conglinne, ocus atnaig trī tomaid dont sos*cē/*a    5 *s.ħoscela* *Ms.*
friss.

Ocus atbert in demun : " Minbad in m-báin
m-bic a cuirrech Liffe, dom' débroth fīa[d] Dīa, a
Cath*ail* mic Fhinguine, dosb*ē*raind do chorp i tal-
*main* ocus t' animm a n-iff*er*n rē nómaide anocht."   10
Ocus folūamnigis i n-ethíar īarsin la muintir iffirnn.    *i.ħiár*


"Cid dogéntar ann hifesta, a Mic Conglinne ?" or
Pichūn.

"Nī *annsa,*" ol Mac Conglinne. " Lémnacht ocus
imm úr a comberba*ſ*d tria mhil, ocus a n-ól do   15    *ri*
núadhig don rīg."


Dorigned sámlaid. Tuccad cori cét combruthi do    *A h Ms.*
loimm lānberbthi dia shainōl don rīg. Conid hī
sáith mōr dēdenach dothomail Cathal īarsan lun int   *ſ aiı srádħ1aoħ1*
sháith sin.    20

Dēraigther īarsin don rīg for colcid clúmdé-
rai[g]thi, ocus æs cíuil ocus airfitig ō etartrāth co
hetrud. Fesſiss in ríg ina shūantórthim chodulta.
Fessaiter in rígrad um Pichūn feib is áibne ocus is
anordha bātar rīam remi.    25


Cáttu mōr ocus anoir for in scolaige leō in adaig[1]
sin.
Atberut eōlaig (.i. scēlaige) co m-bōi in rí teora laa

----

[1] agaid

King was three days and three nights in that one sleep. But the books of Cork relate that he only slept the round of the Hours.

The King arose on the morrow, and passed his
5 hand over his face; and no smaller than a full-fragrant apple was each dark-purple drop of dew that was on his face.

"Where is MacConglinne?" asked the King.

"Here he is," answered he.

10 "Tell us the vision now."

"It shall be done," said MacConglinne.

"However long the tale may be to-day," said Cathal, "it will not appear long to me—'tis not the same as yesterday."

15 Cathal left his grace and blessing on everyone who would read it and preserve it.

"Some boon should be done to MacConglinne," said the chieftains.

"It shall be done," said Cathal. "He shall have
20 a cow out of every close in Munsterland, and an ounce for every householder, and a cloak for every church, and a sheep from every house from Carn to Cork. Moreover, he shall be given the treasure that is better than all these, I mean Manchín's little
25 cloak."

It was then that Roennu Ressamnach came into the house, and Cruitfiach, his son, and Mælchiar, his daughter. And then he made these quatrains:

"Manchín went—a brilliant feat—
30    To plead against MacConglinne,
Manchín they defrauded then
Of the little cloak around him."

ocus teora aidche isi[n] ǣnchodlad sin. Atberat
libair Corccaige nā bói acht ōn trāth co'raile.

Atraig in rīg īarnabārach, ocus tig a láim dar
agaid, ocus nī bā luga oltū uball féta fírchumra cach
banna drúchta dondcorcera bōi trīan[a] agaid.      5

"Cáit hi fíl Mac Conglinne ?" ol Cathal.
"Atā súnd," ol sē.
"Indis int aislinge dún ifechtsa."
"Dogéntar," ol Mac Conglinne.
"Cé fota bé 'ca hindissi indíu, nī fota lemm," ol 10
Cathal.  "Nī hinand ocus indé."

Fácbais Cathal rath ocus bendachtu for cach
n-ōen notlégfa ocus notlessaigfed.
"Maith" ol in rīgrad, "do dénam for Mac Conglinne."                                           15
"Dogéntar," ol Cathal.  "Bó cach liss hi Mum-
aintír dó, ocus uinge cach comathig, brat hō cach
cill, ocus cāera¹ cach thige ō Chárn cu Corccaig
fria thā·b sin.  Dobērthar tra in sét is ferr oltás sin
uile .i. cocholl Manchīne."                        20

Is ann tra tānic Roennu Ressamnach isin tech,
ocus Cruitfhiach a mac, ocus Mǣlchiar a ingen.
Conid ind dosgní na rundn sa :

    "Dolluid Manchīn—monar n-glē—
      d'accra for Mac Conglinne,                   25
    is ē Manchīn melltais [de]
      don chochlín bec bōi imme."
          ¹ bo

" 'Twere not too much for pure Comgan,
    (said the son of the jester)
Though we are not his kindred,
The famous cloaklet which I see,
Although worth thrice seven *cumals*,
Though it were of the ravens' hue,
From Cathal, King of Munster.

" 'Twere not too much for me to give,
Though gold were in its border,
As it was given by his will,
And spoken in pure reason :
For health of reason Cathal now
Receives from Manchin's journey."

Then was given him a cow out of every close, an
ounce for every householder, a cloak for every
church, a ring of gold, a Welsh steed, a white
sheep out of every house from Carn to Cork. Two-
thirds of the right of intercession (one-third being
reserved to the men of Ireland) was accorded to
him, and that he should sit always at the right hand
of Cathal. All these things were granted to him, as
we have said.

Let this be heard by every ear, and delivered by
every chosen tongue to another, as elders and old
men and historians have declared, as it is read and
written in the books of Cork, as the angel of God set
it forth to MacConglinne, as MacConglinne himself
uttered it to Cathal MacFinguine and to the men of
Munster besides. Nothing sorrowful shall be heard
by anyone who has heard it, it will be a year's protection to him.

There are thirty chief virtues attending this tale,
and a few of them are enough for an example.

"Nirb uröil do Chomgān glan, (.i. ar mac in
    druith)
cencobá uánn a bunad,[1]
in cocholl itchiũ co m-blad,
cemad fhiũ trī secht cumal,
cia nobeth fo dathaib[2] bran                                      5
ō Chathal ō ríg Muman.

"Nirb oróil lemm ũaimm fodén,
gémad ór ina tairmchðill,
amail nobeŗad fria rðir,
is itberad tria glanchéill,                                      10
is do Cathal is [s]lán céill
int erriud[3] dolluid Manch[ð]in." Doll. M.

Tecar annsin bó cach liss, uinge *cach* comathaig,
bratt *cach* cille, fail óir ocus ech Bretnach, cũru
fhind *cach* tige ō Charnn co Corccaig. Dũ trīan 15
immpide (ocus trīan d' f[h]eraib Érenn olchenai),
ocus lethlūm Cathail dogrés.
Atagur dó sin uli, feib rorũidsium.

Tidnocul cacha clūaisi ocus *cach* thengad tuic-
sinche di araile, feib atcódutar sruthi ocus senóri 20
ocus senchaide, feib légait*hir* ocus scrībth*air* liubair
Chorccaige, feib roordaig aingel Dé do Mac Conglinne, feib roshluind Mac Conglinne do Chathal
mac Finguine ocus do feraib Muman olchena. Ni
closti ní bes dógra, bat cómga bl*iadn*a da cach ðn 25
atchūala.

Atāt deich prímratha fichet forsin sceōl sa, ocus
is lōr ũath*ad* díb for desmb*er*echt.

─────────────────────────────

[1] buanad        [2] tathaib        [3] leg. in turus

The married couple to whom it is related the first night shall not separate without an heir; they shall not be in dearth of food or raiment.

The new house, in which it is the first tale told, 5 no corpse shall be taken out of it; it shall not want food or raiment; fire does not burn it.

The king to whom it is recited before battle or conflict shall be victorious.

On the occasion of bringing out ale, or of feasting 10 a prince, or of taking an inheritance or patrimony, this tale should be recited.

The reward of the recital of this story is a white-spotted, red-eared cow, a shirt of new linen, a woollen cloak with its brooch, from a king and 15 queen, from married couples, from stewards, from princes, to him who is able to tell and recite it to them.

THE END.

In lānomain dīa n-ind[is]fith*er* i cétadaig,¹ nī
scérat cen comorba, nī bet i terca bíd nō ētaig.

In tech nūa do chētsceōl, nī bērth*air* marb ass, nī
ba terc m-bíd nō étaig, nī loisc tene.

In rīg dīa n-aisnēth*er* rē cath nō comrac, a m-   5
būaid laiss.

Oc taisselb*ad* lenda, oc bīathad flatha, oc gabāil
orbai ocus athardha, in scēl sa do aiss*nēis.*

Is ū lóg aisnēssi in sceōil sea : bó breccfind hóderg,
léne do nūalín, brat longain lómair cona delg ó ríg   10
ocus ō rīgain, hō lūnamnaib, ō mūraib, ō fhlathib,
donti chuingess a fhaissn*ēis* ocus a indisse dōib.

¹ agaid

F I N I T.

H. 3, 18, p. 732.

Cathal mac Findguine .i. rī mōr Muman, co n-gēire
chon, col-longad chapaill. Lon crāis robōe ina
medōn. Satan domeiled leis a c[h]uitigh.
Aniar mac Conglinde, do lucht Athana mōire
5 Muru dō .i. scolaige án, dochūaidh a hAthain Muru
for cōairt Ērend[1] : a Tīr Eoghain, i n-Airgiall*a*, co
hArdmachu, dar Slīab Fūait, dar Magh Muir-
t[h]eimne, hi Cremt[h]aine, hi Crīch Rois, i
m-Mullach Taillten. Ōenscolōc marōen fris .i. Mac
10 na Cairrea. Lotor di[2] Cenandus. Bātar oidchi cen
bīad isin daimliac. Īarnamārach isbert Mac Conglinde i fīednuise an pobail :

　　　" A scolōc,
　　　　cid nā dēnom dā camrand ?
15　　　Dēna-sa rann ar arān,
　　　　digēn-sa rand ar andland."

" Reccmait a les," ar Mac na Cairre, " ocus sind
'nar troscadh 'con sāmad sa irūir." Dorīecht dōcth*ain*
fichet di lind occus di biud dōib rīe n-oidchi. Lotor
20 iernabārach for fud Fer Midi, dar mullach n-Uis*n*ig,
do Dermaig Coluim Cille a Tīr Né[i]ll, dar Slīab
Bladmu, i n-Ele sīar, dar Clār na Muman, dar Machaire
na Clīach il-Lūachair Dedhad.[3]
Is and robātor tīr Muman 'na m-buidnib ic dol do
25 Corcaigh mōir Muman ar⁴fūil Bairre occus Ness*ain*
.i. di[2] trosc*ud.* " Dibērainn comairle maith det, a
Mic Conglinne," ar Mac na Cairrea, " ardīagh cofāg-
bam bīed i Corcaig, .i. abram is fer dāna thū-sa, ocus

<hr />

[1] Ererd　　　[2] leg. do, and so *passim.*　　　[3] deghad

*[margin notes: "lerna barmach", "Bs.", "4 Corrected from iar."]*

nī lēmtor ar m-bet[h] cen bīed." "Dogēntor,"
or Mac Conglinde. Átnagat i tech n-aoiged¹ Corc-
aighe. Sondcū mōr² robōi istoigh. Ticc imach ocus
dibeir cor do Mac na Cairrea isin tonnaig, corānaic
Mac Conglindi.                                                  5
    Atbert Mainchīn .i. ab Corcaige : " Finntor in fail
nech is toigh āiged³ in[n]ocht, dīenad⁴ āil proind di
caithemh." Luidh macclēirech dīe hfis. "In fail
nach ōen sunda?" ar sē. "Nī maith ir-rūidie," ar
Mac na Cairrea. "Atā ollam maith and, ocus nī     10
maith a f[h]rithalom occaib-si. Ēcnaigfid ind eglais,
ar is cīen ō a cenēl andiū." Atfēt in macclēirech
di Mainchīn an scēl sin. "Atāither tene do glas-
chrāibech dōib īertain, occus beror cūachān corcu
doib." Is ann isbert Mac Conglindi :                            15

        " Co brāth nocha n-īsaind-si,
        acht maine bein[n] ri gortæ,
        cūachān corca Corcaigi,
        cūachān Corcaigi corcæ."

    Atfēt in techtaire di Mainchīn sin. "Na mac-    20
clēirich immach !" ol Mainchīn. "Occus cuimrighter
in fer dānai corrocrochtar imbārach i cinaidh āire na
hegailsi." Gabair tra Mac Conglinde occus berair
īerna c[h]engal co Mainchīn. "Nī mochen duit,"
ol Mainchīn. "Notcrochfaider imbārach i cinaid na   25
haoire." "Ascaid dam, a degduine !" or Mac
Conglindi, "ar Bairre asa fēil indocht." "Cīa
hascaid ōn?" or Mainchīn. "Nī ansa," or Mac
Conglinde. "Mo daothain lendu occus bīd, occus
di lepaid-si conu hētach dōib etir colcaid occus broth- 30
raig." "Dibēr-sai ar in ērlam sin," ar Mainchīn.
Luigis⁵ Mac Conglindi īer caithem i folartnaige di
lind occus bīud, occus láighis sūan trom fair. Co n-
acai cuice ind clēirech ina cotlad. Lend finn imbiu,
delcc oír and, lēne mōr sītchu re gelchnes dō, putrall 35
findlīath forchas fair. "Maith, a thrūaig," ol sē.

    ¹ aoided        ² morai         ³ aided
    ⁴ dienat                        ⁵ luidis
                    I 2

"Is maith cotlai, occus tū oc ernaidi būis." "Cīa
atḟtcomnaic-si ?" ar Mac Conglinde. "Muru," ol sē.
"Is dō tānac dot' cobair-si." "Cisi cobair ōn ?" or
Mac Conglinne. "Memraigh ind aislingi si," or sē,
5 "ocus indis i fīednuise Cathail in rīgh, ocus sōerfu
hē don ginaig."
Is and rochan Muru in aislinge, occus bā mebair
lais-[s]im. Berair-sem īerom dá crochad īernabāroch
co hairecht fer Muman .i. dū ir-raibhe Cathal ocus
10 maithi fer Muman. Isbert Cathal nā crochfaide bard
laiss, acht dognetīs fēin na clērich, dāig is īet roītt/r
a ēgōir.
"Ascaid dam-sa, a Chathail," ar Mac Conglinde,
"ocus a maithe Muman !" "Cieisi hascaidh ōn ?"
15 or Cathal. "Mo hsñith de usei, occus mē fēin da
dāil form," ar Mac Conglinne. "Dobērtor det-si
sin," or Cathal.
Beror Mac Conglinde dicum na tiprait, occus lēigis
faon, ocus benais a delcc asa brut, ocus tumais isin
20 tiprait, occus lēigis dirinn in deilge inus [s]in ina
bēul. Indister di Chathal. "Lēicther dāl co matain
dō !" ar Cathal.
Luid Cathal ind aidchi sin co tech Pichā[i]n maic
Māoilfinn, ocus luid Mac Conglinne co m-bōi and ar a
25 cind. Diberor a airigid uball do Cathal. Atnaig
Mac Conglinne ag fūscocnom agaid ind-aghaid fri
Cathal. "Cid sin, a fir dāna ?" or Cathal. "Nār lem
rī Muman oc longadh a ōenar," ar Mac Conglinne.
Dibeir Cathal uball dō.
30 "Nī farcbadh ōen do mes," ar Mac Conglinne.
Dibeir uball aile dó.
"Airim na Trīnōti !" ar Mac Conglinne. Dobeir
in tres n-uball dō.
"Cethor lebair int s[h]oiseēla !" ar Mac Con-
35 glinne. Dibeir in cethramad n-uball dō.
"Cūic lebair Maoisi !" ar Mac Conglinne. Dobeir
in cūiced n-uball dō.
"Sē haosai int shaogail !" ar Mac Conglinne.
Dobeir in seisedh n-uball do.
40 "Secht n-dūnu in Spīrta Naoib !" ar Mac Conglinne. Dobeir in sechtmad n-uball dōn.

"Ocht m-biete int shoiscéla !" ar Mac Conglinne.
Dibeir in ochtmad n-uball dó.
"Naoi n-gráda na hegalsa nemdai !" ar Mac Con-
glinne. Dibeir in nōmad n-uball dóu.
"In dechmad grád na hegailsi tal*mandai* !" ar Mac 5
Conglinne. Dibeir in dechmadh n-uball dó.
"Airem na n-apsdal īer n-imorbus !" ar Mac
Conglinne. Dobeir in n-aonmadh n-uball *dec* dó.
"Dā apstal deg in Coimded !" ar Mac Conglinne.
Dibeir in daru n-uball *dec* dō. 10
"Crīst cend na n-apstal !" ar Mac Conglinne.
Dibeir in tres n-uball *dec* dōu.
"Nī furāil dō so uile !" ar Cathal ic sreud na
seched lāin di ublaib dint shlnāg, occus atraig cāch
isin gribdāil. 15
Atbert Mac Conglinne ri Pichān mac Māilfind, dā
lēged dō airichthi Cathail di lesugud, robad feirde do
feraib Muman. Fūaslaicter di Mac Conglinne for
errudus Pich*āin*, occus nosfothraic ocus gabus fuathrōic
occus līinid n-gil imbiu, ocus atāidh tenid do 20
feolomain uinnsend i fīednuise Cathail cen diaidh,
cen cieig, cen crithir. Nōi n-doirsi fuirri, occus
dobertor nōi m-beru indfodai findcuild a bun cuill
dō, occus dobertor *cethri* aisle senshaille occus dā
muic ūrai, ocus dogni tōchtu dīb, ocus dobeir toocht 25
senshaille etir cech dā toocht ūrsaille occus toocht
ūrsaille etir cech dá toocht sensaille īerna n-esred di
mil ocus do shalond.
"Cīe etir ē-seom ?" ol Cathal. "Duine is eōlach
di lesugud bīd," ar Pichān. 30
"Nach é in bard ?" ol Cathal. "Is hē im*morro*,"
ol Pichān.
"Is maith lesaigther," ol Cathal. "Tairced coll ūath
dam mo bīadh !"
"Ascaid dam-sai, a degduine !" ol Mac Conglinne 35
re Cathal. "Cīa hascaid ōn ?" or Cathal.
"Cen labrai di neoch aile istoig co tair damh-sai
aislingi atconnarcus arrūir d' indisin duit-si."
"Dibērtor," or Cathal, "ocus indis co lūath,
ocus cipē laibērus crochfaid*er* imbārach marō*en* 40
rit-sa."

Andsin atbert Mac Conglinne :

" Aislinge atcondarc arráir,
mo dul ar fecht dís nó triúr,
conn-acai ní in tech finn forlán,
5    hir-raibhi a lommnán di biúdh.

A dá ersaind boccœ brechtáin,
a lebend di gruth is d' imm,
a imdadhœ di blonaic bladhaigh,
*scéi̯t[h]*    scëi[th] immdœ di thanaigh tin.

10    Fir fo sciathraib inda scīeth[1] sin
di maothail mellánaigh mín,
fir cen tuicse gonœ Gaoidil,
gai gruitne cech aoinfir dībh.

Corc romōr lán do millséu,
15    dar lem rolamus ris g'éo ;
braisech bruithe duillech donnbán,
lestor lomnán lán di chéo.

Tech sailli dā fichet tōebán,
caolach caolán, comge clann ;
20    di cech bíad ba maith le duine,
dar lem bātor uile ann." A.

" Aislingi atconnarc arrāir, bā cāin gēbenn,
bā balc brīge cotarfas dam   rīge n-Érenn.

Co n-acai in les m-bilech m-barrach,   bā saill son-lach,
25    caisel carroch[2] do minsceillcib   tanach[3] torrach.

Carna muc is de dorōnta a   colbœ cadlœ,
suaire in sonba occus ñaithne   onba amrœ.

Amra in fīs tarfas damh i   cinn mo tellaig :
fithchell imi cona foirind   blāith bric bendaig.

30    Bendachad Dia mo labra,   līth cen taisi ;
rīa techt damh i Slīabh n-Imbe
rolaad gille fom asœ." *A is.*

[1] scieth*œ*.    [2] imme *add*.    [3] tanai

"Dīa rabā-sai īerom, a Chathail, im' imdai cāin
cumdachtæ cona hūaithnib findruine, cona barreib
forōrdæ, conacolbaibcredumai, conahosair ūrlūachra,
cona colcaid clūmderg and, cona cherchaill clūmdu,
co cūala in guth mo dochum : 'Éirc, a thrūaig, a Mic    5
Conglinne!' occus ní rofregrus-[s]ai indnī sin.
Deithbir ōn, robōi do clithmairi mo lepthu ocus do
sudaile mo chuirp ocus do treisi mo codultu. Cu
n-epert diridisi : 'Fomna, fomna, a Mic Conglinne,
beochail, nā rotrodba achucat in sruth m-belu, teich   10
nū rotbāide!' Atraigim-si annside co hathlamh
imēdrum, occus ní thairisfed cáil form' airenach, is
hē dēne atrachtus. Co n-aca in scūl mo dochum.
'Maith,' ol sē frim. 'Maith,' ol misi fris. 'Cīa ata[t]-
comnaic, a thrūaigh ?' ol an scūl. 'Scolaige trūag   15
sund,' ol mesi, 'occ īarraidh a íccai ar chraos, ar
ithemraighe ocus ar ítaid n-ētūalaing.' 'A thrūaigh,'
ol sē, 'atā sund nech dobērai eōlas duit cosinud-
altōir n-ītha fail inn-īarthar na hecailsi ic a bas tu
for beluch bela i crīch ūa Mochloingthe i fīrdorus   20
dīsirt ind Fūithlegai.' 'Cīæ di comainm-seo ?' ar
Mac Conglinne. 'Mesi ?' ar sē. 'Is tū,' ar Mac Conglinne. 'Bruchtsalach mac Būarandaigh de chiniud
Ulgaibh Esomain, is é fil cot' agallaim dobēri eōlas
duit.'                                                 25
"Atraigim-si andside amail ispert frim co dīrech
dīenmemmnach, co tarpech tindesnech, amail atreisid
sindach do gleith a loing[th]i, nō dam allaid dogleith
guirt cruithnechto, nō aithechān do[sh] leith banrīg-
næ. Ocus lotmur dar cend Slēibi Imi conn-acamar   30
in curchīn beg be[o]chlaidhi bōshailli ind-eocharimill in lochai, cona chodail geired, cona rūma do tiug
tana tuirc, cona eraiss īerslesa, cona braine brechtāin,
cona sesaib sensaille, cona sculmaire smerai, cona
tōescān tainge. Bā cosmail īerum in lestor il-lotmor.  35
Imrāimit dar loch lemnachta, tar trethuaibh tremantæ,
tar bocanfad blāithche, tar baitsiochaibh belæ, tar
ailenaibh māithul, di chaircibh grothæ, d' insibh
drúchtaín, dar moirgrién milsein, corragbomor port
itir Iupior Imbe ocus Sliebh n-Grothæ ocus Louch   40

*[right margin:]*
saidaile Ms.

u/

scolaide Ms.

Lombæ ar beúloibh beloidhe crìche úo Mochloincthi
hi fíordorus diseirt ind Fáithleghæ."
   Mac Conglindi dixit:

        " Aislingi domarfas-[s]u,
5         taidbsi iongnad indisimn,
          hi fíednuisi cáich :
        curchán gered gert[h]ide
        hi purt lochæ lemnachtæ
         uás lind betha bláith.

10       Lotmor isin loechlestor,
        loechdhæ in congaibh conaire
         dar bolcclenna lir,
        cor' bensumm na seisbéimend
        dar moinciond in murtrachtæ,
15       co tocradh a murtorad,
         murgrian amhail mil.

        Cáomh in dúnadh ráncommar,
        cona ráthaib robrechtán,
         risin louch anall :
20       pá himm úr a erdhrochot,
        a¹ chaisiol bá gelchruithnecht,
         a shonduch pá saill.

        Bá suaire segdæ suidiogud
        in tighi tréin trebordæ
25         a n-deachad íertain :
        a chomlæ di tiormcharno,
        a¹ tairsioch di turarán,
         di maithail a fraigh.

        Úaithne slemna sencáisi,
30       sailge saille súgmairi
         serdais imosech ;
        sesa segda sencroithe,
        fairci fin[a]fírgrotha
         folongtís in tech.

35       Tipra d' fín 'na fíríerthor,
        aibne beórc is brocaiti,
         blasda cech lind lán :
        ler do braich[lis] braitlenda
        ós brú topair treamanta
40         dorrói dar a lár.

             ¹ hi

Loch do braisic belaithi,
fa barr uscu olardai
  etorra ocus muir ;
erbe inbe oc imaire
fo cīr blonce bratgile                    5
  immon mūr imuigh.

Ecor d' ablaibh fīrchumra,
fid cona blāth barrchorcra
  etorra ocus slīabh ;
daire forard fīrlosai                      10
do chainnind, do cherrbacān,
  ar cūl tighe tīar.

Muinter enich inicin
d' ōcaib dercaib tendsadchib
  im tenid istaigh ;                       15
secht n-allsmaind, secht n-epistle
do chāisibh, do choclānaib,
  fo prāgait gach īir.

Atconnarc ind aircindech
cona brothraig bōsaille                     20
  'ma mnāi mīadaigh mais,
atconndarc in luchtaire
ōs inber ind ardcoire
  'sa œl ria ais.

Cathal maith mac Findguine                  25
fō fer dīanad[1] airfited
  airscēla bīd brais ;
maith in monar aounaire,
is aoibinn ria indisin
imram lupe laochlesto[i]r                   30
  dar ler Locha Ais.  Ais.

"Lodmor īersin 1 tochortāith, hi crāibech n-geiredh,
hi cepaig sensaille. Āssaidh in dubcheō uscaidhe
immund conā cuingenmair nem nā tal*main* nō áit i
tibremais ar cōir, co tarlai buille dom' cúl frisin   35
elaith grotha bricnói. Beg nach dearna slicrig do
cnāmaib[2] mo cloicne. Sinim mo lámh remom do
athērgi, conamtarlai etir mescāna ūrime co bac m'
uillea. Co n-aca Ugadart gilla in Fáithlegai ic

_____
[1] dianat            [2] cramaib

gabāil čisc il-loch lāin lemnachta, cona dubān smera,
cona riamnaigh uscai, cona slait geirɛd.   Fecht and
bā hūcne sensaille dobered anīs, fecht aile ba hēicne
bōsaille nogebed.   Lorcmaithi mōr di dondmarōicc
5 bruithe 'na lāim.   Is ɛdh nogebed dōib co m-bitīs
ic clesemnaig foa cosaib for in lepend grotha.
   " 'Canas tici, a trūaig?' ol in gillai.   'A cūin a
focraib,' ar misi fris.   'Cid saige?' ol sū.   'Saigim
in dīsertach,' ol meisi fris.   'A thrūaig,' ol sū, 'is
10 it aneōlach.   Ni roiche indocht in dīsertach.   Acht
geib longport etir Slīab n-Imme occus Loch n-Aiss,
t' aiged re Slīab n-Imme ocus di chūl re Slīabh
Tainge fo bun Chroind Chroithe if-ferta Cruind-
Mēsé, im-blenai Guirt Cruithnechtai.   Faidbithir
15 techtæ ōait co toisechu Tūath m-Bíd, cor' gabat di
comairci ar tromtonnaibh beladaigh nārotbāidet.
Tecat dit' frithailem in drochtoisc dōib, ocus tú
cētgnúisid atacommuaic isind ailen sa i tānac.'[1]
   "Gabaim-se longport etir Slīab n-Imme ocus Loch
20 n-Aiss, ocus m' aged ria Slīab n-Imme ocus mo chūl
re Slīaph Tainge fo bhun Chruind Croithe i fert
Cruind-Mēsé, im-blenai Guirt Cruthnechta.   Nirb'
adhaigh i *n*-dris araba bánbídh.   Atraigim *ī*arum i
mochæ laithe iarnabāruch, ocus tēgim co topar n-
25 us*c*ai robæ im' farr*u*d, ocus indlaim mo lāmæ, ocus
slemnaigim moputraill, ocus tēgim co topur tremantæ
robōi din leth aili, ocus ibim mo deich ferlommandæ
fichet ass arnā rolūd in chonair form chridhe.   Ocus
tēgim i cend tsētæ ocus imtechtæ conn-accæ imm'
30 aghaid .i. Beccnat Blāith Būlaithe ingen mBetāin
mBrasslongt[h]ig,senmātha[i]r Thūath m-Bídh,cona
gerrān gerr gereadh foithe,cona dā meallshūil mōethbla
ina cinn, cona srīan sechtairdech do saland [d]ag-
fi*n*d fris, cona brothraigh bosaille immpe, cona cris
35 d' iucraibh fírćisc 'ma tóeb, cona copchaille gaile fo
cend, cona bascmell fo brāgait forsa rabātar secht
mill ocus secht fichet mell do smeruib mucc
mugdornd.
   "Ferais fūlte frim ind rīgan ocus īarfaigis scēlæ
40 dím ocus cíe leth bōi mo shēt.   'Dichum in

[1] tannic

disirtaigh,' ol smē frie.   'Nī cīen óait,' ol sī.
'Acht is cumma duit gan guth ard n-oebela di
dēnamh co fessera rīag*ail* na sruithe filet isin recles.'
   " Is aud bǣ ind recless, isin glind itir Slīeb
n-Imme ocus Loch n-Ais hi crīch hūa Mochlongthe.   5
Is amlaid robǣ ind recless : cona cethri timchōartaibh
do sonduch senshaille imme, cen reincc, cen tuind,
cona blonaic tuirc taisceltu i mull*ach* cech suinn,
cona imdorus cāisi, cona comlu grotha bricnöi, cona
chulaighe imme, cona sabdaib blonge, cona gendibh 10
gered, cona semtille marōce, cona drolom ime.
Benaim-siu in drolom imme frisin comlaidh
n-grotha, co tāncatorna dá doirseōir imach . i. Fūstāibh
mac ui Longthi occus Mulba mac Lonlongēn cona
ceū uscaide dībh.   Is hē greim trēn roghabsat na 15
gemniud geriud dar na saptaibh bloinci conab ar
ēicin dōibh ind oslagad dint semtille marōci.   Araide
tra elaim-si itir clūith occus ursaind.   Co n-acu in
clēriuch ic bein ind cluic metlu for ind ūar alaig i
m-bī secht meda deg di shalonn Sacsanach ina 20
n-öenclō glēgel, bā sī tengu ind cluic.   Ocus co
n-aca in cloch drochdrochat ō tigh cech clērig dib
dia chūile.   Is ē cloch drochat bōi anuside . i. condriced
gach bairg*en* brechtān cruthnechta ria cēile ïerna
n-esrad de blāthsalonn ocus di mil.   Ocus co n-acæ 25
ind eglais clāraid . i. clāir d' aislib sentorc secht
m-bliadan, bā sīat cappair na hegailsi, cona sailgib
sencāisi, cona slinnib gered, cona bendcop*raib* blonce,
cona altōir īthu ina airthir.   Co n-acu in prīmclēriuch
. i. in prīmfāith ic tīechtain asin toig ar dorus na 30
hecailsi, cona choraind secht mescān find fichet i
cl[e]thi a chind, cona secht n-imairib *dec* do borraig
fīrlosæ i mullach a coirne.
   " Ann isbert fris :

" Bennach dūn, a clērig,   a clī cloth co comge,        35
mac milbuilci mela,   meic smeru, meic blonce,
   Meic būadrēn, meic brothc[h]ā[i]n, λ meic brocoiti binde,
meic caindinde caime,   meic saille, meic imme,
   Meic indrechtāin lānmēith,   meic lemnachta imglain,
meic mesæ, meic tor*aidh*,   meic olair, meic inmair,        40

λ   meic barrḟraid breacbāin,
meic barrchroithJe blāithe, meic blāithchi, meic breachtāin,
Meic vēoire (bṷaidh m-bāinde),

Meic īthu, meic ārond, meic clethe, meic gñaland,
meic lonlongōn lānte, meic lārge, meic lñabann,
    Meic lesi, meic lōthcind, meic longæ brond ball[d]ι,
meic inīre, meic lomæ, meic droma, meic tarræ,
5    Meic tremanta thana, meic tainge cen tæthad,
meic ēisc Inbir Indsēin, meic millsēin, meic mōcthal,
    Meic meda, meic fīna, meic carna, meic corma,
meic cruithnechta rigne, meic inbe, meic onba,
    Meic findliten gile   d' ass chairech co n-*glaine*,
10 meic scablīn bhuic blādhmair gona gablaib[1] gaile,
    Meic gruthraigi guirge, meic garbarāin chorca,
meic cræbaca[i]n *cræbaigh* cona chōeraib corcra,
    Meic barr braissce bīthe, meic blogan buicc bānglain,
meic cnōmessa cnāmfhéil, meic Ābōil, meic Ādaimh.
15    Maith do duthaig degbīdh, as milis re[2] tengaidh,
a chēim fossudh fostā[i]n al-lus trosdāin bennaig." Bennach.

Is amlaidh tāinic immach in clēriach for capall
senshaille cona crūaibh[3] cerrboccan, cona moing
murrathu, cona erpall ierslesa. Nolīonfaithis secht
20 n-airmedæ ardcathrach d' airnib cumrai dondcorcra
aipchi a cailech a s[h]rōnæ. Srogell il-lāim in
clōirich forsa rabātar secht n-indrechtāin ocus secht
[ ] fichet. In trāth nodruidedh frisin capall nomaided
bainde dar cend gach indrechtā[i]n i m-bīad sāith
25 sagairt ōn trāth co' raile re harān. Intan nobūailed
co trēn in capall nomaided cāisi ocus tor ( ) ime re
gach m-buille triena iercomla síer. Amlaid do*no*
robōe in clōirech, cona brothraig bōsaille ime, cona
chasair crāibheach*āin*, cona lēni bl*aith*blonce, cona
30 chris d' iuchraibh fo taobh, cona moing glōgil croithi
moa cenn, cona srōin mela dig*res* ic tinsaitin
dar a beōla slemain senshaille sís, cona men*estir*
mæthmetla dar a ucht, cona cristaill do maroicc
dondbruithe foua, cona bachaill buic bruithe bunruisi
35 'na lāimh. Intan nodruted fri lārin bacholl, nomaidhís
secht srebæ triana corr nómeilfcdh muilenn ōn
trāth co arailiu for cech sreibh dībh, ocus bā do
beoil uile inīsin; cona triubhus do bīud scabail fo
cossaibh, cona assaibh ierslesai hi raibe Tāin Bó

          [1] agabraib                 [2] ro
               [3] crudaibh

Cūailgne ocus Bruiden[1] Dā Derg isin asa robōi fo
cois deis, Tochmarc Etaine ocus Tochmarc Emere
isin asa robōi fo a cois clī    A mic lānlēgind int
ĕgna occus in mōreōlus mōr for uball a brāgat occus
for rind a tengad.                                                    5
    " Arōit lem, a clēirich !" ar meisi fris.  Con*ad*
andsin isbert-som : " For foes/m n-degbīd duit, a    o/
thrūaig !" ar sē, " for enech n-deglomæ, for snādad
sensaille.  Canus tice, a thrūaigh ?" ol sē.
    " Ticim, a degduine, a cēin dom' īc ar in n-galor 10
n-*a*ntaigtech fil im' comaitecht."   " Cīa galor ōn ?"
ar in Fāthlieig.  " Nī *ansa* ón," or Mac Conglinne.
" In ginach cona fodlaibh .i. ro-īta ōil, olar, inmar,
caithim, rocaithim co n-gēre con, co longad capaill."
" A thrūaig," ol in Fūithliaig, " nī mō int [sh]āith 15
sin *indās* int shāith domelod mac mis isind ailen so,
ocus fogēbad sund co m-bad crīn.  Is beg do toisc
rē dīthughad m-bīd.  Is lēcad chon re fīed duit.
Is srathor for serrach.  Is sab for sinnach.  Is cuad
do bǣsach.  Is gairm fri fasguth.  Is pōc do crithcenn. 20
Is luindig do bod*ur*.  Is rūn re mnāi n-drūith
n-ētaigh.[2]  Is bos fri sribaill.  Is marcach for sengān.
Is soiget i corthi.  Is dorn im dicidh.  Is gat im
gainim.  Is būalad senclocne.  Is būain mealu a
mecn*aib* iub*air*.  Is tīradh i n-āth diebuil.  Is 25
ierraid ime il-lige con.  Is ierraid olla for gabar.  Is
ecor ti*g*e[3] tolland, a thrūaigh, a Mic Conglinne,
tīachtain do dīthugad duit-si biid ind ailen si.  Ro
ied gortu di choelāna.  Acht dobēr-sa cumgaisiu
duit, mā airige nach treblait it comait*echt*."            30
    " Cīa cumgaisi ōn ?" or Mac Conglinne.   " Nī
*ansa*.  Bī innocht[4] cen bīed bail i m-biæ.  Ēirigh
re muchæ laithi arnamārach.  Ataider tene duit do
foloman crīn lasamhain di chrund gescach forsa
cacait serraig[5] i mullach erslēbhe.  Cōraighter ētgad 35
don leith atūaid din tenid.  Tabrad ben dīen dētgel
desgel masbruindech cōemcolpt*hach* dīt di trī nói
mīrend do bīud somilis soblasdu, bas mēit ogh

---

¹ pruigen          ² etnidh          ³ tege
⁴ intocht          ⁵ serreg

rerchirci cach mīr dīb. Tabrat di trī nói lomand
gach ōen mīïi. In gal*ar* notgēba de, cenmothā in
būarainn, is inisi not- īcf*a*." "Cīa do comainm-si ?"
ar Mac Conglinne. "Nī *ansa*," ar in Fāithlieig :

5
   "Cruit[h]nechtān mac Lcm[u]achtáin
   meic Saille Slemne Sūghmaire
     mo chomainm-si fadēin.
   Brechtān fo mil
   ainm ind f[h]ir
10
     bīs fom' t[h]ēigh.

   Iarslis Caeirech
   comainm mo chon,
     cadla band.
   Blonacc mo ben,
15
   fristibim gen
     dar braisce barr.

   Olar n-Olar
   comainm inalta mo mnā[1] :
   re matne moch
20
   for Loch Lemnachtæ romlā.

   Millsēn m' ingen,
   imt[h]ēit n-inb*er*,
     gīle [a] glonn.
   Bōs[h]all mo mac,
25
   taithinidh dar brat
     n-ītha n-oll.

   Ugadart mo gilla glomar,
     blad ce*n* tuir,
   dā gāi chruithnechta 'na deslāim
30
     lcis di ernguin.

   Ētgud cræibechān immum fadēin
     in cech dū,
   blonacc thinbe occus inbe
     na tcit crū."

35
                     *Cruthnechtān.*

        Gabais a p*ait*r lem in clēirech occus dobe[i]r
     soscēla fom' chenn.[2] Issē soscēla bōi annside .i.

*aiter*

            [1] mnai                    is *add.*

soisc*ēla* do gūalloind aisle shenshaille cen rein*g*, cen
toinn imbe, cona cristall do dondmarōicc bruithi
foa, cona aird blonce fair, et dixit :
" For foesamh duit na saille sleimne sūgmaire !
For foesam duit na croithe crūaidhe cūlbuide !  For   5
foesam doit in[d] aighn*ē*n dīa m-bīadtar nōedlenā[i]n!
For foesam d*uit* na blonce mōre moltraide !  For
faosamh d*uit* na saille tenne truime torcraide !  In
rī robenndach f*ē*in na tortea sea dot' anaccal ar *gach*
n-gūbadhūn.  For a foesam doit, for a snādadān !"  10
For.

Attraigim[1] annside co tōsecha Tūath m-Bīdh .i. co
lūm ar cāch, co turarān ;  co h*ē*t*a*n m-briste, co
brechtān ; co sūa*n*a na dībe, co cōelāna inbe ; co
hairi*g*the taige rīgh, co m*u*cca ūra ; co luna messe,  15
co cāirib teō ;  co h*ē*n croithe,[2] co salunn ; co cimmid[3]
cargais, co gruitin ; co mīan ban n-ō*e*ntu*i*na, co
lemnacht ; co mīan sentuinte, co blonaicc ; co techda
latraigh, co litin ; cosi[n] m-bas lethan m-buicc
m-belaidhe ; co der[b] fiar na sacart, cosin m-braisig ;  20
co r*ē*tlannaib tige rīg, co hugib cercc ; co breith a
n-ucht, co hetne ; co himlūad n-ō*e*naig, co hublaibh
cumra ; co hō*e*nach craois, co hugadart ; co brisc*ē*n
rī*g*hn*æ*, co cerrboccān ; co di*g* suáin, co midh occus
gruit ; co trem*a*nta treisc, co [s]hamaisc ; col-long*ad*  25
rīgh, co bōshaill ; cosna ceit[h]ri sūile finda *fichet*
fīr*ē*na ic*ot*fir fedadh, co henbruithe, luss, gruth,
bīadh m*u*ilt, bīadh tuirc, muc ūr, reng thiu*g*, reng
t[h]ana, ass tiug, ass tana, int ass foloing a sluccad
chocnomh for a reith cūil ciar[b] cet[h]arcosach,  30
dognī sraindmeigil ind reithe frangcaig ic dul dar
do brāgait, co n-apra in bolccum toisiuch risin
m-bolccum n-d*ē*denach[4] : " Sluccud lucadh, tair riuin
remaind, ricub regat, dar in pōlairi saille ocus dar in
min*estir* m-blonce robōi dar ucht in cl*ē*irich sund !  35
cīa beō-se in[n]sin, nī bīu-su sund !  (Cīa thī[s]-siu
anūas, regat-sa sūas !")[5] ar in bolccam tōisiuch frisin

---

[1] *scom add.*       [2] leg. croiche ?        [3] leg. cunnid ?
[4] *deginach*                    [5] *struck out and dotted.*

m-bolcaim n dēdenach.　Is īat sin tra tōisiech Tūath
m-Bīd."

C'onid¹ annsin rochromasdair a lāimh cosna dā bir
bīdh, ocus dosbered co bēl ind rīgh, ocus dūthraicedh

5　a slucud etir chrand occus bīad.　Corrucc fot a lāma
ūad, corroling an lon craois assa brāgait corrabā for
in m-bir m-biidh, ocus corroling don bir, corrogaib
imm-brāgait gilla int s[h]acairt Corcaige robōi 'con
coire for lār in taige, ocus roling a brāgait in gilla

10　for in m-bior cētnae.　Lāid Mac Conglinne inn
m-bior issin² grīsaigh, ocus lāid core ind rīgt[h]aige
corrabā for in m-bir m-biid.　Rucad ind rīg i n-airecal
*codul*tæ, ocus rofolmaiged in tech mōr, ocus roloiscead
īarna folmug*ud*.　Ocus rolēicc in deman teora grēcha

15　ass.

Atracht in rī īarnamāirech, ocus ni bā mōamh a
shāith indāss sāith mic mīos.　"Nach buide lat,
a degduine," or Mac Conglinne, "rot-īccfa-sa ōn
ginaigh ?"　"Nach buide lat-sa," or Cat[h]al, "gan

20　do chrochad indiū dam-sa ?　Ocus in *grei*m rogabais
dam-sa .i. tinme mo chotæ, rotbīa digrēs, occus rotbīa
m' errad ocus fail mo lāma occus ētgud³ mo t[h]aoibh
ocus fīach cēt di chrud."　"Maith, a Chath*ail*," ol
Mainchīn, "in amlaidh sin b*ere* ūaim-si in fer ro-āir

25　ind eglais ?"　"Nī ba haml*aid*," or Mac Conglinne,
"acht dob*er*tor na breth[em]ain sīs, ocus tab*air*-si
gell cēt il-lāimh Cath*ail*, occus dob*er*-sa cēt aile,
occus abrait na brethemain cīa hūain dligius a
enecland."　Isbertotor na bret[h]emain corrodlig

30　Mac Conglinne a dīre occus a enecland, ar nī derna
āir, acht a rād nī īsadh corcu Corcaige.　"Nī
chuingim-si mo dīre nō m' enecland," ar Mac Conglinne, "acht in cochall fil isin cill."　"Rotfīa com'
bendachtain," ol Mainchīn.　Dīe n-epairt in drūt[h]

35　occus a mac ocus a ingen :

　　　"Dolluid Manc[h]īn—monor glē—
　　　d' acra for Mac Conglinne :
　　　is é Manc[h]īn tarras de
　　　'man cochall roboí imme.

¹ conit　　　² inssin　　　³ etcud

Cochall Manc[h]ín, cid maith sē,
ní ró do Mac Conglinne,
ní furáil do Comgan glan,
cencubad úaind a bunad,
in cochall atclu co m-blad,    5
cīa m-bad fīu trī *secht* cumal,
cīa nobeit fo dath*aib* bran,
ō Cath*al*, ō rīg Muman.

Nī bad m*ōr* lem úaim badēin,
cīemad d' ōr andorrum chēill,   10
ocus aicc ris dīa rēir,
mar atberad tria glancēill,
uáir is Cathal is slān cē[i]ll
don tirus[1] dilluid Manc[h]ēn."

Sic tra rohīcad Cathal mac Finnguine din ginaig 15
occus rohordned Mac Conglinne. Finis.

[1] leg. turus

# NOTES.

**2 1** *The four things.* This is the stereotyped beginning of introductions to older Irish prose of every kind. *Cuintesta,* "quaerendus", is a Middle-Ir. corruption for Old-Ir. *cuintechta* (Tur., 4b, 16), the "participium necessitatis" of *cuindgim.*

**5** *Mac Conglinne. Cú-glinne,* "Hound of the Glen".

**6** *Onaght Glenowra.* Hennessy has the following note on this : " A branch of the Onaght (*recte* Eoghanacht), or descendants of Eoghan Mór, son of Oilill Olum, King of Munster in the third century, seated in the district of Glenn-Amhnach ; the name of which is now preserved in that of Glanworth, a parish in the barony of Fermoy, co. Cork." But cf. Joyce, *Irish Names of Places,* p. 440, who would prefer to derive the anglicised Glanworth from the Irish name *Gleann-Iubhair.*

**7** *Cú-cen-gairm,* "Hound without Cry"; *cú-cen-máthir,* "Hound without Mother". The MS. H. 3, 18, p. 570, has the following absurd explanation of the latter name : *Cú-cen-mháthair .i. ic cuifa mháthair robhói intan concibilt in mháthair. Cúccnmáthair a ainm iarsin.*

**9** *Demon of gluttony.* Henn. takes *lón-cracs (sic)* as a compound and renders it by "food-excess". The phrase, however, is always *lon cráis,* or *cráes-lon.*

**25** *Ailech,* or Oilech, in Donegal, was one of the ancient seats of the Kings of Ulster.

**4 4** *Freshford,* co. Kilkenny.

**13** *Kernels.* Thus Moer sends nuts with love-charms to Find mac Cumaill. *LL.,* 200a, 43: "Moer ben Bernsa a Berramain dorat seirc do Fhind mac Cumaill, corodelb nói cnú segsa co n-upthaib scirce intib, ocus focheird

Iburni mac Dádoss dia n-idnacul do Fhind, ocus atbert
fris a teinm ꝝ a tomailt."

4  26  *Charms.* In the *Ancient Laws*, i, p. 202, we read of
such charms made out of the marrow of dead men's
bones.

5  18  *Dia sénad fair,* wrongly translated by Henn. "for hid-
ing it from him".

6  3  *Little creatures.* The Irish *míl* is used as a general
name for any animal, *e.g.*, *míl maige*, lit. "beast of the
plain", *i.e.*, the hare, now corrupted into *míol bhuidhe*,
rectè *míol mhuighe.* But the word is specially used
of insects (cf. *corrmíl, miltóg*), and particularly of the
louse, as on p. 13, 2.

15  Hennessy does not translate this poem. Most of the
eight persons, who are here said to have lived together
at Armagh in the eighth century, are known elsewhere in Irish literature or legend. On Mac Dá
Cherda, see *Corm. Transl.,* p. 7. He is the reputed
author of several quatrains, one of which is quoted by
Cormac, and in *LL.,* p. 201b, another in *LBr.,* p. 92,
marg. sup.

Mac Rustaing, according to a note in the *LBr.* com-
mentary on the Félire (Stokes' ed., p. cxlv), was a
brother of St. Cocmán Brecc. But this cannot have
been the case, for Cocmán died in 615. In the same
note it is stated that Mac Rustaing lies buried at Ross
Ech (now Russagh, near the village of Street, in the
north of co. West Meath), and that no woman can
look at his grave without breaking wind or uttering
a loud foolish laugh. This is also mentioned as one
of the wonders of Erin in Todd's *Irish Nennius*, p. 201,
and a similar story is told in the Old-Norwegian
*Speculum Regale* about the skull of an Irish jester
called Clefsan. It would seem, then, that Mac Rustaing was a famous jester in his time.

Dub Dá Thúath may have been the bishop and
abbot of Rath Acda of that name, who died in 783
according to the *Four Masters.*

25  *Cailleoh Bérre,* "the nun of Beare", still figures in Irish

K 2

legend as a hag or witch of fabulous age.   The Rev. E.
O'Growney informs me that she is said to have lived
near Oldcastle, co. Meath, and that the large cairns of
stone seen there are supposed to have been dropped
by her from her apron.   The following lines are
attributed to her :

" Mise Cailleach Bhéara bhocht,
  iomdha iongnadh amharcas riamh,
  chonnarcas Carn Bán 'na loch,
  cidh go bhfuil sé 'nois 'na shliabh."

" I am the poor old woman of Beare,
  Many wonders have I seen,
  I have seen Carn Bán a lake,
  Though now it is a mountain."

Another quatrain ascribed to her is found in *LBr.*,
p. 89, marg. inf., and in the Stowe MS. 992, fo. 47a,
marg. sup.   I am indebted to Father O'Growney for
the following modern sayings and stories, which he
obtained from a friend residing near Slyne Head.

*Tri saoghal fhada : saoghal an iubhair, saoghal an
iolra, saoghal na Caillighe Béara.*

*Beusa na Caillighe Béara : Nior thug sí salchar
na lathaighe seo thar an lathach eile.  Nior ith sí biadh
an uair a bheidheadh ocras uirre.  Nior chuaidh sí a
codladh go m-beidheadh codladh uirre.  Nior chaith
sí amach ant uisge salach gur thug sí isteach ant uisge
glan.*

*A comairle.  Bhí sí oidhche air fairrge lena clann
mhac, agus bhi an oidhche ciuin dorcha agus é ag sioc.
Bhí an fuacht ag dul go smior ionnta.  Dubhoirt sí
leo iad fhéin a congbhail teith.  " Ní fhéadamuid," ar
siad-san.  " Taoisg an fhairrge amach 'sa isteach," ar
sise.  " Ní 'lmuid ionann sin a dheanadh," arsan
clann.  " Beir air an soitheach taoisgthe agus líon an
bád agus taoisg amach arís é."  Rigneadar sin agus
congbhaidear iad fhéin teith go maidin, go bhfuair-
eadar uain le teacht air dtir.*

*Bhí tarlh ag an Chailleach Bhéara darbh ainm an
Tarbh Conraidh. Ní raibh aon bhó a chluisfeadh a
ghéim nach m-beidheadh laogh óg aici a gceann na
bliadna. Cia air bith áit is feárr agus is milse do
bheidheadh feur, is ann a tiomáineadh sí a cuid ba
agus an tarbh. Lá da raibh sí ag fosuigheacht na m-
bó i d-Tóin na Péice (áit i m-baile Doire-an-Emlaigh)
chualiidh an tarbh géim bó. Rith sé ón gCailligh go dtí
an bhó, agus rith an Chailleach 'na dhiuidh. Lean sí é
agus bhí ag aimsiughadh faoi go dtáinicdear go Mainiu.
Chuaidh sé 'sa tshnámh ag dul thar cuisle brag a
casadh dhó. 'Nuair dh' éirigh asant shnámh air an
talamh tirm bhí an Chailleach de léim thar an geuisle
agus buail sí lena slaitín draoidheacht go n-dearnaidh
sí cloch de. Tá an cloch i gcomharthaigheacht tairbh
le feicsin gusan lá indiu, agus tá lorg an urchair a
chaith sí leis insna carraigibh thart tiompall air.*

Three great ages : the age of the yew tree, the age
of the eagle, the age of Cailleach Bhéara.

The habits of Cailleach Bhéara : She did not carry
the mud of one pool beyond the next pool. She did not
eat when she was hungry. She did not go to sleep
until she was sleepy. She did not throw away the
dirty water until she had clean water in the house.

Her advice : One night she was on the sea with her
children. The night was still and dark, and it was
freezing. The cold went to their very marrow. She
told them to make themselves warm. " We cannot,"
said they. " Bale the sea out and in," said she. " Take
the scoop, fill the boat, and bale it out again." They
did so and made themselves warm until the morning,
when they found opportunity to go ashore.

She had a bull called Tarbh Conraidh. There was
no cow that heard him bellow and had not a calf at
the end of the year. Wherever the grass was best
and sweetest, there she would drive her cows and the
bull. One day the bull heard the lowing of a cow.
He ran from the Cailleach until he reached the cow,
and the Cailleach after him. She followed him until

they came to Mainin.  He swam across a small creek
that lay in his way.  When he reached the dry land,
the Cailleach had leaped across the creek, struck him
with her druid's rod, and turned him into stone.  The
bull-shaped stone is to be seen to this very day.

On Mac Samáin see *Corm. Transl.*, p. 8.

**7    5**  *i m-broind.*  Henn. transl. "in the breast", confusing
*broind*, the dat. sg. of *brú*, "belly", "womb", with
*bruinne*, "breast".

**8    11**  *In the shade of his studies.*  This is Hennessy's translation.  But the Irish *ar scáth* has developed various
meanings.  It means "in the shelter", "under the
protection": *ar scáth arm Hectoir, Tog. Tr.*, 1976 ; *ro-
naidm Muire óg for scáth Iosep, LBr.*, 145b.; *an cuiger
fuil ar do scáth-sa*, 3 *Fragm.*, 74, 17.  "For the protection" : *conid annsin tucsat duille na pailme for a
scáth a féli, LBr.*, 111a ; *ar scathaib a n-ech, LL.*,
264a, 35 ; *nitgonfaidhthar doghresgin bes in sciath ar
do scáth*, Stowe MS. 992, fo. 50b, 1.  "On behalf of",
"on account of": *ar scáth banluirg, Laws*, iii, 412,
15 ; *trian ar scáth a háil, ib.*, 380, 1.  The last is
probably the meaning of the phrase in our text.

**15**  " *Iveagh* (Uí Echach) was the name of a territory in the
S.W. of the present co. Cork, anciently the patrimony
of the sept of O'Mahony." (Henn.)

**17**  *Whitemeats, i.e.*, milk, curds, and the like, opposed to
flesh, eaten as "kitchen" (Ir. *andlann*, W. *enllyn*) with
bread.  Cf. O. N. *hvítr matr*, and W. *enllyn gwyn*.

**9    7**  *Móit mór*, "great pride of mind", Henn., wrongly.

**17**  *Aidche Sathairn.*  This phrase is commonly, but
wrongly, translated by "Saturday night", while
it always means "the eve of Saturday", *i.e.*, "Friday
night".  Cf. *aidche Domnaig*, p. 19, **27, 28** ; *aidche
Lúain* p. 21 1.  This use of *aidche* or *adaig* is perhaps
a remnant of the old Celtic custom of making the day
follow the night, of which Cæsar, *Bell. Gall.* vi, 18,
speaks : " dies natales et mensium et annorum initia
sic observant ut noctem dies subsequatur."

**20**  *Tocht senshaille oo tithfi dar a lár*, "through the middle of which you could see", Henn., reading *cithfi* and taking this for the second pers. conditional of the verb *cim*, "I see". But *tithfi* is, I think, miswritten for *sithfi*. See the Glossary.

10    3    *Who put a gospel around him.* "A 'gospel' is a text of Scripture written in a peculiar manner, and which has been blessed by a priest. It is sewed in red cloth, and hung round the neck as a cure or preventive against various diseases, etc." (Croker, *Fairy Legends*, p. 360.) Henn. misread *soscéla* into *socht*, and translated, "silence was evinced regarding him".

  6    "*Aughty*, now called Slieve Aughty (olim Echtghe), a mountainous district on the confines of Clare and Galway." (Henn.)

  9    *A short time before vespers.* Travelling was prohibited on Sunday, which began at vespers on Saturday night. Cf. the note on p. 18, 30.

  10    *Guest-house.* "Somewhat apart from the cells of the monks were the abbot's house and the house set apart for the reception of guests, called the *tech óiged* or *hospitium*." (Skene, *Celtic Scotland*, ii, p. 59.)

  25    *With its stones.* Such stones, Mrs. Whitley Stokes suggests, were probably heated before being put into the water to make a warm bath.

  30    *In which he dipped his shoes.* "Washing one's shoes" is sometimes used as a term for "making oneself at home", as in a poem ascribed to the dethroned King Diarmait mac Cerbaill, *LL.*, p. 149b :

   " *Raba missi a nuachur cóir*
    *d' ingin álaind hErimóin,*
    *clérig romchursetar di*
    *du chirt Fótla fonnairddi ;*
    *nigfit*[1] *a m-bróca 'na tig*
    *na ríg óca indligthig.*"

  " I was the lawful bridegroom
  Of the beautiful daughter of Erimon,[2]

---

[1] nigfid Fcs.    [2] *i.e.*, Ériu, Ireland personified.

Page Line

> Clerics have thrust me
> From the rule of highland Fotla[1] ;
> Young unlawful kings
> Will wash their shoes in her house."

**12   11**   Diapsalm $= \delta\iota\acute{a}\psi\alpha\lambda\mu a$, synpsalm $= \sigma\acute{v}\mu\psi\alpha\lambda\mu a$. In the old Irish treatise on the Psalter, copies of which are in Rawl. B. 512 and Harl. 5280, these terms arc variously explained.

     **21**   *Manchin*, evidently a nickname, "little monk".

**14   12**   *Spells.* The Ir. word *geiss* rather means a solemn injunction or prohibition to do a certain thing, a taboo.

     **18**   *My God's doom.* St. Patrick's well-known oath. See the Glossary.

**15   11**   *a thachur*, Henn., "to keep it open", wrongly.

     **24**   *dá chammrand*, "two crooked stanzas", Henn. But *camm* here means "duel", "contest". On the custom of making such rimes in contention or rivalry, see *Cormac Transl.*, p. 138, and *Rev. Celt.*, xii, p. 460. Cf. the Skr. *samasyá* and the Portuguese custom of singing *ao desafio*, Latouche, *Travels in Portugal*, p. 47.

**16   8**   *Thy orison, i.e.,* "panem nostrum cotidianum da nobis hodie."

     **17**   *Little boys will sing those verses.* Hennessy here has the following note : " Adalbert von Chamisso, a poet too little known out of Germany, has prettily expressed the idea here conveyed in the lines :

> " Nun singen's auf Strassen und Märkten
> Die Mädchen und Knaben im Chor."

**18   24**   *A party of one.* The Irish *dám*, lit. "company", is often used of one person only. Cf. p. 87, 2, and *LU.*, 86a, 35 : *dám óenmná.*

     **26**   *A little crumb*, lit. "wafer".

     **30**   According to the Irish tract on Sunday called *Sóire Domnaig*, of which there are copies in *LBr.*, Harl. 5280, and the Edinburgh MS. XL, Sunday is to be observed from vespers on Saturday night to sunrise on

---

[1] Another name for Ireland.

Monday morning. (*Sáire Domnaig ó espartu int
Shathairnd co hérgi gréne dia Luain, LBr.*, p. 204b ;
*ó trád esportai dia Sadairnn co fuin maitni die Luain,*
Harl., fo. 38a.) Cf. also p. 28, 30. Some food, but
little only, was allowed to guests who came from afar
on Saturday night. (*Saiged bid do áigedaib, beco araba
di shuidiu,do neuch doteit di céin aidchen-Domnaig,ib.*)

19   2   *Muinter Chorcaige.* Henn. throughout rendered *muinter*
by "people". But it means the aggregate of monks
in each monastery—Lat. *familia.*

21   4   *fuilled ro-immarcraid ind-aithi,* "even to a degree
greater than that", Hennessy, evidently taking
*ind-aithi* as standing for *indás sin.* But no emenda-
tion is required.

    17   *ni frith loc laburtha i n-dligud,* "no instance of illegal
utterance", Henn. evidently reading *indligid.* But
*i n-dligud,* if taken with *ni fhrith,* makes perfectly
good sense.

    25   *fó liúmm ce notisad de,* "I care not what may come of
it", Henn., hardly correctly.

23   7   *Pars.* "Partes dicuntur divinae Eucharistiae vel
panis Eucharistici particulae, quae a sacerdote inter
missæ solemnia fractae in partes minutiores fidelibus
distribuebantur ad communionem." (Ducange.)

    9   *Dol do láim,* "to go to confession, be absolved", mod. Ir.
*dul fa láimh shagairt.* The priest raises his hand in
the absolution. See Reeves, *Culdees,* p. 202.

    24   *ni rochaithes for sét.* Henn. translates, "I consumed
not your food", probably extending the *.s.* of the MS.
into *séire* instead of the usual *sét.*

24   16   "*Ever-full.*" "This is supposed to be the well which
now gives name to the well-known district of Sunday's Well, in the city of Cork. It was also called
*tobar righ an domhnaigh,* or "the well of Sunday's
King", a name applied to many holy wells in Ireland."
(Henn.)

    19   *Supine.* This passage determines the original sense of
the adj. *fáen* (on which see *Rev. Celt.,* xi, p. 456).
It means "outstretched, on one's back, with face up-

wards", and is applied to persons thus lying in bed (*fœn inna imdai, LU.*, 89a, 19), or to dead bodies. (*Eocho Airem fœn arna marbad, LU.*, 38a, 33.)

**25**  22   *a matuda,* "you swine", Henn., confusing *matad,* "dog", with *máta,* "pig". He made the same mistake on p. 27, 19.

**27**  2   *Ni láud form.* The verb *láim* with the prep. *for* or *ar* is used like the mod. *cuirim. Ni chuireadh orm,* "it would not cause me any annoyance, would not affect me". *Cadé tá ag cur ort ?* "What is the matter with you ?" Cf. p. 122, 28 : *arná roláá in chonair form chride. LU.*, 92b, 27 : *ni ralá do chless n-airiut cosinnocht,* "thy skill has never failed thee till to-night".

5   *Barre 'catú,* "St. Barri whose subjects you are", Henn., wrongly. *'catú,* lit. "with whom 1 am". The same phrase is used by Manchín on p. 19, 4.

8   *Ria cách ocus iar cách.* The same phrase p. 55, 7. Cf. Mairg dam-sa ría cách, mairg íar cách! *LU.*, p. 88a, 11.

**28**  9   *The Foxes' Wood,* Ir. Caill na Sindach, "now changed to Shanakiel, a place adjoining Sunday's Well, in the western suburbs of Cork". (Henn.)

31   *The convent.* The Irish *popul,* borrowed from Lat. *populus,* seems to have here and on p. 33, 7, the meaning which it has now, "congregation, community". Cf. populus baptismalis ecclesiae = parochiae incolae (Ducange).

**29**  20   *a brúti nemliterdhai,* "you unintellectual brutes", Henn. But *nemliterda* means "illiterate".

27   *fortgillim.* Following Henn., I translated wrongly "I vow to thee", taking *-t-* as the infixed pronoun of the second person, while it belongs to the verb. See the Glossary.

**30**  19   *Angel's Ridge.* There is a *Casán an aingil* over Cill-Enda in Aranmore, where the angel used to walk with Columcille, and where the grass is always green. (O'Growney.)

**33**  7   *popul,* "populace", Henn. But see note on p. 28, 31, where Henn. rightly renders "congregation".

**33** 12 *a chlt cloth co comgne,* "thou famous shrine of knowledge", Henn.

13 The pedigree of food in Hennessy's translation is full of mistakes, a list of which will be interesting : *bela* "of fat", *borrchrothi bláthi* " thick fresh cream", *brechtán* " pudding", *beoiri búaid mbainde* "strong liquid beer", *cainninde caimme* " tender leek", *hitha* "of corn", *drand* "of bread", *tainge* "of relish", *Inbeir Indsén* " of old waters" (taking *Indsén* to be a compound of *sen* " old", while it probably is a diminutive of *inis* "island"), *inbe* " of flour", *cona gablaib gaile* " with its branches of virtue", *braisce bithe* "of lasting brassica".

**35** 7 *A chéim fosad,* etc. Hennessy gives the following unlucky guesswork :

" As thou walkest in state
With thy staff, while we wait,
That thou bless us, it is meet."

18 *atberut,* " he observed", Henn.

26 *loechlestar,* "shapely boat", Henn.

27 *in chongaib,* " its aid", Henn., who must have confused *congaib* with *congnam.*

**36** 29 *Flowed through the floor.* A house with four doors and water running through its middle is mentioned in the *Laws,* i, p. 130, 20 (*uisce tar a lár*).

**37** 16 *turarán,* " well-baked bread", Henn. But see Glossary.

17 *do mæthlaib,* " of spices", Henn.

20 *imasech,* "all around", Henn.

28 *ós brú thopair thremantai,* " which from the well of nectar came", Henn.

31 *uscai olordai,* " of rich liquid", Henn., who here and elsewhere confused *usca,* "lard", with *uisce,* "water".

35 *immon múr amuig,* "along the sea outside", Henn., confusing *múr,* " wall ", with *muir,* " sea".

**39** 8 *tennsadchib,* " robust", Henn. See Glossary.

17 *fo inbiur in ardchori,* " before the high cauldron's mouth", Henn. But *inbir* is here a compound of *bir,*

"spit", and not the common word for "estuary".
See Glossary.

**39**   21   *airscéla.* Henn. read *ar scéla* and translated "our
            pleasant fiction-tales".

      25   *dar ler Locha Áis,* "across the sea-wide lake", Henn.

**40**   23   *For which they fasted.* "There is here an allusion to a
            practice that seems to have obtained among the an-
            cient Irish, of fasting *against* a person from whom
            something was sought to be extorted. See *Senchas
            Mór,* vol. i, Pref., xlviii." (Henn.)

**41**   25   *eter Corccaig ocus a termund,* Henn. translated "be-
            tween Cork and Thomond". Here, as so often, he
            was misled by his habit of reading the older language
            with modern pronunciation. The MS. has *tmūd.*
            Henn. extended this into the modern Thomond, which
            would be *Tuathmumain* in older Irish.

**42**   14   *Dún Coba.* "The situation of this place is not at pre-
            sent known; but it was near the town of Dromaleague
            (in the barony of West Carbury, co. Cork), which is
            on the confines of the ancient Corca-Laighde, or
            O'Driscoll's country." (Henn.)

**43**   27   *Bragitóracht,* which I have rendered by "buffoonery",
            really means "farting". It is a derivative from
            *bragitóir,* a kind of buffoon who entertained his
            audience by farting. See the Glossary.

**44**   19   *Welsh steed.* Cf. *gaillire,* "a Welsh stallion"; *gailliti,*
            "a Welsh mare", O'Dav., p. 95; *cullach .i. ech bret-
            nach, ib.,* p. 68; *ech allmardha,* Stokes, *Lives,* l. 3128.

**46**    7   *Maidens began to serve.* The Ir. *fósaic,* better *ósaic,* is
            borrowed from Lat. *obsequium* (Stokes, *Lives,* Ind.),
            and probably refers here to the service of washing
            the feet.

**48**   17   *Humanity.* The Ir. *dóennacht* often means "generosity",
            "liberality", as in the following passage from the
            *Book of Fenagh,* 310, 20: *gan diultud re dreich n-
            duine, acht sé ina oil nemchumscuigthi a n-daonnacht
            tré bithu,* "not denying the face of any man, but he
            like an immovable rock in ~~humanity~~ for ever". It is
            thus explained in *LL.,* 294a, 38: *issed is dóennacht,
            dilsi ocus diute.*

Page Line

49  22  *Mysi*, more usually *Moysi*, but the same spelling occurs in the *Félire*, p. lv, 3.

50  4  *The seven things.* Cf. *LBr.*, p. 74b : *ar ecnairc in sechta rotairngircd duit i talmain .i. do choimpert, do genemain, do chruchad, t' adnacul, t' ésergi, do fhresgabáil dochum nime, do shuide for deis Dé athar in-nim, do thidecht do mess for bíi ocus marbu il-ló brátha.*

8  *The eight Beatitudes of the Gospel, i.e.,* Matth. v, 3-11. "Of the Gospel" is added to distinguish these beatitudes from that of the 119th Psalm (" Beati Immaculati"). See Stokes, *Lives*, p. 406.

17  *After sin, i.e.,* the sin of Judas.

23  *Christ with his apostles.* In *LBr.*, p. 74a, Christ is invoked "a thaissig apstal ocus descipul núfhiadnaise !"

22  *Pet crane.* Such a creature is mentioned in the Life of Ciaran, Stokes, *Lives*, p. 270.

51  14  *Anfhurmithi*, bad spelling for *anfoirbthe.*

24  I do not know how to extend the mark of abbreviation after *frith.*

52  6  *Thy foot and thy check under thee.* Literal translation, obscure to me.

13  *Malediction.* Ir. *osnad*, lit. "groan".

15  *Emly-Ivar.* " Emly, in the county of Tipperary, anciently a bishop's see, but now a very poor village." (Henn.)

53  10  *Dorala dam fri muintir C.*, an idiomatic phrase, meaning "I fell out with". Cf. *darala eturru ic imbert fhidchilli ⁊ Fergus*—"He and Fergus fell out in playing *fidchell*," *LL.*, 103b ; *noco tarla etorra i Temair Luachra imman muic Slanga*, CC., 8 ; *dorala itir Luicet ⁊ Aed mac Morna isin chath*, Mcgn. F., 2; *conad impi sein tarla eturru*, Tog. Tr., 1900.

13  *Luid dó.* Here *luid* must be an imperative form. It would seem that a present stem *luid-* was developed from the perfect. Cf. *conludim*, p. 89, 3.

18  *Bóinni*, "striped", Henn.

22  *Tic lán dó do blogaib*, "came forth loaded with fragments", Henn., wrongly.

Page Line

53  27  *In slúaigcd*, etc.   The construction of this period is very
        obscure.

54  14  *He was the first that exempted clerics from going a-
        soldiering.*  "This exemption of the clergy of Ireland
        from military service is ascribed in other authorities
        to Aedh Ordnidhe, King of Ireland *circa* A.D. 800.
        See *Annals of Ulster*, ad an. 803." (Henn.)

59  4   *Sámaigis in mac légind i tulg i tœb n-ursainde*, " the
        student fixed a beam beside the door-post", Henn.,
        wrongly.

60  32  *English salt.*  The export of salt from England to
        Ireland is mentioned in Higden's *Polychronicon:*
        " Also Flaunders loveth the wolle of this lond, Ireland
        the oor and the salt."

61  24  *Atbér fir*, " Thou speakest truly", Henn., reading
        *atbir.*

        *Co bruinde m-brátha*, " to the front of Doom", Henn.

    30  *Fetta*, lit. " brave", here used merely for alliteration.

63  9   *Fri gáith*, etc.  Cf. *LL.*, 83a : *ra sidi répgáithi erraig
        il-ló Mártai dar muni machairi.*

    13  *Crithir chonnli*, " candlewick", Henn., wrongly.

64  8   *And dipped it in the honey.*  Honey was used as a
        seasoning with all kinds of food.   It was given to
        the children of kings as a flavouring (*tummud*) with
        their stirabout of new milk, *Laws*, ii, p. 150.  A broiled
        salmon is dressed with honey, *Táin Bó Fráich*, p. 152.

65  8   *A thosach ar míl firend so*, " here's the first for male
        honey", Henn., reading *mil* instead of *míl.*

    24  *Ní dernad fair-sium.*  Cf. *ní dersat fair*, " they did not
        do it for him", *LU.*, 39b, 9.

66  22  *Puddings fresh-boiled*, lit. " after their first boiling".
        Father O'Growney remarks on this : " These would
        be pigs' intestines stuffed and boiled.  They are
        boiled and hung up to dry, and then cooked for the
        second time, as needed."

68  14  *Topped with trees.*  The earthen walls of raths and
        lisses seem to have been planted with trees.  Cf.
        *tuittid cnói cuill cáinmessa do robilib ráth*, *LL.*, 118a,
        16.

## Notes. 143

Page Line

**68**  28  The translation should be : *When I get to Buttermount, may a gillie take off my shoes !*  This is, I believe, a skit on a custom of the early Irish Church, which, as far as I know, has not been noticed before.  It would seem that it was a rule for the priest in approaching the high altar, and before passing through the chancel, or sanctuary, to take off his shoes, or to have a gillie in attendance to perform this service.  The following passage is at present the only one known to me, from which I can infer the prevalence of this custom in the Irish Church.  *Intan bui Colum Cille isin iarmérgi oc dul tar crandcaingel* (*saingel* Fcs.) *siar is é Scandlán rosfrithoil a assa dhe*, *LBr.*, 238d. a, 64—"When Columcille passed at matins through the chancel westward, Scandlán performed the service of putting on his shoes."  Scandlán had been imprisoned by King Aed, and though he was fettered and closely watched, Columcille prophesied that he would perform this service for him in the morning whereever he was (*co n-erbairt-sium dana fri Aed is é nongébad a assa imme imm iarmergi cebé bale nobeth, LU.*, 5b, 38).  See the same story in Stokes' *Lives*, p. 313.

The custom (which is also found in the Coptic Church) was no doubt of Eastern origin, based on such passages as Exodus iii, 5 : "Solve calceamentum de pedibus tuis ; locus enim, in quo stas, terra sancta est"; Josua v, 15 ; Act vii, 33.  In our passage, Butter-mount takes the place of the altar.

**69**  1  *Lán do luaibn,* "full of herbs," Henn.  But see the Glossary.

19  *Grbend,* lit. "fetter, bondage".  It is the W. *gefyn,* and should have a short *e*, though it here rimes with *Erend.*  It is *géibhenn* in the mod. language.

22  *Ongha.*  Henn. translates "unctuous", prob. reading *ongtha.*

28  *Lith cen tassa,* "with fame increasing", Henn.

29  Henn. translates : "And when I go to heaven's mount, may brightness be shed round me !"  He read *Sliab Nime* for *Sliab n-Imme,* and *gile* for *gille.*

Page Line
**70** 13 *The gravy.* The Ir. word is *beochail,* which is glossed
by *beoil,* "meat-juice". This was a favourite drink
with the Irish as well as the Scottish Gael. Cf.
Walter Scott's description of the Highland banquet
in the *Fair Maid of Perth :* "The hooped cogues or
cups, out of which the guests quaffed their liquor, as
also the broth or juice of the meat, which was held a
delicacy."

17 *Phantom.* The Ir. *scál* is a general word for a superna-
tural apparition. It is formed from the same root as
*scáth,* "shade". See the Glossary.

32 The transl. should be "Dining on grains of pepper".
See the Glossary s. v. *scell.* Henn. has "eating in a
pepper-box".

**71** 6 *Im' lepaid cháin chumdachta,* "in my soft well-shaped
bed", Henn.

12 *Beochail nárotbáda,* "that *beochail* ruins thee not",
Henn., wrongly.

20 *Robad do throich,* "giving warning to a miserable",
Henn. But *troch* f. originally means, I think,
"doomed to die, fey", then "coward". Cf. the
development of Old-Germ. *reige* in the former sense
to Mod.-Germ. *feige,* "cowardly". See the Glossary.

22 *Tusliud clochi fria crand,* "deriving a stone from a
tree", Henn., confusing *tusliud* with *tusmiud.*

23 *Sanais fri bodur.* Cf. *céol do bodur,* Book of Fenagh,
p. 106.

24 *Dibad for dubach,* "oppressing the sorrowful", Henn.
But see *dibad* 2, in *Wind. Wörterb.*

27 *Esorcu darach.* Ci. *nirba hesorcon darach do dirn,
nirba saiget i corthi, nirba buain mela a mecnaib
ibair, nirba cuindchid imbi il-ligi con,* Rawl. 512,
fo. 113b, 2. *Esorcu* is the Middle-Ir. form for O. Ir.
*essorcun.* Cf. *persu* (p. 3, 5), *Mórrígu,* for *persan,
Morrígan.*

**73** 5 *Táeb fri coin fholmnig,* "favouring a mad dog", Henn.
For the phrase *tóeb fri,* "trusting", cf. *nint i n-Erind
áin risi tabraim thóeb ingi Atha[i]r, Mac ocus Spirut
Náem, LU.,* 119b, 36. *ferr duiná taeb do thabairt fri*

Page Line

*fer dorosat nace omnia*, Laws i, 22, 20. *Folmnech* should have been translated by "roped". See Gloss.

**73** 10 *Lind do bóethaib*, "ale to the vulgar", Henn. For my rendering of *bóeth* by "infant", cf. *Laws*, ii, p. 62, 20; *ib.*, 64, 27.

12 *Coland cen chend*. Cf. *is coland cen chend duine cen anmcharait*, LL. 283b, 26.  ✳.

15 *Athlaech*, lit. "an ex-layman". See Gloss.

17 *Cen lái*, "without an oar", Henn. Impossible.

21 *Caera for gaimen*. Henn. does not translate this, just as O'Donovan, *Magh Rath*, p. 124, 14, leaves the phrase purposely untranslated. It might mean "a sheep on a hide".

22 *Taidbsi .i. messa*, "judgment", Henn. But see Gloss.

24 *Aisec*, "lending", Henn., wrongly.

26 *Tarcud*, "proposing", Henn. See Gloss.

**74** 32 *The Wizard Doctor*, Ir. *Fáthliaig*, "vates medicus", "seer-leech". Cf. Pliny, xxx, 4, 13 : "Tiberii Caesaris principatus sustulit druidas eorum et hoc genus vatum medicorumque per senatus consultum." A *fáthliaig*, who is at the same time a judge (*brithem*, *fáthbrithem*) is mentioned in *LL.*, 200b, 2; *ib.*, 192a, 1.

**75** 5 *Can deitt fén*, "who thou art thyself", Henn., wrongly.

7 *Mac Eleaib Essamain*, "son of Joyous-Welcome", Henn. See Gloss.

**77** 3 *Do dulas*, "thy appetite", Henn.

9 *Brasslongthech*, "quick-eating", Henn.

13 *Do ithascaig*, "of frumenty", Henn.

19 *Airnechán* "purveyor", *Bairgenach* "baker", *Fastaib* "retainer", *Lachtmarán* "cook", *Lámdóitech* "ready-handed", Henn.

**79** 9 *Cadla band*, "of hardy bound", Henn.

14 *Imthét n-inber*, "traverses rivers", Henn., repeating the same mistake which I stated in my note on p. 39, 17.

24 *Sall bocc braincch*, "a soft fat leader", Henn.

26 *Is din sœthra*, "part of whose load is", Henn.

29 *Oirech mœthla*, "a cheese-chief", Henn.

31 "On his ribs are greasy trappings", Henn.

**81** 7-8 Henn. does not translate these lines.

10 *Nita tuir*, "not mean are these," Henn.

L

**81** 11-12 Not translated by Henn.

15 *Imbert inbe*, etc., "Take thou these that spells come not from uncooked food", Henn.

**83** 12 *Sithaltai*, "long-preserved", Henn.

26 *Co herard cendfhœlid*, "to Irard Cinnfaeladh", Henn.

**85** 2 *Do leith œgaire*, "approaching a fold", Henn. *Acgaire*, which usually means "shepherd", may here, as Stokes suggests, mean "a flock of sheep", as *damgaire* means "a herd of deer".

4 *Ag allaid*, "a wild ox", Henn., wrongly.

7 *Corrmil*, "wasp", Henn.

**87** 24 *Ticimm bulli*, lit. "I come a blow". Cf. p. 109, 3.

**88** 22 *Dulse*, Ir. *duilesc*. "Duleasg, or Salt-leaf, is a weed growing on sea-rocks, and preserved by drying it on stones in fair weather, and soon after, when occasion serves, for eating. There is scarce any sea-shore whereon it grows not." O'Flaherty, *Iarconnaught*, p. 99.

23 *Every ordinary* (lit. *natural*) *day*. Cf. Marlowe, *Faustus*:

> "Let this hour be but
> A year, a month, a week, a natural day,
> That Faustus may repent and save his soul."

**89** 5 *Oclach*, "youth", Henn., wrongly.

10 *Cona secht cornib*, "with his seven horns", Henn., confusing *corn*, "horn", with *corann*, "crown". See Gloss.

24 *Do métail tiug*, "of hard-pressed cheese", Henn., taking *métail* = *márthail*.

**90** 2 *Bundrish*, Ir. *bundraiss*, some kind of edible sea-weed.

11 *With their shovels*. Cf. LL., 353a: *Bái Dirmaid oc glanad urdrochit a thaigl, ocus a shliasat 'na láim.*

**91** 8 *Cona m-brotharlumnib*, "with their bare garments", Henn.

9 *Boc-brechtáin*, "of egg-fritters", Henn., reading *og-brechtáin*.

10 *Ic fochartad*, "tossing", Henn.

**93** 13 *'Os tuil*, perhaps leg. *ós t' shúil*, "over thy eye".

14 *'Os t' ingnib*, "over thy joints", Henn.

**95** 16 *Midchuine*, "an antidote", Henn.

20 *Comelfi dorni fri détu*, "rub thy teeth with brambles", Henn., thinking of English "thorn".

Page Line
95  27  *Nárotbena a dé*, " that its heat may not scorch thee",
        Henn., wrongly.
97  4  *Banamail*, "modest", Henn.
    5  *Muncach.* Henn. read *maccach*, and translated " rich
        in sons".
    6  *Nároshera*, for *nárosfhera.*
99  4  *Adochrat*, for *a d-tochrat.*
    11  This difficult and partly obscure list of *kennings* has
        occasioned much indefensible guesswork in Hen-
        nessy's translation. Throughout he treated *co* as *co* n-
        and translated " with" instead of *"to"*. The follow-
        ing mistakes are worth noticing. *Co luna hitha*
        " the food of the hungry", *co lunu messi* " with the
        food of judgment", *cosnait na slóig* " that sustains
        multitudes", *cosin sercoll sochenelach* " with the
        noble drink of the love-sick", *co héill fir célide* "with
        the deceiver of a guest", *coilech circe* " hen's tripe"
        (taking *coil-* to stand for *cóclán*, but cf. *coilech circce*,
        LBr., 222b, 49), *co hingur cingir cicharan* " with the
        restraining anchor of the hungry", *co hén crossi*
        " with the sauce of excess", *co brafud nochta* " with
        betrayers of the heart".
101  14  *A charrmatraid*, "my friend", Henn., thinking of *cara.*
    15  *Ar mataidecht ar n-ilis*, "our mutual opposition", Henn.
    16  *Isin istadluc sa*, " in this lowly place", Henn., thinking
        of *is* and *isel.*
103  18  *Iss asu chách lind*, " all things are urgent", Henn.
    22  *Lúag cossi cenbair*, " the value of a hen's leg", Henn.
        See Gloss.
104  11  *Monk.* Ir. *manach* is sometimes humorously used in
        this way. Thus St. Moling, most humorous of Irish
        saints, addresses a ragged piece of cloth : *Airg, a*
        *manaig út, ar Moling frisin certán*, LL., 283b, 49.
105  9  *Oibell*, " wicked", Henn., perhaps thinking of Engl.
        "evil".
106  7  *Thrice threatening him with the Gospels.* Another in-
        stance of lifting the Gospels to scare the Devil is
        found in the *Félire* of Oengus, p. civ.
    9  *The little fair woman from the Curragh, i.e.,* St. Bridget.
109  4  *Féta.* See note on p. 61, 30.
111  19  *Tidnocul.* Cf. *tidnacul clúaise di araile*, Laws I, 30, 25.

## Page 114.

[In order to enable those students of folk-lore who do not know Irish to compare the two versions for themselves, I subjoin a translation of that of II. 3, 18, omitting only those portions which agree with *Leabhar Breac*, or which I am unable to understand.]

Cathal Mac Findguine, a great king of Munster, with the greed of a hound, with the appetite of a horse. A demon of gluttony was in his inside ; Satan consumed his food with him.

Aniar Mac Conglinne, of the people of great Fahan-Mura,[1] a splendid scholar. He went from Fahan the round of Ireland, into Tyrone, into Oriel, to Armagh, across the Fews Mountains, across the plain of Louth, into Criffan, into Crioch Rois, to the hill of Teltown. He had one attendant with him, Mac-na-Cairre (the Scabbed Youth). They went to Kells, and spent the night without food in the stone-church. On the morrow Mac C. said in the presence of the congregation :

"My lad,
Why should we not have a duel in quatrains ?
Make thou a quatrain on the bread,
I will make one on the relish."

"We need it," said the Scabbed Youth, "having been left fasting by the community here last night." Before evening enough for twenty came to them of drink and food. On the next day they went through Meath, across the hill of Usnech, to Durrow of Columcille in Tír Néill, across Slieve Bloom, into Ely (O'Carroll) westward, across the plain of Munster, across Machaire na Cliach, into Luachair Dedhad.

There were the men of Munster in their bands going to Cork for the festival of St. Barre and St. Nessan, in order to fast. "I would give you good advice," said the Scabbed Youth to Mac C. "that we may get food in Cork. Let us say that you are a poet and they will not dare to let us be without food." Mac C.

---

[1] Now Fahan, co. Donegal, "where St. Mura, the patron saint of the Cinel-Eoghain, was held in the highest veneration" *O'Don. FM.*, 1101.

agreed to this, and they came to the guest-house of Cork. There
was a large dog in the house, which came out and jumped at the
Scabbed Youth, sending him into the quagmire (?), (where he
lay) till Mac C. came up to him.

Manchín, the abbot of Cork, said : " See whether there is anyone in the guest-house to-night who would like to eat something."
A young cleric went to see. " Is there anyone here ?" said he.
" Not good is what you say," said the Scabbed Youth. "There
is a good ollave here, and he is not served well by you. He will
revile the Church, for he is far from his kindred to-day." The
young cleric reported this to Manchín, who ordered a fire of green
branch-wood and a bowl of oats for them. Then said Mac C. :

> " Till Doom I would not eat,
> Unless I were famished,
> The oaten ration of Cork,
> Cork's oaten ration."

The messenger repeated this to Manchín, who ordered out the
clerics and had Mac C. bound in order to crucify him on the next
day for his having slandered the Church. " A boon for me,"
said Mac C., "for the sake of Barre, whose festival is to-night.
My fill of drink and food, and your own bed with its bedding,
both quilt and cover."[1] " For the sake of our patron I will grant
it," said the abbot. After having eaten and drunk his fill, Mac
C. lay down, and a heavy slumber fell upon him. Then in
his sleep he saw a cleric approach him. He wore a white mantle
with a golden brooch, a large silken shirt next his white skin,
and long white-grey curly hair. He said : " You sleep well, and
you awaiting death." " Who are you ?" said Mac C. " Mura,"
said he. " I have come to help you." " What help is it ?" said
Mac C. " Remember this vision," said Mura, "and recite it in
the presence of King Cathal, and you will cure him from his
craving."

Mura then sang the vision, and Mac C. remembered it. On
the morrow he was taken to a gathering of the men of Munster
to be crucified. Cathal and the nobles of Munster were there.
C. said he would not crucify a bard, but the clerics might do it
themselves, for it was they that knew the wrong he had done.

---

[1] Here *dóib* seems out of place.

" A boon for me, O C., and ye nobles of Munster," said Mac C.
" My fill of water, and let me draw it myself !" This was
granted by C. Mac C. was taken to the well, and proceeds as on
p. 24, 15-23. When C. was told of this, he granted him a respite
until morning.

That night C. went to Pichán's house, and Mac C. followed him
there. Then follows the apple-scene, as on p. 48—p. 50, 23.

" The whole would not be too much for you !" said C., scatter-
ing the hide full of apples to the host. And everyone arose. . .

Then said Mac C. to Pichán, if he were allowed to prepare the
food for C., it would be the better for the men of Munster. On
Pichán's guarantee M.'s fetters are loosened, he washes himself,
puts on an apron, etc., as on p. 62.

" Who is this ?" said C. " A man who knows how to prepare
food," said Pichán. " Is it not the bard ?" said C. " It is he indeed," said P. " It is being well prepared," said C. " Let me have
my food quickly !" " A boon for me !" said Mac C. " What
boon?" said C. " Let no one else talk in the house until I have
finished telling you a vision that I saw last night." " It shall
be granted," said C., " and tell it quickly. Whoever speaks shall
be crucified to-morrow together with you."

Then said Mac C. :

" A vision I beheld last night," etc., as on p. 66—p. 70, 14.

" When the voice had spoken to me again, I arose so quickly
and lightly that a fly could not have stuck on my forehead. Then
I saw a phantom approaching me. 'Well,' said he to me.
ｨ Well,' said I to him. 'Who are you, wretch ?' said the phantom. 'A poor scholar', said I, ' seeking a cure from greediness,
from voracity, and intolerable thirst.' 'Wretch,' said he,
' there is here one who will direct you to the Altar of Fat, which
is in the west of the church. . . . . on the Pass of Meat-juice in
the land of the Children of Early-eating, right in front of
the Hermitage of the Wizard Doctor.' 'What is your name?'
said Mac C. 'Is it I ?' said he. 'It is you,' said Mac C. 'Dirty-
belch, son of Fluxy, of the race of Elcab the Fearless, it is he
that speaks to you, that will direct you.'

" Then I arose," etc., as on p. 84, 1-4. "And we went across
Butter-mount, and saw a juicy little coracle of corned beef on
the border of the lake, with its hide of tallow," etc., as on p. 84,
13-28.

Then said Mac C.:

" A vision that appeared to me," etc.,
as on p. 34—p. 38, 25.

" Thereupon we went on to a causeway of curds, into a copse-
wood of lard, into a field of old bacon. A dark lardy mist arose
around us, so that we could see neither heaven nor earth, nor any
place to which we might fairly go, so that I struck with my back
against a tombstone of ... curds. It almost shattered the bones
of my skull to pieces. I stretched out my hand to raise myself
again, and fell between pats of fresh butter up to the bend of my
elbows. Then I saw Egg-pillow, the gillie of the Wizard Doctor,
catching fish in a full lake of new milk," etc., as on p. 90, 20-28.

Where do you come from ?' said the lad. ' From afar, from
near,' said I to him. ' What do you seek ?' said he. ' I seek
the Hermit,' said I to him. ' Wretch,' he said, ' you do not
know your way. You will not reach the Hermit to-night. But
camp between Butter-mount and Milk-lake, your face towards
Butter-mount and your back towards Cheese-mount, at the foot
of the Tree of Cream, in the Trenches of the Round Dish (Altar?),
in the Hollow of the Field of Wheat. Send messengers to the
chiefs of the Tribes of Food, that they may protect you against
the heavy waves of the Gravy, lest they drown you. They will
come to attend you on an evil journey,[1] as you are the first face
that appears in this isle to which you have come.'

"I encamped as I was told. It was not ' a night in thorns',
what with the white-meats. Early in the morning I arose and
went to the well of lard that was near me, and washed my hands,
and smoothed my hair. And I went to the well of *tremanta* that
was on the other side, and drank thirty draughts out of it, so that
my heart might not fail me on the road. And I set out on my
road until I saw before me Becenat the Smooth and Juicy, the
daughter of Betan the Monstrous Eater, the grandam of the
Tribes of Food, with her short garron of lard under her, with
two pleasant eyes of cheese in its head, with a seven-peaked
bridle of good white salt, with her mantle of corned beef, with
her girdle of salmon-roe, with a coif of the caul of a stomach on
her head, with a necklace from her neck, in which were seven
score seven beads of . . . . pigs' marrow.

---

[1] Here again *dóib* seems out of place.

"The queen bade me welcome, and asked tidings of me, and whither my way was. 'Towards the Hermit,' said I. 'You are not far,' said she. 'But I advise you not to utter any loud sound until you know the rule of the elders that are in the church.'

"There lay the church, in the glen between Butter-mount and Milk-lake, in the land of the Children of Early-eating. And thus it was : with four circles of palisades of old salted meat around it, without a wrinkle, without skin, with the lard of a choice boar on the top of every stake, with a porch of cheese, with a door of . . . . curds, with its *culuige* of butter, with its posts of lard, with its wedges of lard, with its beetle of pudding, with its knocker of butter. I struck the knocker of butter against the door of curds, so that the two door-keepers came out, Hollowsides, the son of O'Eating, and Mulba, the son of Gullet, with their lardy . . . . .[1] However, I escaped between the door and the door-post. Then I saw the cleric tolling the . . . . bell on the cold . . . ., in which were seventeen measures of English salt in one pure-white mass—that was the tongue of the bell. And I saw the stone-dyke leading from one cleric's house to another. This is the sort of stone dyke that was there : every wheaten cake would grow together with another, after having been strewn with fine salt and honey. Then I saw the wooden church. Boards of flitches of seven-year-old boar were the rafters of the church, with props of old cheese, with tiles of fat, with domes of lard, with an altar of fat in its west. And I saw the chief cleric, even the chief prophet, coming out of the house in front of the church, with his crown of twenty-seven fair butter-lumps on the top of his head, with seventeen ridges of bunches of genuine leek on the top of his crown.

"Then I said to him :

"'Bless us, O cleric,'" etc., as on p. 32,14—p. 34, 10. "The way in which the cleric came out was on a horse of old salted meat, with hoofs of carrots," etc., p. 88, 17—p. 90, 5. "With his trousers of pot-meat round his legs, with his shoes made of a hind-quarter, with Táin Bó Cúailgne and Bruiden Dá Derga in the right shoe, and Tochmarc Etaine and Tochmarc Emire in the left.

---

[1] Here I omit a sentence which I understand but partly.

" 'A prayer for me, O cleric !' I said to him. Then he said : Be thou under the safeguard of good food, O wretch !' said he ; under the protection of good drink, under the guardianship of old bacon ! Whence do you come ?' said he.

" 'I come, O noble man, from afar, to be cured from the insupportable sickness that accompanies me.' 'What sickness is it ?' said the Wizard Doctor. 'It is easily told,' said Mac C., 'greed with its subdivisions, even great thirst of drinking, juice and relish, feeding, great feeding, with the greed of a hound, with the appetite of a horse.' 'O wretch,' said the Wizard Doctor, 'that meal is not greater than what a child of one month would eat in this island, and would remain here till it grew a withered old man. Small is your intention of destroying food. It is letting a hound at a deer, it is a saddle on a colt, a bitch on a fox, talking to a foolish person, a cry against . . . ., a kiss to a palsied head, music to the deaf, a secret to a lewd jealous woman, a hand against a stream, riding on an ant, an arrow against a stone pillar, a fist grasping smoke, a withe around sand, beating an old skull, gathering honey from the roots of a yew-tree, warming in the devil's kiln, seeking butter in a dog's kennel, seeking wool of a goat, setting in order a house full of holes, O wretch, O Mac Conglinne, for you to come to this island to destroy food. Hunger has closed up your entrails. But I will give you a cure, if you feel any trouble.'

" 'What cure is it ?' said Mac C. 'Not hard to tell. Go to-night without food wherever you may be. Rise early to-morrow. Let a fire be kindled, of withered flaming branch-wood, on which colts drop dung on the top of the hill-side. Let a garment be spread out on the north side of the fire. Let a quick, white-toothed, white-handed, fine-breasted, fair-thighed woman give thee thy thrice nine morsels of sweet tasty food, each morsel as big as the egg of a heath-fowl. Let her give thee thy thrice nine draught with every morsel. The disease that will seize thee from it, except loose bowels, I will cure it.' 'What is your name ?' said Mac C. 'Not hard to tell,' said the Wizard Doctor. " Wheatlet, son of Milklet," etc., as on p. 78, 1—p. 80, 16.

" The cleric sang his paternoster for me, and put a gospel ound my neck, a gospel of the shoulder-bit of old bacon, without a wrinkle, without skin about it, with its crystal of brown boiled sausage around it, with its point of lard on it, and said :

" Be thou under the protection of smooth juicy bacon ! Be thou under the protection of hard yellow-backed cream ! of the pannikin from which infants are fed ! of the great lard of wethers ! of the strong heavy lard of boars ! The King, who has himself blessed these cakes to save thee from every danger, be thou in his safeguard, under his protection !'

"Then I arose to the chiefs of the Tribes of Food, viz., to Hand-upon-all—Dry Bread, to Broken-Brow—Butter-roll," etc., as on p. 98, 12. " To Thick Milk, Thin Milk, Milk that needs chewing, that makes the snore and bleat of a French wether in rushing down the gorge, so that the first draught says to the last draught: 'By the tablet of fat and by the service-set of lard that was on the breast of the cleric here ! though I be there, you shall not be here !' Those are the chiefs of the Tribes of Food."

Then he bent his hand with the two spits of food and put them to the lips of the king, who longed to swallow them, wood, food, and all. So he took them an arm's length from him, and the demon of gluttony jumped from his throat on to the spit, and jumped from the spit into the throat of the priest of Cork's gillie, who was by the cauldron on the floor of the house, and jumped from the throat of the gillie on to the spit again. Mac C. put the spit into the embers and upset the cauldron of the royal house on to the spit. The king was taken to a sleeping-chamber, and the great house was emptied and burnt afterwards. And the demon let forth three shrieks.

Next morning the king arose, and what he ate was no more but what a child of a month would eat. "Are you not thankful, noble man," said Mac C., "that I have cured you from the craving ?" "Art not thou thankful," said Cathal, "that thou art not crucified by me to-day ? And the service which thou didst for me, viz., carving my food, shall be thine for ever, and thou shalt have my dress and the ring of my hand, and the garment of my side and the value of a hundred of chattels." "Well, Cathal," said Manchín, "is it thus you take from me the man that slandered the Church ?" "Not thus shall it be," said Mac C., "but let the brehons be brought hither, and do you place a pledge of a hundred in the hands of Cathal, and I will place another hundred, and let the brehons say which of us deserves his honour-price." The brehons said that Mac C. deserved his fine and honour-price, for he had not made a satire, except saying that he would not eat the oats of Cork. " I do not wish my fine nor my honour-price," said Mac C., " but the cloak which is in the church." " You shall have it with my blessing," said Manchín. Hence said the jester, and his son, and his daughter :

" Manchín went," etc., as on p. 108, 29—p. 110, 12. Thus was Cathal Mac Finnguine cured from his craving, and Mac Conglinne honoured.


FINIS.

**abb**, an interjection of defiance. 85, 29. ab, ab! ab ab ó! *if you dare*, P. O'C. Cf. abú, the ancient Irish war-cry, O'R.

**accobrach** *desirous, greedy.* 75, 24.

**achad** m. *field.* 5, 4. t'úr ꝝ t'achud, LL. 193a, 10. gen. achaid aird, LL. 43a, 8. dat. ar cach achud, LL. 192b, 57. pl. nom cóic achaid Uisnig, LL. 295b, 32.

**achucat** *towards thee.* 119, 10.

**adastar** *halter.* 81, 3. Rev. Celt. xi, 493. Laws i, p. 124, 14. 138, 37. Manx cistyr.

**adúaid** (perf.) *he ate.* 25, 6. Wind. s. v. duad. opund di*du* atuaid Eua in uball sin, LBr. 111a, 18. atúatár, LU. 34a, 5.

**áel** (dissyllabic) m. *fleshfork.* achel 39, 18. int áel a!-lus in bíd, LL. 300a, 49. aiel ꝝ caire, Laws I. 122, 13. áel co m-bennaib braine, LL. 300b. gen. fri búim n-ácla, LL. 300b, 24. beim n-aeóil, ib. 46.

**áer** f. *satire.* 9, 5. 21, 7. gen. áire 115, 26, 27. de gaaib úire ꝝ écnaig, LL. 81a. dat. áir 45, 28. acc. áir 87, 10.

**ácraim** *I satirise.* 9, 3.

**agfind** 122, 33, leg. dagfhind? Or = aig-fhind *as white as ice.* trí chét da chrud cach elgga, síat aigfhinda óidergga, LL. 27a, 25.

**aicíd** *sickness, distemper, disease; a sharp ache, pain or stitch, pang,* P. O'C. gach tinneas agus aicíd dá leanann síol Adhaimh, Hardiman I. 18. pl. gen. na n-aicidi 83, 31; but see the note. Manx cighid.

**aicsid** m. *observer.* 97, 20.

**aigen** *paten, pan.* oighen gl. patena, Ir. Gl. 86. gen. aigin 83, 7.

**aignén** *a small paten, pannikin.* 127, 6.

**ail** f. *stone, rock.* Stokes, Metr. Gl. acc. darsin oilig cloiche, LBr. 126b, 23. pl. acc. ailcchu 5, 6. Hence ailchide *stony,* LBr. 203a, 17.

**áil** *asking, seeking, request.* a áil, LL. 266a, 27. pl. gen. ail 49, 8.

**ainmne** f. *patience*. Atk. LU. 118a, 20. LL. 343a. LBr. 261a, 42.

**ainmnetach** *patient*. Atk. Wb. 26b, 7. LL. 147b, 31. Alex. 839.

**ainmnidach** cach gaeth, Aibidil Cuigni.

**airecal** *apartment*. 128, 12. gen. airicuil, Ann. Ulst. 809, 837 From Lat. oraculum.

**airech** .i. ech imchuir, H. 3, 18, p. 650a. 79, 23.

**airerda** *delightful, pleasant*. 81, 17. 101, 23. taige ardda airerda, LL. 298b, 23.

**airerdacht** *delight, pleasure*. 101, 22. Cf. airuras : is crich bidbad so ꝛ ni faidchi airurais, LL. 66b, 3. aururas, LL. 162b, 10.

**airigid** f. *honorific portion*. Wind. gl. delibatio, Wb. 5b, 23. Ir. Texte ii, 1, p. 173, 4. pl. airigthe bíd ꝛ lenna, LL. 56b. 109b, 40. 253b, 47. Mer. Uil. 121.

**air-límaim** *I file, polish*. 77, 3. Cf. ic límad a lorgfertas, Cath Catharda.

**airmed** *measure*. Stokes, *Lires*, 1. 2921. pl. nom. airmedæ 124, 20.

**airne** *sloe*. gen. leth ind airne, Rev. Celt. viii, 57, n. 10. pl. nom. na háirni a hEblind, LL. 297a, 38. gen. a lán áirneadh, Tor. Dh. p. 124. dat. d'airnib 124, 20. M. airn. W. eiryn (en). Airnechán, a diminutive of airnech *sloey*. 77, 20.

**air-shlíab** n. *mountain-side*. 95, 24. 125, 35. Hy. 5, 11. airm i n-adnacht 'sint aurshléib, LL. 198b, 34.

**airtecul** m. *article*. 49, 24. From Lat. articulus.

**aisc** *gift*. pl. gen. aisc 49, 8.

**aisec** *restitution, delivery*. Tog. Tr. Ind. Trip. Life 12, 18. 434, 24. assec, LL. 162a, 13. 73, 24. fria aisec 43, 3. fria aisic beó *to restore him alive*, 3 Fragm. 36, 2. Hence aiscim *I restore :* aiscis a mac do Diarmait, LL. 358, marg. sup.

**aislinge** f. *vision*. 65, 26. as í sin an aislinge. Moy Leana, p. 6, 21. do breith breithe na haislinge, ib. 14. M. ashlins.

**áith** f. *kiln*. gen. dat. for thírad i n-áith no loscud na hátha, LBr. 204b, 3. criathar atho gl. cribrum areale, Berne MS. 34a. condochaid issin áith, LL. 286a, 51. Laws i, 162, 23. Manx aie. W. odyn f.

**aithe** *retaliation*. 21, 5. O'Don. Suppl. gl. talio, Wb. 14c. gl. focnus, Karlsr. 42a. *revenge*, Trip. Life Ind. Tog. Tr. Ind. 45, 14. dá athe nó da dígail, LL. 91a, 6. fri hathi na n-gním, LBr. 72b.

**aithindlat** *washing-tub*. 11, 25. Echtra Nerai, 37.

**alaig** 123, 19, l. g. cluid ꝛ

allsmand *knot, bead.* allsmaidhn for allshnaidhm, by metathesis,
*a large or clumsy knot,* P. O'C. pl. nom. allsmaind 39, 10.

ammaig *into the house;* Germ. *hinein.* 91, 5. LL. 286b, 30.
287a, 51. Salt. 2575.

ana m. *plenty.* 55, 14. Stokes, Metr. Gl. inna n-anæ gl. opum,
Ml. 28a, 3. Ana ⁊ Indmas ⁊ Brugus a trí n-dúine, LL. 30d, 62.
*bounty?* 97, 7. orddan ⁊ ana, LL. 294a, 18.

an-amail *incomparable.* 83, 19.

an-fíal *shameless.* 87, 7. ar in galar n-anfial n-olc, Chalcidius
68b.

annland *anything eaten with bread, opsonium, 'kitchen'.* 15, 26.
LL. 285a, 48. LBr. 9b, 15, 17. pl. nom. andlaind 99, 7. W.
enllyn.

antaigthech? 125, 11.

antem 83, 19 ; for an-timm *not feeble?*

apaig *ripe.* Asc. Trip. Life Ind. LBr. 133a, 1. cnuas abbaig,
LL. 206a, 41. metaph. intan as apaig fuil námat do thesin
di, LU. 95b, 7. pl. aipchi 124, 21. is ann ba háibche mesa ⁊
toirthe, Bk. of Fermoy, 29a. Manx appee.

áru f. *kidney.* gen. arand 33, 21. pl. nom. na hairne toile,
Laws III. 354, 16. dat. cusna hairnib gl. cum renibus, Gild
Lor. 175. Manx aarey. W. aren f.

aradain shróin *the reins of a bridle,* P. O'C. acc. aradnu 81, 5.
rogabastár ćsi astuda a ech ina thuasri .i. aradna a ech, LU.
79a, 15.

arba *corn.* Old Ir. arbc n. gen. Ind. arbc, Wb. 10d, 6. cacha
orbaind 99, 6. pl. nom. orbaind 99, 3. acc. na harbhanna,
O'R. Ir. Gl. 213. Manx arroo.

ard-choire *a high cauldron.* 39, 17.

ard-gabáil *lifting up high.* 9, 25. 63, 29.

ármide adj. *numeral.* 49, 24.

arráir *last night.* 117, 39. 118, 4. LL. 59, 11. irráir LU. 58b,
11. aráir 67, 10. 69, 11. 71, 6. LL. 298a, 6. arræer, Rev.
Celt. x, 66, 1. arćir 19, 20. 39, 31. arćr 33, 2.

ass *milk.* deg-ass .i. loim, Rev. Celt. x, 50, 6. ass a máthar
atib, LL. 285b, 31. gen. aiss 39, 25. dat. d'ass 33, 29.

assa *shoe.* 69, 30. 125, 1. 3. da assa co foráib óir impu, LU.
55a, 41. pl. is ć nongćbad a assa imme LU. 5b, 39. dat.
assaib 89, 6. 124, 39.

atáim *I kindle.* 63, 5. 115, 13. 117, 20. ra addái tenid, LL.
287b. rohatád torc mórtheined, LL. 300b, 31. atáither torc
tened, LU. 87a, 13. ataifes. LL. 287b.

ath-érge *rising again.* 121, 38.

ath-gére f. *greed.* 81, 32.

ath-láech m. *an ex-layman.* 73, 15. Fel. p. iii. 10. LL.358, ma rg. pl. nom. adláig, Wb. 9c, 11.

**B.**

bacc (1) *hook.* pl. baic 63, 27. LL. 168b, 30. 329a, 39. (2) *bend.* 121, 38. go bac a tónai, go bac a dí ullend. Harl. 5280, fo. 66b. Cf. cu air-baccaib a dá ochsal, LL. 266b. W. bach.

bachall f. *crozier, staff.* Wind. nom. in bhachall sa, LBr. 278b, 74. gen. bachla, Ann. Ul. 910. dat. bachaill, 89, 30. acc. in m-bachaill, LBr. 177b.

báesach *capricious.* O'R. 125, 20.

bainne *drop.* 33, 17. 124, 24. banna 23, 23. 25, 19. 109, 5.

Bairgenach *cakey.* 77, 21. From bairgen f. *cake.*

baitsech *pool?* 85, 18. 119, 37. baisteach now means *rain.*

ballda *spotted, speckled.* 33, 23.

banamail *womanly.* 97, 4.

bán-bíad m. *white-meat.* 9, 14. 15. See note.

band *motion, movement.* 79, 9. banu .i. gach cumhsgugadh O'Cl.

bán-méth *white-fat.* gen. f. bánméthi, 89, 27.

barr *bar?* 119, 2.

barrach *topped.* 69, 15.

barr-bind *sweet-crested.* 7, 26. barr-chorcra *purple-topped.* 39, 2.

basc-mell *a chain or necklace of round balls or globes.* 122, 36. Cf. Corm. p. 7.

belach m. *pass, passage.* gen. belaig 85, 24. dat. 119, 20. oc beluch da liac, LU. 39a, 38. dar belach Mara Rúaid, LL. 134a. pl. acc. belgi, Alex. 206. dat. for bernadaib ⁊ belglb, LL. 93a. 93b.

beladach? gen. beladaigh 122, 16.

belaiche 37, 30 ; for belaide?

belaide *juicy.* 81, 20, 24. 85, 19. 99, 27. belathi 77, 8. 87, 15. Cf. beólaide, LU. 85a, 29. 113a, 38. From beoil.

bend f. *the top or tip of a cloak.* 65, 2.

bendach *peaked.* 35, 7. Trip. Life, 34, 10.

beochail, glossed by beoil *meat-juice,* 71, 13. 119, 10. beochoil 83, 20. gen. beochla 83, 23.

beochlaide *juicy.* 85, 11. 89, 29. 91, 2. 119, 31.

bcoil *meat juice*. Stokes, *Lires*, Ind. LU. 12a, 33. gen. bcla
85, 19. 119, 10. 20. dat. beoil 124, 38.
bcór f. *heer*. gen. beóiri 33, 17. beóri 37, 25. From Old Norse
bjór n.
bertaim *I hurl ; draw*. berdais 65, 5. bertais, Macgním. Finn
24. bertis-seom co cloich conid romarb, LU. 675, 36.
bilech *covered with ancient trees*. 69, 15. LU. 134b, 21.
bille *boss, stud*. 89, 13.
binit *rennet*. dognither gruthrach dóib, acht ni théit binit ind,
LBr. 9. Beuntraige .i. binit-ríge .i. de millsen dliges rí Caissil
díb indsin, Corm. p. 7. ib. p.
bíthe *female, effeminate*. O'Cl. 35, 4. Salt. 5814.
bladach *famous, glorious*. 118, 10. ropad bl. a dígail, LL. 258a,
2. uli Ulaid ollbladacha, ib. 64a.
bladmar *famous*. 35, 1. LL. 157a, 4.
blassachtach f. *smacking the lips*. 47, 12.
blasta *tasty*. 37, 26. 77, 6.
bláthach f. *buttermilk*. Wind. gen. bláithche 33, 16. dat.
blathaig, LBr. 11a, 4.
blén (1) *groin*. Wind. (2) *a creek, a hollow or curved place*.
O'Don. Suppl. Joyce, ii, p. 258. dat. i m-blenai 122, 14, 22.
Blichtucán, a diminutive formed from blicht *milk*. 77, 23.
blonoc f. *lard*. 87, 15. blonag 79, 10. gen. bloince 33, 13.
blonci 37, 36. blongi 85, 12. dat. blonaig 67, 24. pl. n.
blonoca, LBr. 9. blongi 81, 24. dat. blongib 81, 26. 83, 24.
W. bloneg. Manx blennic, blonnic.
bocc m. *buck*. 79, 24. LL. 116, marg. Trip. Life, p. 466, 13.
W. bwch.
bodar-usce *stagnant* (lit. *deaf*) *water*. 19, 11. 55, 6. Cf. bodar-
sháith d'usci 17, 24.
boinne .i. blaithgel, Egerton 90, fo. 17a, 1. 33, 18.
bolcach *bubbling*. 99, 26. 101, 10.
bolcsón *middle, midst*. boilsceán O'R. See bolgán. cutruma
for bolcsón 11, 2.
bolcumm m. *a sip, mouthful*. 101, 12. 13, Ir. Texte ii, p. 126.
gen. bolgaim 101, 6. gen. ac ól trí m-bolgama, 3 Fragm. p. 12.
bolgán (1) .i. builgsean no meadhon *the mean or midst, bulge,
belly of anything, centre, middle*, P. O'C. rogab nathraig
m-bí ar bolgán ina glaic, Cath Catharda. of a spear, LL. 80b, 25.
a barr trinna bolgan, Bk. of Fen. 194, 5. (2) *midriff*, O'R.
gen. bolgáin 35, 4.

bolg-shliss *middle, midst* ? 63, 9.

borr *a bunch, knob, swelling; puffed, bloated, swelled*, P. O'C.
in tond baeth borr, LL. 88b, 41. *proud*, Salt. Ind. Comp.
borr-óclaech, LU. 92b, 17. borr-chroth f. 33, 16. borr-thorad
n. 33, 14. metaph. máthair Chonchobair, in borrthoraid rath-
mair réil, LL. 138a, 15.

borrach f. *bunch.* dat. borraig 123, 32.

bóthar m. *a made road.* dat. 'sin bothur eter dá mag, LL. 193a,
4 (rhymes with tóchur).

brá f. *eyebrow.* 97, 11. dí broí duba, LU. 55a, 43.

brafad *twinkling, winking.* brafud 101, 4. See Rev. Celt. x,
p. 57, n. 2. la brafad n-oenúaire, LU. 34b, 7.

bragitóracht *farting.* 43, 27. From bragitóir m. *farter, a kind
of buffoon.* pl. n. braigetóri, LL. 29. Cf. cáinte ᴊ braigire, ib.
fuirseoraigh .i. doníad an fhuirseoracht asa m-béalaibh,
br[a]igedoiri .i. doníad in bruigedóracht asa tónaib, II. 2. 16,
col. 936. Petrie, *Tara*, pp. 179, 180.

braich *malt.* Wind. gen. bracha, Stokes, *Lives*, l. 2921.

braichlis, from braich, *wort of ale*, P. O'C. 37, 27. Laws ii,
p. 242, 12, where it is translated *mash.*

braine *prow.* 85, 11. Wind. Rev. Celt. x, p. 80, 11. 92, 6. inna
braine na bárce, LU. 85b, 33. for braine in churaig, LL. 108a.
*front, edge :* álaind do brúach, do braine (of a dún), LL. 193a.
37. áel co m-bennaib braine, LL. 300a, 47.

brainech *leading ; leader, chief.* 79, 24. Cf. brainech *proreta*,
Ir. Gl. p. 147.

braissech f. (1) *kale, colewort.* (2) *potherbs, pottage*, P. O'C. *ka'e*
Scotice. Stokes, *Lives*, Ind. LBr. 9b, 15. gen. braisce 35, 4.
69, 3. 79, 12. oc bein nenntai dochum braisce, Fél. p. c, 11.
dat. braisig 87, 30. W. bresych, from Lat. brassica.

brass-longthech *eating mightily.* 77, 10.

bratach *mantled.* 97, 5.

brat-gel *with a white mantle.* gen. f. bratgile 37, 34. do brú
Banba bratgile, LL. 34a, 32.

brecc-bán *speckled white*, 33, 14.

brechtán *custard.* P. O'C. 33, 16. 79, 4. gen. brechtáir. 67, 22.
123, 24. Cf.

> Carna, cuirm, cnóimess cadla,
> it ó ada na samna,

M

tendál for cnucc co n-grinne,
bláthach, brechtán úrimme.

Rawl. B. 512, fo. 98b, 2, and Harl. 5280, fo. 41a.

breó f. *flame.* gen. inna briad gránna gl. pirae dirae, Goid. p. 65, 8. dat. briaid 105, 3.

Bretnach *Welsh.* 45, 16. 111, 14. ra táeb ech m-Bretnach m-blathmín, LL. 49b, 6.

bretnusach *wearing a brooch.* 97, 5.

bricnói ? 121, 36. 123, 9.

briscén *mash ?* 99, 20. P. O'C. has briscín, dimin. of briosca, *a small haunch or buttock, the arse or breech.*

brocóit f. *malt liquor, bragget.* Corm. p. 6. gen. brócoti 33, 17. 37, 25. 89, 18. baeth briathra brócoite, LL. 203b, 32. See Stokes, *Linguistic Value,* p. 26.

broimnech f. *farting, cracking, bouncing,* P.O'C. dat. broimnig 73, 1. From broimm m. *fart.* broimm crúaid iar n-ithi arba i timnu anma Concluchair, LL. 285a, 50. Broimm, ni focul fand saide (the name of a jester) LL. 28a, 10. W. bram, Manx brem.

brothar-cert *a hairy rag.* 91, 8. Cf. bruth *the hair, beard, or down of the body ; fur, shag, rag* or *cloth ;* brothaire *one that has much hair or fur on,* P. O'C. brothairne *hair,* LL. 252b.

brothar-lumman f. *a hairy cloak.* 91, 8.

brothchán *pottage.* LL. 286b, 32. Mer. Uil. 280. LBr. 11a, 52. gen. brothcháin 33, 14. 99, 18.

brothrach *fried ?* 87, 15.

brothrach f. (1) *bed-cover.* acc. brothraig 115, 30. Alex. 873. ni bid tuigi no pell no brothrach no breccan no croicenn anmanna fui isin lebaid sin, Cath Catharda. LL. 144a, 36. 297a, 44. (2) *a royal garment.* Ir. Gl. 180. 124, 28. brothrach colluibnib finnaib im chechtar de, LL. 252b, 26.

brothrachán 91, 8. gl. sabribarra, Ir. Gl. 180. sarrabarra gl. esclavine (Ital. schiavina) *a pilgrim's cloak,* Ducange. Isid. Orig. xix, 23, uses the word for wide and long pantaloons (fluxa ac sinuosa).

Brucht-shalach *Dirty-belch.* 119, 23.

brusgarbán? 87, 22. brus *the cleaning or refuse of corn; small lopping of trees,* P. O'C. brusghaineamh or sbrusghaineamh *gravel or rough sand,* ib.

brút f. *brute.* pl. voc. a brúti 29, 20.

búaidrén *stirabout?* 33, 14.

búar *flux, diarrhœa.* 101, 20. buar .i. buinnech, ut est : buar
brucht broim .i. buinn[e]ach do beth ar in cáinti, O'Dav.
p. 61.

búarann f. *flux.* acc. búarainn 126, 3.

Búarannach *Flury.* 75, 7. 119, 23.

buinde *spouting, squirting forth; stream, wave.* 89, 18. *corruption flowing from an ulcer*, P. O'C. Hence buinnech
*diarrhœa ;* also *the dirty wool about a sheep's tail.*

bulbing *a cudgel?* 87, 22.

bunatta *original.* 13, 16. From bunad, W. bonedd *origin.*

bundraiss f. *bundrish,* an edible seaweed. gen. bundraisse 91, 1.

buptáid 85, 18. Cf. fubtad feirge, LL. 371a, 16. i fubtud cach
omnaig, Laws i, p. 174.

búraim *I roar, bellow.* 65, 23. dobúirestar amail tarb, Bk. of
Fermoy, p. 34b. bid amnas dombúrfet chucaib in damrad sa
Bretan ⁊ Alban, LL. 290b. bursit Ulaid, LL. 161a, 37.

## C.

cacc *dung.* gen. a chonu cacca 23, 25. 29, 20. Cf. W. cachgi
*coward.*

caccaim *cacco.* 95, 25. 125, 35. conid 'na chend cacait na huli
coin, LU. 117b, 32. cacfam i n-esaib ⁊ i n-inberaib in choigid,
Eg. 1782, fo. 32b, 2. LL. 117a, 10.

cadla *comely, graceful, beautiful, charming,* P. O'C. 69, 20. 79,
9. Fél. Ind. comharba cadlai Colaim, FM. 979. delm cadla,
LL. 35b. cadla cuuird, LL. 204a. cœmcadla uile, TB. Reg. 3
(Lec.) tír chadla, LL. 161a, 41. Salt. 5427, 5991.

cadla .i. caolán, *one of the small guts, chitterlings,* P. O'C. 69, 19.

cádus m. *honour, respect, reverence.* LL. 148a, 50. LBr. 140b,
9. gen. in chádais, LBr. 156b, 23. cádusach *venerable*, LBr.
149b.

cáemna *food, good cheer.* 93, 26. coemna Alex. 974. 982. 985.
ni thormailt biád no bronnud no cœmna no comlongud, LL.
192b, 17. cach coemna ⁊ cach airfitiud forsin talmain, LL.
279a, 8.

cainnenn f. *leek.* dobeir déra a suillb an fir au chaindenn

M 2

Rawl. B. 512, fo. 52b, 1.　gen. cainninde 33, 18.　dat. cainnind 39, 5.　89, 11.　W. cenin(en).

cáintecht f. *satirising.* 43, **26. 29.**　ba cáinti ar cáintecht .i. ar gcri ⁊ gorti ⁊ amaiusi, Rawl. B. 512, fo. 114b, 2.

cairde f. *respite, truce.* 29, 4.　35, 15.　cath can chardi, CCn. 7, " guitter cardi chlaidib úadib for Coinculaind," or Ailill, LU. 70b.　72b, 16.　conomraib cairte lat frim budin, LU. 67a, 39.　Cf. cairdigter gl. foederari, Ml. 126c.

cairre (pl.) *scabs, scald.* 114, 10. 17. 27.　115, 4.

caisel *a stone wall,* or *an earthen wall faced with stone.* 37, 10. maceria, Bk. of Arm.　gen. ic dénam caisil, Fél. acc. conderna caisiul caem cloch, Bk. of Fenagh, p. 124.　pl. n. caissle, Coimp. Concul. 2.　dat. eclas chruind eside co tri caslib impc, LBr. 157b.

cáith f. *chaff, husks.* bid caith cách .i. bid éttarbach, Harl. 5280, fo. 41b.　M. caih, W. coden.　Comp. síl-cháith.

caithfid *it behoves,* O'R.　rocaiter 87, 5.

calath m. *port, harbour.* 85, **22.** Tog. Tr. 852.

camm-rand m. *a quatrain made in contention.* 5, 3.　15, 24. 114, 14.　dorignius-sa camrand certchóir, LBr. 101 marg. inf. Rev. Celt. xii, p. 460.

cantaicc f. *canticle.* 13, **12.** Atk.　acc. rochansat immund ⁊ cantaicc lógmair dó, LBr. 177a, 31.

capall m. *horse.* 89, **15.** gen. capaill 114, **2.** M. cabbyl, W. ceffyl.　From Lat. caballus.

cappar *dom*. pl. n. cappair 123, **27.** sg. dat. isin capur airther-descertach, LBr. 278a, 44.　isin capor n-descertach aniar, ib. 53.　Cf. bend-chopar.

carrach *having an uneven surface,* Highl. 69, 17.　*mangy, bald.* tanig imbuile tairis-[s]im co n-derna carrach de, Mcgn. F. 7.

carr-matrad m. *a mangy cur.* 101, 14.　Cf. ba mellach cnámach carr-garb a druim, LL. 117b, 20.

cartaim *I send.* 5, 28.　rocartad, Fél. cii, 13.　rochart Find éseom for inrraid usci, LL. 208a.　I.L. 152b, 19.

cartaim *I cleanse.* cartad raite, cartad acnaig, Laws i, p. 122, 14.　cartfait clanna Iareoil dia cóille, dia clár, LL. 147a, 39. Comp. fo-chartad.

carthain *love.* 93, **26.**

casar *brooch.* dat. casair 124, **29.**

cass-draigen lit. *twisted thorn ; a fence.* 87, 14.

cáttu *respect.* 107, 26.

cel *death.* 23, 8. Salt. Ind. mithig dam-sa dul for cel, LU.
40a,39. cach ina cinaid cingid ar chel, Laws i, p. 10, 25.

célide *visit.* co m-buí for célidi occo, LU. 20b, 26. fer célide
*visitor.* 99, 21. áes célide *advenae,* Alex. 935.

cenbar *a chafer?* cenbar gl. caphia, Ir. Gl. 51. gen. cenbair
103, 22.

cend-fháelid *with exultant head.* 83, 27.

cend-ísel *low-headed.* 29, 22. a byname, Fél. p. lxxxv, 12.

cend-phart, lit. *head-piece.* (1) *the capital of a column,* Alex. 578
cenn-bart gl. capitulum, Sg. 47a, 5. epistilia .i. supermissa
cennbartæ columnarum, Reg. 215. (2) *introduction,* corthind-
scain in molad ⁊ rochan in cendport iartain, LBr. 238d, b, 50.
cennpurt 31, 19, 21. cennport, 35, 14. pl. nom. tairngire
remfhastini ⁊ cendphairt in sceóil, LL. 56b, 3.

ceó (1) *vapour, steam; mist.* 121, 33. 123, 15. acc. ciaig 63, 6.
117, 22. LU. 80a, 18. 19. (2) *milk.* 69, 4. Manx kay *butter,*
*cream of milk.*

ceppach f. *a plot of land laid out for tillage,* O'Don. Suppl.
Joyce, p. 220. acc. ceppaig 121, 33. LL. 285b, 41.

cerc f. *hen.* 101, 3. gen. circe 99, 22. M. kiark.

cernach *four-square, angular.* O'R. 75, 17. Cath Finntr. Ind.

cerrbaccán *carrot.* 39, 5. 99, 20. cerboccan 124, 18. gl. eruca,
Rev. ix, 232.

cert *a rag.* 91, 9. Laws i, p. 178, 2. hi certaib ⁊ lothraib, LL.
274b, 1. acc. na ceirte, ib. 11. Hence certán *a small rag.* LL.
283b, 50.

césad-chrand *passion-tree.* 29, 9.

cót-gnúisid m. *the first face.* 122, 17.

cethar-chossach *four-footed.* 127, 30.

cethir-doirsech *having four doors* or *apertures.* 63, 5.

cethir-druimnech *four-ridged.* 63, 5.

cethir-ochair *four-edged.* 75, 17. cetharochair 81, 31. Cf.
cethareochrach, Alex. 181.

cethir-scoltigde *four-cleft.* 63, 6.

cét-sherous *first love.* 3, 21. ros-car i cétshercas, LL. 152b, 18.

ó chíanaib *a while ago, just now.* 27, 3. Rev. Celt. x. 52, 19.
LU. 69a, 4. a chianaib, LL. 267a. There is a mod. dimin.
ó chianaibhín.

cicharan ?  99, 30.

cimmas f. *border, edge, rim.*  Corm. Tr. p. 31.  Tog. Tr. 1531.  LU. 79a, 44.  dat. chimais 55, 2.

cingir ?  99, 30.

cír f. *the crest of a fence.*  37, 34.  in chír draighin, Laws iv, p. 70, 26.  ib. 112, 15.  úas figi min ag urcomair círe draighin .i. ag dénam in fáil, O'Dav. p. 86, s. v. fenamain (from Laws iv, p. 114, 3).

cláraid *made of wooden boards.*  123, 26.  tech cláraid, LL. 254a, 1.  268a, 26.  268b, 21.  Tog. Tr. 1868.

cló-boss f. *the left palm.*  103, 15.

cló-lám f. *the left hand.*  53, 19.

clessemnach f. *playing, juggling.*  dat. clesemnaig 122, 6.

cleth f. *stake, rod.*  cleth cáirthind, LL. 35a, 27.  clethchur fiacal imma chend, LL. 34a, 38.  in cú araig do nómad cleth ón dorus, Laws iii, 412, 19.  gl. tignum, Ir. Gl. 485.

clethe (cinn) *the crown of the head.*  63, 4.  pl. dat. clethib, 93, 4.  Salt. na R. 5871.  a fírchlethe a chendmullaig, LU. 80a, 17.

clí *house-post,* fig. *prince.*  Salt. Ind.  ib. 7483.  33, 14.

clíab-galar *chest disease.*  99, 17.

clíath f. *the valve of a door* (made of wicker-work).  123, 18.

clith .i. clúda, ut est : rofeas cid dech édach, clith álainn étrum, O'Dav. p. 71.  29, 23.

clith .i. dlúth, *close, tight, compact,* P. O'C.  *sheltering, comfortable,*  im chót m-brat cungas clithetach, LU. 83b, 1.  inmain cathir is chlithrúaim, LL. 201b, 21.  W. clyd *sheltering, comfortable.*  Hence clithaigim *I shelter* : 'ca chlithugud int shotha sain, LL. 160b, 42.

clithmaire f. *shelter, comfort.*  71, 9.  119, 7,  Cf. W. clydrwydd.

cló *nail, pin, peg.*  O'R.  123, 21.  Let. clavus.

clochán *causeway.*  Wind. for clochánaib ┐ srátib, LBr. 156b, 15.  Trip. Life p. 458, 20.

cloch-drochat *stone-bridge, stone-dyke.*  123, 22, 23.  Sic leg. 91, 10.

cloicenn f. *skull.*  gen. cloicne 121, 37.  dat. cloicend 99, 1.

cluicín *a small bell.*  89, 25.  Alex. 81.  clucíne prainntige, LBr. 261b, 85.  LL. 267a, 36.  Manx cluigeen *handbell.*

clúmda *downy.*  119, 4.  Cf. clúmdaide, LL. 109b, 31.

clúm-derg *downy red.* 119, 4.

cnáim-fhíal lit. *bone-generous.* 35, 5.

cnám *gnawing.* 93, 27. for cnám na hemi, Corm. 30, 13.

cnó-mess *nut-crop.* . 35, 5.

cochlín *a small hood or cloak.* 109, 27.

cocnum *chewing.* 101, 11. 127, 30. Cath Finntr. Ind. Pass. part. coganti, LBr. 156a, 60. Comp. fás-ch. 116, 26.

cóel *rattling.* Ir. Texte iii, p. 195.

cóelach *rattling.* Stokes, *Lives*, Ind. 69, 6. eter chuallc ┐ chailach, LL. 198a, 20. Three Hom. p. 108, 5. ib. p. 76, 27. dorigned cró coelaig imme can conair ass, LBr. 238c, b, 30.

cóelán *entrails, tripe.* 69, 6. 91, 15. 99, 31. Manx colane.

coic m. *cook.* Rev. Celt. x, p. 82, 1. Stokes, *Lives*, Ind. gen. coca 93, 18. pl. acc. for coice ┐ bligre ┐ cuchtrori, LBr. 9b, 30.

coiclim *I spare.* 99, 3. inf. cen nech do chocill, LBr. 120a, 35. Stokes, *Lives*, Ind.

cóicthiges *fortnight.* cóicthiges ria Lugnasad, LL. 2a. cóicthiges for mís, LL. 23b, 5. gen. 29, 26. i cind cóicthigis ar mís, LL. 23b, 8. LU. 55a, 28. LL. 172b, 49.

coidlide adj. *made of hide* (codal). 9, 23.

coile-dírech *straight-bladed.* 53, 19.

coilech m. *cock.* 99, 22. pl. n. cailig fheda, LL. 227b, 44.

coimdetta adj. *dominicus.* 107, 4.

coin-tell *dog-whip.* Cf. tailm .i. toll-fhuaim .i. tobcim na n-iall, Corm. pl. nom. cointóill 107, 1.

coma f. (1) *gift, bribe.* 57, 21. Stokes, *Lives*, Ind. Tog. Tr. Ind. ragelta comada móra dó ar in comlond do dénam, LL. 81a. nochar gab si coma cruid, Hy Fiachr. p. 206, 13. (2) *condition.* ni maith cath can choma tind, LL. 203b, 5. ni ba coma acht cath mór mer, LL. 299a, 14. naiscset a coma fair. LBr. 188a, 13. acc. na gabaid comaid n-aile, ib. 20. pl. d. ar sámchomadaib sída, Magh Rath, 194, 19. gan beith fa chomadaib claena, ib. 120, 25.

com-aithech (1) *neighbour.* Wind. LL. 188b, 45. (2) *dweller.* 57, 11. 109, 17. 111, 13. *plebeian,* 3 Fragm. 202, 10.

comarc *consultation, council.* 27, 13. Comp. lúath-ch. 27, 12. W. cyfarch *address.*

com-berbad *boiling together.* 107, 15. W. cymmerwi.

comga, coimge *protection, support.* 111, 25. 123, 25. Crist dia

chomge, I.L. 201a, 60.　comde nimi núi, mo chomge is mo chri,
LL. 307a, 15.　mo chomla nach camm dom chomga ós mo
chind, LBr. 262b, 45.　do choimgi mo chuirp, ib. 47.　coimge
conaire, Moy Leana, p. 36.

bid comga cruid is cethra,

bid dín dogra *ocus* debtha, $\mathrm{p.}\ 3^{23}$ fo. 17a.

bricht comga, LU. 79a, 22.　celtar comga, ib. 79b, 20.

comgne .i. fis cach ríg robui i comamsir fria ceile .i. comgene,
H. 3. 18, p. 67.　.i. senchas, O'Dav. p. 62.　*synchronism, know-
ledge of universal history*, O'Don. Suppl. 33, 12. Trip. Life,
Ind.

com-longud *eating*.　ni thormailt biád no bronnud no cœmna no
c., LL. 192b, 17.　LBr. 108b, 70.

commur *meeting*.　7, 33.　Wind.　dar commur a chráis [chraes
Fcs.] ꝺ a bráget, LL. 108a, 30.　Commur na trí n-usce.　Hence
O'R.'s " vale".

comroircnech *erring, mistaken*.　29, 21.　isin sét cian fhota comroircnech sa, LBr. 118b.

comrorcu *error*. 13, 16. 91, 7. 57, 6.　comrurgu. i. sechrán,
H. 3, 18.　Alex. 584.　acc. comrorcuin, Ml. 56b. 9.　tre
comrorgain, O'Dav. p. 124.　gen. roásaiset driessi inna
senchomrorcan tar sodin, Ml. Goid. p. 31.

com-scísachtach f, *wagging together?* 49, 9.

com-thromm *equipoised*. 11, 1. Stokes. *Lives*, Ind.　gl. par,
Ir. Gl. 960.　Cf. ib. 903.

congab f. *seizing, taking*. 35, 27.　nucu n-olc in chongab chruid,
LL. 296a, 21.　dat. 'na congaib ágmair fhassaid, LL. 192a, 47.

con-gninim *I recognise*.　connar cungain nem na talmain, FB.
39.　conná cungnétar nem na talmain, LL. 277b, 27.　coná
cuingenmair nem na talmain 121, 34.　Cf. comgne.

conicim *I can*.　cuinges 113, 12.　s-aor. nir choem, 105, 5.

conludim *I go*. 89, 3.

cop-chaille f. *a woman's coif or kerchief;* also *a priest's cope or
cowl*. 122, 35.　in chopchaille .i. bréit, LBr. 158b.

corann f. *crown, wreath, garland*. gen. coirne 123, 33.　dat.
coraind 89, 12. 123, 31.　acc. a m-bith cen chorin gl. non
uelato capite, Wb. 11c, 10.　pl. acc. coirnea gl. coronas, Bk. of
Arm. 180a, 2.　dat. cornib 89, 10.　Hence coirnigim *I tonsure*,

**3 Fragm.** p. 114, 2. 4. From Lat. córona, while coróin is from coróna. Cf. W. coryn and coron.

corcca *oats.* 15, 1. 2. 19. 17, 5, 6. 35, 2. W. ceirch. M. corkey *oaten.*

coréu *a small caldron.* 99, 9. coirin P. O'C. Comp. lon-ch. 77, 13.

corgas *lent.* gen. corgais 99, 22. in dominicis in chorgais máir, LBr. 9b, 7. dat. hi corgus erraig, LL. 285b. samchorgus nó gemchorgus, LBr. 261b, 74. Manx kargys. From Lat. quadragesima.

corr (1) *round.* cnoe corra códergga, LL. 200a, 15. dá chíoch chorra chruinn bhánmhilis chúmbra bhreágh, Hardiman i, p. 355. corrchíchech, LL. 210b. im Crúachain cuirr, LU. 38b, 3. Compar. cuirrither[1] hog luin a dí shúil, Corm. p. 36, 27. bátir cuirridir og (viz. their eyes), LL. 252b, 20. (2) *pointed.* 9, 23. 89, 1. marbthar do chorrlannaib, Hy Fiachr. p. 210. oide Conaill na corrshleg, Bk. of Fenagh, p. 322, 18. ar los chloidim chuirr, ib. 400, 11. legga corra clochbána, ib. p. 188, 21. corrchend *some sea-monster,* LL. 172b, 10. na corrgabla siúil *a pointed fork,* LL. 172b, 26. Compar. cuirre iná córr auróchala a dhá grúad, Corm. p. 36, 29.

corr f. *a pit of water.* gen. na cuirre 55, 6.

corr f. *any bird of the crane or heron kind; also a stork or bittour,* P. O'C. gen. cuirre 51, 28. 99, 8.

corrach *unsteady.* 29, 21. Atk. Cath Finntr. Ind. collud c., Ir. Texte ii, 2, p. 128, 164. ib. p. 180. suidhe an athar a dtigh a mhic, suidhe cruinn corrach, Ulst. proverb.

corrán *hook, sickle.* = baccán, Mart. Don. p. 318, 3. LBr. 191a, 13. Fél. p. cxlvi. pl. acc. corránu 63, 27.

corr-míl *gnat.* 85, 7. LU. 98b, 12. Cf. Atk. s. v. míltóg. corr *a worm, reptile; fly, insect.* corrchuil *a fly,* P. O'C.

cosnamaid m. *contender, defender.* 5, 1. 51, 11. Comp. ard-ch, 49, 3.

coss-lúthmar *with vigorous feet.* 83, 27.

cráebach *loppings or branches of trees, brushwood or firewood,* P. O'C. Comp. glas-craibech 115, 13. *copse-wood:* cráibech 121,

---

[1] Windisch, Gramm. § 72, and Wörterb. p. 455, puts this with cruind *round,* wrongly, I think.

**32.** adj. *branchy, curly.* uói monga crœbacha cassa foraib LU. 94, 8.

cráibechán *pottage.* 35, 3. 81, 12. 83, 5, 7. craoibechan .i. caro bechan .i. feoil min no bec, no caro dona bechanuib .i. no dona lenmaib, quia est bechan bec no lenum, H. 3. 18. tria craes romill Iesu a prímgendacht ⁊ rorec [ri]a bráthair re hIacob ar craibechan, Harl. 5280, fo. 41a.

crebar *a kind of fly called a blood-sucker,* P. O'C. 85, 7. crebhar gl. lucifugia, Ir. Gl. 201. pl. n. crebair, Stokes, *Lives,* 1. 3652. W. crüyr.

credb *shrinking, withering.* crcadhbh .i. creapall no ceangal, P. O'C. gen. credba 93, 25. Cf. W. crebach *shrunk, withered.* fidbæ .i. nemuech rogab credbad, H. 3. 18, p. 81.

críathar m. (1) *sieve.* gen. cróthir 73, 3. (2) *honey-comb* 61, 29. Manx creear.

cristall f. *crystal.* 127, 2. But cf. criostal .i. iris, *a suspender whereby anything hangs,* P. O'C.

cross f. *cross.* gen. crossi 101, 1 (market place?).

croth f. *cream.* gen. crothi 83, 3. croithe 122, 13, 21. Comp. borr-chroth 33, 16. sen-chroth 37, 21.

crúad-charric f. *a hard stone.* 85, 20. in charruc, LBr. 157b, 53. carrac, LL. 278a, 9. acc. for carraic, LU. 25a, 29. pl. nom. carrce, LU. 80b, 5. acc. cairrgge, LL. 358 marg.

Cruind-mías f. *Round Dish.* gen. -móse 122, 13. 22.

cúachán *a small bowl* or *basin.* 15, 1. 17, 5. 6. 115, 14. W. cogan.

cúachán *oats.* .i. corcca 15, 1. 45, 10.

cúadh .i. innisin, O'Cl. 125, 19=cúadh do bhaos .i. sgél d' innisin do duine bhaoth, O'Cl.

cúarán (and cúaróg) f. *a shoe made of untanned leather ; also a sock,* P. O'C. 9, 23. 11, 25. 26. 27. asaite imthecht a tribuis ⁊ a cuarain imc, O'Dav. p. 96, s. v. hais.

> fada la nech mar atú,
> can fer cumainn acht a chú,
> gan gilla acht a láma,
> gan cúach acht a chúaróna.

Harl. 5280, fo. 46b, marg.

cuchtair *kitchen.* 91, 17. 24. Stokes, *Lives,* Ind. cochtair gl.

coquina, Ir. Gl. 283. Cf. cuchtartech, LL. 263a, 38. cuchtróir *kitchener*, LBr. 9b, 31.

cuil f. *fly, gnat.* 85, 6. 119, 12. Fel. p. clix, 2. nosblathiged connatairised cuil forru, LL. 68a, 45. tri cuile, L.Br. 108b, 68.

cuitig f. *portion, ration of food.* 13, 27. 31. 114, 3. caith do chutig, LBr. 151a, 34. ósna lothraib asa tomlitis na coerig a cuitig, ib. 114a, 23. Comp. prím-ch. 45, 8.

culaige *some part of a door*, 123, 10.

cúl-buide *yellow-backed.* 83, 3. 127, 5.

cumgaise *help?* 125, 29. 31. roling in fúir demnachda .i. Tesiphone i cumgaise a chride "entered the cavity (?) of his heart," O'Don. Fled D. na n-G., p. 32.

cummaim *I shape.* 9, 22. 31, 19. Stokes, *Lives*, Ind. rochum in n-Gaedilg asna dá bérla sechtmogat, LL. 2a. a fhir do-chumm in cruinde, Gael. Journ. iv, p. 42. in cháin sin racummad and, LL. 206a, 6. cumsat ratha, LL. 162b, 50. M. cummym.

cummascaigim *I mix.* 91, 23. Cf. ro cumaiscthea na bérlai, LU. p. 16, 14. cumaiscther for grutin, LBr. 9b, 27.

cumra *fragrant.* Stokes, *Lives*, Ind. 101, 2. 124, 20. Goid. p. 180, 16. i n-aballgort chumrai, LL. 253b, 33. Comp. fír ch. 39, 1. 109, 4.

cundrad *contract, bargain.* cach cunrad cen dichell, Aibidil Cuigni. dlegar cuudradh do chomall, Bk. of Fermoy p. 81. gen. cundartha 73, 28. M. coonrey.

cunnid m. *support, sustenance.* 99, 22. la cunnid comairle, LL. 119b, 18. ba hé cunnid na cúane, LL. 273a, 32. Muridach mac Domnaill daith, Cunnid in chomlaind chóicdaig, LL. 185a, 9.

curchán, curchín *a small coracle.* 35, 23. 119, 31.

## D.

dag-choic m. *a good cook.* 93, 18.

dáig co *in order that.* 83, 11. Atk.

dál báis *a meeting with death.* 29, 26. 81, 11. darsin n-dáil i tiag-sa .i. dál báis, LL. 272b, 30. Cf. ni rach i coinne in báis, LBr. 144a, 50. *Sentence of death:* tucsat na dúle dáil báis do Loegaire, LL. 299b, 40. tucsat dáil báis forsin ríg, ib. 45.

dó f. *smoke.* 95, 27. dé do thig, LBr. 156a, 51. acc. diaid 63, 6. 117, 21.

dó-broth *God's doom.* Wind. mo d. 15, 16. dom d. 45, 18. 67, 3. darom d. 61, 3. dar mo d. 83, 9. debrad ! is crúaid do chomlond, LL. 87b. debrad ! Stokes, *Lives,* l. 2246.

decaid *a set of ten psalms.* 13, 12. From Lat. decad-.

dénmus *making.* 9, 19. gen. denmusa, Bk. of Fen. 118.

deóin *free will, pleasure, consent.* 29, 19. dia n-deóin, LL. 193a, 46. a deonaib Dé, LL. 164b, 18.

deol *sucking.* 71, 28. oc a diul, Fól. p. xxxiv. M. dy yiole.

dergnatach *full of fleas.* 11, 19.

dermitnech *irreverent.* 105, 9.

dethach f. *smoke.* Cath Finntr. Ind. is dethach do muchad, LU. 32, 15. dat. dethaig 55, 3. Manx jaagh.

dethbir *hasty.* 43, 14.

díbad *property of a deceased person, legacy.* Wind. 71, 24. Laws ii, p. 406. *spoil :* ic roind in fhuidb ⁊ in díbaid persecda, Alex. 377.

díbe f. *denying, refusing ; niggardliness.* 95, 7. ar dibe ⁊ ar dochill, LL. 117a, 43. tria duba ⁊ díbi, LL. 188b, 33. ib. 121a, 19. 188a, 2. gen. na díbe 127, 14.

dí-chonnercle f. *uncharitableness.* 95, 3. díchondirclech *merciless,* Alex. 311.

dí-chumce f. *incapacity.* 75, 13.

didiu, didu *however.* Written out :

> marbais tricha díb didu,
> rofácaib 'na chróligu.    LL. 202a, 18.

O rachruthaig didu uili anmand in talman do criaid, LLec. 529b. ronfuid didu Dia súan sadail sámchotalta i n-Adam, ib. atchondairc didu in ben corbo maith in crand re thomaltos, ib. 530a, etc.

dí-fhrecra *unanswerable, unspeakable, enormous.* dirccera 63, 2. Salt. Ind.

dírinn *dropping.* 116, 20. dirain .i. geinomain (?), ut est : tobair imda ag dirain asin tobur sin, Harl. 5280, fo. 42a. diorain .i. snighe no sileadh feart[h]ana no fleachaidh, O'Cl. Salt. Ind.

dísert n. *hermitage.* dísert .i. desertum .i. derechtae, H. 3. 18. dísiurt 87, 12. a n-dísert sa, LU. 15b, 8. gen. dísirt 119, 21.

120, 2. díserta 75, 27. 85, 25. dat. dísiurt, LU. 15b, 2. W. diserth *desert*. From Lat. desertum.

dísertach m. *hermit*. 122, 9, 10. Reeves, Adamnán, p. 366.

díthaigim *I destroy*. inf. díthugud 125, 18. 28. LU. 76a, 23.

díthait *repast*. cotormalt feiss ⁊ díthait, LL. 59b, 6. gen. díthata. 75, 20, 21.

dlai f. *a wisp (of thatch)*. 53, 4. dásachtaig .i. fo tabair dlai fulla, Laws iii, p. 12, 2. In Arann bun-dlaoi or bun-tshop means the eaves of a house. feib raléiced dlai omthanaig ar aithi ⁊ ótrummi, LL. 267a. (sic leg. with the Edinburgh copy) *as quickly and lightly as he would fling a thistle wisp*.

doccair *troublesome, uneasy, miserable*. Atk. Comp. doccrn 17, 18. Used as a noun : cen doccair, LL. 197b, 34. Oppos. soccair.

dochosail ? 95, 21.

dochta *tightness, closeness, strictness, narrowness, niggardliness*. 95, 3. bríg cen docta, LL. 2a. From docht *tight, close, niggardly*. ciarbo docht for rúne in rí .i. ciarbo balb remi sin, LU. 9a. Three Shafts, Ind. Bk. of Fen. p. 240.

dóennacht *humanity, kindness*. 49, 13.

dóethain *sufficiency*. 114, 18. 115, 29. LU. 25b, 20. Mer. Uil. Ind.

do-fil *he comes*. 5, 5. dofuil in fer chucut, LU. 20b, 14. Stokes, *Lives*, l. 499. frithalid na firu dosfil far n-dochum, LL. 116b, 7.

do-fochellim *I promise*. doruachell 5, 23. Ann. Ulst. 963.

doichell f. *grudging, inhospitality*. 95, 3. Rev. Celt. v, p. 243, gen. doichle 97, 8. LL. 117a, 42. rodochell, LL. 188a, 2. Oppos. sochell, LL. 345b. sochall, Trip. Life, 149, 9 ; whence soichlech and soichlige f., LL. 343c.

do-idnaim *I give*. dobérthar in talam duit doidnais ar t' anmain, LU. 116b, 4. tidnais 49, 21. tidnus 71, 18.

doinmech *unfortunate, unhappy*. 9, 9. doinmecha gl. adversa, Ml. 32b, 1. doinmech cach daidbir, Aibidil Cuigni. Hence doinmige f., Alex. 640.

doirrseóir m. *doorkeeper*. 89, 4. 91, 5. 123, 14. pl. acc. dorscori, LL. 51b, 4. Hence dorscoracht, LL. 263a. W. drysor.

dóit-gel *having white forearms*. 97, 3. LL. 161a, 37.

dond-bán *dun-white*. 69, 3.

drech-ongdás *face-band ?* 89, 22.

dressán *spleen*. 89, 23. gl. splen, Ir. Gl. 1012.

**drolam** m. *a hook or ring ; handle* or *knocker of a door.* Salt. 4309. 123, 11. comla ibair ꜩ dá drolam íaraind esse, LU. 19a, 17. it remithir sliastæ fir cech dubdrolom cetharchoir fordadúna, LU. 95b, 36. of a cauldron : trascarthair in trénfher forsin coire co memaid a dóeláma forsin drolam iartharach, LL. 292b, 31. of a cup : coilech argait hé ꜩ dí drolam da cech leth ass, LBr. 158a, 20. Cf. drolmach f. missi bias fon drolmaig de eter chomlaid is choire, LL. 34a, 16. M. drolloo *pothooks.*

**druchtán** *cheese-whey.* 119, 39. LBr. 9b, 23.

**drús** f. *lust, lewdness.* LU. 68b, 1. LL. 208b, 50. dí ingin báeissi .i. drús ꜩ doairli, Harl. fo. 74b. dat. drúis 73, 2. From drúth *lewd*, Wind.

**dubán** m. *fishing hook, angling rod.* 91, 18. 122, 1. ruaimnech dubain, Ir. Gl. 428. M. dooan *hook.*

**dubánacht** *angling.* 91, 21.

**dublaithe** adj. *melancholy.* 87, 5. dublaithe a n-deoid au domain, Harl. 5280, fo. 42a.

**duilesc** *a sort of edible sea-leaf, dulse.* in duilesc fiuch, Laws i, p. 170, 13. femnach no duilesc, ib. fithrech .i. dúilesc, Rawl. B. 512, fo. 52b, 1. gen. dulisc 89, 19.

**duille** f. *leaf.* Wind. dulle ꜩ bláth ꜩ mess, LL. 156a, 21. of a book : 53, 25. W. dail.

**duillech** *leafy.* 69, 3. gaim dullech, LL. 188c. rosc duillech, LL. 97b, delg d., ib.

**dulas** 77, 4. For dolas *grief*, the opposite of solas ? Henn. translates *appetite.* Cf. dulasach *greedy*, Three Shafts, Ind. dúlda, dulmhar *greedy. desirous ;* iondula *desirable*, P. O'C.

### E.

**éca** f. *death ?* 93, 15. A by-form of éc ?

**écin** *some, a certain.* 61, 14. Tog. Tr. 835. ni búi (scil. Titus, lá cen mhaith écin do dénum, LBr. 150b. Trip. Life, p. 558, 19.

**ecnaide** f. *wisdom.* 105, 28.

**ecnaidecht** f. *wisdom.* 105, 22.

cithre *tail.* 79, 18. .i. dered no forbern no err, Three Ir. Gloss.
p. 136. *end :* eithre na slabraide, LL. 393b, 44.

elath f. *a calvary or charnel-house, a carn, a heap or pile of bones
in a churchyard*, P. O'C. *a stone tomb.* m' ilad ⁊ m' uág,
LU. 119a, 40 dat. atá corthe oc a ulaid, LU. 134a, 6. ·a
cloch thall for elaid úair, LL. 150a, 26. acc. elaith 121, 36.

Elcab 75, 8 = Ulgabh 119, 24? Cf. benais béim n-ulgaib lcóman
don charput úachtarach for a forcli, LU. 79b. 43 ?

ellach *trappings?* 81, 3. Or *load, burden,* O'R.?

emeltius *tediousness, tardiness, prolixity*, P. O'C. 13, 3. is emil-
tius fri héstidib tíachtain dar na nechaib inundaib fo dí, LU.
97b, 39. iar laxu ⁊ emeltus ⁊ torsi, LBr. 256b. ionmhoille ⁊
cimioltas, Moy Lcana, p. 44, 1. Chron. Scot. p. 4. emilte f.
Rev. Celt. ii, p. 382. From emilt *tedious:* is emilt engnam
cach fhir folcith díb d' innisin, LL. 74a. LBr. 10a, 40. ib.
156b, 53. Tog. Tr. Ind.

eochar-immel *border, edge.* 119, 31. Rev. Celt. x, p. 365. ochor-
immel, Tog. Tr. 1131. ind-eocharimill in lochai, H. 3. 18, fo.
736a. bratt glefind imni co n-acharimlib argit, LL. 267b.
Cf. ós bordimlib in beatha, Magh Rath, p. 112, 7.

epaid f. *poison, philtre, charm.* Wind. gen. eptha 7, 4. 71,25. pl.
nom. auptha ⁊ felmasa ⁊ fidlanna, LBr. 258b, 82. dat. gan
credium do chrandchoraib na d' upthaib ban, LBr. 243a, 26.
Manx obbee.

epistil f. *epistle ; necklace, collar.* gen. episle, 89, 14. pl. dat.
epislib. 89, 12. 14. See O'C. Manners and Customs, iii, p.
105. sín Maic Máin .i. epistil bói ima brágait fri forgell
fírinde .i. intan ba fír atbered ba fairsing dia brágait, intan
ba gó ba cumac, Corm. p. 41.

eraiss *stern, poop.* Rev. Celt. x, p. 52, 11. dat. 119, 33. erus
85, 12. earais .i. deireadh, O'Cl.

er-ard *very high.* 83, 27. 95, 26. echrada ána aurarddai, LU.
85a, 17. fossad airard, LL. 33b, 13.

er-dorn *hilt.* e. claidib, LL. 173b, 43.

erdracaigim *I honour.* LL. 187a, 53. 187b, 22. LBr. 176b, 22.
By metathesis for erdarcaigim ; cf. erdraicc 91, 26.

er-drochat *front-bridge.* 87, 9. gen. bái Dirmaid oc glanad
urdrochit a thaigi, LL. 353a. dat. for irdrochiut, LL. 272b, 35.
pl. nom. it salcha ua herdrochait, Rawl. 512, fo. 115a, 1.

érnaim *I escape.* ní érna acht óenchoiciuir díb ass, LU. 98a, 42.
érnaba 5, 10. noco n-érnába cern ná cárna dít asind áit hi
tudchad, LU. 86a, 20.

errandus *part, particle.* 55, 2. LU. 37a, 47. LBr. 188b, 8. is
irrandus dom churp thusa, a Eua, LBr. 112a.

errchaide *vernal.* 63, 9.

errudus *responsibility, guarantee.* 117, 19. cach urrudus co
deoraidecht, cach deoraidecht co hurrudus, Aibidil Cuigni.
Laws, passim.

esrad *strewing.* 123, 25. esred 117, 17. ic esrad tigi, LL.268b.
rohesrad a tech di cholctib 7 brothrachaib, LU. 19a, 19.

essamain (1) *fearless.* Wind. Trip. Life, 456, 1. W. chofn.
(2) *welcome,* from bidding the stranger be "without fear"
("μὴ φοβηδῆς"). 75, 8. 119, 24.

essamna *welcome.* 95, 7. ferais esomni fris, Tochm. Em., l. 68.

étaid *jealous.* 125, 22. LL. 54a, 8, 12. 844a. edaigh .i. tnuth-
ach, ut est : nirbu edaigh, H. 3. 18, p. 415.

etar-aissnćis *inter-relation, interlude.* 55, 17.

etar-tráth *twilight.* 107, 22.

etrad *noun?* 107, 23. See Corm. Tr. 68 s. v. etsruth.


**F.**

fáball f. *fable.* gen. fáible 71, 5. dat. fábull 69, 31.

fáen *supine.* 25, 16. 116, 19. O. Ir. fóin.

fail f. *arm-ring* (fainne *finger-ring*). LL. 267a. 111, 14. acc.
falaig 45, 16. pl. gen. coica falach, LL. 206b. dat. co failgib,
Stokes, *Lives,* 4573. a di foil do airgit, LU. 134a, 4.

fáith-liag m. *vates medicus.* passim. ar cend ind fháthlega
'sin Mumain, LL. 329a.

fannall f. *a swallow.* Wind. LU. 62b, 6. acc. fannaill 63, 9.
W. gwennol f.

fannaigim *I grow weak, relax.* 93, 12.

farr *post, prop, pillar.* .i. colbha leptha, O'Don. Suppl. pl.
nom. fairre. 37, 22.

fás-chocnom lit. *empty chewing.* 116, 26.

fasguth ? 125, 20. Cf. ni chuala comrád no fas cud gotha
Cellaig. LBr. 274b, 56.

fóic 105, 4 = féice *ridge-pole, roof-tree; lintel.* Wind. cotarla
feci in dorais i mullach a chind corusmarb, LBr. 128a, 8. feci

dou tig, LBr. 260b, 36.   dochúaid ar ettelaig for fégi in
tige, LBr. 223a, 1.   a féci for airlár, LL. 263b.   ling dar féice
in tige, LL. 301a, 16.
feolomain 117, 21.   foloman 125, 34.
fer-glacc f. *a man's grasp.* 3, 14.   Trip. Life, p. xxii. 7.   Cf.
glacc 89, 20.
ferna *alder.* gen. ferua 97, 2.   W. gwern.   M. faarney.
féta *brave, generous, heroic,* P. O'C. 61, 30. 109, 4.   Ir. Texte ii, 2,
p. 132, 254.   athair féta fírfhíal, LL. 34a, 4.   fer féta farsaid
findlíath, LL. 267b.   Findabair fhéta, ib. 138a, 27.   féta a
rath, ib. 205a, 17.
féth *aspect, look.*   93, 11. 17. 19.   olc féth fíl fort, LL. 117b, 36.
Cf. anféth : boi anfeth na gorta lee, Corm. p. 37, 15.   FB. 29
(Eg.)   deigfhéth, Fél. C, 27.
féthán *a poor aspect.*   93, 10.
féth-shnass lit. *a smooth cut.* gen. féthshnais 93, 10.   From
féth *smoothness.* .i. ciúnas, O'Cl.   *a calm,* Tog. Tr. 982.   co
n-dénad a féth ⁊ a snass, LL. 68a, 44.   ba féith in snass
dédlinach, Corm. p. 32.   féth dar fudbu, LL. 55a.   ba feth dam
iu muir, Rev. Celt. x, p. 84, 9.   Hence féthugud *smoothing :*
faithche .i. fethcai .i. conair iarna fethugud .i. réidhugad,
H. 3. 18.   LL. 188a, 11.
fíad *welcome.* 23, 24.   ní fhuarus-sa fiad n-óiged, LL. 62b.
dorigned fiad mór fris, Bk. of Fermoy, p. 31a.
fiadain *wild.* 49, 14.   M. feayn.
fiad-uball *a wild apple.* 45, 11.
    dar fiar-láit *athwart, across.* 43, 17.   47, 15.   ar fiarlaid
críchi Saxan, Rev. Celt. x, p. 188, 7.   ar fiarlaoid dá chóiged
Muman, Moy Leana, p. 60.
    dar fiar-ut *athwart, across.* 13, 25.
fidbach *some kind of corn.* 99, 5.
figlim *I watch ; study.* 53, 22. 24.   figell a uigilia .i. frithaire
H. 3. 18.
findach *hairy.* 95, 23.   findech, LL. 266b.
find-choll m. *white hazel.* 63, 1.   117, 23.
fír-dírech *quite straight.* 63, 1.
fíre f. *truth.* 5, 21.   W. gwiredd.
fír-íasc m. *salmon.* 89, 9.   122, 35.   bratán fíréisc, LL. 283a, 24.   ⊁
Cf. fír-én *eagle.*

                                                                                N

**fithir** *tutor.* .i. aite, 11, 3.   Laws ii. p. 128, 8.   Cf. fithithair fria felmac, Laws ii. p. 344, 4.   do chungid derscaigthe dia fithithir, LL. 188c, 24.   cona urerset felmaic a fithithre, ib. 22.

**fo-chartad** *scouring, cleansing,* 91, 10.

**fo-chóim** *gait.* 97, 17.   Cf. fochengat, LL. 295b.

**foigdech (fo-guidech)** *beggar.* 71, 21.

**fo-immthecht** *gait.* 97, 17.

**foithe** *under her.* 122, 32.

**folartnaige** f. *sufficiency.* 115, 32.   Cf. ar lórdataid 7 ar fholortnaige, Alex. 865.

**follus** gnóthech *plain-working.* 13, 17.   19, 8.

**folmaigim** *I empty, evacuate.* 128, 13. 14.   falmaigter an tech umpa, Bk. of Fermoy, p. 34b.   *lay waste:* dofalmaigemar in chrích 7 in ferann, Laud 610, fo. 123a, 1.

✗ **folmnech** *roped, tied by a rope.* 73, 4.   From folomna .i. róithéud *a strong cord or rope,* P. O'C.   LU. 80a, 25.   LL. 67b, 11.   Cf. cú lomna leu, LL. 251b, 43.   Cf. W. llyfan *rope.*

**foltnide** *hairy.* 95, 22.   From foltne *a single hair:* cach foltne ina chend, LU. 59a, 35.   ni rothesctha oenfhoiltne dia moing no dia fhult, LBr. 127b.

**fo-lúaimnigim** *I fly.* 107, 11.

**fomnaim** *I beware, guard myself.* Imper. fomna 71, 11.   119, 9.   eimdhe .i. fomnæ no bith do menma, H. 3. 18.   = cave, Ir. Nenn. p. 82, 7.   fomna in láech, LU. 73a, 14.   Laws iii. p. 414, 24.   maine aightis ina piana, ni fomnibtis, 23. P. 3, fo. 16a.

**fomtiu** f. *precaution, guard.* acc. fomtin 87, 26.   ar fomtin 7 ar imgabáil, LU. 35b, 24.   asbert in liaig fri Conchobar co m-beth i fomtin .i. arna tísad a fherg dó, Aid. Conch. 65.   Atk., *Ir. Lexicogr.,* p. 22.

**for-ard** *very high.* 39, 4.

i **forcipul** .i. i filliud, LL. 266b.   9, 27.   LU. 133a, 26.   55a, 12.   dá nathraig for leimnig 7 for banganaig a forcipul a bairr, Cath Catharda.

**for-lán** *very full.* 118, 6.   Wb. 3a, 7.   LL. 268a.   W. gorlawn.

**forrgim** (*for-fhragim, root vrag, Stokes) *I strike.* 29, 25.   forraigim *I crush, overpower,* Tog. Tr. Ind.   cóica foirrged digail, LL. 207b, 11.   forrgither andsin ó ó chnedaib, LL. 193b, 24.

**fortgellaim, fortgillim** *I declare.* 7, 15.   27, 4.   29, 27.   67, 5.

Wb. 4b, 27. is taid ocus is lator, fortgella in rí, LBr. 261a, 47.
fortgellat, Ml. 23c, 15. LL. 43a, 45.

for-tócbalta *uplifted.* 9, 27.

fostán *steadiness.* 35, 7. tre dúire ꝛ fostain, Alex. 32.

francach *French.* 127, 31. Cf. coileach no cearc francach *turkey.*
luch fhrancach *rat,* cnú fr. *walnut,* aitean fr. *great furze or
gorse,* bolgach fhr. *the French pox,* P. O'C.

frith no frioth .i. slighe *a road, way, passage,* P. O'C. 51, 24?

frith-airigid f. *fore-meal.* 3, 17.

frith-pían f. *preliminary torture.* 31, 2.

fúathróc f. *apron.* ro fhuaigsedar duillinda na fice ꝛ dorindsedar
fuathroga doib dona duillennaib, LLec. p. 530a. Comp. lín-fh.
63, 3.

fuillim (fri) *I add (to).* 45, 18. osin immach ni fullim-sea,
LU. 126a, 8. combad fhuillite a gráin, LL. 193b, 2.

fuirseóracht *juggling.* 43, 24. fuirsirecht gl. mimi, August
Carol. 12c.

furachair *wary, vigilant, watchful,* P. O'C. 97, 20. co fichtha
f., LL. 256b.

## G.

gábadán *a small danger.* 197, 10. A humorous dimin. of gábud
*danger,* M. gaue.

gabáil f. *profit.* 95, 2.

gaile *stomach, cawl.* 122, 35. Three Fragm. p. 124. M. gailley.

gal f. *smoke, rapour, steam.* gen. gaile 35, 1. M. gaal.

galbech *peevish, testy, angry, stormy, tempestuous, outrageous,*
P. O'C. 93, 16. sidi gáithi géri galbigi, LL. 253b, 50. ria
n-dílind gailbig glúair, ib. 136b, 47. A frequent epithet of
the "Saxon", e.g. ri báig Saxan n-galbech n-gand, LL. 154a,
20. 393b, 14.

garbán *a grain of coarse meal, a single bran, a grain of sand,* etc.
P. O'C. gen. garbáin 35, 2. Comp. brusgarbáu 87, 22.

garr *dung or ordure in the paunch,* P. O'C. *garbage, offal,* O'R.
gen. gairr 85, 3.

gat *a withe.* 71, 26. M. gad.

gebbad *cropping?* 85, 4.

gebend f. *prison, confinement, any great distress,* P. O'C. 69, 12.
fo góbind gibsig (rhymes with Érind), LL. 5b, 30. Alex. 1098.
Cf. the proper name Geibennach, FM. 970. W. gefyn.

N 2

geir f. *suet.* gen. gered 35. 23. 85, 11. 20. 121, 32. 122, 2. geriud 87, 25. Cf. W. gwer.

gelbund *sparrow*. Comp. pl. nom. min-gelbuind 95, 25. W. golfan.

gel-chruithnecht *white wheat*. 37, 10.

gem-shecal *winter-rye*. 85, 4.

genelach *genealogy*. 38, 10. LBr. 185, 2. pl. nom. genelaich, LL. 144b, 20.

gentlecht m. *heathenism*, also *magic*, P. O'C. 5, 26. genntliucht, LBr. 128a, 30. Cath M. Tuir. 1. dat. apair fris nacha n-erbbad i n-gentliucht, nan-erbbad i fírinne, LL. 294b, 20. Cf. draidecht 7 génntlidecht 7 sénairecht, LBr. 258b, 81.

gérait *warlike, heroic*. Eochu Garb, gerait Gædel, LL. 161b, 12. Compar. gératu 83, 22.

gére f. (1) *sharpness, acuteness*. 105, 15. Cf. 17, 11. (2) *greed*. 3, 12. 114, 1. Ml. 75b, 1.

gerrcend *bolt, bar*. 87, 19. From Lat. gergenna, Ducange. Reeves, Adamnan, p. 126, note c. Changed by popular etymology as if "short-head".

gerthech *suety*. gen. f. gerthige 35, 23. 85, 21.

gillim = gellaim *I vow*. Wind. 21, 6.

ginach m. and f. *craving, greed*. 125, 13. gen. teidm cróeis 7 ginaig dochumm a chota, LBr. 143a, 2. dat. ginaig 116, 6. 128, 19. From gin *mouth*. 105, 19.

glámm *guest? assembly*, used like dám of one person only? glaim 87, 4. greas 7 glamh (leg. glam?), Magh Rath p. 104, 1. pl. glámma 7 clíara, LL. 109b, 11. glamaigim *I gather!* rosnglamaigit leis a grega 7 a damrada, LL. 304a, 41.

glas-chráibech *green branches*. 115, 13.

gnidim *I fling?* gnidis 51, 15.

grían m. *gravel or sand of a sea, lake, or river*, P. O'C. 17, 1. Rev. Celt. x, p. 54, 5. dat. ar úir 7 grían, FB. 52. acc. fil and grian Glindi hAi, Rawl. B. 512, fo. 52b, 1. deotar eter úr 7 grian 7 fér, ib. 112a, 1. Comp. murgrían 37, 5. 85, 26. W. graian.

grianad *to expose to the sun, sunning*. 11, 20.

gribda *pleasant?* 49, 5. mná glana gribda, LU. 38b, 25. gillai gribdai gráda, LL. 201b, 19. griabhdha (leg. griobhdha?), 3 Fragm. p. 34, 11. Cf. grib: an maidin chaom go n-glóir n-gribh "glorious", Moy Leana, p. 126, 11.

# Glossary.

grib-dál f.? dat. gribdail 117, 15.

gríss f. *embers, hot ashes, heat, fire, sun;* also *pimples, rash pimples, blotches, spots on the skin,* P. O'C. 95, 26.

gríssach f. *burning embers.* acc. grisnig 128, 11. M. greesagh.

gruiten f. *the small curds which remain mixed with the whey after the removal of the thicker substance,* Reeves, *Culdees,* p. 203. Corm. Tr. p. 86. grus grot gruiten, a groso cibo .i. dagbiad .i. scaiblin no braisech, H. 2. 16, col. 114. gen. gruitne 67, 29. acc. gruitin 127, 17. LBr. 9b, 28.

grut *curds.* grut bruithe, LL. 117b, 23. acc. gruit 127, 25.

gruth *curds.* 67, 23. rop gilithir gruth, Stokes, *Lives,* l. 4075. gen. grotha 85, 11. 24. Comp. fír-gruth 37, 22. sen-gruth 85, 21. 99, 18. M. groo.

gruthrach f. *curds.* LBr. 9b, 24. gen. gruthraige 85, 2.

guilbniugud *nibbling, biting.* 13, 3. From gulban, W. gylfin, *beak,* Wind. gl. *aculeum* Ml. 20d, 10. 32c, 11. 122b, 8.

## H.

Hirophín *Cherubim.* 41, 10.

## I.

Iar-comla f. *foramen podicis.* 85, 7. Alex. 705. LL. 64a, 5. dat. iarcomlaid 89, 19.

íar-shliss *hind-quarter.* 79, 7. 124, 39.

idnocul *delivering.* 43, 6. idnacul, LU. 133b, 9. Cf. ronidnacht, LL. 285a, 19.

il-blassa *many sweet things, dainties.* 5, 13. 27. di énaib ┐ lubaib ┐ ilmblasaib, Ir. Texte ii. 1, p. 173, 8. *many tastes* or *fancies,* 93, 27.

imbert? leg. inbert? 81, 14.

immasech *crossed* (of legs). 65, 4.

imm-chassal m. *cover, coating.* 85, 10. cassal, from Lat. casula, is fem. in the Trip. Life, Ind., but masc. in the following passages: gen. ic figi chasil, LL. 358 marg. sním casil, ib. dat. dom chassul, Three Hom. p. 38, 7.

imm-chíallda *very sensible.* 97, 3.

imm-dorcha *very dark.* 15, 6.

imm-líge *licking.* 101, 26.

imm-lomm *very bare.* 63, 9.

imm-naiscim *I bind around, twist.* 11, 29. nonimnuisc 'mo chend fcib imnaiscthe*r* lathranna staible, LL. 110b, 40.

immorro *but, however.* Written out: immoro, LL. 238a, 40. ummoro, LL. 257b, 13. imora, Alex. 931. imuro, Laud 610, fo. 82b, 1. imoru, Harl. 5280, fo. 22b.

imm-thús *contending?* 73, 11. Cf. fá anghlonn ioma re triath, Moy Leana, 146b. morthu fri ríg, LL. 344b.

inbe *entrails; tripe.* indbe .i. biadh i n-indib .i. isna cœlanaib, H. 3. 18. 33, 28. 81, 7. 15. 91, 20.

inbert *horsecloth?* 81, 7.

ind-ber *a large spit.* 39, 17. 79, 14. indbe*r* íarind ar in dá drolam sin LU. 19a, 19. remithir inbe*r* cairi crand cach*œ* dib, LU. 88a, 28. bert inbe*r* in chorc .i. inber iairnd, LU. 97b, 17. dobert nói m-bulli dond inbi*ur* iarind, ib. 19. comemaid a choeldruim immon inber, LL. 292b, 32. gen. cend ind inbir, Trip. Life, xxii. 5. From bir *spit;* bir ia[i]rn ina láim, LL. 89a. gen. in bera, LU. 69b, 14. acc. biur, ib. 13. dat. den bir culind, LL. 74b. pl. gen. coica bera, LL. 207a.

indco, an interjection. 51, 21. 55, 8.

ind-fhota *having a long point.* 117, 23.

indlaim *I wash.* 59, 17. 122, 25.

in-dligthech *unlawful, illegal.* 101, 24.

indmaim *I wash.* inf. indmad, 71, 15. 95, 20.

indorsa *now.* 61, 7. indorsai, Alex. 155.

indraithim *I invade, attack.* 77, 3.

indrechtán *pudding, sausage.* 33, 19. 89, 27, 29. .i. putóg, O'Cl.

indsén *an islet.* 33, 26. Cf. indsech, LL. 5b, 31.

indsmaim *I rivet, fasten, fix.* 47, 17. 87, 28. inf. cride in choimded iarna indsma isin croich, LBr. 158a. bui Conall ac indsma gai forsin ráith, H. 2. 17, fo. 475b. indsma slog, 3 Fragm. p. 34, 12. *engagement, pledge* (of marriage), 73, 6.

ingerta *greasy.* 91, 10. See gcir.

ingur 99, 30 *anchor?* Wind. Or *matter, pus, filth, dirt?* Or cf. forsgath no ingar gl. enigma, Ir. Gl. 137?

inichin? 39, 7. 121, 13.

inmar *juice, dripping, condiment.* 125, 13. Stokes, *Lives,* p. 316, 26. LBr. 11a, 6. gen. inmair 33, 20. gan mir n-ionmair, FM. 534. dat. inmar 63, 14. Cf. inmaire, Ml. 20a, 25.

inmarda *juicy.* 29, 23. Stokes, *Lives,* Ind. gabaid for ongad-

*inviud 95,8*

chomailt a chuirp do ola ⁊ do neithib inmar[d]aib eile, Cath
Catharda.

innram *service, attendance.* O'R. 55, 18.

ir-chuitbed *mocking, deriding.* 71, 21.

is-at *thou art.* 57, 8. isit, 122, 9. Cf. itib *you are,* LL. 281b, 28.

istad-loc m. *treasure-house.* 101, 16. Salt. 4198. As to istad,
O. Ir. etsad (1) *treasure,* (2) *treasury,* see Ir. Texte iii, p. 280.
autsa[dh], O'Dav. p. 51.

íth *fat.* O'Don. Suppl. 79, 31. gen. ítha 33, 21. 77, 12. 81, 5.
119, 19. bó co n-ocib ítha, LL. 358, marg. sup. M. eeh.

ithamail *greedy, voracious.* 87, 7.

íthascach f.? dat. íthascaig 77, 13.

ithemraige f. *voracity.* 95, 1. 119, 17.

ith-lann f. *corn-yard.* 73, 25. lann .i. ithlann no ferand, O'Dav.
A Mid. Ir. nom. form ithlu (cf. persu, Mórrígu) also occurs:
ithla choitchend, Laws i. p. 140, 12. ni facbatís tech na uaim
na ithlu innte cen iarrair ⁊ cen tochailt, LBr. 154b. M.
yllan, yllin. W. ydlan.

ítmaire f. *thirst.* 95, 1. From ítmar *thirsty,* Alex. 647. 667.

iuchair *fish-spawn, roe.* pl. dat. iuchraib 122, 35. 124, 30. Manx
oghyr.

iuchua *pale red.* pl. iuchanta 97, 16.

### L.

lachtmar *rich in milk.* 93, 18.

lúi f. *steering-oar, rudder.* 73, 17. lúi, Rev. x, 86, 21. claideb
sithider loí churaig, LU. 68b, 11. sithithir a lám ri læ, LL.
44b, 29. *tail, brush:* il-lái cecha sinnaig, LBr. 127a, 33. W.
llyw.

láid form *it troubles, harms me;* also *I am unable, I fail, miss.*
27, 2. 122, 28. Cf. lai (!) .i. foimed ut est: rolæi fiadnaise
fair fuirmed, H. 3. 18, p. 62.

láinte *filled.* 33, 22. 124, 2.

láir f. *a mare.* Wind. gen. lára (for lárach) 73, 1. M. laayr.

lán-berbthe *fully boiled.* 107, 18.

lán-méth *full-fat.* 33, 19. 91, 14.

lassamain *inflammable.* 125, 34. ba lond lassamain lándían,
LL. 224b, 19. As a noun: da chrín ⁊ do lassamain, LL. 268a,
28.

latrach *l*  gen. latraigh 127, 19.

lebar-thecht *long and clotted, viscous.* 101, 9.

leibend *dais, platform, bank.* 67, 23. 118, 9. 122, 6. *a raised road,* LBr. 109a, 58. lebend sciath, LL. 120a, 55. léibend, LL. 43a, 46.

léir-gním *arranging.* 67, 16. 91, 15. Cf. colléir, du léir (LU. 126a, 24) *de industria.* di léir gl. *diligenter,* Ml. 68a, 15. Cf. léir-thinol, 3 Fragm. p. 32, 9.

lemnacht *new milk.* Wind. 99, 19. gen. lemnachta 33, 19. 35. 24. loimm lemnaicht, LBr. 9b, 49.

il-leth fri *in the direction of, towards; with reference to.* 57, 7. (cf. p 53, 12.) 55, 1. Alex. 437.

less f. *thigh, haunch.* Wind. gen. lessi 33, 23. cnám lessi, LU. 86b, 43. Cf. Manx craue-leshey *haunch.* dual : a di leiss, LL. 117b, 22.

lethar *skin.* 89, 9. Cath Finntr. Ind.

leth-ard lit. *half-high ; uneven.* 73, 28. lethard condarta, Harl. 5280, fo. 41b. measam laigi lethard, Aibidil Cuigni.

lethind 33, 23, leg. lethcind ? cf. 124, 3.

lettromm lit. *half-heavy; onesided, partial.* 73, 29. is breth lettrom lesmathar, LL. 34a, 12. Hence lettruimme f. *partiality.* Gael. Journ. iv, p. 42b.

lilaice *a milch cow.* gen. lilicca 93, 18. caire lulaice, Laws ii, 254, 2. pl. nom. secht lilica, LL. 286b, 37.

línaide adj. *linen.* 63, 4. a léine ligdæ linide, LU. 91a, 23.

lín-scót *a linen sheet.* pl. nom. -scóti 103, 15.

lista *slow, tedious, heavy,* P. O'C. *oppressive, importunate.* 95, 4. lista in slúag, LBr. 224 marg. at fer'saignesach-su lista, LL. 66a, 13. Trip. Life, 32, 31. Hence listacht (*Lires,* Ind.) and lisdatus (Three Hom. 78, 22) *importunity.*

littiu f. *stirabout, porridge.* Wind. littu, LL. 214b, 27. lite, Laws ii, 148, 20. gen. litten 33, 29. acc. litin 127, 19. Comp. find-litte 99, 29. W. llith.

ló *a lock of wool, a blade of wool, a single hair.* P. O'C. Cf. O'Cl. 97, 6. cét lend lóchorcra, LL. 51a, 20. coic bruit corcra do caemlaeib, Bk. of Fen. 368, 6. 370, 4. *a flake :* loa snechtai, Rev. iii, 183.

loan, see (2) lon.

lóech-lestar n. *warrior-ship.* 35, 26. 39, 24. 120, 10. 121, 30.

lómar *nappy.* Tog. Tr. Ind. 113, 10.

(1) lon m. *demon.* 3, 12. 115, 2. gen. luin 3, 8, 20. 7. 7. 103, 24. dat. lun 107, 19. lon cráis, LBr. 143a, 4. Comp. cráes-lon 103, 5.

(2) lon .i. leis *hip, thigh,* P. O'C. loan 77, 12. pl. acc. luna 99, 12. Cf. O'Cl. s. v. lon lairge.

(3) lon m. *a wether.* pl. acc. lunu 99, 13. 127, 15.

lon charna f. *rump-steak.* 91, 14.

lón-choire *a food-caldron.* lónchore mór, LU. 95a, 39. Dimin. lón-chorén 77, 14.

lón-fheiss f. *a meat-feast.* 29, 25.

long f. *the cartilage of the chest.* gen. loinge 33, 23. 124, 3. acc. dar loing a ochta, LL. 64a, 1. Cf. O'Cl. s. v. longa bronn.

longan? gen. longain 113, 10. Cf. lendanach longanach, Ir. Texte iii, p. 98.

lon-loingén, lon-loingín *the gullet, weazand.* 33, 22. 77, 13, 22. 91, 22. 99, 15. Cf. LL. 187c, 18. Also the name of a musical instrument, the flute or recorder. See Walker, *Irish Bards* i, p. 124. O'Dav. p. 103, glosses the word by taob *side.*

lorg f. *a peg.* 11, 27.

loth-ommar *a washing tub.* 11, 22. pl. n. -ommair, LL. 54a. Cf. loth *a lotion or washing,* P. O'C.

lúabann (gen.) *loin?* 33, 22. 124, 2.

luabin? 69, 1. Cf. luabainde gl. casiatum (quoddam cibi genus ex caseo farreque confectum, Duc.), Ml. 81b, 5?

lúasc *a swinging.* 97, 24. Cf. lúascad *a swinging, jolting, rocking,* P. O'C. ni luaisced gáeth caircech m-bó, II. 2. 18, col. 718.

lúb-diabalta *double-looped.* 99, 31. Cf. lúp.

luchtaire m. *a caldron-man.* Boroma, Ind. 39, 16. 121, 22. gl. lanista, Ir. Gl. 10. d'iarraid airigthi barsna luchtairib, LL. 300b, 44. Ir. Texte iii, p. 196, 9.

luchtairecht *taking food out of the caldron.* robáttur na Danair ag l., 3 Fragm. p. 122. fuine na l., LBr. 155b. gair na n-aithech ósna coirib ac l. dona slúagaib, Bk. of Fermoy, p. 169a.

luidim *I go.* Imper. luid 53, 13. Cf. conludim.

luindig *some kind of music.* 125, 21. duchonn .i. loinniucc no ceól, O'Dav. p. 73. oc luindiucc, LBr. 188b, 4. luinneag *a song, ditty, chorus.* Highl.

lumman f. *a coarse cover, a large great-coat, sackcloth,* P. O'C. acc. lummain 9, 27. 25, 15, 17. gen. hi fola na lumne, LU. 134a, 19. a n-ucht mo luimne, Bk. of Fermoy, p. 85a.

lúp f. *a winding, meander, maze.* gen. luipe 39, 24. 121, 30.

luric ? 93, 19.

## M.

✠ máelán *beare, a kind of coarse barley.* 99, 4.

máelán *sandal, shoe.* Rev. ix, 490, 4. pl. acc. maelanu LU. 3b, 45 (in medio ficonis sui, Nennius).

máer m. *steward.* 57, 12. 113, 11. *keeper:* maoir na croisi Athracht, Hy Fiachr, p. 40. From Lat. maior.

mairgócán, a dimin. of mairg *woe !* 95, 14.

maith *well !* 17, 15. 19, 19. 71, 16. 115, 36. 119, 14. Interrog. *well ?* followed by the answer *ní anse,* LL. 282b, 42.

maithe 122, 4; for maide *stick?*

maithem *remission.* Wind. 29, 18. Cf. mathim n-anacuil do Diarmait, LL. 358 marg.

mál, adj. *noble.* 3, 11. Salt. 865.

'mana *around his.* 63, 10.

mang f. *a fawn.* O'Cl. acc. maing 63, 8. Cf. lúaithi mang ina máthair, Corm. s. v. mang.

maróc f. *pudding, sausage.* gl. iolla, Ir. Gl. 55. gl. trolliamen, ib. gen. maróce 87, 19. 123, 11. dat maroicc 122, 4. pl. maróca 67, 20. See Rev. xii, p. 461. Comp. dond-m. 122, 4. 127, 2.

Marta *March.* Marta la nuna, LL. 188c, 59. gen. 63, 10.

matad m. *dog, cur.* gen. mataid 27, 19. pl. gen. tech matad, LU. 74a, 13. adba maddad m-birach, Fél. lxxxv, 23. voc. matadu 23, 25. 25, 22. Hence the proper name Matudán, LL. 184a, 39. M. moddey. Cf. W. madog *fox.*

mataidecht f. *doghood.* 101, 15.

matra m. *dog.* voc. a charr-matraid 101, 14. madra allaid *wolf,* Ir. Gl. 275. Eachtra an Mhadra Mhaoil, Jubainv. Catal. p. 119. Cf. W. madryn.

mát-roga *a swinish choice.* 27, 19. Cf. mátt *pig,* Corm. pl. nom. mátta, ib.

medg-usce *whey water.* 15, 1. Rev. x, 86, 18. LBr. 9b, 37.
megill *bleating.* 101, 11. Cf. Germ. meckern, mecke *ram.*
Hence ro meglastar, Trip. Life, 180, 24.
mellánach *small-lumped.* 118, 13. From mellán *a small lump
or mass,* P. O'C.
memraigim *I remember.* 17, 11. 116, 4. W. myfyrio, from
Lat. memor.
menistir *a service-set.* 124, 32. 127, 35. From Lat. ministerium,
sacrorum vasorum congeries et apparatus, Ducange.
mescaim *I dip, plunge.* 11, 26. Rev. x, 79, n. 2. mescthus
isin duiblinn í sin, LU. 95a, 40. Trip. Life, 70, 27.
mescán *a small dish or roll of butter,* O'R. *a ball, lump, or mass
mixed,* P. O'C. mescan .i. do mescad in loma ásas, H. 3. 18.
87, 16. 121, 38. 123, 31.
(1) messe *boiled.* .i. bruithe 99, 13. 127, 15. messe no bruth-
nigthe .i. forloiscthe gl. argentum igni examinatum, Ml.
31c. 28.
(2) messe *apparition, phantom.* taidbsi .i. messa 73, 22. messi
.i. aurdraighe .i. aurdracht, Eg. 1782, fo. 15b, 2. meissi, O'Cl.
métail? dat. métail 89, 24. gen. metla 123, 19. 124, 33. Perh.
for móetal *paunch, stomach.*
méth adj. *fat.* Comp. lán-méth 33, 19. 123, 39. M. mea.
mether *a covering.* 17, 25. meithir bís im cairig claim .i. for-
brata míl, Laws i, 188, 17. cen mether imbi, LU. 68a, 14 =
gan meither (.i. étach) ime, H. 3. 18, p. 538. *a head-covering
for women :*

ní holc lim
ce beth calle finn form' chinn :
bái mór mether cech datha
form' chinn ic ól daglatha. H. 3. 18, p. 43.

Cf. the proper name Calb-mether.
metríne *a small measure.* 101, 6. Cf. metrén fochœl folethan
a hind ferna fodluigthe, Rawl. 512, fo. 115a, 2. A dimin. of
metar. See Rev. xii, 465.
mí-altromm *bad nursing or feeding.* gen. -altromma 93, 20.
mí-chæmna *bad cheer.* 93, 26.
mí-chuirdech? 85, 1.
mid-builc *belly.* Stokes, *Lives,* Ind. gen. -builce 33, 13. builc,

originally the nom. pl. of bolc, has passed into a feminine singular. Cf. the origin of Engl. bible, chester, Germ. zähre, thräne, schläfe, etc.

mid-chúartach *having a mead-hall.* 87, 11.

midchuine f. *medicine.* 93, 16. From Lat. medicina. Cf. midach from medicus.

mifech = mifrech ? 45, 2.

mí-fhocul *an evil word.* 17, 14. mífocul mná di araile, Laws i, 146, 32. dobreth a mífhocla do Choinculaind, LL. 119a, 16.

mifrech *dejected, miserable.* miffrech 93, 25. Corm. 37, 7. LL. 45a, 32. Hence mifrige f. LBr. 108b. 134a, 13. 224a, 28. Cf. mifre f. oc derfadaig ┐ oc mifri, LL. 256b. cen miffri, ib. 134a. See Stokes, Rev. x, 57, n. 2.

míl *a louse.* Rev. x, 74, 21. pl. n. míla 17, 26. M. meeyl.

mílach *lousy.* 11, 17.

mil-builc f. *honey-bag.* 123, 36. Cf. midbuilc.

millsén *any sweet thing ; sweet whey, cheese-curds,* P. O'C. O'Cl. 33, 26. 79, 13. 85, 27. LBr. 9b, 23.

min-chirrad *a subtle gnawing.* 93, 27.

minde = minne *a small particle, speck?* 11, 15. From min *flour.* Cf. folt-ne, cuis-ne, etc.

min-scellic *a small rock.* 69, 17. 118, 27.

min-scomartach f. *small broken pieces.* 91, 19. briscbruan ┐ minsc. LL. 61a, 4. Cf. doringni minbruan ┐ minscomart din charput, ib. 61a, 1.

Mithemain lit. *midsummer ; June.* 85, 4. domnach im-mís M., LL. 44a, 37. Corn. mes metheven, Meriasek 4303. Bret. mezeuen, W. mehefin *June.* The Irish word seems borrowed from the Welsh (th = h).

moch-loingthech *eating early.* 87, 7.

moch-longad *early eating.* 85, 24. 93, 24. 119, 20. 123, 50.

moethal f. *biestings, also thick milk curdled,* P.O'C. 33, 26. 85, 20. 81, 26. 119, 38. gen. mæthla 89, 2. 93, 9. 122, 32. dat. moethnil 67, 27. 120, 27. ní do moethail no do chnisse, LBr. 9b, 18. pl. dat. mæthlaib 37, 17. 81, 26.

moethal *fruit.* for mæthla matha .i. forsna maethla mathi .i. mess ┐ torud, LL. 187c, 4. Cf. O'Cl. and P. O'C. *the goodly fruits of the earth and of trees.*

móit *wish, desire.* 9, 7. Alex. 1101. is ed rofhiarfaig in budh *m̄ onuar̄ 29, 7     m̄ onar̄ 3? 22*

móid le rígh nime ⁊ talman a beith-sium ag éisdecht re scélaib
na féinne, Agall. na Sen.

moltrad f. *wethers.* LL. 296a, 21. gen. moltraide 127, 7.

múch f. *smoke, vapour;* also *gloom, darkness, dreariness,
heaviness, weariness, fatigue;* .i. tóirse, *sadness, dulness,* P.
O'C. gen. ar mét am-muiche, Goid. 158. dat. fo múich 93,
20. betitt huili fo muich marb *in mortal sadness,* Bk. of Fen.
374, 4. i n-doccomul ⁊ i muich iffirn, LBr. 256b. W. mwg.

mugdorn 122, 38. This is the place-name Mugdorn, Stokes.
*Lives,* l. 2788.

muirn f. *high spirit, courage, wantonness,* P. O'C. 45, 2. Moy
Leana, 12, 30. caide na cuirn no caide in mhuirn dobí 'cot
athair? Gael. Journ. iv, 106b. gen. for aba fhledóil no
múirne dímáinige in domnáin duthain, LBr. 273b, 69. M.
moyrn *pride, conceit.*

mulba? 123, 14.

mulcháu *cheese-curds pressed (but not in a cheese-vat) and baked   .ʌ.
by dairy people for food,* P. O'C. 81, 1. gl. glassia, Ir. Gl.
243.

muncach *wearing a necklace or collar.* 97. 5.

mur-grían m. *sea-gravel.* 85, 26. 119, 39. cluid ⁊ cairthe ⁊
carroc ⁊ táthleca ⁊ mur-grían in talman, LU. 80b, 5.

mur-raith *sea-fern?* gen. murrathu 124, 19. Cf. dá mecon do
muráthaig, Fél. p. lxi, 44.

## N.

nár *high.* .i. úasal, unde dicitur Nár mac Gúaire, H. 3. 18.
O'Dav. p. 107. A frequent epithet of nem *heaven.* Salt. Ind.
for nim nár, LL. 161b. gen. náir 7, 29.

nás *death.* .i. oel, H. 3. 18. .i. bás, O'Cl. gen. náis 7, 31.

nem-brisc *infrangible.* 105, 17.

nem-literda *illiterate.* 29, 21.

nert-lia *a stone on which to try one's strength?* 47, 16. n. gáise,
SC. 38. ba n. fergi, LL. 255b, 16. Cf. M. clagh-niart *a load-
stone, a putting-stone.*

nimtá *it is not so.* pl. nimtát 85, 29. See imtha, Wind. imta
.i. is inann leam, Laws iii, 30. amal file tra deochair eter
laechu ⁊ clerchu, eter maccaillecha ⁊ laichesa, imtha samlaid
deochair eter a sæthar ⁊ a pennain, Rawl. 512, fo. 42b, 2.

*Cid is ressen dún?103, 17*

*remaind 97, 13*

190 *Glossary.*

nóedenán *a small child.* 127, 6.

nómaide f. *an ennead of nine hours=three days and three nights.* 27, 1. 3.   107, 10.   Cf. nómad, Stokes, *Linguistic Value,* p. 9. ro áinius nómaid, LU. 16b, 37.

## O.

ochar f. *legging, hose,* eochra (ochra O'Cl.) .i. bróga, ut est : rogab a dí eochra ime, H. 3. 18. O'Dav. p. 83.   pl. dat. ochraib 89, 7. Ir. Texte iii, p. 238, 101.   From Lat. ocrea.

ocht-shlisnech f. *an octagonal log.*   95, 24.   Cf. ·slisnige, LL. 216a, 20.

odarda *dun.*   53, 18.   odorda LL. 266b.

ó-derg *red-eared.*   113, 19.

og f. *egg.*   Wind.  Sg. 8b, 10.   3, 16.   og thirimm, LBr. 9b, 18. acc. uig, Magh Rath, 128, 19.   gen. cloch i n-inad uigi, Bk. of Fen. 138.   pl. n. oga, LBr. 9b, 29.   dat. ugib 127, 21.

oibell adj.?   105, 9.

oirbire f. *reproach.*   119, 26.   21, 2.

oirfitech *musical; a musician.*   87, 4.   binnius airfitig inna guth, LL. 267b.

olar *juice?*   79, 19.   125, 13.   126, 17.   gen. olair 33, 20.   risin mnæ n-olair abbæth, LL. 210b, 4?   Cf. the river-name Olor, LL. 24a, 2.

olarda *juicy?*   29, 22.   37, 31.   121, 2.   olorda 85, 20.

onba ?   33, 28.   118, 29.   *meal,* Henn.

onfad = anfod *a storm at sea.*[1]   anfud, Wind.   bolg-onfad 85, 18. bocanfad 119, 37.   anboth, Ml. 125d, 11.

ongha ?   69, 22.

ordnim *I honour.*   129, 16.

oróit f. *prayer.*   17, 8.   aróit 125, 6.   dobcrat a n-oráit úadib, LBr. 258b, 52.   From Lat. oratio.

## P.

pater f. *the Lord's prayer; any prayer.*   13, 12.   81, 32.   acc. cen phatir, cen chreda, LL. 309b, 4.   M. padjer, W. pader.

ponc m. *point.*   Wind.   is minphonge ⁊ is nefní, LBr. 157a, 31. dat. punc 41, 8.   ina pongcaib, LBr. 280b.

[1] doinenn *a storm on land.*

popul m. *a people or congregation, the public,* also *a tribe or sept,*
P. O'C. 29, 29. 33, 7. aircinnig anettlaide, popul fodardach,
Harl. 5280, fo. 42a. gen. pobail 114, 12. M. pobbyl, W. pobl.
putrall f. *the hair of the head.* 115, 35. Corm. Tr. 138. Stokes,
*Lives,* Ind. acc. putraill 122,'26. co pudrallaib imgerra
urardda, LL. 268a, 1.

### R.

ráma *oar.* 119, 32. LL. 12b, 26. M. maidjey-raue.
refeda *cords.* 31, 4. réfeda 63, 18. refóda 63, 24.
rell *a block?* 47, 16.
(1) reng f. *the waist, the lower part of the back near the hips;
one of the loins,* P. O'C., who quotes the quatrain :

> A rígh nimhe na naomh,
> as tinn liom mo cheann,
> cidh leabhar mo dhruim,
> ni reamhar mo reang.

127, 28.
(2) reng f. *a wrinkle, string, welt, cord,* P. O'C. acc. reing 123,
7. 127, 1.
rer-chero f. *a heath-poult.* 3, 16. O'Dav. 112. ib. 118, s. v.
sallann. rer .i. lon, Corm. Tr. 145. Laws iii, 380, 7.
ressamnach? 109, 21.
ríamnach f. *a fishing-line.* dat. riamnaig 122, 2. gen. rogab in ✸
gilla bratán ríamnaige, LU. 116b, 24. M. rimlagh.
ro-brechtán *a large custard.* 37, 7. 120, 18.
robud *warning.* 71, 18. 20. gen. tendál robaid, LU. 87a, 14.
M. raaue.
ro-chaithem *great eating.* 125, 14.
ro-immfharcraid *great excess.* 21, 4.
ro-ítu *great thirst.* 125, 13.
ro-thé *very hot, too hot.* 31, 15.
ro-thecht *very clotted, viscous.* 101, 8. 9.
rúadán .i. cruithnecht rúadh .i. maolcruithnecht, O'Dav. 112.
*buckwheat?* 99, 5. There is a sea-weed now called ruadh-
ánach.
ruaimnech f. *a hair-line for fishing.* r. dubain, Ir. Gl. 428. dat.
ruaimnig 91, 18. 21. Cf. ruaimne *a long hair; a fishing-line,*
P. O'C.

*ruth 79,30*

S.

sab 125, 19 ;   bad spelling for sad, sod *bitch.*

sab m. *staff, stave, block,* O'R. Rev. xii, 462.   pl. dat. sabdaib 123, 10. 16.

Sacsanach *English.*   123, 20.   Saxanach 61, 29.

sadail *comfortable, lazy.*   sádhail *luxurious,* Three Shafts, Ind. Uath Beinne Etair, 45.   slóg saidbir sattail, LL. 155a, 30. rochodal co sadail 7 co súantrom, Magh Rath, 110, 20.

sadall m. *saddle.*   dat. sadull 89, 21.   pl. acc. sadli, Rawl. B. 512.   Rev. xi, 494.

sail f. *beam, prop, joist,* O'R.   pl. n. sailghe 37, 19.   nói sailge sin Senchais Móir, Corm. 32, 6.   dat. 123, 27.   for sailgib na n-eclais, I.L. 188b, 24.

sain-ait *something specially pleasant, a dainty.*   77, 6.

sainchan *on all sides, everywhere.*   105, 2.   Atk. Ir. Lexicogr. p. 21.   sancan .i. anunn 7 anall, II. 3. 18, p. 538.

sain-ól *a special drink.*   107, 18.

sall ?   79, 24.

saltair m. *the Psalter.*   13, 7.   59, 18.   pl. acc. saltracha, LL. 298b, 15.

sám-fhind *gentle and fair.*   87, 8.

Sarophín *Seraphim.*   41, 10.

Satan *a Satan.*   143, 3.   sattan, 3, 12.   is ina étun bís a satan comaitechta, LL. 282b, 25.

scaiblín *pottage.*   35, 1.   See quotation under grut.

scaiblíne *a small caldron.*   89, 7.   From scabal f. .i. aighean no coire, O'Cl.   Rev. xii, 86, § 92.   Laws i, 124, 4.   134, 1.   gen. scaibaile, ib. 170, 5.

scál m. *an apparition, phantom.*   71, 15. 18.   nidom scál-sa ém 7 nidom urtrach, Baile in Scáil, Harl. 5280.

scell *kernel, grain.*   71, 30.   Cf. sceallan *a kernel,* also *a thin slice ;* also *a thin pepple, a coin,* P. O'C.

sciathrach *a shield strap.*   67, 26.   cró sciathrach, Alex. 470.

sciathar *a shield strap.*   118, 12.

scibar m. *pepper.*   Z. 10, 780.   gen. scibair 71, 30.   grainne scibair, H. 3. 18, p. 6.

scób f. = scúap, Wind.   *the tail* (of a horse).   dat. scoíb 89, 19. W. ysgub, M. skeah.   From Lat. scōpa.

scolóc (1) timthirid, gilla *a man-servant, attendant.* 13, 21. 15, 23. 17, 10. 11. 114, 9. 13. eiric giunta co lomad a ciabaib na crosan 7 na scoloc, Laws iii, p. 354, 6. *A farm-servant,* Lismore Lives, Ind. The word is now fem. and means *an old man, an elderly farmer,* P. O'C. Manx scollag *lad, stripling.* (2) *a scholar, student.* Fél. cxxix, 1. In O'Curry's MS. Dictionary (now preserved in Clonliffe College) the following passage is quoted from the Bk. of Ballym. 41b, b (?) : tréde as mó menma bís .i. scolog ar légad a shalm 7 gilla iar legadh a erraidh úadh 7 ingen iar n-dénam mná dhi.

scor *a stud of mares.* 79, 25.

scúabad *sweeping.* 11, 15. scópthe *swept,* Goid. p. 4, p. 14. M skeabey, W. ysgubo.

sculmaire *a sculler,* O'Don. Suppl. scemgal na sculmairi ic a scoltud, LL. 236a, 10. *a rowing-pin?* 85, 13. 119, 34.

sóbcaide = sebcaide *hawk-like?* 97, 15.

sechtach *sevenfold.* 105, 16.

secht-airdech *seven-pointed.* 122, 33.

secht-fhillte *sevenfold.* 9, 13. Cf. sechtfilltech, LBr. 277a, 48.

secht-trumma *seven times heavier.* 61, 16.

secul *rye.* 99, 4. M. shoggyl. From Lat. secale.

seg *strength, pith.* 55, 4. cin seg, cin súg, LBr. 163b, 8.

sel *a while.* 11, 9. Wind. sol bec, LBr. 8a, 45. Rev. ix, 18. andara sel *alternately,* 3 Fragm. 26, 24. dális dóib sel cach thrír lee, LU. 25a, 15. W. chwyl.

semtille *a beetle or mallet,* P. O'C. *the knocker of a door :* 123, 11. 17.

sénaim *I refuse, deny.* 5, 18. Inf. séna. Mer Uil. 9. Rev. vii, 302, l. 206.

sen-cháisse f. *old cheese.* 37, 18.

sengán *ant.* 125, 22. Alex. 687. From seng *slender.* M. sniengan.

serbán *wild-oats.* scruán 99, 4. serpan .i. conel n-arbha .i. ba doich bidh é in corco, H. 3. 18, p. 637d.

sessar *I sat.* 93, 2.

sótige *blanket.* 11, 18. 28. 17, 25. From sót *bedding.* deich cind ina rosétaib, LU. 81b, 5. do cholcthechaib 7 brothrachaib 7 di sétaib ingantaib, ib. 134b, 26.

sifind? 11, 15.

o

síl-cáith f. *seed-husk.*  gen. sílcátha 15, 2. 19.

sinchán *a young fox.*  85, 2.  Cf. sinchénac gl. vulpecula, Sg. 47a, 6.

sítach *silk.*  gen. 115, 35.

síthalta *strained, clarified.*  83, 12.  *transparent :* 97, 16.  From síthal, W. hidl.

síthfe *rod, wand, switch,* P. O'C.  9, 21.  Cf. ar ropé in síthbe óir dar in clár findruini síl Aeda Sláni dar Bregmag, LU. 52b.

slaimegil.  101, 11.  Prob. miswritten for sraindmegil.

slatt f. *rod.*  Wind.  dat. slait 122, 2.  M. slatt, W. llath.

sleith *having carnal communication with a woman without her leave or knowledge,* O'Don. Suppl.  85, 3.  hi sleith do mná .i. cen forba n-gníma, Laws i, 162, 26.  gen. lánamnas óicne no sleithe, Laws ii, 404, 14.

slemda *smooth, slippery.*  85, 1.  From slim.

slemnaigim *I smoothe.*  122, 26.

slemne f. *smoothness.*  47, 26.  metaph. slemna fria garbu, LBr. 260b, 88.

slicrech f. *small shells, thin pebbles, bits of broken glass or other ware, potsear, potsherds,* P. O'C.  acc. slicrig 121, 36.  From slice *a shel'.*

slithemda *stealthy ?*  85, 2.

sluccad-chocnom *swallowing and chewing.*  101, 10.  127, 29.

smé *I.*  71, 17.  123, 1.  Rev. x, 82, 17, 24.  ib. 85, n. 7.

snadadán, a humorous dimin. of snádud *protection.*  127, 10.

snedim *I fling ?*  snedis 49, 17.  sncid slaitt forru, LL. 111b, 31.

so-accallaim f. *affability.*  gen. 93, 7.  atchonnarc and in suid sulbair soacallma, LL. 116a.

so-accallmach *fair-spoken, affable.*  99, 14.  LL. 343d, 6.

so-accobrach *easily moved or moving to desire.*  9, 15.  LL. 343d, 6.  Cf. oldate ina suaccubri gl. quam *speciosa,* Ml. 59c, 7.  suaccobrib *pretiosis,* Ml. 130a, 3.

so-bucc *affectionate ?*  87, 8.  Cf. buca : ni himond buca na báig daib-se do chlannaib Colmáin, LBr. 277a, 14.

soccair *steady, safe, sound, comfortable.*  85, 15.

sochla ?  97, 3.

sod f. *bitch.*  int sod maic thíre, LL. 301b, 39.  LU. 77a, 5.  sogh allaid gl. lupa, Ir. Gl. 297.  sodh co cuileanaib, Ir. Texte iii, p. 36n.  Cf. so[d]tech gl. lupanar, lit. *bitch-house,* Sg. 64a, 7.

# Glossary. 195

so-dethbir *very right, natural.* 93, 17. 21.  Trip. Life, p. 6, 15.

so-fhulaing *pleasant to bear.* 31, 15.

so-mesc *intoxicating.* 29, 23.

so-milis *very sweet.* 29, 23. 83, 12.  LBr. 142a, 3.

sonba *beams?* 69, 21.

sond-chú *a dog tied to a stake.* 115, 3.

soscéle (1) *gospel.* Wind.  (2) *the book of the gospels.* 107, 5.
(3) *a text, particularly John* i, 1. in tau atbcrtin soscela
erdraic : In principio erat verbum, LBr. 145a, 29.  (4) *the
leathern bag in which the gospel-text was put.* 11, 4. 81, 28.
20. 126, 37. 127, 1.

so-tor-chutbide *easily moved or moving to laughter.* 87, 8.  Cf.
cuitbide. (1) *laughing :* LU. 96b, 37.  forchuitbidc, ib. 32.
(2) *laughable :* gl. frivolus, Sq. 49b, 10.  cuitbide cach
denmnetach, LL. 344c.  cuitbide cach n-uallach, Aib. Cuigni.

spírtalda *spiritual.* 13, 10.  LU. 34b, 2.

spled, for spleg *play, sport.* 43, 30.  From A.-S. plega.

spréid f. *possession, stock.* gen. sprédi 9, 19.  From Lat. praeda.

sraind-megil *snoring and bleating.* 101, 11.  srann *snoring*
Corm. Tr. 153.  srand .i. srón ann. .i. isin sróin bís, H. 3. 18,
p. 83b.

sreb f. *stream.*  Salt. Ind.  a fhir imthéit sále sreb, LL. 265b.
dat. maigre 'na srib, LL. 297b, 50.  There is a sister-form srib,
Corm. Tr. p. 97.  tar an Sinainn sribhghlain, Rawl. 512, fo.
121b, 1.

sriball f. *stream.*  acc. sribaill 125, 22.

srón f. (1) *nose.*  (2) *ness, headland.* 85, 21.

stacc f. *pile, piece.* gen. na staci 63, 12.  dat. staic 65, 5.  pl. n.
staci 81, 20.  acc. stacci 63, 2.  From O. N. stakka f. *stump.*

stúag-lerg f. *an arched slope.* 9, 29.

súan? 127, 14.  Cf. súan cech slemon, LL. 344a.

súan-torthim *deep slumber.* 107, 23.

súgmar *juicy.* 37, 19. 77, 21. 83, 1.

## T.

tachur=tochur, Wind.  *placing, setting, sending.* 5, 22.  bárca
do thochur i port, LL. 343a.  *putting in order,* 15, 11.

taisec *restoring; delivering.* 45, 23. 73, 24.  Rev. xii, 124.
gen. diablud taisic *double restitution,* Laws ii, 64, 27.

o 2

tanach f. *cheese pressed and formed.* 69, 18. 85, 22. 99, 25.
gen. tainge 33, 25. 119, 35. dat. tanaig 67, 25. LL. 125a, 19.
pl. acc. tangea gl. formellas, Reg. 215, fo. 95b (Kuhn, 30, p. 556).

tarcud *acquisition, gathering, acquired wealth,* O'Don. Suppl.
73, 26. Laws ii, 356, 9. targud, ib. 396, 28.

tarsund *condiment.* O'Don. Suppl. pl. acc. torsnu 99, 7.

tarthrann (pl. n.) *flitches?* 81, 25.

tascaid (sg. dat.) 89, 10. *flummery,* Henn. *fat heifer-beef,* O'C.
iii, p. 104.

tassa f. *weakness.* 69, 28. A sister form of taisse.

táth .i. mulchán, *cheese unpressed made of sour milk curds,* P.
O'C. biad cosmail do chássi nó tháth, LU. 25a, 11. gen.
táith 121, 32. Cf. táth *solder or glue, cement ; a knot or joint*
P. O'C. M. taa, cf. W. todi.

tecbaim *I lift.* 11, 27. tecbaid in fial, LL. 212b, 19. tecbaid
Beccan súas a aenláim. 23. P. 3, fo. 11b.

techt *coagulated, viscous.* 101, 10.

téith-milis *smooth and sweet.* 97, 18. srotha teithmillsi, Ir.
Texte, p. 133, 3. Cf. teith .i. bláith, ut est : teithgela caema,
H. 3. 18, p. 51. lem .i. cach téith, Corm. Tr. p. 100. lemh .i.
gach maeth, ut est lemhlacht, Eg. 1782, fo. 15b.

tenga f. *the tongue of a bell.* 89, 24. 123, 21.

tenn-sháthach *fully satiated.* 39, 8. Cf. teannsháth *plenty,*
*abundance, enough,* P. O'C. a tennsuith dona bochtaib, Laws,
iii, 20, 3. im úr dia tumad ꝝ a tennsaith dóib di, ib. ii, 150, 3.
The opposite seng-sháith, ib. 150, 1. sathach gl. satur, Ir. Gl.
402. LBr. 143a, 5. Compar. sathchu, LL. 203b, 12.

teó *vigour, strength, power,* O'R. 127, 16?

termund *limit or precinct ; glebeland, sanctuary, asylum, refuge,*
P. O'C. 41, 25. LL. 201a, 27. termon cell, LL. 147b, 34. From
Lat. termon-, as W. terfyn is from Lat. terminus.

tesc f. *dish, paten.* med no thesc no slice gl. lanx, Sg. 20a.
dut. teisc 65, 6.

tét-bind *sweet as string music.* 97, 18.

tíag libuir f. *book-satchel.* 9, 21. 11, 26. 13, 6. cotorchratar
tiaga libair hErenn dia n-aidlennaib, LL. 371c. cuirset na
manaig in cend ina téig libair, LBr. 188b, 52.

tibrecht? 81, 7. 15.

tibrón *a small spring or fountain.* 85, 19.

ticcim *I come*, used idiomatically = *I gire.* 51, 6. 13. 87, 24.

tigadus *housekeeping, husbandry.* 73, 20. gen. gan adbar a thigedais leis d'ór ┐ d'airget, Cog. G. 118, 17.

timm *tender, soft.* 67, 25. nirbat rochrúaid, nirbat rothim, LL. 345e.

tinbe? 126, 33.

tindrum .i. sgél, ut est: tindrum mac Miled dochum n-Erenn, H. 3. 18, p. 46¼. 105, 18.

tinme *cutting up, carving.* 128, 21. in lúathletrad 7 in lúath-tínme, Tog. Tr. 2, 1653.

tinmim *I cut up, carve.* 65, 13. Rev. v, 379. tuarsena tinmthi don ár, Bk. of Fen. 376, 7.

tírmaide *dry.* 29, 24. 85, 22. 95, 25. Ml. 123d, 3.

tírm-cháise *dry cheese.* 81, 30.

tírm-charna *dried flesh.* 37, 15. 77, 22. A byname : Aed mac Echach Tirmcharna, LBr. 238c, a.

tochar *a fight or fray, a battle or skirmish*, P. O'C. 121, 32. tachar, Stokes, *Lives*, l. 3289. i tochur risna clérchib, LL. 150a, 8. nirbu gaine dom' athair-si tochur (.i. indsaigid nó iarair) fri Coinculaind, H. 3. 18, p. 601. Hence tochraim *I quarrel, fight.* mairg thochras ri clérchib, LL. 149b, 26. ib. 38. mairg triallas is tochras, ib. 150a, 10.

tocrád *injury, offence, insult.* 77, 8. Trip. Life, p. 394, 20.

tóeb fri *trusting.* 73, 4. Cf. ferr duind taob do tabairt fri fer dorosat heo omnia, Laws i, 22, 20. iontnobha *fit to be trusted*, Three Shafts, Ind.

tóebán *small side-beams on the roof of a house*, P. O'C. 69, 5. taebhán tellaigh no comladh gl, *trabecula*, Ir. Gl. 71.

tóescán *a spill of water, a flush*, P. O'C. 119, 35. Cf. a tóesca fola trethu, LU. 94, 22. in tóescach 7 in tinsaitin na fola, LL. 291a, 17.

tolg m. *bedstead, cot.* .i. lebaidh, H. 3. 18. Boroma Ind. tolg creduma ima leapaidh 7 seisium inti dogrés, Fled D. nang. p. 42. dat. tulg 59, 5. pl. n. tuilg adnocuil, Alex. 887. Hence tolcda *bedding*, which occurs in a quatrain quoted s. v. medb .i. serb, H. 3. 18, p. 82 :

> " tolcda di coilcthib simenn,
> gáir peinn di dromaib duillenn,
> lind serb a béluib debenn,
> mid medb di bratuib cuilenn."

tón f. *the bottom* (of a sieve). dat. tóin 73, 3. W. tin.

tonnach *covering?* tonnach crédumi forsin taig, LU. 134b, 24.

tonnach f. *quagmire*, O'Don. Suppl. acc. tonnaig 115, 4.

tor *tower.* dat. tuir 105, 3. doróne tor tened dermaire i n-dorus na huama, Cath Catharda.

torcrad f. *boars.* gen. torcraide 127, 8.

torsigim *I weary.* 25, 21.

torsnu, see tarsund.

tort f. *cake.* .i. bairgen, Corm. Tr. 156. pl. acc. tortea 127, 9. W. torth f. from Lat. torta.

tracht *strength.* 55, 7. Cf. díthracht *without strength*, díthrachtaim *I weaken:* romdithracht a díbad, LL. 123b, 17.

trebar *strong, firm, robust*, P. O'C. 87, 15. fer tailc trebur co sonairte ballraid, LU. 82b, 28. Comp. trebar-glan 87, 11.

trebarda *strong.* 37, 13.

tremunta *some beverage.* 33, 25. 37, 28. 85, 17. 119, 35. 122, 26. Cf. treabhantar *a syllabub, sour milk*, P. O'C.

tresc *refuse, offal.* ait in rocuired a tresc dorigne cnocc mór de ba hé a ainm Tresc in Máirimdill, Tochm. Em. Cf. treiscach *draffish, full of swine-wash*, P. O'C.

tresse *strength.* 71, 70. 119, 8. Alex. p. 94, 15. is é tressi inn anfaid raċrig dóib, LL. 172b, 12.

trilis f. (1) *hair.* Wind. (2) *a sheep-fold?* gen. trillsi 45, 21.

triubhus *trousers.* 124, 37. Scot. trews.

troch f. *one doomed, fey; coward.* dat. troich 71, 20=ba rabhadh do throich a dteagasg, Moy Leana, 18, 15. Lorcán Laigen i treib trcch ṛ.the dead, FM. 941. mairg gusa tiagar, it troich (.i. mairb) gusa tiagar, Brud. Dá D., H. 3. 18, p. 531 = LU. 88a, 17. troich imda 7 mórchoscuir, LL. 120a, 27. fo thaidbsin troch, 108b, 2. ba turus troch tromthuitted, 198a, 24. ba teidm teined tar trocha, 7a, 3. gai glas gona troch, FM. 917. fri demnu troch, LL. 150a, 46. 191b, 34. 211b, 40. ná tabair táib ri troich, LL. 148b, 8. pl. acc. tollais trocha, ib. 184a. Hence trucha *short life*, O'R. cen trucha, LL. 11a, 2. fuair trucha 7 trénaithbe, LL. 129b, 4. 184a. 184b. 193a, 58. LU. 119b, 38.

tromm-tonn f. *a heavy wave.* 122, 16.

túathe *charm, spell.* 5, 25. 27.

*tuir* 81,11     *um at öit* 13.4.

tuicsinech *chosen.* 111, 19.  tuicsenach 99, 14.
tur-arán *dry bread,* i.e. without condiment.  37, 16.  91, 9.  Cf.
 bargenai turai, Rev. xii, 70, § 39.  Now arán tur.

### U.

úatha f. *scarcity?*  93, 15.
ug-adart *some dish ; egg-fritters,* Henn.  127, 23.
úr-móin *fresh turf or peat.*  gen. -mónad 15, 20.   dat. -mónaid
 15, 3.
ursann f. *door-post.*  gen. ursainde 59, 5.  W. g-orsin.
usca *lard.*  37, 31.  85, 19.  122, 2.  usca quasi súsce .i. geir suis     -ᵡ-
 .i. na muice, II. 3. 18.   tumud na cainnell a geir 7 usca in
 carna, Laws ii, 252, 2.   From Lat. axungia.
uscaide *lardy.*  121, 33.  123, 15.

# INDEX OF PERSONS.

# INDEX OF PLACES AND TRIBES.

# CORRIGENDA.

## TEXT.

P. 5, 20. For *ōmun* read *omun*. The shortness of the *o* is proved by the word frequently rhyming with *domun*, *e.g.* LBr. 91, marg. inf. So *omnaig* rhymes with *fodluig*, Salt. 7763.

P. 7, 23. Read *bá[i]n*. ib. 24, read *Samá[i]n*.

P. 11, 2. Read *for bolcxén*.

P. 13, 10. Read *spírtalda*. ib. 11, read *annālaib*.

P. 31, 11. Read *nocho* n-*damad*.

P. 33, 23. For *lethind* read *leth[ch]ind*. ib. 26, read *Indsé[i]n*, *millsé[i]n*.

P. 34, 1. Read *bladuāir*. ib. 5, read *Ābéil*, *Ādaim*. ib. 7, read *fostá[i]n*, *trostá[i]n*.

P. 41, 6. Read *Ādam*. ib. 7, read *Ābēl*.

P. 43, 18. Read *Múil[e]finde*.

P. 57, 23. For *ēcna* read *ecna*. That *e* is short is proved by such rhymes as *ecna : ecla*, LBr. 255, marg. inf. *ecnae : Teclae*, Fél. Feb. 22, etc.

P. 65, 12. For *fódén* of the Fcs. the MS. has *fodén*.

P. 67, 7. For *fobrais* read *fóbrais*.

P. 73, 2. For *bóithe* of the Fcs. the MS. has *boithe*. ib. 10, read *bæthaib*. ib. 17, the MS. has *lái*.

P. 75, 17. After *comlethain* insert *cernaig cianfhota cethirláin*. ib. 18, for *trē* read *trī*.

P. 77, 3. The MS. has *itchótamur*, *láife*. ib. 6, for *blásta* read *blasta*. ib. 7, the MS. has *corís*. ib. 21, the MS. has *fastáib*.

P. 79, 24. Read *Sall*. ib. 26, read *Is dīn*, etc.

P. 89, 23. The MS. has *bá bragait*.

P. 91, 4. Read *osslaiether*. ib. 7, *clti* MS. ib. 10, read *c[l]ochdrochat*. ib. 19, for *lurgān* read *lurgan*. ib. 24, for *'ma* read *ina*.

P. 93, 14.　For *ōs tuil* read *ōs t'[sh]ǎil.*　ib. 17, *trómyalair* MS.
ib. 18, *dagchoca* MS.
P. 95, 6.　Read cethri *fodlaib* fichet.　ib. 21, *dochosail* MS.
P. 97, 1.　Read *fhót.*　ib. 4, *si* MS.　ib. 6, *dá* MS.　ib. 14, *segda*
MS.　ib. 20, *risimbenfa.*
P. 99, 3.　*nidoscoicela* MS.　ib. 6, read *cacha orbaind.*　ib. 12,
*hitha* MS.　ib. 18, *senyruth* MS.　ib. 21, *cclide* MS.　ib. 23,
*hétan* MS.
P. 101, 14.　*this* MS.　ib. 28, *doberthi.*
P. 103, 10.　Read *sin fil.*　ib. 11, *lebruih.*　ib. 14, *deisi* MS.
P. 105, 15.　Read *col-léri.*　ib. read *ccnai;* 22, *ccnaidecht;* 28,
*ccnaide.*
P. 107, 5.　*shescela* MS.　ib. 11, *ethiár.*　ib. 15, *comberbad* MS.
ib. 17, *chombruthi.*　ib. 23, *fcsiss.*
P. 109, 10.　*ni* MS.
P. 114, 20.　*iernabarmach* MS.　ib. 25, *ur* corrected from *iar.*
P. 115, 12.　*aniu* MS.
P. 116, 2.　Read *atatcomnaic-si.*　ib. 22, *or* MS.　ib. 35, *upull*
MS.
P. 117, 20.　Read *atāidh.*
P. 118, 9.　Read *scēit[h].*　ib. 34, after *asœ* insert *A is.*
P. 119, 8.　*saidaile* MS.　ib. 12, read *euil.*　ib. 15, *scolaide* MS.
P. 123, 22.　Read *in clochdrochat.*　ib. 23, read *clochdrochat.*
ib. 34, after *brothchāin* insert:

meic borrt[h]oraid breacbāin,
meic borrchroit[h]e blāithe, meic blāithchi, meic breachtāin,
Meic boóire (bñaidh m-bainde).

P. 125, 4.　Read *cgna.*　ib. 7, *foesom* MS.
P. 126, 36.　Read *paitir.*

## TRANSLATION.

P. 10, 3.　Read *who put a gospel.*
P. 28, 29.　Dele *to thee.*
P. 42, 13 and 21.　Read *Maelfinde.*
P. 56, 7.　For *and it was—on me* read *and this is what caused
that misunderstanding between me and thee.*
P. 68, 28.　Read *When I get to Butter-mount,*
*May a gillie take off my shoes.*

P. 70, 32.  For *the husks* read *grains.*

P. 72, 4.  For *mad* (?) read *roped.*

P. 86, 8.  For *niggardly* read *shameless.*

P. 90, 13.  For *lake-bridge* read *stone-dyke.*   ib. 22, for *leg* read *shanks.*

P. 92, 15.  For *brow* read *eye.*   ib. 17, for *sharp* read *fierce.*

P. 96, 22.  For *slender* read *transparent.*

P. 98, 6.  Dele *fair.*

P. 104, 15.  For *can* read *cannot.*

# ADDENDA.

## NOTES.

P. 132. *Mac Dá Cherda.* There is a poem on Femen in LL.
p. 209b, which Mac Dá Cherda or Comgán is said to have composed together with Cummine.

Ib. *Dub Dá Thúath.* In H. 3. 18 the well-known poem
beginning *Dia m-bad messe bad rí réil* is ascribed to him.

Ib. *Caillech Bérre.* After the notes were printed, I found so
many further references to this Protean character, that there
would be materials for a monograph on her. In H. 3. 18, p. 42,
there is a long poem ascribed to her, with the following introduction : Sentanc Berre, Digdi a [h]ainm, di Chorco Duibne di
.i. dá Uaib Maic Iair Conchinn. Is dib dana Brigit ingen
Iustain. Is diib dono Liadain ben Chuirithir. Is dib dono
Uallach ingen Muineghain. Foracaib Finan cel doib ni biad
cin cailli*g* n-amra n-áin dib. Is de robói Caillech Berre fuirre :
cóica dalta di a m-Berri. Secht n-ais n -aith*edh*[1] a n-decha*id*[2]
cond*e*ged cech fer óc críne uade, comt*ar* túathe 7 chenél*a* a húi
7 a iarmúi 7 cét m-bliadan di fo cail*le* iarna shenad do Cuiminiu
for a cend. Dosnanic si œs 7 lobræ iarom. Is and asrubard sii.

"The Old Woman of Beare, Digdi was her name, of Corco
Duibne (Corkaguiny), viz. of the Uí Maic Iair-Conchinn. Of
them too was Brigit, the daughter of Iustán, and Liadain, the
wife of Cuirithcr, and Uallach, the daughter of Muinegán.
Finan left a prophecy for them that they should never be without a famous illustrious old woman of their race. The reason
why she was called the Old Woman of Beare, was that she had
fifty foster-children in Beare. She had seven periods of youth
one after another, so that every man reached death by old age

---

[1] leg. úitedh — óited ?        [2] leg. i n-degaid.

before her, so that her grand-children and great grand-children
were tribes and races. And one hundred years she was under
the veil, after Cuimmine had blessed it on her head. After that
~~she reached~~ old age and debility. It was then she said"—
Then follows a poem beginning :

> " Athbe dam-sa bés mara,
> senta fomdera croan."

> " My life ebbs from me like the sea,
> Old age has made me yellow."

From this poem, a second copy of which is found in the same
MS., p. 764, it appears that she had been a famous hetaira in her
time. She compares her present life with that of her younger
days :

> " It máine
> charthar lib, nitát dáine :
> i n-inbuith im-marsamar,
> bátar dóini carsamar."

> " It is riches
> That you love, not men :
> In the time when we lived,
> It was men we loved."

> " It fálte na hingena,
> ó thic dóib co Beltene :
> is dothberiu dam-sa brón,
> sech am tróg am sentane."

> " The maidens rejoice
> When Mayday comes to them :
> For me sorrow is meeter,
> For I am wretched and an old woman."

> " Ni feraim cobra milis,
> ni marbtar muilt im' banais,
> is bec is liath mo trilis,
> ni liach drochcaille tarais."

> " I hold no sweet converse,
> No wethers are killed at my wedding
> My hair is all but grey,
> The mean veil over it is no pity."

"Rombui denus la ríga
ic ól meda ocus fína :
indiú ibim medguscc
itir sentanib crína."

"Once I was with kings
Drinking mead and wine :
To-day I drink whey-water
Among withered old women."

In the same MS., p. 38, marg. inf. the following quatrain is found, in which she is said to have been the mother of St. Fintan (cf. Fél. p. liii) and of the fénnid Finn who fought at Cromglenn :

"Caillech Bérre, brígh go m-blad,
máthair fíralainn Fintain,
ocus in fennedha Fhinn
dochuired cath i Cromglinn."

The following lines in LL. 139a make her the wife of Fothud na Canóine, a well-known poet of the eighth century :

"Callcch Bérri búan bind bunaid,
ben Fhathaid Chanóine na cét."

Father O'Growney has also collected several further modern stories about Cailleach Bhéirre, some of them from Castlebeare itself.

P. 135. As to the custom of making the night precede the day, cf. O'Dav. p. 114, s. v. saboit: lá reimtćit adaig nocotáinic núafiadnaise 7 adaig reimtcit lá ossin illé. "Day preceded night until the New Testament came, and night precedes day from that till now."

Ad p. 43, 23. Cf. girri cach n-uachtarach, libru cach n-ichtarach, LL. 266b, 30. With the whole scene compare the following description of a nebulo, in William of Malmesbury, ii, p. 438 : praeter ceteros ludo mordente facetus, obscenos quoque gestus imitari peritus, si quando verbis minus agentibus destitueretur . . . primoque nudato inguine incestavit aera, tum deinde crepitu ventris emisso turbavit auras.

Ad p. 51, 11. Cf. LL. 45b, 34 : Nói n-grád nimi ocus in dechmad grád talmau tilchaig Is iat dilsi lúagi lemmghair dúani Crimthain.

Ad p. 103, 18. Cf. messu a chách lciud do dál, Boroma, 139.

*Addenda.* 211

# GLOSSARY.

áer *satirising.* Sg. acc. bá-sa maith frim' áir, LU. 114a, 34.

ammaig lit. *out of the plain.*

annland *opsonium.* anlond, LL. 206a, 8.

arráir *last night.* areir, LL. 285b, 30.

assa *shoe.* gl. soccus, Sg. 22b, 9.

beoil *meat-juice.* beóil *grease,* Corm. s. v. mugeime.

bíthe *female, effeminate.* Olla sétig Scim bláith bíthi, LL. 136b, 38.

cliathán *the breast or side,* O'R. 99, 32.

cocnam *chewing.* in cocnam, Ml. 75b, 7.

comroircnech, Sg. 6a, 11. 26b, 7.

comrorcu *error,* seems a Middle-Ir. form for Old-Ir. comrorcon. Cf. connabí comrorcon and, Ml. 82d, 6. ib. 25d, 12.

cundrad gl. *merx.* Sg. 68b, 5. huanaib cundradaib cissib gl. *mercedibus,* Ml. 122a, 3.

dísertach *hermit.* LL. 281b, 3.

emnach *double.* 99, 31.

erdracaigim *I honour.* Cf. erdaircigidár gl. *concelebrat,* Ml. 28b, 15. erdarcaigfes, Ml. 89b, 4.

fail *arm-ring.* foil gl. *armillam,* Sg. 64a, 17.

fairci 120, 33 = fairre 37, 22.

fithir *tutor.* faig ferb fithir, LU. 10b, 36. it [fh]idera for fid-chellaib, LL. 276a, 17.

folmugud *to lay waste.* Bk. of Fenagh, 312, 26. *to evacuate.* Ann. Loch Cé, 1315.

fomnaim *I beware.* fomnid-si, Wb. 33a, 15. foimnide, Trip. Life, 42, 9.

forlán, Wb. 3a, 7.

forrgim *I harass.* Cf. ní forrúich, LU. 86b. nachamforraig, LU. 71a, 13. 21. díanamforgea, ib. 22. romfhorraig, LL. 205b, 21.

fortgellaim. Cf. fortgellait fellsaim, LBr. 181b.

ginach *craving.* Such derivatives in *-ach* used substantively are either masc. or fem. Cf. Z. 810.

lái *steering-oar.* Better lui, dat. luith, Corm. s. v. prull. W. llyw points to urkelt. *levo- or *lïgo-.

muirn *high spirit.*    Hence muirnech *cheerful*, Bk. of Fenagh, 276.

og, *egg.*    The pl. dat. *ugib* shows that the word was still declined as an s-stem when the original of LBr. was written.

síthfe.    sithbi isin brutt ós a brunni, LL. 231a.

slicrech *small shells.*    Cf. sligre ꝛ turrscar, Fél. xxxviii, 36.

soccair *comfortable.*    m'inar, édach sídama*il* soccuir, Eg. 1782, fo. 33a. 2.

somilis *very sweet.*    Hence somailse gl. *dulcedo*, Sg. 52a.

spirtalde, Wb. 15b, 2. The *i* is short.    Cf. the rhyme ilulc : spirut, Maclísu's Hymn, 6.

LONDON : CHAS. J. CLARK, 4, LINCOLN'S INN FIELDS, W.C.